THE VOYAGES OF TRUEBLOOD CAY

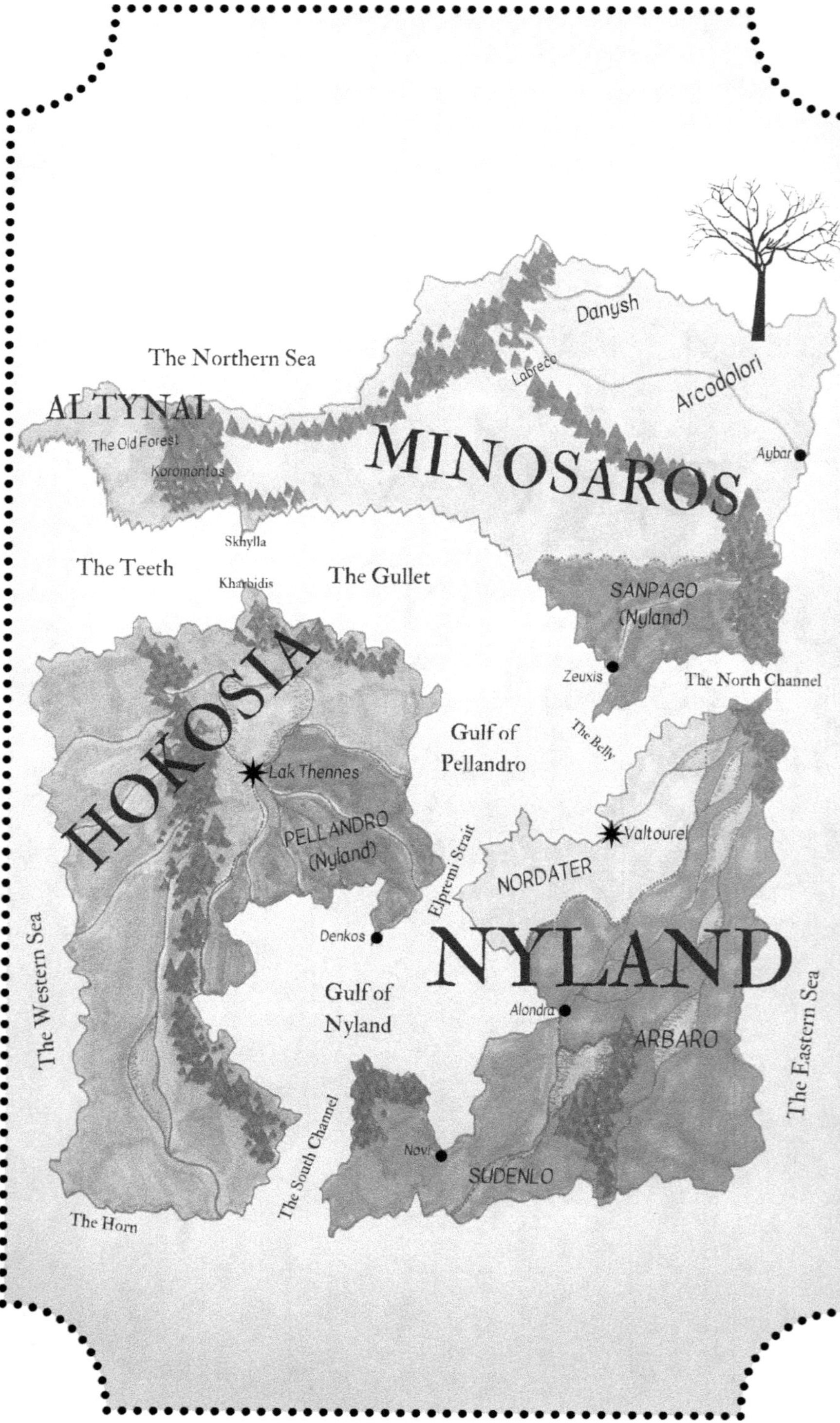

Danysh
The Northern Sea
ALTYNAI
The Old Forest
Koromontas
Labreco
Arcodolori
MINOSAROS
Aybar
Skhylla
The Teeth
Kharbidis
The Gullet
SANPAGO
(Nyland)
Zeuxis
The North Channel
HOKOSIA
Gulf of
Pellandro
The Belly
Lak Thennes
PELLANDRO
(Nyland)
Elpremi Strait
Valtourel
NORDATER
The Western Sea
Denkos
NYLAND
Gulf of
Nyland
Alondra
ARBARO
The Eastern Sea
The South Channel
Novi
SUDENLO
The Horn

The Voyages of Trueblood Cay

Being an Especial Accounting
of his Life and Times at Sea,
as Told by Gil Rafael

Suanne Laqueur

Suanne Laqueur/Cathedral Rock Press Somers, New York www.suannelaqueurwrites.com

Cover Design Art by Tracy Kopsachilis
Book Design by Ampersand Book Interiors LLC
The Voyages of Trueblood Cay/ Suanne Laqueur. — 1st ed.

ISBN 978-0578448879 (paperback)
ISBN 978-1737981466 (hardcover)

For Naroba, my sister and queen, who started the story.

For Rafael, my father, who said I told a good story.

For Mr. Durante, my English teacher,
who made me submit the story.

For Philip Trueblood, my friend, who
gave the story a face and a name.

But mostly for Stef.
My man, my finch, my kepten, my
gelangos and my love story.

*"In those days, we finally chose to walk like giants
& hold the world in arms grown strong with love
& there may be many things we forget in the days
to come, but this will not be one of them."*
—Brian Andreas, *Awakening*

"Yo no soy marinero. Soy capitán."
—La Bamba, Mexican folk song

*"So I'm sailing for tomorrow my dreams are a-dyin'
And my love is an anchor tied to you,
Tied with a silver chain."*
—Crosby, Stills & Nash

The Voyages of Trueblood Cay

Prologue

THE KHEIRON FLEW west across the desert with a human boy on his back.

Kheirons, dear reader, are half man, half horse. But don't equate them with centaurs. Kheirons fly. Centaurs do not. Furthermore, centaurs are eternally hybrid while kheirons can shift between *equos*—pure horse—and *humos*—pure man. Or they can rest as *kheiros*—the half-and-half form which appears like a centaur.

The kheiron in the sky above the desert was in humos, his human form. He could not shift, for he'd lost the magic stone that allowed him to morph between horse and man. Locked into the latter, helpless to flee or fight, he'd been cruelly abducted from his homeland and sold into captivity.

But he was free now.

Almost, he thought as his wings sliced through the night sky, moving in a gentle cadence on either side of the boy strapped to his back. The boy was dressed in the rough clothes of a slave. The mark of his master was branded into his neck, the seared flesh not yet healed.

The kheiron had known two masters, so he bore two different brand marks on his neck. Both had long turned to raised, pink scars in his tanned skin. The years enslaved had stripped him down to wiry, lean muscle over bone. The stress of planning this escape had shredded his nerves to a trembling fringe. Carrying the boy's extra weight cut miles off the distance the kheiron wanted to cover. The sun would rise soon and it would be too dangerous to travel in the heat of daytime. They'd need to find shelter. And a well. They fled the slave compound with just one waterskin between them and a third of it was gone already.

One more mile, he thought, looking back between wing beats to check the streak of pink at the eastern horizon. Solos, the sun god, hadn't yet ridden his steed above the edge of the world. They had a little more time.

The kheiron flew west while the boy slept on his back, arms wound tight around the kheiron's chest, their fingers entwined.

Below them undulated the desert floor, sapped of her daytime heat and rolling like an endless field of snow under the moon's waning light. The kheiron followed the old trading route through the desert, straining his eyes for any sign of scrub or vegetation where there might be water. Any crumbling caravanserai remains where they could take shelter from the unforgiving sun. When not trained on the ground, his desperate gaze squinted ahead, toward the faint bulge of the Altyn Mountains. Not until he put that range between himself and slavery would he even consider the idea of relief.

One more mile, he kept thinking. *One more behind us is one closer to freedom.*

His back and abdomen ached with the effort to hold his body parallel to the earth, stay tight and streamlined and let the wind carry him like an arrow. Flying long distances in human form was impractical. His four equine legs would've provided additional power and thrust, letting him literally gallop across the sky. If he hadn't lost his moonstone—*You fucking gave it away, remember?*—he and the boy would be over the mountains by now. But the stone was gone, along with its power to let him shift. The bell couldn't be un-rung, but at least he had his wings.

One more mile, he thought. *Put one more behind you.*

"Can I give myself a new name?" the boy asked.

"Good idea," the kheiron said. "New names for our new life."

The boy rubbed his brow along the back of his steed's neck. "What will you call me?"

"Why am I picking?"

"Because I want you to."

"All right," the kheiron said. "Your name is Alon. Do you know what it means?"

"It's a giantword. It's what they call a lark."

"Yes. Larks bring souls to newborns. And you, my friend, are newly born. You are the lark bringing your own soul to yourself. It's never been done before. You're the first."

Alon's cold hands squeezed the kheiron's fingers. "I like it," he said. "What's your new name?"

"You pick."

A long silence, save for the wind whistling through the kheiron's feathers.

"Fen," Alon said. "Your name is Fen."

It was the giantword for finch. Finches returned the souls of the dead.

"I see," Fen said slowly. "Am I a goldfinch, who returns the souls of the righteous?"

"No," Alon said. "You're a redfinch."

"They return the souls of the damned."

"Yes." The boy tightened his arms around Fen. "They'll tell stories about you forever. Any slaver who crosses your path is damned and doomed. You'll get them all, Fen. You'll never let anyone do this again. Not to anyone."

Fen ate and drank the prophetic words. *Damned* crunched between his teeth, splintering like bone. *Doomed* burst on his tongue, liver-rich with a rusty edge, like biting a sword still hot from battle. *Get them* slid deliciously down his throat. *Never again* warmed his belly and numbed the pain in his back and shoulders. *Stories* stirred up his strength and *forever* shone ahead, pointing the way. At his temples pulsed *Fen, Fen, Fen* like a bell that could never be un-rung. As he chewed on *Finch* and let the juice run down his chin, he imagined his old name was a shell encasing the past two years. He cracked it, felt the broken husk fall away beneath him. A delicate puff of sand rising as the name Tehvan il-Kheir was swallowed by the desert, dead and buried and forgotten.

I am Fen, he thought, putting the miles behind him. *I am The Finch. Cross my path and you are damned. None will escape. Never again.*

They found shelter in the remains of a caravanserai whose well, thank Gods, was full. A tenacious fig tree gave them a bit of breakfast before they lay down in the shadow of a broken wall and slept the day away. When the sun god began his descent to the west and the sand began to shiver, Fen filled the waterskin, lifted the boy on his back and took to the skies once more.

They flew west, the finch and the lark. Through the hot days and cold nights, Alon seemed to grow quieter and weaker while Fen, fed on a diet of revenge and legacy, filled with a greater resolve.

"There," he cried on the third evening, when the Altyn range began to take over the sky. "We're nearly there, Alon. Through those peaks."

Alon sighed against Fen's back. His body was icy deadweight. The only active part of him was the hand curled around Fen's thumb.

"We're almost there," Fen said. "Hold on just a little longer."

"Will they want me back?" the boy said.

The cadence of Fen's wings stuttered. "Who?"

"My family. Will they even want me back, knowing what I was doing?"

"You weren't doing anything," Fen said between gritted teeth. "Things were being done *to* you."

"I know. But..."

"Don't talk anymore. I need to think."

The updrafts grew colder and sharper as they began to cross the peaks. Gusts knocked Fen sideways and his body howled as he righted their course again and again.

"Hold tight," he kept saying, an ugly panic boiling up from his stomach. "Alon, you *hold on*. Don't you fucking let go of me."

"What if they don't want me back?"

"They want nothing more than to have you back," Fen said, gasping. "They'll tell stories about it forever."

He was so tired, he felt outside himself. Here and not here. The cold lulled him to the edge of sleep, then it shocked him awake. Somehow, his wings kept moving and the mental fatigue began to work to his advantage. His body zigged when the wind zagged. He mastered the dance of the updrafts and let the gusts partner him instead of pummel him. Nearly there. One last ridge. He could see the Old Forest now. A swath of dead trees like a hundred witches' hands reaching upward. The skeleton branches magnificent against the gray skies.

"Look," he said between heaving breaths. "These were the tallest Nye trees that ever grew. See the platforms in the upper canopies? The ancient ones built houses in the branches. They'd live up there weeks at a time, picking the spice flowers. Lowering them down in big baskets on pulleys. Did you ever think you'd see something like this?"

"You won't forget," Alon said, barely audible above the wind.

"See those birds circling the treetops? They're called caracaros. They're a kind of falcon and they won't nest anywhere but Nye trees. They're the best messenger birds in the world but they only live up here in Altynai. When you get home, tell all your friends you saw caracaros. They'll drop dead from jealousy."

"You'll tell this story." The fist tightened, white-knuckled around Fen's thumb. "Won't you?"

"Forever," Fen said. "They'll write songs about us. Epic poems. How the lark and the finch escaped from—"

The boy slid from his back.

"No," Fen cried over the empty tree tops. He pulled up short, life and death separated by one small fist clinging to his thumb. His wings pounded the air to a fury as his legs reached long, trying to snag Alon between his calves and haul him in close.

"Hold on. Look at me. *Alon...*"

But the boy's eyes were closed and his little fist was sliding, wrenching Fen's knuckle in its socket until, with a smooth tug, the silver band on his thumb slipped free.

The scream of the caracaros tore the sky open and echoed off the mountain peaks.

Absolute power doesn't exist, dear reader. All creatures of the gods have their frailties and limitations. A kheiron's wings are bound to the nine silver rings he wears on his fingers. All nine must be present for flight. One left off, lost or stolen, and his wings will not extend.

Fen's master knew this, and took the rings away the day he bought Fen at the slave market. It took two years for Fen to buy eight of them back.

On my face, he thought in a split second that stretched into infinity. *On my knees. I bought them back with my mouth and my body. Two years as a whore to buy back what was mine.*

The ninth ring he stole from the master. Or rather, Alon stole it, earning himself a ride to freedom on Fen's back.

What if they don't want me, knowing what I was doing?

Fen hovered over the dead forest, watching with incredulous detachment as Alon fell away from him like a forgotten name, Fen's ring still in a fist. A hot, liquid rush down his back as his wings began to retract beneath the skin. Instinctively he threw his human arms out, as if they could take over the job.

We were nearly there...

Tehvan il-Kheir, now renamed Fen, was not yet fully grown. His wingspan was nowhere near the epic proportion of his father's. Still, it took time for nine feet of tiered feathers to shrink, fold down and pull within. Time enough for him to glide a small, silent distance, reflect on how close he'd come and wonder who would tell the story now.

Then the wind filled his ears as his body plummeted through a wheeling cauldron of falcons and into the upraised hands of dead spice trees.

PART ONE
SOLOS
God of the Sun

# THE STORY

May I call you *legantos*?

It's an old giantword. It means "beloved reader" and it allows me, the storyteller, to address you throughout the tale-telling.

Shall we begin?

The story of Pelippé Trueblood starts and ends on a ship.

His life at sea was shaped by his decisions and the choices made by those who came before him. His voyage was shaped by legends that began centuries before his birth and the tales he left in his wake.

His life is written and his is a love story.

So listen, legantos.

Listen to learn it. Learn it to tell it. Tell it to teach it.

NYE

Once, on a ship called the Cay, a boy called Pelippé True-blood sailed with his father.

Trueblood once asked a sailor called Rafil, "Why do most stories begin with *once?*"

"Because once can mean something that happened one time and never again," Rafil said. "Or once can be the same thing happening for a long time and gradually, never again. Once can be a precise moment in time. Or a way of saying a long time ago."

"Once is just a place to start," Trueblood's father said.

Rafil nodded gravely. "Once," he said, "a ship called the Cay sailed the high seas. The kepten of the Cay was called Ikharus-Lippé True, and every evening he invited the crew into his quarters to hear stories. His only son was among the crew."

"But that's happening *now*," Trueblood said, looking around the large sitting room.

The Cay was built by giants and Kepten True's quarters in the aftercastle had room for all. The crew lounged in the big chairs and long couches, or sprawled on the floor. During the long weeks at sea, everyone could take a turn at being *rakontistos*, the story-teller. Some read from books. Others told from memory. A few could make up tales as they went along. And of course, there were those who preferred not to tell at all, but to just be *aŭskul-tantos*—beloved listeners.

"Once," Rafil said, "all was One, and One was called Os."

Rafil was the Cay's oldest sailor and considered the best rakontistos onboard, if not the world. The youngest of the crew, including Trueblood, sat at his feet and crowded the arms of his chair. The ship's newest member, barely nine years old and terribly homesick, sat in Rafil's lap, eyes drooping with the effort of holding tears back all day.

"Of all the children of Os," Rafil said, "Nyos was the greatest and most loving. When Os divided into sky and land, Nyos planted a tree to bridge the two. Rooted deep in the earth, the tree's nine branches touched the sky, where Nyos anchored each one with a star."

Abrakam, the Cay's wise and wonderful centaur, passed a book around, beautifully illustrated with pictures of Nydirsil, the great Tree of Life.

"As she anchored the ninth and tallest branch to the ninth star," Rafil said, "Nyos accidentally tore a hole in the sky, releasing the winged horses. The pegasos."

"What was on the other side of the hole?" Trueblood asked.

The sitting room hissed with shushing noises.

"The hooves of the winged steeds tore another hole in the sky," Rafil said, "releasing the birds, who came to earth and build nests in Nydirsil."

Trueblood was unwavering in his curiosity. "Where were the birds before?"

"Nobody cares," the ship's cook said. His name was Seven, because after bearing six children, his mother had given up on names. Seven's younger brother Eleven was among the crew, and their youngest sibling, Sixten, was the lad dozing in Rafil's arms.

"I care," Trueblood said.

"Well, I don't," Seven said. "If I wanted scientific explanation, I would've gone to university. I became a sailor and the face value of stories is enough for me."

"Lad, it wasn't so long ago *you* were the one asking questions," Rafil said to him. He jostled Sixten against his arm. "And it won't be long before your brother starts challenging every story that crosses his ears."

"I just wondered where the birds came from," Trueblood said.

Kepten True's golden eyes twinkled at his son. "Not many things are to be taken at face value, Pé," he said. "Legends are one of them. Let's enjoy the tale."

The book passed hand to hand. Few could read the ancient text but the pictures coupled with Rafil's voice were all they needed.

"Nydirsil's roots were fastened below the ocean floor, down into rock and through lava to the core of the earth. The birds nested in the lower branches while the upper canopy, among the stars, was home to the pegasos.

"Nyos took no mate, for her one great love was for the tree. Nydirsil drew love up like sap, into her trunk and branches and leaves. Nydirsil swelled with buds and the buds opened to release Nye, the spice of life, the source of love and the birthplace of happiness."

Sixten was asleep now, mouth parted against Rafil's sleeve. Kepten True stood by the fireplace, which the giants had cleverly built into an exterior wall and vented out to the weatherdeck. The fires it held were kept prudently small, but the two-stepped, tiled hearth was wide and a favored place to sit for story hour.

True rested an elbow on the mantel, gazing fondly at his crew. His eyes lingered on Pelippé, his only child. As usual, the boy sat between the *Ĝemelos* brothers, Raj and Lejo. Their shoulders touching and their six outstretched legs stacked like wood.

"Forests of Nye trees grew thick over the land," Rafil said. "They swelled with buds and released clouds of Nye spice. But no seeds fell from their spent flowers. No seedlings or saplings grew at their feet. For only Nydirsil dropped seeds to grow into new trees. The birds took the seeds all over the land and planted them in the earth."

The book closed. Rafil said no more, but the wheel of his story continued to spin in the quiet room. Trueblood stared at the pile of his feet, Raj's ankles and Lejo's calves. Keenly aware the story of Nye was still being written and it could end in his lifetime.

Once, the ship called Cay transported Nye to every port city in every part of the land. A special hold in her hull called the *nyellem* was stacked to the ceiling with casks of the beautiful spice. But that *once* was long ago. Beyond the time of Kepten True's father and grandfather and his grandfather's grandfather. The Cay's history was built from generations of mariners from House Tru, stretching from this sitting room back to the time of the giants. All the stories told in past tense led up to today's present truth: Nydirsil was gone.

"What happened?" Trueblood asked. He knew. He only asked to fill the swollen silence. And because it was polite to the rakontistos to pretend you never heard the tale before.

"Once," Rafil said, "a great feud was fought between Nyos and her twin brother Truvos, god of the sea. It started when Truvos climbed Nydirsil, stole the nine stars that held her branches to the sky and gave them to his lover, Khe. Loosened from the sky, the tree toppled and swayed, until her roots began to pull free from the earth. Nyos begged her brother to return the stars, but Truvos would not.

"Nyos slew Khe," Rafil said. "But before she could take the rings, Truvos slew his own sister. Nydirsil was torn from everything she loved and everything that loved her. Truvos sailed away in his mighty ship, towing the Tree of Life behind, vowing he'd never give back the nine stars until the love he knew with Khe returned to the earth threefold.

"Truvos took Nydirsil away, and all the seeds for new trees went with her. Now when a Nye tree died, nothing took its place. Less spice was in the world. Year after year, a little less. Decade after decade, less spice in the holds of ships. Century after century until Nye grew too scarce to be traded, and it began to be hoarded."

"But what does Nye do?" Trueblood asked. "What's it *for*?"

"It makes the world beautiful," Abrakam the centaur said. "Simply by existing."

A collective sigh went around the kepten's sitting room, each crew member thinking of the nyellem, deep in the Cay's hull. They could only imagine the golden age when it would've been crammed full of casks. Today the Cay sailed with her nyellem dark and barren, only the scent of Nye lingering in its walls. Some believed the spice hold was kept empty out of respect. Others felt it was a sign of hope. One day spice would again be as abundant as air and water, instead of a scarce commodity and the cause of so much trouble in the world.

"Every year a little less love and a little more trouble," Rafil said, and Sixten whimpered in his sleep.

"Enough," said Kepten True, who regarded the empty nyellem as a sign of hope. "Larks still bring the souls of newborns, even if no seed is dropped to mark the beginning. Finches still return souls of the dead, without a seed to mark the end. Even as the trees die and Nye decreases, we live and we die. One day, Nye will be no more. Which means what?"

He paused for effect, meeting each of his crew's eyes.

"It means we can't take beauty and love and goodness for granted," he said. "We can't sit around and wait for the world to be made beautiful for us. We must find beauty in a troubled world. We must *be* the goodness Nye once granted. And what are things beautiful and good, lads?"

"Stories," Seven said, and other crew members chimed in.

"Truth."

"Respect."

"Friendship."

"A job well done."

"Ships built by giants."

Hands thumped the floor and table tops in appreciation.

"Never forget this ship is made from the wood of Nye trees," Kepten True said. "Who better to live as Nyos intended if not us? Trouble and despair and greed are for lesser men. Not mariners. Do you understand? Answer your commander."

"Aye, Kep," his crew said, shaking their heads and limbs out of the melancholy. They got up and one by one, approached the kepten to say goodnight.

Kepten True believed in a day's beginning and ending. He liked evening biddings to be something sweet to lay your head on. He liked a formal greeting in the morning, to show the day was new and the slate clean and the possibilities endless.

The kepten knew not every ship's commander took the time to open and close the day. But it had been his grandfather's way. Then his father's way. The True Way. It was one of the few things he took at face value and didn't question.

"Good night," he said to each sailor. "Rest well."

"*Amatos*, Kep," they all said in return. *Until the morning.*

Pelippé was last. He didn't sleep below decks, but in a room off the foyer of the kepten's quarters, across from Abrakam's cabin. This, too, went unquestioned. After the murder of his wife, nobody faulted the kepten for wanting his son close by, or accused him of favoritism.

Kepten True looked forward to the day when his son would retire at an adult hour and be the last person True said goodnight to. For now, Pelippé was last among the *minoros*, the crew under the age of sixteen. True folded the boy into his long arms and kissed his head.

"You are my story," he said. "And I love nothing the way I love you."

ESPECIAL

KEPTEN TRUE NAMED his son after Pel, the giant who built the Cay. *Ippé* was an ironic suffix meaning "little," often given to those who already stood head and shoulders above other men.

Ikharus-Lippé True was eight-and-a-half feet tall and giants of old would've considered him a runt. His height was a rarity in the modern giantsbloodline, which grew more diluted with every generation. Pelippé was over six feet and still a growing boy, but he doubted he'd reach his father's height. His mother was a Treeblood, a family known for being petite.

Noë Treeblood had been a *vicreĝo,* one of the elected regents of Nyland. Her marriage to Ikharus was regarded as a superb uniting of two dynastic houses, and everyone approved Trueblood as the surname for their only child.

From an early age, he was known by his surname alone. Those closest to him called him Pé, but because his resting expression was either curious worry or worried curiosity, many of the Cay's older crew called him Troubled.

"What's on your mind, Troubled?" they'd ask, jostling him out of deep thought.

Or, "What's troubling Trueblood?" as they startled him from the pages of his leather notebook, which he always quickly closed.

Trueblood was seven-almost-eight when Abrakam Centauros gave him his first journal. It was right after Noë died, when Trueblood's troubles robbed him of his voice. Into the pages he put all the words he couldn't speak aloud, framed by little drawings in the margins.

He was twelve now, and on his fourth notebook. No longer silent, yet he still liked to end his day by filling a page or two. He was a skilled artist, and he considered writing to be an extension of drawing. The flow of hand to pen to paper and the construction of letters and words was satisfying work, but he found stringing words together to express himself difficult. He almost never read what he wrote out loud. He cared less about how his thoughts sounded than how they looked on the page.

He inscribed the flyleaf of each notebook with the same words, in his especial beautiful penmanship:

The Most Private Journal of Pelippé Trueblood
An especial accounting of his life
and voyages on the Cay.
As written by Pelippé Trueblood
(Me)

"ESPECIAL ISN'T A word," Abrakam said, glancing over the boy's shoulder as he started a new tome.

"Yes it is," Pelippé said. "My mother said it." It was one of the few things he could remember in Noë's voice.

You do have especial beautiful handwriting, Pé.

The old centaur's eyes filled with love and sadness. "It was her accent, lad. People from Alondra often put an E in front of words that start with S."

"Well, I'm from Alondra, too."

Whenever Trueblood spoke of his destroyed birth city, his voice felt too big for his throat. The sack of Alondra robbed him of both mother and motherland. He didn't like talking about it. Not on paper, not out loud.

Abrakam put a hand on this serious boy's head.

"Well-argued, Troubled. It'll be your especial word."

From the Most Private Journal of Pelippé Trueblood

These are the people I love.

My father. His full name is Ikharus-Lippé True. He has a title that comes before the name, which is Kepten. He owns and commands this ship. He is my father but also my commander. When he asks a question, I say "Yes, Da." When he gives an order, I say, "Aye, Kep."

Da has gold eyes and long black hair he wears in many braids, as is the way of giants. My hair is being trained for braids so they are short right now, and red-gold at the tips. Da says this is because my mother's soul kissed each one.

Da is tall, because men descended from giants are of a very magnificent height. The bed in Da's cabin is the longest bed on the ship and also the longest bed I have ever seen. It was made for giants because they were so very tall.

One day I will be kepten of the Cay. My father is teaching me about it. It's a lot of work to command a ship and the people on it. I have lots to learn but Da is patient. I ask a lot of questions, because Da likes people who are curious. He doesn't like people who boast or brag. He is strict, but he doesn't punish mistakes. He only punishes disrespect.

Da took me aboard the Cay when I was seven-almost-eight. Usually boys don't go to sea until they are nine. But after my mother died, Da wouldn't let me be anywhere but with him. He is my home and the person I love most in the world.

TOP OF THE WORLD

ONCE A YEAR, the Cay invited youngsters over the age of nine to take the ship's single entrance exam: climbing her main mast. It was made from the trunk of one of the greatest Nye trees ever to grow on earth. Five men could embrace its base and touch hands, if they stretched their arms.

From its ironbound foothold in the bottom of the ship, this wooden needle stretched to pierce a hole in the sky. The anchoring shroud lines holding it straight were bigger around than a man's clenched fist. The ratlines, strung like ladder runs between the shrouds, were broad planks of wood for the first fifty feet, then became braided rope the rest of the climb. Floating like a cork hundreds of feet above the deck was the crow's nest, where six men could sit comfortably as they kept watch.

The *maristos*—crew members over the age of twenty-one— took turns climbing behind the candidates. coaching where to step and grab. By tradition, a kheiron hovered close by, ready to swoop in if there was a fall. Or a panic.

These children who tried to climb the Cay were the stuff of family legend. Stories and tales abounded, detailing success and failure, courage and surrender, near misses and close calls. But none recounted death on the mast. There never had been a fatal fall.

For a week, the Cay threw her gauntlet at the world's youth. A hundred might accept the challenge, but when the ship set sail again, only four or five new faces would be among the minoros.

Most of them stayed for life.

PELIPPÉ TRUEBLOOD CLIMBED the Cay's main mast when he was six. No crowd cheered him on. No kheiron circled his ascent. Only a few early-rising crew members watched quietly from the deck.

"And your mother watched, too," Kepten True said. "She looked through her telescope outside her bedroom window. Do you remember?"

"No," Trueblood said. He remembered his father below him the whole time, advising a little here, coaching a bit there. He praised good technique and chided careless missteps. Trueblood winced at the admonishments and never made the same mistake twice.

"Are you afraid?" his father occasionally asked.

"Yes."

"Good boy."

The fear was healthy, and more for not being able to finish than falling. Trueblood wasn't afraid of the height. He needed little encouragement above the topsails. The view was exhilarating. The climb felt natural. He paused once to put arms around the mast and hug it, his smiling cheek to the rough wood. He *loved* the Cay's impossible dimensions and her siren call upward, farther and farther, beckoning him to touch the sky.

The day was beautiful, perfect and superlative. He was young and brave, still two years away from the tragedy that would wipe his childish memory banks nearly clean. Today, however, would remain in the basket of his heart like an un-cracked, unblemished egg. Every detail intact.

"This is the best thing I ever did," he said when they reached the crow's nest and the earth stretched on either side of him, as far as the eye could see. Like a humungous pair of arms flung wide, declaring, *I made all this for you. Do you like it?*

"You are the best thing I ever did," Kepten True said, swinging Trueblood up in his arms. Perched like a bird in the nest of his father's hip, Trueblood gazed at the top of the world. True's long black plaits blew around in the wind. The air was thin, clear and salty. The rock of the ship as comforting as a mother's cradling embrace. Wanting for nothing, stretched wide with happiness, the boy turned his face into his father's shoulder and wrapped arms around his neck.

"I love you, Da."

His father hugged him tight, one large hand heavy on his head.

"You are my true blood," the kepten said. "And I love nothing the way I love you."

The descent felt more precarious. Trueblood didn't like not being able to see where he was going. Climbing up was a test of courage, but climbing down was a lesson in trust and prudence. He relied more on his father's guidance. He thought twice before he stepped once. His father praised him for resting often. By the time he made the awkward scramble past the futtocks shroud, his body was wrung out. In a mixture of elation, relief and bravado, he jumped the last ten feet to the deck below. His exhausted legs buckled and he toppled on his bum, somersaulting over one shoulder and sprawling on his stomach. Accomplishment burst out of him as hooting, gasping laughter. A crowing triumph that abruptly stopped when his father seized his arm and hauled him roughly to his feet.

"Do you know what that was?" he asked in a quiet, dangerous voice. His fiery topaz eyes turned Trueblood inside-out. His grip around Trueblood's upper arm immutable.

Trueblood opened his mouth and shut it, not understanding.

"That was lazy," True said. "And it was showing off. You didn't finish the job properly. You let your emotions finish, you took an unnecessary risk and that's when things go wrong. That's how people get hurt or even killed at sea."

He let go his son and crossed his arms over his broad chest. Unable to bear that reproachful stare, Trueblood looked down at his feet, which were blurred by tears. His skin burned under the benign gaze of the crew members and shuddered beneath the weight of his father's disappointment.

A horrible moment passed.

"Look at me, Pelippé."

Chin wobbling, throat tight, Trueblood looked up.

"I've seen too many sailors achieve excellence on the open sea then grow careless once land is in sight. I and you don't have the luxury of assumptions. We do not strut as the end of a task is near. And when the job is done well and completed properly, no strutting is required. Excellence needs no announcement. Do you understand?"

"Yes, Da."

True's head tilted slightly. "Answer your commander."

"Aye, Kep," Trueblood said.

The next day, he climbed the main mast again. He remembered everything his father taught him and finished the job properly, staying on the rigging until the very last step onto the deck.

"Well done," Kepten True said. He hugged the boy tight to his side a moment, then let go and headed toward the gangplank. Trueblood followed, not strutting. The accomplishment didn't laugh or crow this time. It sat dignified and pleased in his heart, knowing it was a far better thing he'd done today than yesterday.

Once on the wharf, Trueblood slid his hand into his father's. The strong, warm fingers folded around his and squeezed. The twinkling golden eyes smiled down at him and whispered, *Excellent.*

MEMORY

PELIPPÉ TRUEBLOOD DID not remember many things from his childhood.

When he was seven-almost-eight, his mother was murdered and his brain simply decided to forget nearly everything and start over. When people told him stories of his tender years, he believed them, but the faith was disconnected and detached. These things surely happened, but he doubted his role in them. The doubt made him ask the same questions over and over.

Ikharus-Lippé True was a patient father, and treated every repeated inquiry as if it were the first.

Trueblood asked, "Who killed my mother?"

He knew the historical answer, the account put into books and taught in lessons. The radical Cult of the Bull had secretly organized into an army and shocked Nyland with a surprise attack on Alondra. They came up through the sewers, leaving a sunpowder trail in their wake that blew the ancient city apart. The minotaurs looted, sacked, raped and pillaged their way to the palace, their red eyes on the prize of Alondra's Nye vault. The lock of the vault's main door had one and only one key. It hung at the belt of Noë Treeblood and the minotaurs killed her to get it.

The Vicreĝo of Arbaro died at the hands of the minotaurs, the history books read. But Kepten True understood his son wanted a name. *Who* had struck the death blow?

"I couldn't tell you exactly who," True said. "I wasn't in the palace that day."

"Where were you?"

"Here on the ship. We were anchored beyond the harbor. You know Alondra's port wasn't deep enough for us."

Few port cities in the world could accommodate the Cay's vast hull. Everywhere else, including Alondra, she had to anchor at sea and the crew rowed in by longboat.

Trueblood often imagined his childhood was a ship anchored far beyond his conscious memory, and his father's stories the dinghies that rowed in the information he wanted.

He asked, "Where did they find me that day?"

"In your mother's bedroom," Kepten True said. "Do you remember at all?"

"No."

Whenever he tried rowing himself out to that distant, anchored ship, he found it permeated with the acrid scent of smoke, the coppery stench of blood, and something even worse. Something foul and violent, something done to his mother, something terrible and not to be remembered.

"The kheiron guards found you curled up next to her," True said. "You had a piece of her torn skirt in your hands."

This was a detail Trueblood had full faith in. The piece of his mother's skirt was still in his possession, a remnant of green velvet with an embroidered tree dripping gold and red leaves. The Cay's sail makers sponged away the bloodstains and lovingly tacked the torn fabric to a piece of soft wool, binding the edges with strong, expert stitches. Trueblood clutched it for the better part of a year, dragging it around the ship until the sail makers had to replace the wool backing. Gradually he let go the need, or the need let go of him. Now he kept it smoothed on top of his pillow during the day, then folded it carefully and put it under the pillow when he went to sleep.

Sometimes, when sleep eluded him, his hand slid beneath to caress the softness and finger the beaded leaves, but that wasn't anything anyone needed to know.

"What happened after the kheirons found me?" he asked his father.

"Sevri il-Kheir scooped you up and flew you out to the Cay." Kepten True's voice always tightened at this part of the story, the words making themselves tiny so as to emerge with as little pain as possible. "He brought you back to me."

Trueblood wished he remembered this. Sevri il-Kheir was the Horselord, king of the kheirons. Trueblood sketched picture after picture of the heroic rescue in his notebook, drawing himself wrapped in green and clutched in il-Kheir's human arms. He took great pains with every feather of the Horselord's spectacular wingspan. He held the tip of his tongue tight in his teeth as he struggled with the equine body, trying to get the legs just right. Abrakam often helped him by posing, holding a leg or hoof still for Trueblood's anxious pencil.

From the Most Private Journal of Pelippé Trueblood

Abrakam is someone I love. He has sailed with my father for many years and they are good friends. Abrakam teaches me all the things Da can't, like music and archery and languages and history. His cabin has lots of books with pictures, which are the books I like best. He is wise and good with problems. If I am worried and Da is busy, I talk to Abrakam and I feel better.

Abrakam is the smartest person I know, even though he isn't exactly a person. He is a centaur. That means he is one half of a horse and one half of a human. The bottom part of him is horse, which is good. He says it wouldn't be as nice a life if he were a horse head on two legs.

"Do kheirons live forever?" Trueblood asked. After stories about himself, he liked tales of horsefolk best, especially ones about the kheirons.

"Not forever," Abrakam said. "But still much longer than humans and they age much slower."

"How old is the Horselord?"

Abrakam had to close his eyes to think. "I believe Sevri il-Kheir is one hundred and forty-two. But he doesn't look much older than your father."

"Are he and Da friends?"

The centaur took a long time to answer. "It's difficult to be il-Kheir's friend," he finally said. "The Horselord is a complicated creature."

"But he saved me," Trueblood said. "When my mother died and the palace was on fire, il-Kheir brought me back to Da. He must have cared about him to do that."

"Yes. But also, once upon a time, il-Kheir lost something precious and your father brought it back to him."

"So they *are* friends," the boy said, crossing his arms in the way he did when he decided something was settled.

The centaur laughed and rumpled Trueblood's head. "Well-argued, lad."

"Can I look at the book?"

"Certainly."

Abrakam had a beautiful book about horsefolk in his cabin. It had more pictures than words, which meant Trueblood only had to turn pages and ask questions, and Abrakam made it come alive.

"See how the kheiron's hooves are silver?" the centaur said. "It's not like ordinary silver. It comes from the stars and it's what empowers his wings."

The kheiron in the illustration had a blue-black horse body and a human torso packed with muscle. Trueblood couldn't *stop* seeing him.

Abrakam turned the page. "When a kheiron shifts into humos, or human form, those silver hooves become rings. See them on his hands?"

"He only has nine fingers," Trueblood said, letting go the book to stretch his ten digits long.

"Because each symbolizes the nine branches of Nydirsil."

Trueblood thought about his best friends, Raj and Lejo. They were twins and they both had six fingers on one hand. It seemed significant to Trueblood. His friends having eleven fingers and kheirons having nine ought to mean something. But no matter how he overlapped the manual peculiarities and did the math, he never got a satisfying answer.

"What if a kheiron loses a ring?" he asked.

"Ah. That's a serious matter. A kheiron can't fly unless he has all his starsilver with him."

Trueblood's brows knitted. "So if you took one of his rings, you could capture him?"

"Well, no, not capture him," Abrakam said. "He just wouldn't be able to fly. He could still turn his lower body into a horse and run you down, though."

"Oh."

"Whether on four legs or two, a kheiron is a formidable warrior, Troubled. They're the best archers and swordsmen in the world. Stealing or taking one of their rings would be next to impossible. If you managed it, you'd be sorry."

Trueblood chewed on his bottom lip. "What if a kheiron *gave* you his ring?"

Abrakam lifted his head and blinked at the boy. "Well, that would…" His mouth curved in an upside-down smile and his head tilted to one side. "That would be a great honor indeed. It would mean he trusted you." The tilted head nodded now. "Or even loved you."

Trueblood turned a page. "If the starsilver controls the wings, what controls the horse part? I mean, can a kheiron get stuck as a full man and not be able to change back?"

"The power to shift lies in the moonstone," Abrakam said. "Every kheiron is born with one and wears it somewhere on his body. See, this one has it hanging around his neck. And this one has it on his wrist."

"And if you take it away or he loses it, he'll be stuck?"

"Indeed."

"Stuck as a horse or stuck as a man?"

"As a man."

Trueblood's fingertip traced the feathers of the kheiron's stretched wings. "If a kheiron lost a ring *and* lost his moonstone, he'd really be in the shit."

His glance up at the centaur was naughty, but no frown or raised eyebrow looked back at him. "Aye, he would," Abrakam said, staring off into some immeasurable distance or memory, his head faintly nodding again. "Your father can tell you a story about it."

"He can?"

"Ask him one day. Say, 'Da, tell me the tale called *The Kepten and the Kheiron.*'"

ONES WHO WERE THERE

IT'S ALWAYS BEST to hear a story from the ones who were there. So come with me, legantos. Let's sail back twelve years in time, when a slightly younger Kepten True navigates the Cay on her last voyage of winter. He's impatient to get home to Alondra, for he's soon to be married and has a child on the way.

Listen to learn it. Learn it to tell it. Tell it to teach it.

The Kepten and The Kheiron

Twelve years earlier

A MAN CAN CRAVE adventure and change yet still cling to his little rituals. After story time, Abrakam Centauros always uncorked a bottle of wine and poured out two glasses for the kepten and himself. Other crew stuck to ale, cider or rum, but Ikharus-Lippé True favored a thick port Abrakam called "Altynian plonk."

"Look at the shoulders on that," True said, swirling the goblet.

He laughed when Abrakam made a sour face. The centaur hated the wine but he loved the kepten, and the hour they spent alone after stories was True's favorite time of day.

They hadn't taken more than a few sips when they heard voices raised outside the aftercastle doors and a sailor burst into the sitting room. "Kep, a falcon just came in."

"At this hour?" True said.

"It's a caracaros."

The kepten unfolded his body from the chair, both wary and curious. Caracaros were only found in Altynai, a land closed tighter than a fist.

"Did you invite the Altyn headman to your wedding?" Abrakam asked.

"Of course," True said. "And he declined with regret."

"Of course."

"Maybe he's sending a gift."

A glance between the two friends, followed by laughter. Altyns did not give gifts of any kind.

The quartermaster came in, his burly forearm covered with a leather glove. On it perched a light brown falcon with a head of shimmering purple feathers and an extremely haughty expression. She snapped at the quartermaster when he tried to untie the red leather pouch on her leg, then held the claw out to Kepten True, dainty and patient.

"You're out late tonight, my beauty," True said, his heart soft with love for these majestic couriers.

Abrakam's expression was harder. "I don't have a good feeling about this," he said. The bird glared at him with yellow eyes that replied, *Don't shoot the messenger.*

The kepten unfurled the scrap of paper, took a cursory glance and handed it to Abrakam. After a lifetime at sea, Ikharus-Lippé True spoke three tongues fluently and could trade in a half-dozen others, but the pictographic language of Altynai was beyond him.

"Come quickly," the centaur said slowly, brow furrowed in concentration. "We found something."

True blinked, waiting for more.

Abrakam looked up. "That's all it says."

"Are you sure?"

They'd been friends too long for Abrakam to take offense. "Come quickly, we found something," he repeated.

Kepten True pinched the bridge of his nose. He'd already squeezed the Cay past Skhylla and Kharbidis into the angry, chopped waters of The Gullet. They were moving at an excellent clip along the coast of Hokosia and True didn't relish turning around and letting the bay vomit him back out again. He *was* in a bit of a hurry. He had a wedding to get to—his own. After months of disciplining the howling needs of his body, he was just starting to allow thoughts of his bride to loiter around the edges of his daily business. To thumb through memories of Noë's sound and scent and taste, imagine her in his bed and want her to distraction.

"Godsdammit it all." He stomped into his study, muttering his choicest words at the Altyns, who aggressively kept the world at a distance, or sent out passive messages that couldn't be ignored.

"We found something," he said. "I suppose it would kill them to say what."

"Then again, it might," Abrakam said.

Their eyes met. Unspoken words shimmered between them. The Altyns were obscenely wealthy from gold and gemstones they mined from the mountains. The range of impossible peaks separating their land from the desert was pockmarked with caverns and caves. What the Altyns discovered in those caves would've been the stuff of pure legend, if they hadn't allowed just enough of it to make its way across the world. They'd achieved the perfect balance of sensational rumor and documented credibility. Three casual words from the tribes—*we found something*—could make even the most cynical of men think of one, and only one thing: Nye.

And the thought of Nye made Ikharus-Lippé True turn his ship around.

ON THE OPEN seas, Kepten True trusted the wheel to a half-dozen of his best men. But he alone brought the Cay toward a coastline and away again, which was when things had the most potential to go wrong. If they did, the responsibility was his.

It was his father's way.

The True Way.

Sailors referred to the channel between Altynai and Hokosia as The Teeth, with good reason. Many a ship had been chewed up and spit out by her treacherous waters. Within the jagged rock fangs of Altynai's coast was a single, accessible inlet. One sea chart for this harbor existed in the entire world and it was owned by Kepten True. The Cay had an exclusive invitation to Altynai. Everyone else had to sneak in.

"The Teeth are aching this morning," Rafil said.

"No shit," True said, white-knuckled at the helm. His nerves were shredded but he kept his face composed and his commands smooth as he wrestled the ship into the inlet. He and Rafil took one longboat to shore with a second following. They might need it for whatever *something* the tribes found.

His discomfort increased when he saw a group of tribesmen waiting for him on the shore. At their feet was a makeshift litter, two long poles with a canvas sling. Whatever they carried on it, it wasn't Nye.

This can't end well, he thought. In all his voyages to Altynai, the tribesmen never met his ship. He always made his way up the mountain trail to them.

"Zornin, is that you?" he called through the ring of his hands.

"It's I," Zornin yelled back. "You and your man come with us. Send the other boat back, you'll need your crew. And rope."

"What the fuck is going on?"

"Looks like they have a body," Rafil said.

"Hurry, Ikharus," Zornin bellowed.

True hopped over the side and splashed to shore. Two Altyns went out to help Rafil beach the longboat.

"We found him in the forest," Zornin said, indicating the shroud-wrapped body on the litter.

"Who is it?"

"Let's go. Come." Zornin hustled True and Rafil off the beach and up the steep trail. The two seamen, not conditioned to mountaineering, wisely saved their breath and their questions.

They reached a natural rock outcropping that overlooked the forest. Here the Altyns built a stone tower for a greater vantage, and the three men clambered up to its observation deck. Zornin passed Kepten True a telescope and pointed toward the forest.

"Not the tallest tree but the one just north. On the harvest platform. Do you see?"

True exhaled as he turned the tubes of the scope and the circular field of vision tightened. "Holy *horses,*" he whispered.

"What is it?" Rafil said.

"Another body."

"Dead?"

"I can't tell. Wait. I think he just moved."

"How did he climb up there?" Rafil said.

"He didn't," Zornin said. "He fell out of the sky."

Kepten True lowered the telescope and looked at the Altyn. Dark liquid eyes peered back from the rugged, lined face, the gaze unwavering as Zornin reached into his tunic and drew out his closed fist.

"We found this with the corpse," he said. His fingers opened to reveal a silver ring in his palm. Beautifully carved in the shape of feathered wings that curved around the wearer's finger. Between the wingspan was the head of a horse.

True's eyes widened, flicked across the valley, then back again. "It's a kheiron up there?"

Zornin nodded. "Not just any kheiron. Look at the inside."

True took the ring and tilted it so he could read the engraving behind the silver wings. "Oh my Gods," he breathed.

Rafil's far-sighted eyes squinted over True's shoulder. "What's it say?"

"Tehvan il-Kheir."

"*What?*"

Heart pounding, True passed the ring to the boatswain. "It's the Horselord's son."

"Fuck me," Rafil said softly. "I thought he was dead."

"We sent the messenger birds out right away," Zornin said. "Two caracaros to you and two to Nyland. We counted on you being closer than the Horselord."

"He's alive," Kepten True said softly. His throat was tight but a little bubble of amazed laughter squeezed out as he said again, "He's alive."

The slimy anxiety coiled in his stomach dissolved, replaced by hard, bright purpose. He knew his job now, knew why he'd been summoned. Nothing on earth rivaled the height of these Nye trees. Nothing except the mast of a ship built by giants. If you needed something retrieved from an old harvest station in the spice canopy, you didn't call for a mountaineer.

You called for a mariner.

A GOOD KEPTEN took the helm and brought his ship to and from the coast, when things had the most potential to go wrong. He shouldered the blame ahead of time. It was the True Way, and Ikharus viewed the Nye tree no differently. He climbed first and climbed alone, establishing the route and tying the lead rope as he went.

His minoro crew watched from the lookout station, telescopes pointed up and out, like a many-headed, long-nosed monster. Among them was an inquisitive galley cook called Seven.

True took little on that first ascent. Two thick blankets strapped to his back. A waterskin. The kheiron's ring in his buttoned pocket. In another pocket, a bead of a powerful narcotic called *fadara*. No bigger than his little fingernail, yet if sold on the black market, True could purchase a house.

"Put it under his tongue," the Altyns' witch told him. "Let it dissolve before you give him water."

True also carried pen and paper, for once he got to the kheiron, the fastest way to communicate to the ground would be by caracaros. One circled the tree now, watching as branch by branch, choice by judicious choice, Kepten True climbed the mast of this earthly ship. He paused often to rest and think. Several times he stretched his arms around the mighty trunk, as far as they could reach, and inhaled the faint scent of Nye.

Right now I am a flower, he thought. *A single flower on a tree that used to bloom in love. I must be the goodness the forest can no longer give. And what is good and beautiful in this world?*

Respect. Friendship. A job well done.

"And stories," he said under his breath, hauling himself at last onto the harvest platform. "They'll be telling this one forever."

On hands and knees he crawled to the foalboy sprawled on the warped, splintered wood. His hair was white, his face dirt-streaked, bruised and battered. His torso was bare, the skin over his bones blue with cold. Loose breeches twisted around his human legs and through the bloodied canvas poked the evil edges of broken bone.

One of his rings came off, True thought, unrolling the pack from his back. *His wings retracted. The passenger, whoever he was, fell to his death. The kheiron aimed for a platform, took the brunt of it with his legs.*

He shuddered at the unprotected edge of the deck. It was a miracle the kheiron hadn't landed and rolled right off again.

He draped the blankets on the foalboy's shattered legs, touching them as little as possible. He took off his thick blue coat and tucked it tight around Tehvan's arms and chest.

"Tehvan," he said. "My one, can you hear me?"

The kheiron's head flopped side to side. He moaned softly, but didn't open his eyes.

"I'm here, lad. I've come to take you home."

The cracked lips parted, loosing a single sound. "Da?"

True's throat constricted. It was a saying among his people that *Da* was the most giant of giantwords. It meant more than just father. It meant the steel-hearted courage required to be a father.

"It's I, Tehvan," he said. "Kepten True. I'll get you down and take you home. I'm taking you back to your Da."

Two years, he thought. *Sevri il-Kheir has been taking the world apart two years looking for him.*

He got the fadara under the foalboy's tongue, then scribbled a note for the waiting falcon: *Alive. Both legs badly broken. Start my men coming up.*

"Fly, my beauty," he said. With a scream, the caracaros launched to the ground. True got some water down Tehvan's throat, then sat cross-legged and took Tehvan's cold hand between his large, warm palms.

Men have a right hand and a left hand, each with five fingers. Kheirons, my legantos, have nine fingers. One for every branch of the great Tree of Life. One for each star that held those branches to the sky, until the god Truvos stole them for his lover, Khe.

Khe, who was the father of the first kheirons.

Instead of right and left, the nine-fingered kheirons orient themselves toward their fourhand or fivehand. Kepten True blew his warm breath on the bare thumb of Tehvan il-Kheir's fivehand, then he slipped the lost ring from his pocket and returned it solemnly to its owner.

"You'll fly again, my beauty," he whispered.

IT WAS TWILIGHT when the litter holding Tehvan il-Kheir was loaded onto one of the Cay's longboats. An icy rain had moved in, and Rafil unfolded the oiled leather cover to shield the foalboy.

True watched with Zornin as the corpse was loaded onto a second longboat. "I hope we can find out who he is. Was."

"Whatever you do, don't look in that shroud," Zornin said. "Whether he fell out of the sky or fell out of the tree, he broke every bone in his body. And that was before the vultures came to feast. If the boy has a mother, she'd die of a broken heart."

"Gods," True muttered, the enormity of the day dropping a heavy fatigue on his shoulders. "Any idea which way they came from?"

Zornin rolled his lips in tight. "Both have slave brands on them. You do the geography."

True didn't need a map. The northeast corner of Minosaros was the last outpost of human trafficking on earth. It both bewildered and angered him that a place so wretched had such a poetic name: Arcodolori. It meant "arrow of sadness."

"We sent out new caracaros toward Nyland," Zornin said. "Telling the Horselord that Tehvan's on the Cay. You should send your own birds as well. Strange things are afoot, Ikharus."

"What do you mean?"

"Mother called upon the pegasos for help. They wouldn't come."

Kepten True hadn't the slightest idea how one would call upon the mysterious winged steeds, but it made a certain sense the elusive Altyns would know how to contact the most invisible of the Horsefolk creatures.

"They refused?" he asked. "When Tehvan's own dam was a pegaso? He's practically one of them, how could they not come?"

Zornin tugged at his chin hairs. "They didn't so much refuse as decline with deep regret. Mother said it wasn't that the pegasos wouldn't come, but they were forbidden to come. She has the same feeling about the birds we sent toward Nyland. Meaning it wouldn't surprise her if none of them arrived."

"But my birds might?"

The Altyn nodded. "It's as if something wants you to be right here, right now."

True snorted. "You haven't taken up smoking fadara, have you?"

"I don't touch that shit. But speaking of which…"

Zornin pulled a small, paper-wrapped package out of his tunic. He unwrapped a corner and showed True a small block of *kyrrh*—the rare resin that dripped from the Altynai's evergreen trees, known for both its healing properties and its high price. After Nye and fadara, kyrrh was one of the most valuable things in the world and it was not simply *given* away.

Yet Zornin handed it over like a bit of lunch. No price, no negotiation, no haggle, no expectation of anything in return. "Spread it on the wounds if he can stand it," he said. "Mother says you can shave a bit into hot water and make a tea. It won't obliterate the pain as well as fadara, but it won't fix him with a habit, either. Godsdammit, what that foalboy needs is Nye."

For a moment, the experienced, worldly Kepten True stood lost and bewildered, as if the sun had reversed direction in the sky. Then he reached an arm out to Zornin, elbow bent with fingers high, offering the ritual handshake called *gelango*.

Zornin clasped True's hand. Their palms shifted and slid to hold forearms. Each free hand rested on the other's shoulder and their brows came together for a single, shared breath.

"Take him home, Ikharus," Zornin said gruffly. "Give him back to his Da."

And so, legantos, Kepten True sailed out of the inlet with a very different idea of the Altyns than when he arrived.

RAFIL

From the Most Private Journal of Pelippé Trueblood

Rafil is the oldest person on the Cay. He is seventy-seven and has been at sea since he was ten. My grandfather was Rafil's commander and Rafil knows just a little bit more about the Cay than my father does. When Da has to make important decisions about sailing or fixing the ship, he will ask Rafil's advice.

Rafil is the only person on the Cay allowed to call my father by his first name. Sometimes he calls my father "lad." But only in private.

Rafil used to be the boatswain, which is a hard job and takes lots of time. He got too old to do it and now he just takes care of the rope for the ship. The giantword for this job is ŝnuromastisto, which is the dumbest word anywhere, ever. I like rope master better.

Rafil is an especial wonderful rakontistos. He knows more stories than stars are in the sky. I asked how he knows so many and he told me it's because he listens.

I try to listen to things carefully because I would like to tell stories someday.

THE CAY WAS anchored in Zeuxis, a port in Sanpago. Before this region was annexed by Nyland, Zeuxis was a crossroads bazaar of slave and drug trafficking. The invasion by Queen Nysiema and Sevri il-Kheir—a conflict commonly known as Tehvan's War—had rid the city of its worst vices. Ten years after the hostilities, Zeuxis' reputation still preceded. Especially the penchant for young boys.

Kepten True kept a strict curfew in Zeuxis and forbade sailors under the age of thirteen from leaving the ship. Older minoros and *majoros* had to stay in pairs or groups. Nobody walked around Zeuxis alone. No excuses, no exceptions. Any sailor who broke the restrictions got thrashed. And not a private hiding in the kepten's study, but nine bare-assed lashes in front of the crew.

One such beating happened only yesterday and Trueblood's stomach still hurt thinking about it. One day he'd be Kepten. He'd make rules and when they were broken, he'd be holding the strap and leaving welts on naked skin. His ears would have to shut out howls and moans, ignore snot and spit dripping on the deck as the offender sucked in air and cried between stripes.

A lesser boy might have relished such a prospect.

"What's troubling Trueblood?" Rafil said.

"Nothing." Trueblood shivered back to the present. He and the twins were on the weatherdeck with Rafil, sorting out and inspecting rope. On the wharf below, a vendor was selling nuts and seeds. The air was full of birds, scavenging, begging and thieving. A particularly cheerful goldfinch flew laps from the vendor to the Cay and back. It perched on the rail to warble and Rafil perfectly mimicked its song.

"The larks bring souls of the newborn to the earth," the old sailor said. "But finches return souls to the moon."

Lejo went statue still, holding out his six-fingered hand. The finch regarded him a moment, then flew into his palm. Trueblood watched with sour jealousy. He could hold his hand out for three days and no bird would come to him. But all animals seemed to love Lejo.

Lejo brought his palm close to his thoughtful gaze and a finger stroked the bird's bright yellow head.

"Where do they keep the soul?" he asked. "In their beaks?"

"They carry it in their feet," Raj said.

Lejo glanced at Rafil for confirmation. If Raj didn't know the answer to a question, he didn't hesitate to make something up.

"Now goldfinches," the old man said. "They carry souls of the righteous. Live a good life and a goldfinch will take you back to the moon when it's time. Live an extraordinary life and a charm of them will bring you home."

The little bird was sitting on Lejo's shoulder now. "What about redfinches?" he asked.

"Ah," Rafil said. "They deliver the souls of the damned."

"Deliver them where?" Trueblood said.

The old boatswain sighed as he finished coiling a length of rope. He eased himself to sit on the bulkhead. "Once," he said, "redfinches took souls of the damned to Nydirsil, the Tree of Life. Nyos would bury them in the roots so they could learn."

"Learn what?" Raj said.

"Where they'd gone wrong. When they atoned, Nyos would send them back."

Lejo's eyes rolled up as the goldfinch walked across his head. "Back where?"

"Back here," Rafil said, spreading his palms. "On the wings of a lark, newborn with a second chance."

Trueblood squinted his eyes at this information. "You mean, some people walking around have been here before?"

"It used to be. But when Nydirsil was broken off her roots and lost, souls of the damned had nowhere to go." Rafil held out his wrinkled, rough hand and the goldfinch flew onto it. "Live a good life, lads," he said. "Because when Truvos took Nydirsil away, it was the end of second chances."

The goldfinch flew away, leaving a quartet of sober men on the wharf.

"I'll tell you something about your father's soul, Troubled," Rafil finally said.

"What?"

"When your Da brought Tehvan il-Kheir home to Nyland, the Horselord was so grateful, he made an extraordinary promise. He vowed when Ikharus-Lippé True died, il-Kheir would take his soul home."

"Really?"

"He can do that?" Raj asked.

Rafil nodded. "It used to be il-Kheir always took souls home to the moon. Until there got to be too many people. So he got the finches to help him and soon they were doing it for everyone. But sometimes, for a rare soul, il-Kheir will take it himself. It's a great honor."

The twins wore identical expressions of awe. Trueblood, on the other hand, had mixed feelings. Pride that his father was a rare, righteous and extraordinary man. Trepidation that one day, not today but one day, his father would no longer be there.

FLY FOR NO MAN

KEPTEN TRUE CONDUCTED business swiftly in Minosaros. He liked to anchor early in the morning, offload and settle accounts before the sun was overhead, then take on new cargo as fast as possible. With a ship the size of the Cay, they could be at sea a little after sunset if everyone hustled without stopping and snatched bites of dinner between jobs.

Attendance at the evening story hour was sparse, most of the crew already fallen into their bunks. Only the most indefatigable souls showed up, or the sticklers for routine no matter how exhausted. Trueblood sat at the big round table with his most private journal, weary to his young bones, but valiantly trying to write a few words about the day. He was behind in his "People I Love" entries.

"Merevhal, you read us a tale tonight," Abrakam said.

A tiny rumble of hands thumping the floor as the Cay's boatswain chose a book and took the place of honor in one of the big chairs. Minoros pushed and shoved for the prime spots on the arms and at Merevhal's feet.

Merevhal is the boatswain, Trueblood wrote in his especial penmanship. *Which is the second-most important job on the ship. When my father is busy or resting, Merevhal is in charge. She is the first woman to be boatswain on the Cay in the whole history of the world, anywhere, ever.*

"Settle down, twerps," Merevhal said. She glanced up at Sixten, who leaned over the chair's back. "Gods, lad, if you're going to breathe down my neck, close your mouth."

Loud laughter, which Trueblood didn't share. His relationship with the boatswain was complicated. He felt strange giving her an entry under "people I love" when he wasn't even sure he *liked* her.

He wrote, *Merevhal is a good sailor and an important person, but I must tell the truth and say I am a little afraid of her.*

She was hard on him, much harder than the other minoros in Trueblood's opinion, though he could understand why. She was training him for command as well as service, which meant every move he made in Merevhal's presence made its way back to the kepten. Her demand had all the exacting and relentless scrutiny of his father, but with none of the biased, indulgent love. She let him get away with nothing.

"Your boatswain must be the person you trust most in the world," True often said to his son. "Your future crew is in his or her hands."

Trueblood understood his father's implicit confidence in Merevhal, but the understanding didn't sustain him in the long, arduous hours of the day when it seemed he could do nothing right. Or when he perched on a tight-throated, frustrated edge of rebellious anger, hating Merevhal with every ounce of his being.

One day he'd have a son of his own, and he'd have to put him in the charge of a boatswain and stand back, keeping his indulgent emotions out of the way.

He sighed hard, trying to break up the knot in his chest. The future leaned heavy on Pelippé Trueblood tonight. Breathing open-mouthed down his neck and making him feel he was behind, unprepared, and he should be making decisions about his command *now*.

He turned to a new page. His especial penmanship wobbled as he wrote, *When I'm Kepten, I would like Lejo to be my boat-*

swain. Da says your second-in-command must be the person you trust most.

He glanced at Raj with a twinge of disloyalty. He trusted Raj, but in a different way.

I want Raj to be my pilot, he wrote. *He always knows what direction to take, while Lejo always knows the right thing to do.*

Raj switched the cross of his ankles in Trueblood's lap. His expression was intent over an atlas. Raj lived for maps. Occasionally he jotted on a scrap of paper with the two pencils he held in his six-fingered hand.

Raj can write two different things with his sixhand, Trueblood wrote. *It's very wonderful to watch.*

On the floor by the hearth, Lejo sat center of a group of minoros, because he lived for company. One lad held Lejo's sixhand, eyebrows furrowed as he examined its extra finger.

Lejo's sixhand is his non-dominant one, Trueblood wrote. *He can't do anything useful with it, but when people hold hands with him, which is often, it's always his sixhand they take.*

He stared at the lines he penned and felt better. As Merevhal started to read, he sketched a goldfinch in the margin.

"This is the *Truviad,*" the boatswain said. "The epic of Truvos, god of the sea."

She held open the book to show a two-page illustration of the ocean. The foaming crest of every wave was the head of a white stallion, with the black-skinned Truvos riding the highest wave. Bands of gold scales clasped each ankle and wrist. His triple-spear pointed ahead. Fish and shells tumbled from his long hair, braided in hundreds of thin plaits.

"He looks like the kepten," little Sixten said.

All eyes swiveled to Ikharus-Lippé True, asleep in the other big chair, one side of his dark face melted into a palm. His big feet rested on a hassock and three minoros perched on the bench made of his long legs. A thick gold bracelet clasped each wrist.

Around his shoulders spilled his braids, each plait tied with a bit of blue thread.

He was so magnificent, so immutable with power and so soft with fatigue, it made Trueblood's gaze blur around the edges.

"Truvos created the kepten's people," Merevhal said, turning the book back around to read. "The sea god heaved mighty stones from the ocean floor and set these monoliths into the earth. They drew off essence from the great Tree of Life and became the giants.

"As Nydirsil dropped her seeds and forests of Nye covered the land, the giants took the tallest and strongest trees to make ships. House Tru became a great mariner dynasty, the only ones permitted to transport Nye around the world."

Merevhal's voice, so strident and overbearing across the decks of the Cay, softened around the story. The lamp glinted along the strong cross of her nose and eyebrows and blurred her face into something almost beautiful.

"Now, lads," she said. "Once a man called Khe was the devoted servant of Truvos. The sea god loved Khe best, often doing foolish things for his attention. Khe became fascinated with the pegaso that nested in the highest branch of Nydirsil. He called to the winged mare to fly down to him so he might adore her.

"'I fly for no man,' the pegaso replied.

"Khe asked Truvos to turn him into a horse. Truvos hesitated. All living creatures on the earth, including men and horses, belonged to his twin sister, Nyos, who did not like her creations changed or altered. But after Khe pleaded for nine days, Truvos relented.

"The sea god knew Nyos had made horses from a rock taken from the moon. He climbed to the top of the Tree of Life, chipped away a small bit of the moon and gave it to Khe. Whenever Khe held the stone, he could shift from man to horse and back again.

"Delighted, Khe showed himself in his horse form to the pegaso. He begged her to fly down to him so he might adore her.

"'I fly for no steed who is bound to the earth,' she said.

"Khe now asked Truvos for wings. Truvos again climbed the Tree of Life and stole the nine stars holding her branches to the sky. These he made into rings which he placed on Khe's human fingers. The starsilver made great wings open up from his back, allowing him to fly.

"'Come to me now,' Khe said to the pegaso. 'I who am no mere man, nor a steed bound to the earth.'

"But Nydirsil, not anchored to the sky anymore, was toppling and swaying and the pegaso was frightened from her perch. She flew away and Khe gave chase, forced himself upon the winged mare and sired the first kheirons, twins female and male. Each born with a moonstone that allowed them to shift between horse and man. Each born with the power of flight bound either to silver hooves or nine silver rings."

Merevhal turned the book to show the illustrations of the first kheirons. "Here is ele-Kheir, the Horsedam. The immortal female kheirone. She stayed with her mother, with a secret purpose kept safe on the side of the moon never shown to man."

A page turned. "And this is il-Kheir, the Horselord. He lived on earth as king of all the steed races. His mortal descendants threaded through time and his reign passed in an unbroken father-to-son line, looped like a string of beads around the centuries."

"Who is the Horselord now?" Sixten asked.

"Sevri il-Kheir," Abrakam said. "And Tehvan is his heir."

"Fen," Kepten True said behind his closed eyes. "He likes to be called Fen il-Kheir now."

"Why?"

True's chest swelled wide as he yawned and stretched. The boys perched on his legs rose up and down. "Fen is the giantword for finch. The Horselord's son defied death so many times, maybe he felt like he delivered his own soul."

"You delivered him," Trueblood said. "You rescued him from the top of a Nye tree and brought him home."

And il-Kheir promised to bring your soul home when it was time.

The kepten opened his eyes and looked at his son. Trueblood's heart pulled in two and twisted around itself. Love and pride tangling with the fear of growing up and watching his father grow older until the inevitable day when...

"Aye," True said. "But I'm not a finch, Pé. I'm just a single flower on a tree."

Trueblood wanted to run to him. Knock aside the lap usurpers and fling himself against his father's strong chest. But now the kepten was getting up, spilling boys onto the floor and bidding everyone goodnight through enormous yawns. Merevhal closed the book and smoothed it with a palm before handing it back to Abrakam. "To your bunks, twerps," she said.

THE SISTERS

From the Most Private Journal of Pelippé Trueblood

Osla, Sayenne and Rona are the only other women on our ship. They are not related, but everyone calls them "the Sisters." Actually Rona was born a man, but lives as a woman. Da says to call her anything but a woman is disrespectful. I've seen him dress down a few sailors for doing so, and none of them are with the crew anymore. Da does not suffer disrespect.

Once, a lot more women used to sail on the Cay. But in the four years I've been at sea, no girls have come to climb the main mast and join the crew. Da told me that given a choice between sailor or soldier, girls typically choose the army. "Nyland's endured this long because of the women who protect her," he says.

The Sisters are the Cay's sail makers. This is an important job because without sails, the ship can't go anywhere. Osla weaves the sail cloth. Sayenne measures it and Rona cuts it. Then they sew the sails together. Most ships have plain white sails but ours are different colors. This shows my father is an important man.

I like climbing the masts and rigging the sails, and I like learning how to tack and beat and get the sails to obey the wind. Once, I thought making sails would be easy work but it isn't. Canvas weighs a ton. The huge grommets that go in the corners of sails are stacked high and chained together so they don't roll around. When those chains are opened, everyone gets nervous. Sayenne is missing two toes after a grommet broke free and rolled on her foot.

The Sisters' workroom is a smelly, noisy place. The stench of the dyes can make you barf and the racket of the looms wears on your nerves. Sewing can be done on deck, thank Gods, but a sail has to be double-hemmed on all sides and you can spend a week on just one edge. Lejo likes the work, but I and Raj are probably the worst sewers in the history of the world, anywhere, ever.

The Sisters also sew clothes for the crew. We all wear white clothes and black boots. Everyone's breeches and shirt are a little different, but they are all white. I don't know why. Sometimes things are done on the ship and Da says, "Because that's the True Way."

Da has an especial blue coat he wears when he goes ashore because he is the kepten. One day it will be my coat, but I'm not sure I will fit into it.

EVERY YEAR, THE Sisters took Kepten True's blue coat apart. Removed every button, ripped every seam, washed and dried every piece and then sewed it all back together again.

"Why?" Trueblood asked. It was his job to clean and polish the buttons.

"The salt spray is bad for the dye," Osla said.

"Too much exposure and it can fade," Rona said.

Sayenne bit off a thread with her teeth. "It's the only coat of its kind."

"This shade of blue, Pé? It's from *ukhor* stones."

"Ukhor was only found in the ground at the roots of Nydirsil."

"It doesn't exist anymore."

"Nowhere else on earth will you see this color blue, Pé."

Trueblood followed the conversation around the circle. "Not unless someone finds Nydirsil."

The Sisters exchanged a glance, nodded as one and then bent over their work again.

"Maybe Da will find it," the kepten's son said.

"If anyone can find it, he can," Osla said.

"Have you heard the *Truviad*?" Rona asked.

"No," Trueblood said, because it was polite to the rakontistos to pretend you hadn't heard a story before. And he liked this one.

"Truvos stole the stars that held Nydirsil's branches to the sky," Sayenne said. "He made them into rings for his lover, Khe. The tree became unmoored, the weight of her branches making her trunk sway dangerously this way and that. Until her roots began to pull free from the center of the earth."

Around the circle the story grew, each sister sewing her part to the whole.

"The ocean floor cracked open, releasing a horde of demons and monsters into the sea. Leviathans. Sea serpents. Kharbidis, who sucked ships into her whirlpool mouth. Aspida, the giant turtle who disguised himself as an island and lured sailors to their doom."

"Worst were the twin kraken, Murder and Misery, who roam the waters to this day."

"Her foundation broken, the earth divided. Quakes and volcanoes rearranged the terrain. Old mountain chains crumbled into sand while new mountains punched to the skies like the fists of giants. Tidal waves flooded the land, wiping out much of the Nye forests and reducing farmland to salt flats. People began to starve. Famine brought war and disease."

"Nyos begged her brother Truvos to return the nine rings to Nydirsil before all was irrevocably lost. But Truvos would not relent. Nyos strung her mighty bow with an arrow fletched with peacock feathers, which contain the eyes of the stars."

"The feathers made her aim impeccable and true. Nyos never missed a shot. The arrow impaled Khe upon Nydirsil's trunk. He hung there nine days while the tree continued to pull free from the earth."

"In a rage over his slain lover, Truvos slew his sister. He took Khe's body down from Nydirsil and put it onto his ship, the Khollima. He chained the tree behind and sailed away forever. But not before leaving the world a message."

"Upon three monoliths uprooted by Nydirsil's roots, Truvos chiseled his conditions. He would not return the nine stars..."

"Until a love like he knew with Khe..."

"Came to earth threefold..."

"And hung bound with silver in Nydirsil's branches for nine days."

Trueblood had forgotten to breathe at the end. He exhaled beneath a furrowed brow. "That makes no sense."

His head wrestled with the image of a man and woman caught in a tight embrace, wrapped in silver chains and dangling from a branch like a piece of fruit. Threefold? Did that mean three couples had to hang from the tree?

"The great stones with the original *Truviad* were moved first to the library of Alondra," Osla said. "And after the sack, they were taken to Valtourel."

"Two of them, anyway," Sayenne said. "The third was lost."

"A bit of the second stone is missing, too," Rona said. "It broke off right in the middle of a sentence."

"That's why every copy of the *Truviad* is printed with its last page torn in half."

That night, before story hour, Trueblood slid the book off the shelf and turned to the back. Just as the Sisters said, the last page of the *Truviad* was torn across. Its rough edge had been touched with silver foil, making it a serrated blade that sliced through the last sentence:

He must begin his voyage where...

And then the story stopped.

Trueblood asked his father what he thought the rest of the sentence said.

"I don't even know who Truvos was talking about," the kepten said. "*He* who?"

Trueblood shut the book and slid it back on the shelf. "I don't like mysteries."

"Neither do I. But I'll tell you what my father said about the beginnings of a voyage."

"Don't leave port angry."

"Oh, I've told you this one?"

Trueblood leaned a little, letting his shoulder press against Ikharus's side. "Don't go to your bed with anger in your heart. And don't let land out of your sight if anger is filling your sails."

"Sage advice," Ikharus said. "When Truvos loaded Khe's body on his ship, chained the tree behind and set sail, he was *pissed*. And look what happened."

Part Two

LUNOS

Goddess of the Moon

Down...There

From the Most Private Journal of Pelippé Trueblood

Dhar is Osla's son and one of the sail makers. After my father, Dhar is the biggest person I know. He is both tall and wide. It is funny to watch him sew because his giant hands swallow up the little needles and make especial tiny stitches.

Dhar has a great big voice, too. If he is down in the holds and I am on deck, I can still hear him. Sometimes when I am in my cabin at night, the last thing I hear before I fall asleep is Dhar laughing, somewhere on the ship. This is something I love.

Dhar and Merevhal are gelang. This means they are together and love each other and sleep in the same cabin.

"DID YOU GET it?" Raj said.

Trueblood flipped up his loose shirt to show the book tucked in his breeches. "Come on, let's go."

The best way to appear invisible on the Cay was to act like you were working. Trueblood and Raj grabbed buckets and brushes, then clomped down the stairwells of the ship, grumbling loudly about a scrubbing assignment. Lejo followed, a mop over his shoulder, saying nothing.

Lejo, Trueblood once wrote in his most private journal, *is the worst liar in the whole history of the world, anywhere, ever. If you tell a secret to Lejo, he will keep it until he dies. But he won't be able to keep secret that he has a secret.*

The boys closed themselves up in a hold filled with iron ore they were shipping from Hokosia to Nyland. All the rest of his days, the sharp, rusted odor of metal would make Trueblood start to sweat in a nostalgic arousal.

The boys lay on their stomachs, Trueblood in the middle, and opened the tome at random. A bonanza of full-color illustrations lay before them. Couples half-clothed or unclothed. Faces with wide eyes, stiff smiles, strange expressions. An onslaught of bodies and limbs and...*parts.*

A long, page-turning silence, broken only by dry swallows.

"So that's what gelang looks like?" Raj finally said.

"I thought it would be..." Trueblood trailed off, not having the first idea what he thought. The wood of the hold pressed all along his thighs and knees and stomach. It was an effort not to squirm. To *rub* against it. He knew how good that would feel. Lately he was spending a lot of nights discovering how good it could feel.

"This is stupid," Raj said. "I mean they look ridiculous. They're just posing. Is that really what Dhar and Merevhal do? Stand around naked in strange positions, looking at each other like fish?"

"You don't stand still," Trueblood said. "You're supposed to move."

"They're not moving. He's just putting it in there and holding still."

Trueblood jammed his elbow hard against Raj. "They're not moving because it's a picture. You don't put it in and do nothing."

"How do you know?"

"Because that's how it feels good, you idiot. What, do you take it out at night and just hold it in your hand and do nothing?"

Please say no, he thought. *I can't be the only one.*

"No, but…" Raj's teeth closed with a click and his face flamed crimson.

Lejo, silent all this time, laughed against his crossed arms.

"You shut up," his brother said, turning the page.

"Huh," Lejo said. "That's interesting."

They stared a long time. Interesting wasn't the word Trueblood would've chosen, but this picture was certainly calmer. A man lay on his back and the woman knelt over him. Her hands rested on his shoulders and Trueblood closed his eyes a moment, imagining soft palms on his collarbones, pressing him down. Leaning on him with all that lush weight. Would it hurt? The man in the picture didn't look in pain. He smiled as he reached a hand up to the woman's cheek, as if reaching for a faraway star. Now Trueblood focused on his own palm, a girl's smooth cheek within. It would be flat at first, then grow round when she smiled. Her smile would curve right into his hand, like a tiny apple.

He squirmed. And rubbed. Just a little.

"She's pretty," Raj said quietly. A fingertip traced down the ripples of the woman's hair.

"Women are so round," Lejo said. His own pointing finger traced the woman's limbs, moving in and out of the curve of her tiny waist. Its delicate narrowness sat above an ample backside.

It's in her, Trueblood thought, slowly pushing his hips down into the floor. *That's why it gets hard. So he can put it in her. And reach up to touch her face while it's in her. He can touch all of her skin and she lets him. Because they're gelang. They're together and they love each other. They take their clothes off and sleep in the same bed and when he gets hard, he puts it in her.*

What does that feel like?

Would it be warm or cool? Dry or wet? Loose or tight? Would it be as tight, wet and warm as his fist could be when he spit in it and curled into his palm like a smile…

Raj turned the page.

Trueblood was light-headed. All that skin and nakedness. He was so confused. Tongue bone dry in a watering mouth. Head buzzing with something he didn't have a name for.

"Grown-up men are so hairy," Lejo was saying, drawing along this man's splayed legs. "Their bodies don't hide anything. They keep it all outside. Everything's on display, even their hair."

"She has hair under her arms," Trueblood said, pointing at the female who was as wide open as a wind-filled sail. "And hair down...there."

Lejo chuckled. "Raj has hair on his balls."

"So?" Raj said. "Why are you looking at my balls anyway?"

"Yeah, how do you know?" Trueblood asked Lejo.

"I sleep with him, dumbass."

Lejo, Trueblood once wrote in his most private journal, *is terrible at name-calling. Because he never means it.*

"I don't sleep with my balls in your face," Raj said.

"Ew." Trueblood shook his head hard to break up the visual.

"Anyway, women are more secretive," Lejo said, unperturbed. "Everything's tucked inside and invisible. You can't see anything."

"Well holy horses, these aren't inside," Raj said, pointing to the women's breasts.

"I think the artist was exaggerating," Trueblood said. "No woman I've seen has tits that big."

"Merevhal doesn't stick out like that," Raj said, nodding. "She'd tip over."

"Maybe women can control how big they get."

"Sure. Like I can control how tall my mast gets."

"You cannot."

"Oh yeah? Watch." Raj rolled over and went for the laces on his breeches. The other two boys howled laughing, shoving him off, yelling at him to put that *thing* away before he hurt himself.

"They'll be looking for us soon," Trueblood said. "We should go."

A lot of shuffling and throat-clearing as they got up, Raj and Trueblood casually arranging their shirts outside their trousers. Lejo was a little flushed along his cheekbones, but otherwise seemed unfazed by the whole episode.

The boys gathered their unused bucket and brushes and mop, opened the door of the hold and walked smack into Kepten True.

"*Héjo*, Da," Trueblood said, his voice shrill and guilty in his ears.

Raj gave his most dazzling smile and a grand wave behind him. "Well that hold doesn't need scrubbing," he said.

Lejo's eyes rolled toward his twin and closed briefly. "We were just reading, Kep," he said.

Raj kicked the back of his calf.

"Ow. What?" Lejo said. "It's the truth."

True's face was impassive but his eyebrows were having a hard time holding still. He glanced to the book tucked under Trueblood's arm and his chin rose slowly, then fell again.

"Reading's a fine thing but not when work's to be done," he said.

"No, Kep," Raj said.

"Put the book away and get up to the quarterdeck. That's where scrubbing is needed."

"Aye, Kep," Trueblood said.

"It's Abrakam's," Lejo said. "I mean, it comes from his library."

A corner of the kepten's mouth danced. "Well, we know how Abe feels about his books. Be sure to return it when you're finished. And don't get it wet."

"We'll be careful," Lejo said.

"Hop to it, now."

"Aye, Kep." The boys stampeded up three flights of stairs before saying anything.

"Can you believe it?" Raj said. "I thought for sure he'd have our hide."

"Why?" Lejo said. "Because we were lazing off?"

"Because of the book, stupid."

"You're the stupid one. Rafil always says, 'What's for you won't pass you by.' Right?"

"So?"

"So if this book weren't for us, it wouldn't be on Abrakam's shelves."

"But it's got dirty pictures."

Lejo stopped dead, wearing the closest thing to disgust Trueblood had ever seen on his face. "Gelang isn't *dirty*," he said. "Skin and bodies and tits and hairy balls are weird, but they're not… Honestly, Raj, you're such a horse's ass sometimes."

He sounded like he meant it. He stomped up the next flight of stairs. His brother and Trueblood followed, humbled and confused.

GELANG

“W HAT DOES GELANG mean?” Trueblood asked Abrakam.

“It has two meanings, Troubled. Sometimes it means at hand. Someone who is always there when you need him. Or it means together with. When you belong to someone. That’s a little more romantic.”

What’s romantic? Trueblood wanted to ask, but didn’t. Lately his words were a burden to him. He couldn’t say or ask anything he meant. Everything came out sounding stupid. He was so *frustrated* all the time. His body felt coiled like a spring, his skin too tight over his bones. He had one nerve and, holy horses, everyone and everything was on it. He bit his tongue hard in the presence of superiors, which meant he snapped at the twins and the other minoros, who snapped right back. The slightest provocation and they were in each other’s faces like feral horses, rearing and snorting and shoving.

Once, they fought so bad, Merevhal threw the lot of them over the side of the ship to cool off. They had to work together to haul themselves back out, which made them forget their grievances.

Until next time.

The minoros drove the boatswain demented, but Kepten True largely ignored the below-deck altercations. He only punished disrespect and as long as none of the aggression and foul language was aimed at him or the senior-ranking maristos, he viewed the posturing and head-butting as healthy.

"You're growing boys," he said. "You're doing what you're supposed to be doing."

Sometimes Trueblood was tempted to mouth off. Tell Merevhal to stick it on the dark side of the moon. Because maybe whatever was wrong with him was nothing a good hiding couldn't fix. Maybe if his outsides smarted as much as his insides, he'd feel better.

Gods, he needed something. He couldn't say what. His soul flung up its hands without the slightest idea what ailed it. He was hard in his fist every night, sometimes even sneaking off during the day to deal with this impossible need. Twice. Three times. It left him sated, but confused. He knew the ferocious release and its hot spurting result meant *something,* but not this. Or at least more than this. More than him alone in the dark with his damp hand.

Lately he couldn't stop staring when Dhar and Merevhal went to bed and their cabin door closed. He was consumed with what they were doing in there. Right here on the ship. Right *now.*

THEY. ARE. DOING. IT.

So fixated were his thoughts, so persistent and so *loud,* he was sure everyone onboard knew what he was thinking. How he looked at every maristo and wondered what he'd look like lying on his back with the woman from the book astride him.

Does he do it? Has he ever done it? Does he like to do it? When does he do it?

When his bewildered gaze fell on his father's tall body, he felt a mixture of revulsion and fascination that left him unable to look Ikharus in the eye.

Da's done it. Of course. He did it with my mother.

This was unexpectedly sad.

Does he miss her? Does he lie on his back and look up at nothing, and reach up to touch a face that isn't there anymore?

If you lose the one you belong to, are you still together and gelang?

Can your hands still feel them?

From the Most Private Journal of Pelippé Trueblood

Beniv is Sayenne's son and also a sail maker. He was very sick when he was little and the sickness made one of his arms so bad, they had to cut it off. The other arm was sick, too, but he still has it. It isn't a strong arm and his fingers are twisted, so Beniv learned to sew and do other things with his feet. It's a very wonderful thing to watch. His stitches are even tinier than Dhar's.

Da is quite fond of Beniv. He says it was a sight to see when Beniv climbed the Cay's main mast. Eleven years old, with only one weak arm and his two incredible feet. He made it to the top, but halfway down he was exhausted and asked the guarding kheiron to take him the rest of the way. Da says he took Beniv aboard because he knew when to ask for help.

Beniv always works hard and likes to do a good job. He doesn't want pity for the way his body is. He asks for help if he needs it and never complains.

Once, Trueblood watched Beniv whip the finished hem of a sail with thousands and thousands of criss-cross stitches.

"Is that to secure the edge tighter?" Trueblood asked.

"Gods, no, lad," Beniv said. "Fine linen cord like this doesn't add strength." He bent toward the thread stretched from the canvas to the needle held in his toes. He bit it off and smoothed the hem. "It's just because."

"Because why?"

"Because I like how it looks."

Trueblood glanced up at the Cay's main mast. "But you're the only one who will know how it looks. And only if you're up in the crow's nest inspecting it."

Beniv smiled. "That's fine."

"But why bother?"

"Because it makes a good job into an excellent job." His weak, withered hand reached to pat Trueblood's shoulder. "Whatever job you're given, Troubled, be *excellent* at it. Even if you're the only one who knows. Especially if you're the only one who knows."

It made no sense to Trueblood until he wrote about it in his notebook that night, adding a little sketch of a sail rigged to a mast. He took his time bordering its hem with dozens of tiny Xs. As he hummed under his breath, the conversation with Beniv clicked into his soul like a lock turning. When Trueblood put things in his most private journal, he always did an excellent job, even if no one else would ever see it. He spent the effort *because* nobody else would see it. The pride he took in his especial beautiful penmanship and the pleasure derived from drawn details was for him alone.

Everything Good in The World

THE FOOD ON the ship was good, but plain. The bread was dull in taste and texture. Fruit was dried and cloyingly sweet. Meat smoked, fish salted and vegetables pickled. Trueblood was never hungry, but the extreme food left him perpetually thirsty. The fresh water stored onboard grew stale in its barrels and never slaked to satisfaction. Rainstorms offered a welcome break, but often it wasn't until the ship pulled into port that the crew got to drink their fill of truly fresh water.

Trueblood and the twins knew the location of the finest well in every port city. They'd rush the gangplank and make a beeline for the square or plaza or market. They'd drink and drink and drink and drink, bellies growing round under their breeches. The kepten would find them draped on the cobblestones, sighing and moaning in icy, sweet relief.

Water came hot in port cities too, and the crew had its favorite bath houses. Kepten True ran a clean ship and nobody was permitted to go unwashed. Bathing at sea, however, was an infernally chilly business. Quick shivering sponge-offs in the galley or a brave plunge off the side of the ship when they were anchored. What luxury to strip down and submerge to your chin in steaming hot water, lathering up properly with well-made soap and lingering until you were wrinkled.

Slaked and clean, the three boys went in search of their favorite goods and foods. In the sketchy ports of Sanpago, they had to stay with the kepten at all times. Trueblood held one of his father's big hands, Raj held the other. Lejo held his twin's hand, his five fingers firmly yoked between Raj's six. The boys craned their necks, looking up at obelisks topped with golden bulls. They passed modest temples Kepten True said sprawled underground in an endless warren of catacombs, passages, labyrinths and mazes. Unspeakable things hiding in their depths.

The marketplace vibrated with sights and sounds and scents. After years of war and strife, Sanpago was under the protection of Nyland and striving to turn over its soil and reinvent itself. Most of the region baked under a shadow-less sun, but along the coast, terraced gardens grew figs, dates and olives. Hectares of sunflowers turned their heads to follow Solos across the sky. The burgeoning Apiary Guild was gradually cornering the honey market.

Since cattle were revered in this land, and consumption of pork forbidden, nearly all the cuisine in Minosaros was vegetarian. Sanpago was becoming renowned for its superb milk and cheese exports. After a week at sea with a hold full of dairy goods, the lower decks of the Cay let off a pungent aroma that could knock you on your ass.

Desert traders came to the Zeuxis markets, too, tying camels by their brightly-colored tents. They sold stained-glass windows and priceless rugs and tapestries. With the former wrapped carefully in the latter, the Cay crossed the Gullet and made its way to Hokosia, moving clockwise around the giant continent. First to the east coast, with its marble quarries and clay-rich soil. Calvo, the quartermaster, stacked the clay according to group, and Trueblood loved the names: kaolinite and illite and chlorite. The chunks and bricks lay damp and dank in the hold, heading to the eager hands of potters and sculptors.

Next was the south coast with its forests of oak and pine and its fields of indigo. This was the realm of the Printer's Guild. The Cay took on timber but Abrakam took on books. Trueblood always bought his leather notebooks, pens and pencils at the same shop and Raj prowled the markets for old maps.

Around The Horn of Hokosia to the west coast, a cornucopia of farmland produce, fruit orchards and vineyards. Sheep herders and flax farmers supplied the textile cities. Here the Sisters purchased the raw materials to weave the Cay's sails and the crew's clothing, along with dyes and sewing implements.

Finally, the ship reached the foundries and seafood markets of the north, which made the holds reek of rusty metal and fish.

From Hokosia, the Cay sailed to Altynai, and weather permitting, dropped anchor in her secret inlet. They sailed away with a hold full of gold and jewels, which smelled of nothing.

"Wealth has no scent," Kepten True always said.

Pelippé Trueblood was never as full of questions about gelang as when the Cay pulled into port.

"Why are brothels always built near the wharves?" he asked Abrakam.

"Convenience," the centaur said.

"That makes no sense."

"It will one day."

The houses of love were sumptuous and sparkling buildings, towering up two, three, sometimes four stories. Trueblood watched as some majoros ducked beneath signs advertising women, and others slipped through doors in search of men. Seven, the Cay's cook, picked establishments that offered both.

"At the same time?" Trueblood wondered to the Ĝemelos. Raj's expression was twice as curious while Lejo's was somewhere between trepidation and distaste.

Lejo, Trueblood once wrote in his most private journal, *is rather funny about matters of gelang. Raj has a bold and fearless mouth and can make any situation gelang-y. Lejo makes crude jokes the same way he calls names. He just can't mean it.*

The boys wouldn't be allowed into brothels until they were sixteen. In fact their presence wasn't even welcome on the streets where the courtesans lived. Once shooed away, Raj's sense of direction would find the way to fun, while Lejo's went in search of misfortune.

If the needle of Raj's compass turned in all directions, Lejo's only pointed to right and wrong. He led his brothers away from trouble not worth their time, guiding them toward trouble they could fix.

Lejo sniffed out lost children and people dying unaided in alleyways. His needle had a keen edge for stray animals. Kepten True drew a firm line against pets on the ship, so Lejo was always bereft when they set sail. He'd stand forlorn at the rail as the city pulled away, his hands aching for kittens and puppies and birds.

"You're our pet," Abrakam said.

Which was true, whether it consoled Lejo or not. His was a tactile nature, and every crew member unconsciously reached an arm or hand when Lejo walked past. Not a beat of conversation missed as Lejo was drawn into crooks of elbows or under a shoulder. He never minded hands running through his hair or circles rubbed on his back.

Women are always handing their babies to Lejo to hold, Trueblood wrote in his most private journal. *Not because they need a favor, but because they want a blessing. They think whatever makes Lejo so simple and kind will rub off on their own children.*

Raj wasn't averse to being cuddled, he simply didn't hold still long enough. He only went still in his sleep, his body wrapped around Lejo's as the ship rocked them in arms and the ocean cradled the ship. Far beneath them, the holds of the Cay swelled with goods and riches.

One hold was closed off and empty. The thick door fit in its jamb without the slightest crack. The walls, floor and ceiling were gorgeous, honey-colored wood. The smell within defied description.

This was the nyellem. The hold that once transported nothing but casks of Nye. Empty now, save for a single bed and the scent that had buried itself in the grain of the wood.

A night's sleep or even an hour alone in the spice hold was a reward for a well-done sailor. The one time Kepten True whipped his son in front of the crew was when the boy went into the hold without permission, then failed to shut the door properly.

Trueblood did his share of foolish things, but he rarely made the same mistake twice. Particularly when the lesson made him eat on his feet and sleep on his stomach for a week. After that hiding, he always asked permission to go into the nyellem. He often asked twice. When allowed inside the hold, he rubbed his hands along the smooth walls, filling his pores with the lingering scent. He carefully closed the door, checked it twice, then raced on deck to find Abrakam or Rafil or his father, and press his redolent hands to their faces.

"What a gift," the centaur always said.

"That's the scent of everything good in the world," old Rafil said.

Kepten True closed his eyes, inhaling deeply. "Thank you, Pé. I needed that."

MONSTER

From the Most Private Journal of Pelippé Trueblood

Calvo is the quartermaster. The giantword is kvartermas-tisto. He is in charge of all the holds in the ship and all the casks and crates that go in them. He must store food correctly so it doesn't spoil—both our rations and the foodstuffs we ship. Textiles like cloth and rugs can't get wet. Boxes and barrels must be precisely stacked so the ship is balanced, and secured tight so things inside don't get broken.

Nothing comes onto the ship or goes off the ship without Calvo knowing about it. When we come into port or are leaving port, Calvo is very impatient and short-tempered because he worries about the things in the holds. Once we are at sea, he is a much calmer person. But I must tell the truth and say I am a little afraid of him. His job is difficult and I get more tired working with him than anyone else. He yells at me a lot, but he always apologizes after.

Calvo and Beniv are gelang. That means they are together and love each other and sleep in the same cabin.

I T WASN'T OFTEN Trueblood and his father spent time alone. Leisure was a scarce commodity at sea. Days were long with arduous work and nights were for sleeping the work off.

One rare evening, Trueblood sat with his father in the aftercastle's sitting room. Typically this was the social hub of the Cay. The exterior doors were always open and the crew went in and out as they pleased. The smaller study and the kepten's bedroom were off limits. Even Trueblood had to knock on those doors and wait to be invited inside.

Tonight it was only father and son. Kepten True sat reading in his large chair, with a glass of the thick, port wine he loved.

"Look at the shoulders on that," True always said when he poured out his evening tot.

Trueblood tasted it once and screwed up his face as it burned from tongue to gut.

"Vile, right?" Abrakam said, laughing. "Like liquid prunes."

His father laughed harder. "Altynian plonk keeps the cargo moving, my friend."

Trueblood sat in the other big chair with his notebook. He found being alone with his father a wonderful thing. Their long, socked feet kept company on one hassock. The quiet, intimate evening made his mind reach into the closet of memory, open drawers he kept deliberately shut and draw out a carefully-folded garment.

I remember Mami sitting in her chair by the great fireplace, his pen wrote. *The light from the flames shines on her red hair. She leans to look at something I wrote and says, "You do have especial beautiful handwriting, Pé."*

"What's troubling my Trueblood?" the kepten said, pouring a little more wine into his glass.

"Nothing."

"Ah. My mistake."

Trueblood stared at the little fire crackling in the hearth, pen slowly twirling in his fingers. "Da?"

"Aye, lad."

"Do you miss Mami?"

"Oh." A big sigh. "Yes. To my bones."

"How did you know... I mean, when did you find out she died?"

True closed his book around a finger. "When il-Kheir flew you out to the Cay. He told me."

"Did you cry?"

"You don't remember?"

"No," Trueblood said. No drawer existed for that particular memory. He couldn't bear to even invent one. He had enough trouble imagining his father being gelang. His father *crying* was inconceivable.

"I cried until I thought I would die," True said. "My heart was broken."

Trueblood nodded. He knew this, but sometimes he needed to hear it. "You didn't get to say goodbye to her."

"No. No, she disappeared from my life. It was perhaps the cruelest thing ever done to me. When I wasn't crying, I passed the time being angry. Do you remember that?"

"No."

"Good," the kepten said with another sigh. "It wasn't my finest moment."

A polite rattle of knuckles on the half-open door and Calvo leaned in. "Saying goodnight, Kepten."

"Goodnight, lad," True said, raising his glass. "Beniv's feeling better?"

"Aye. Abrakam gave him a bit of something or other and he's asleep."

"Good, good. Both of you rest well."

"Goodnight, Troubled," Calvo said.

"Amatos," Trueblood said.

He counted ten before speaking. "Da?"

"Pé."

"Why do some men bed other men?"

The ceiling didn't collapse, so he went on in a rush. "And some bed women and some bed both?"

"Lad, you can bed anyone who wants to be bedded by you," True said. "But *why* one prefers men or women, or has no preference…" He smiled as he turned up his large, brown hands. "I always tell you few things in life are to be accepted at face value. Gelang is one of those things. It has no reason. It just is."

"But how do you know what kind of gelang you want? How will I know which I prefer?"

"That, Pé, is something else that just is. In fact, your mind already knows what it is and what it likes and what it wants. It's a part of your mind that sleeps while you're young, because gelang doesn't concern children. It wakes up as you get older."

"When?"

"Right around now," True said, and his smile grew broader. "All of you hairy monsters are starting to wake up. That's why you're at each other's throats all the time and driving Merevhal up the mast. Every one of your minds is trying to figure out what just happened, who it is and what it wants."

"Oh," Trueblood said.

Kepten True slid his silver hoop from his ear and rubbed the lobe thoughtfully. "If I remember correctly, it feels a bit like you're going mad."

With an exhale that could've filled one of the main sails, Trueblood slumped in his chair. "Lately I feel like a monster about everything."

He stared at the flame of the oil lamp, letting his vision split it into two flames and then merge into one again. He glanced over to see his father had been watching him all this time.

"I wish your Mami could see you right now," he said, eyes full of love and sadness. "She'd think you were an especial monster."

ĜEMELOS

THE CITY OF Alondra lay in ruins. Her wells poisoned, her streets abandoned. The miles of stone walls had long been scavenged away and the old palace was a pile of rubble. After the sack, Nyland moved her capital northeast to Valtourel, where the kheirons had always buried their dead and giants once had their shipyards. The Cay had been born in Valtourel, and she had no trouble anchoring in the harbor.

"Like a baby in a cradle," Kepten True said as he brought her in.

He had a house in Valtourel. Not as large as the old one in Alondra, but a caretaker kept it cleaned and maintained, and rented some of the rooms while True was at sea.

With each trip home, Valtourel was a little more built up, a little more thriving. A new palace reached spires into the sky. Trade was brisk in the marketplaces. The military barracks swelled with warriors. The new library was almost finished, as well as the crypt House Tru built to replace the one destroyed in Alondra. It took years to excavate and exhume the remains of so many mariners, their spouses and honored crew, but at last the bones were at rest.

The kheirons were constructing a new pavilion near the palace. The winged steeds strutted along the cobblestone streets or filled the skies over the harbor. As usual, Trueblood and his father called on the Horselord and as usual, Trueblood shrank into awed silence in the king's presence.

All kheirons were tall and muscular, their bodies built to support four legs and two wings. But one would think a giant had snuck into Sevri il-Kheir's lineage somewhere, for he was nearly as tall as Kepten True. Unfurled, his wings stretched eighteen feet from tip to tip.

Da once told me that many scholars hate kheirons, wrote Trueblood in his most private journal. *That is, they hate the idea of kheirons because they make no scientific sense. Not only are their wings built all wrong for flight, but their wings are in the wrong place for flight. One scholar wrote a three-hundred-page thesis proving a kheiron's wingspan would have to originate at the base of his spine and be eighty feet wide to support his equine body in the air. His calculations showed, without a doubt, that kheirons have no business being a foot off the ground, let alone flying hundreds of miles. He published the dissertation and then admitted himself to an insane asylum.*

Kheirons find this hilarious.

Sevri il-Kheir didn't give the impression of one who appreciated a good joke. Trueblood rarely saw the Horselord smile. Still, he was a splendid creature. His equine body was one shade darker than white. A pale gray that shimmered faintly blue in certain light. He wore his moonstone on a thin, black braid around his neck. His fivehand crushed Trueblood's fingers when he offered gelango, and the palm that dropped on Trueblood's shoulder felt heavier than a rolled-up sail.

"He's becoming a man," the Horselord said.

"Little by little," True said. "Is your son at home?"

"No, he spends most of his time up in Arcodolori," il-Kheir said. Then added under his breath. "Exacting revenge."

His icy blue eyes flicked to the ceiling and his tone dripped contempt. Kepten True cleared his throat and Trueblood studied a crack in the floor, uncomfortable. The relationship between his father and the Horselord confused him. Each had rescued the other's son. Theirs ought to be a legendary friendship. Certainly Il-Kheir always seemed glad to see the mariner and had never been anything but kind to Trueblood. But Ikharus's face didn't mirror the geniality. His smile around the Horselord was tight, his shoulders stiff and his manner tense.

"Is il-Kheir your friend?" Trueblood asked as they left the pavilion.

"Yes. But…" True took a long time to continue. "I respect him in all ways but one. I don't like how he treats his son."

"Why not?"

The mariner sighed. "In my mind, Fen il-Kheir is one of the bravest, most resilient souls to walk this earth. Yet his father treats him like a common pony." His long braids swept across his shoulders as he shook his head. "I don't understand."

"Because it's not the True Way."

Ikharus laughed and put an arm around his son. "Not at all."

Together they loped through the burgeoning city. Trueblood's stride had a bit of swagger in it. He'd just had his thirteenth birthday, and while he was still considered a minoro and would be for another three years, thirteen heralded a significant change in dress code—new black boots that reached his knees. The heels bumped importantly on the cobblestone streets. He glanced sideways at his reflection in shop windows, admiring how his white breeches were tucked smooth and trim within the boot's tops. He looked good. He looked even better after a visit to a jeweler's shop, where Ikharus allowed him to get his ear pierced. Just one ear, with just a plain silver hoop, just like Ikharus.

"Should we go see your mother?" True asked afterward.

Noë Treeblood was interred in the new mariners' crypt and Pelippé always took flowers to her. Tulips in season, for they'd been her favorite. Or poppies, though they didn't last long, dropping their papery petals before he could get them arranged nicely.

Sometimes, father and son arrived at the crypt to find an apple next to Noë's tomb.

"Who left this?" Trueblood always asked.

"Someone who knew her well," Ikharus always answered. "She loved apples."

Trueblood dreaded the visits. Not so much for the sadness, but because one half of the tomb's façade was inscribed with Noë's name and dates, while the other half was blank, patiently waiting for his father's death. Something about that smooth blank space was smug. It curled a lip and said, *You'll only have a short time. Then I get him forever.*

Trueblood was relieved when they set sail again. He didn't like the sojourns in Valtourel. The city was filled with courage and becoming more beautiful every year, but it didn't feel like home to him.

THE SHIP HAS many other crew members and I like everybody, Trueblood wrote in his most private journal. *But the ones I have written of here are the crew I especially love. Or especially fear, but out of love.*

He wore his troubled face as his thumb fanned the pages of the leather book. This narrative had a glaring gap in it. He hadn't written much about the Ĝemelos.

He loved Raj and Lejo best of all. More than anyone else and just a little less than his father. And yet he couldn't put that love into words. Still, he should try.

He chewed the end of his pen, then wrote, *My father found the twins on an abandoned ship. This was before I was born. Nobody knew where they came from or who they belonged to, so Da brought them back to Alondra and became their guardian.*

When he was younger, the simple story of how Kepten True found the twins was sufficient for Trueblood's curiosity. He only wondered who the twins' mother was, and what could have driven her to abandon the boys.

As his years piled up, he fixated more on the ship. What ship? Where? Why was it empty save for two babies?

Trueblood sighed and went on writing. *Our house in Alondra was quite large. Two of my mother's sisters lived with us, with their husbands and children. Raj and Lejo were always considered part of the family, but they were funny about calling my father Da. They called him Kep, and instead of taking the surname True, they wanted to be known as Ĝemelos. It's a giantword that means "the twins."*

I think they picked the name because deep down, they only belong to each other.

He was avoiding his feelings. Fiddling with his new earring, he fished in his heart, to the deep waters where his love for the twins ran like a constant current.

Sometimes the space between Raj and Lejo sparkles like stars, he wrote carefully, for he'd never attempted to describe this phenomenon. He was five when he realized the Ĝemelos had an aura, and ten when he realized he was the only one who could see it.

It's not visible dead-on, he wrote. *I can see the aura best when I look sideways at the twins. It's white-yellow around their silhouettes, hard and glinting like sunlight, while the space between their bodies is soft and it twinkles.*

The only person I ever told this to was Da, and he looked at me so strangely, I never spoke of it again, anywhere, ever.

He still wasn't describing how he felt.

Raj and Lejo are my brothers. We do not share blood, but we are brothers the way Osla, Sayenne and Rona are called the Sisters.

But that wasn't what he meant.

They are my friends.

He may as well have written the sky was blue. He nearly felt ashamed of the trite words.

We are gelang.

This was closer, which confused him. What he felt for Raj and Lejo seemed to fit his definition of gelang. He loved them and they loved him. They were together all the time and they slept in the same cabin. It *sounded* gelang. But Trueblood slept in his bed and the twins slept in theirs. They kept their hairy, monstrous parts to themselves which meant, Trueblood was sure, they were most certainly *not* gelang.

I love Raj and Lejo, he finally wrote, and threw the pen down in frustration. He took up a pencil and began to sketch around the paragraph.

He drew a compass rose for Raj, with his love of maps, his uncanny sense of direction and a preternatural ability to read the skies. Like any sailor, he knew all the major constellations. But he knew the minor ones too, plus he saw pictures in groups of stars no one had ever grouped together before.

For Lejo, Trueblood drew a different compass. No directional markings around the circumference. Instead, he shaded half the face black and left the other white, trying to convey right and wrong. To capture Lejo's guileless decency, the way he could divine the perfect thing to say or do in any situation.

His shoulders relaxed. Drawing always soothed Trueblood's soul and let his thoughts spin out a little more clearly.

Raj has simple tastes and emotions, he wrote. *He never worries. He pats problems on the head and tells them to run along. If he's cold, he puts on a coat. If he breaks something, he sweeps it up. If fear strikes, it's a sign he's doing something wrong and he changes direction. I never feel lost knowing Raj is in the world. If we're ever separated on the streets, I just stand still and he always finds me.*

Lejo worries. His mind goes down fifteen flights of stairs into a warren of secret rooms and passageways. But only love and kindness live down there. He's the most gentle person I know. Even on my worst days, when I do the stupidest things, I know Lejo always loves me. The time I left the nyellem door open and Da whipped me in front of the crew, I didn't let anyone see me cry afterward except Lejo.

Biting the corner of a sudden smile, Trueblood imagined a future Cay with himself at the helm, Raj and Lejo on either side. His pilot and his boatswain. His two compasses. His pen moved across the page, experimenting with a third-person narrative that might be told a hundred years from now.

When Kepten Trueblood needed direction, he sent for Raj. When the heart of Trueblood was troubled, he sent for Lejo.

THE TRUTH

RAJ AND LEJO had no memory of their origins and neither seemed to care where their mysterious ship came from.

Trueblood tried asking the older crew members who would've been with Kepten True at the time—Abrakam, Rafil or the Sisters. Oddly, none of their answers matched. They put the twins' ship in five different waters and described it five different ways. The only consistent aspect of their separate recollections was a distracted, almost dreamy expression in the telling.

When Trueblood asked his father about finding the Ĝemelos, the Kepten took on that same abstracted look.

"It was right after we rescued Tehvan il-Kheir in Altynai," he said. "We came across the ship and found Raj and Lejo. It was remarkable."

Each time, Trueblood waited for more. Sure more details would be forthcoming.

"Remarkable and wonderful," True said, his gold eyes looking through the air and into next week.

That was all.

This was his only version of the story.

Of course, legantos, the truth has a reason for disguising herself in five different costumes.

She'll tell you the tale. Just remember it's not always best to know the truth when others don't.

The Ancient Scent of Nye

Twelve years earlier

I T   W A S   A chore to keep the Cay's minoro crew out of the cabin where Tehvan il-Kheir lay. Few had ever seen a kheiron before, and none had seen one in pure human form.

"Where's his horse half?" they asked Abrakam. "He's supposed to look like you."

"He can look like whatever he wants," Abrakam said. "That's what makes him a kheiron. Now run along. Leave him be."

No sooner had one youth been shooed out than another snuck in, wide-eyed and full of questions.

"Where are his wings?"

"They're put away," the centaur said. "Does it look like he should be flying now? Stop hovering over him. And don't touch that."

"What is it?"

"It's kyrrh and it's not for you to muck with. Put it down and go back to work."

Shaking his head, the centaur turned around, and now Seven's questioning face looked up at him. "What was he doing in Altynai?"

"We don't know, lad. He was stolen away from his family two years ago and disappeared. Then the Altyns found him."

"Where was he?"

"In a tree."

"I mean before that?"

"We don't know."

"How did he get hurt?"

"*Out*," Abrakam roared through clenched teeth. "I don't have the answers to everything."

The kheiron burned with fever, his shattered legs neither improving or worsening, only holding him in a fixed place of pain. He lay in one of the cabins within the foyer of the aftercastle. When the crew gathered for evening stories, the young ones insisted Tehvan's door be kept open.

"He'll want to hear, too."

To honor their suffering guest and assuage the crew's curiosity, Abrakam read from the *Truviad* that evening, retelling the story of the first kheirons.

"The pegaso living atop Nydirsil flew away," he read. "Khe gave chase, forced himself upon the winged mare and sired the first kheirons, twins female and male.

"Il-Kheir, the Horselord, lived on earth as king of all the steed races. But ele-Kheir, the Horsedam, stayed with her mother, with a secret purpose kept safe on the side of the moon never shown to—"

"Kepten, are we moving?" Rafil asked.

Every head looked up and every body stiffened, dialing into the ship. They were bobbing, not moving.

"Odd," True said, striding out of the quarters and onto the deck. Beneath a sliver of moonlight, the wind was silent. The water barely made a noise.

"The air feels tight," Rafil said.

Indeed the night had contracted, leaning on the ship, heavy and dense. The bowl of the sky looked odd to Kepten True, as if it were turned inside-out. He searched for the familiar constellations of Nyos and Minos and found them right where they were supposed to be, but it brought no comfort.

"Strange things are afoot, lads," he said under his breath.

Kheirons falling out of the sky. Pegasos forbidden to help. Kyhrr gifted without a price. Now the wind ran away and the hand of night pressed the ship under its thumb.

Something wants you to be right here, right now.

"I don't like this business," he said louder. "Not one bit."

Rafil stepped closer to him, eyes on the sky. "This is a right cruel development."

"Zornin said something wanted me in that place at that time," True said. "But right now, it seems something doesn't want Tehvan il-Kheir ever to return home."

"Balls," Rafil said. "What's for him won't pass him by. Not while he's on your ship."

By morning, dead calm surrounded the Cay. The sails on all five masts lay limp, marooning the ship in a waveless, windless bubble.

Kepten True sat by Tehvan's bed, holding the boy's fivehand in both of his. He thought about the caracaros the Altyns sent to Nyland. He thought about the Cay's own messenger birds, dispatched toward Alondra, heralding the rescue. The memory of Zornin's words made him sigh over and over against the anxiety in his throat.

We called upon the pegasos for help. They wouldn't come.
Not that they refused. They were forbidden to come.
Wouldn't surprise me if our birds never arrived in Nyland.

"One will get through, lad," True said, patting Tehvan's hand. "Your Da will know soon I've got you. He'll be flying out to meet us. I'd like to see anything try to get in his way. He might even be coming right now."

Right here, right now.

He shivered in his skin, fearing the foalboy might not live to see his father again. Ikharus would have to face Sevri il-Kheir and tell him his only son died so close to home.

He freed one hand to dig fingers between his plaits, pulling hard at his scalp. They were so *close*. They'd flown over the waters from Altynai, the breath of the gods filling every sail. The Teeth barely grazed them. They slipped through the Gullet like a sip of sweet wine. The ocean flung itself out of the way, urging them on. *Home. Home. Hurry. Hurry.*

But then the wind disappeared, the ocean turned to rippling glass and the Cay sat still, staring at her own reflection.

"Godsdammit it all," the kepten said.

Tehvan stirred, his head turning from one side to the other and words under his breath.

"What's that, lad?" True said.

"Alon."

"Alon?" It was the giantword for lark. The birds who brought souls to the newborn.

"Those are caracaros," the kheiron whispered. "Alon, do you see them?"

He must mean the boy, True thought. *That poor wretched child whose bones were picked over by vultures. If he has a mother, her heart would break.*

"I'm sorry," Tehvan said. "It wasn't me, it was him."

"Shh." True put his hand on the foalboy's burning head. "None of it was your fault."

"Tell the story. Don't let it be forgotten."

"Hm? You want me to read, lad?" The kepten reached at random from the stack on the floor and came up with one of his childhood picture books. The spine tattered and the corners of the covers worn round. His thumb fanned the soft pages until he found an old favorite.

"Truvos, god of the sea, built three great ships from the wood of Nye trees," he read. "The Khollima, the Kaleuche and the Khe."

He balanced the book in his lap and kept tight hold of Tehvan's hand. Kept his voice rolling and soft as he read about those magnificent vessels.

The Khollima wasn't the largest ship, but she was the sole transporter of Nye for centuries. Then came the *Nyvosok*—the titanic feud between Nyos and Truvos that pulled the Tree of Life from her roots. Truvos sailed away on the Khollima, his slain lover Khe on a bier, towing Nydirsil behind.

"Never to return," True read, "until a love between giant and kheiron bloomed threefold on earth.

"The Kaleuche was the second giantship. Truvos built it with the help of the mighty twins, Ra and Lé. They built it bigger and taller and faster. After the *Nyvosok,* the twins became the leaders of House Tru. They surpassed all other mariners in skill, reputation and wealth. But then they sailed away one day and didn't return. Neither them, nor their crew, nor the Kaleuche was ever seen again."

Kepten True leaned toward the bed as if confiding a secret. "My grandfather swore he saw the Kaleuche once, and I've heard more than a few salty dogs say the same. Always at dawn, usually shrouded in mist. Funny thing is, two people who see the ship at the same time describe the experience in utterly different ways. What do you make of that, lad?"

Tehvan's fingers were limp, his breathing slow and deep.

"Rest now, *valentos,*" True said. "My brave one. You marvelous, gallant foalboy. You flew across a bloody continent. You rescued yourself and I'll make sure everyone knows it. Hear me? You saved yourself. I just helped finish the job."

He cleared his throat and read the last part on the page.

"The third ship, the Khe, endured. She was built with the help of Pel, the gentle and wise nephew of Ra and Lé. Pel brought honor and respect to House Tru. Some even said he was the embodiment of Nye, and this made the Khe endure. The ship passed from mariner to mariner's son, over generations of giants. And when the giants were no more, the ship sailed on, steered by half-giants. Then quarter-giants. Until the original blood of the race ran thin in the veins of House Tru. Yet it ran deep. And it endured."

He closed the tome, crossed his arms over it and closed his eyes.

Nobody remembers when the ship's name morphed from Khe to Cay, he thought. *Or when the dynasty's name morphed from Tru to True. Names come and go, lad. But we endure.*

We make our own beauty in the world and we endure.

WHILE THE BROKEN kheiron burned with fever, the sleeping Kepten dreamed of his bride. Noë Treeblood, sumptuous and sweet in his bed, winding him up in her arms and legs and her red-gold hair. The future beckoned his heart into the depths of her wide, gray eyes, pointing to a child who would call him Da.

"Your heart must be strong, Ikharus," Noë said, pulling free from his arms and climbing up a great tree. He followed her, resting often and choosing wisely. Nine branches spread from the massive trunk, each anchored to the sky with a single star.

"Eight branches for the eight gods," Noë said, pointing up through the canopy. "The ninth and tallest for Os, who is One. Anchored with Estelos, the greatest star. It takes a heart of steel to keep it safe."

True pulled her to him and she wrapped arms around his neck.

"Come home," she said. "I want to live in your heart."

She was liquid on his tongue and he swallowed her kiss, consumed his bride, the truth of his blood. She said his name and it was the most giant of giantwords. She plucked a star off the ninth branch, held it out to him like a silver apple. He went to bite it but instead she put it on his finger like a kheiron's ring and married him...

He woke and knew something was wrong.

He's gone. Tehvan's dead. He died in the night.

His startled lungs softened as Tehvan stirred in the big bed. His closed eyelids were violet and trembling, the lashes damp. A blue vein flickered in his temple.

"She's here," he whispered. "Go see."

Kepten True walked out of the aftercastle. A thick mist surrounded the Cay. His entire crew stood on deck, every pair of eyes transfixed and staring off the starboard side.

True slowly pushed through the shoulders of his men. Looking out, then up.

"My Gods," he said.

It was bigger than the Cay. Bigger than the sky. The top of its main mast shrouded by the clouds overhead. The hull stretching right and left as far as the eye could see. Every member of the Cay saw it, but no two would describe it the same way.

The air was perfectly still and silent as the Kaleuche pulled alongside her sister.

No one hailed them from its decks.

The Kaleuche bumped the Cay's hull. Precise. Almost delicate. She bumped their side again, soft as a kiss but deliberate with curious affection. As if to say, *Is it you?*

Tears sprang to Kepten True's eyes. All his life, he'd only known the power of the Cay. A thorough and intimate knowledge, but singular. It never occurred to him two giantships had a power and energy of their own. A personality. An affinity.

They're alive, he thought. *They know each other. Did the Cay call out for help?*

The Kaleuche stopped bumping and the wall of her hull began to move.

"Is she sinking?" Abrakam said. "Or are we rising?"

Nobody tore their eyes away to check. They stood mute and staring as the top decks of the sister ships came to the same level. The ships shuddered still, their sides caressing.

"Rafil," Kepten True said. "Come with me."

Boarding the Kaleuche was like stepping into a painting. Everything was preternaturally still. The ship was emptier than a cup. Not a scrap of humanity in the neat cabins or the Kepten's quarters. Not a book, a bottle, a candle stub, a shoe, a rag, not one object anywhere. The galley had no pots or pans, no dishes or knives. The workrooms echoed. The holds didn't even contain dust.

"It's so clean," Rafil said.

"I don't understand," Kepten True said, skin crawling with a strange sensation. Something between arousal and fear. "There's nothing here." His voice had conviction but his soul was in doubt.

Rafil's expression had gone soft. As if he'd fallen asleep behind open eyes. His rough hand slid into the crook of True's elbow.

"What's for you won't pass you by, lad," he said.

True clasped the boatswain's fingers, grateful for his presence. Rafil was the last of the crew who had sailed with True's father, and he was allowed to call True "lad" in private. If Rafil gave advice, True took it. If Rafil gave his word, True believed it.

If nothing for him were on this ship, it would've passed him by.

They walked the decks again. Slower this time, working from the top down.

They found the twins in the nyellem.

Two sleeping baby boys lay on a bed in the spice hold. The small room was wreathed in the scent of spice that ceased being transported in this ship centuries ago, yet its odor clung to the wood in the walls. It crept into True's nose and under his eyelids and along his tongue.

"Remarkable," he said. "Just like the story. The mighty twins built the Kaleuche, sailed away and disappeared. But here they are again. Reborn."

Time joined hands in a beautiful circle as True breathed in the ancient scent of Nye. His heart pressed against the wall of his chest and happiness like a cresting wave broke from the top of his head because *oh,* wasn't the world *wonderful* and these boys, *these beautiful boys* sleeping *and weren't they remarkable and wonderful and for him, of course for him and they hadn't passed him by, no, they were here, these boys, they glowed like starlight and if only he could climb the mast of the world and set them in the sky, set them at the tips of nine branches, they would bring Nye back to the world and wouldn't it all be wonderf—*

The door to the hold slammed shut, plunging Kepten True into darkness.

One of the babies whimpered, then fell silent.

"Rafil?" he called.

"No, Ikharus," a woman's voice said. "It's I."

He knew her. So strange this knowing—her identity certain in the most trusting parts of his heart. His faithful soul recognized her, yet his human, secular brain, so comforted by what he could give a name, needed more than this.

"Are you real?" he said.

"Of course. The centaur read my story two nights ago. Don't you remember?"

True reached open-eyed into darkness, as if to slide an imaginary book off a shelf. Pages fanned beneath his thumb, beautifully illustrated. Ancient script he could not read, only recite from memory.

Khe gave chase, forced himself upon the pegaso mare, and sired the first kheirons, twins female and male. Each born with a moonstone that allowed them to shift between horse and man, and the power of flight bound either to silver hooves or nine silver rings.

"Yes," she said.

The male kheiron was a mortal creature who lived on earth as il-Kheir, king of the horsefolk. His descendants threading through decades and centuries. The heir to that unbroken line lay dying on True's ship, the needle of time pierced through two fractured legs.

But the female, the kheirone…

The female stayed with her mother as ele-Kheir, with a secret purpose kept safe on the side of the moon never shown to man.

The Horsedam moved in darkness and legend. She was heard but rarely seen. Full of doubt and belief, Kepten True felt her cold gaze press his shoulders, heavy with intention. She had a purpose for him. She must, or the ship would've passed him by.

"What is it?" he whispered. "What do you have for me?"

"It's what you have for me." Her voice was silvery, cold and mournful. "I'm pleased it's you. And I'm sorry."

"It takes a heart of steel," Rafil said.

True stiffened. "Rafil, are you in here?"

"It's I, lad," ele-Kheir said. "I need a strong heart to keep my sons safe."

"Mine?" True said, beginning to shake. "Safe?"

She laughed in the dark, yet even her laughter was tinged with sadness. "You've made your heart into a beautiful thing, Ikharus. Your heart protects the Cay, but I need it now." A hand touched his shoulder. "The world needs it. Help me, Kepten True. This is for everyone."

"Can I see you?" True asked, his voice tiny and *afraid, so afraid of how wonderful-remarkable the world is for him, all for him…*

"None can see me," the kheirone said. "I live on the side that never shows its face to man. I came a long way for you."

"What's for you won't pass you by, lad," Rafil said dreamily.

"Yes," said the Horsedam. "He's right, Ikharus. And what's for me mustn't pass me by."

True had no idea what she was asking or why.

He only knew he could not refuse.

He breathed in the scent of Nye and turned around in the dark.

A mouth kissed his mouth.

O wonderful, remarkable, beautiful, you are mine, my lovely, scented like spice and silvery cool like the moon that—

Something plunged into his chest and tore his heart apart.

HE WOKE.

He lay in bed. His own bed on the Cay. The largest bed onboard. Possibly in the world. It was built for giants.

Drifting in and out of dreamless sleep. In and out of waves of pain breaking and cresting in his heart.

It burns, he thought. *Burns hotter than the sun. Burns like a star in my heart but isn't it wonderful and remarkable though it burns…*

He woke once and realized a sleeping baby boy was on either side of him, then the pain—*it burns so bright*—was on him again and he slipped underneath it.

When he woke again, he was curled on his side like a crescent moon, the twins nestled in the arc of his lap. His woozy eyes blinked and focused on the windows. Pure white clouds in a blue sky slid past the panes.

They were moving.

Good.

Home.

He looked down at the boys. Each slept with a little hand on the other's head. Each hand had six fingers. One infant's sleeping face exuded a quiet confidence, the air of one who isn't easily rattled.

You're not a giant, Kepten True thought, *but I will call you Raj. After the mighty pilot Ra, who steered the Kaleuche. He was the compass. The wheel. Some stories say his strength and self-assuredness were the ship's sixth mast.*

The other babe slept with his eyebrows slightly furrowed, wreathed in deep, complex thoughts. The little mouth pursed in a worried frown, then smoothed into a pleased smile.

You will be called Lejo, Ikharus decided. *Stories say Lé was the Kaleuche's rudder. His conscience was clear as water, his integrity unimpeachable, his compassion boundless.*

His large hand spread wide across the twin boys.

Ra and Lé sailed away and never returned. They disappeared forever into legend and lore. But I will never let you be lost again, my ones. My heart beats with yours. This day and every day.

The twins sighed together. The space between the little bodies seemed to twinkle. When True closed his eyes, pinpoint sparkles of light danced beneath his eyelids.

Far-away voices touched his ears. Raised high somewhere in the ship. All over the ship, shouting and calling, "The Horselord! The Horselord!"

"Il-Kheir is coming!"

"Clear the deck, stand aside, lads."

"It's the Horselord! Here for his foalboy!"

"Watch those hooves, stand back…"

Remarkable, Ikharus-Lippé True thought. He heard a rumbling clatter of hooves on wood before pain took him under again. *Remarkable and wonderful and lovely and…*

WHERE A HARD MAN COULD GO

THE YEAR CAME when Raj and Lejo turned sixteen and became majoros. At their next port-of-call, Raj boldly went to one of the brothels. Lejo did not follow. He stood on the street outside, making a visor with his sixhand and squinting up at the shuttered windows.

Fifteen-year-old Trueblood thought he'd feel wildly jealous when this day came.

He felt strangely indifferent.

Curious, but indifferent.

"You're not going in?" he asked.

"No. It's not for me." Lejo turned with a smile both shy and dazzling. "I'd rather be with you."

The words made Trueblood's heart whip around and stare.

Me?

Lejo took his hand. "Where should we go?"

We? Trueblood thought.

You mean, I and you without Raj?

The notion shivered deliciously. Lejo was walking now, pulling Trueblood's arm out long, wanting him to come. Trueblood followed, willing and intrigued. As they wandered the city, he found he liked the feel of Lejo's six fingers between his five. He let go to point at things, to purchase and peruse, but when they set off again, Lejo's hand went looking for his.

He liked being looked for.

His young bones stretched with a new aplomb. When they passed shop windows, he noticed the reflection of a black man following them. Tall with broad shoulders beneath white clothes and long legs ending in black boots. His hair was shaved close from the temples down, with a corona of short plaits above, each touched copper-red at the tips. Handsome, composed and confident.

Wait, he thought, each time he caught sight of the man in the glass. *That's me.*

He became aware of appraising, admiring eyes on him and Lejo. From both women and men. He liked it. Sometimes the gazes were glazed with jealousy.

He liked that, too.

As the day passed without Raj's enormous presence, Trueblood quietly studied the nape of Lejo's neck and how the light caught the fine hairs there. He'd known forever that Lejo had dimples but why hadn't he *noticed* how they winked in and out of sight and beckoned a fingertip's touch? Did breeches hang on every boy's hips that provocative way, or just Lejo's? Would any boy's head feel good lolling against his, or only Lejo's particular head and its soft, sunshiny smell?

Something's happening, he thought, every time his glance collided with Lejo's direct gaze. Or whenever Lejo held a finger out to shy birds, crouched down for stray cats and scratched the ears of sober, old dogs. Then he'd hold his hand out to Trueblood. Balance his chin on Trueblood's shoulder to look at the world. Dig his fingers between Trueblood's plaits and scratch.

Something's happening.

Raj didn't come back to the ship that night. Lejo moved over in his bed and folded the blankets back. Trueblood blew out the lamp and got in with him.

They didn't do anything but laugh and make stupid jokes at first. Then they kissed a little, which neither had done before, but they'd seen it in Abrakam's books.

"Hold still, Pé."

"Sorry."

"And stop laughing," Lejo said, laughing.

Trueblood felt a little dumb about the kissing. The nervous laughter wasn't helping and he wondered, *Is this it?*

"Hold still." Lejo rolled on top of him, crushing Trueblood into the mattress, all of his body warm and hard.

Oh, Trueblood thought. *Oh, I see. This is… Oh.*

When his mouth parted in discovery, Lejo's tongue touched his and he felt a little less dumb. He closed his eyes and tilted his chin. Lejo had been eating oranges before bed and Trueblood could taste them.

"Gods," Lejo said. He seemed bigger. Bolder. The same sweet Lejo and yet…not. As if the absence of his twin had let some secret self off the leash to run wild. His hands holding Trueblood's head were both soft and hard. His kissing had a rhythm. It came in waves as he turned Trueblood's mouth this way and that through each crest and swell.

You could kiss fast or slow, Trueblood discovered. You could kiss an upper lip independently of a bottom lip and each felt different. Kissing made little noises squeeze through your chest and made your thoughts do somersaults.

This is…

He put one tentative arm around the new, strange and wonderful thing. Then the other. Lejo shifted his hips and suddenly what he had was up against what Trueblood had.

Oh, Trueblood thought. His brave hands slid down the long plain of Lejo's smooth back. They dipped beneath the loose waist of his sleep pants. His palms curled around and filled themselves and pulled it all in, getting Lejo to lie against him the right way. Getting that hard heat to *rub* in just the…

"Oh," he said out loud, as the secrets of the universe whispered in his ears.

"Holy horseshit," Lejo said against his neck, sounding like he meant it.

They laughed again, but the laughter was deep, wicked and daring. And when they pulled off their clothes and let their hands explore, they stopped laughing.

It wasn't anything Trueblood hadn't done to himself before. But to have *someone else* do it was an entirely different ship on an entirely different ocean.

Oh, he thought with a mixture of wisdom and relief. *Now I understand.*

"What are you smiling about," Lejo said afterward, nibbling the cap of Trueblood's shoulder.

"I once wrote in my journal that you couldn't do anything useful with your sixhand," Trueblood said. "I was wrong."

The night unfolded into an I-and-you-without-Raj map. Together they co-piloted this private ship, following the course of first desire. Navigating feelings big as boulders. Charting lands that had no name. Their bodies clanged like magnificent bells, then shuddered into humbled stillness.

They were young. They trusted each other implicitly. All they knew of sex was what they read in Abrakam's books or heard the crew joke about. Some things they knew instinctively. Others seemed logical. After all, if a woman had a soft place where a hard man could go, it stood to reason that...

"Oh," Trueblood said in the dark, and now his voice was a knife's edge. "Lé, stop."

"What's wrong?"

"It hurts."

Lejo froze. "Are you all right?"

"I don't like this. Let's stop."

"I'm sorry." Lejo moved off him a little too fast and Trueblood sucked in air with a hiss. "Oh Gods, I'm sorry," Lejo cried, and the night crashed in pieces on the floor. "I'm sorry, it's my fault. I probably did something wrong."

This was tantamount to Lejo saying he'd committed murder.

"You didn't do anything *wrong*," Trueblood said. "I just didn't like it."

"Pé, I'm so sorry."

"Stop saying that."

"I didn't mean to hurt you."

"I know. It's all right. Let's just do something else."

But Lejo had gone small and soft and didn't want to do anything. All that beautiful wildness was back on the leash, secured tight like a stack of grommets in the sail room. His face filled with love and worry as he made Trueblood lie down. Then he wanted to *look* where Trueblood was clenched and smarting and Trueblood pushed him off, laughing anxiously.

"Lé, stop."

"You want to put some cold water on—"

"It's fine."

"You sure?"

"Holy horses, quit fussing over my ass."

"I'll fuss if I want." Lejo stretched out and gently shoved Trueblood around a little, like he was a pillow. Finally he got his head in just the right place between Trueblood's shoulder and chest and sighed. "I'm sorry."

"It's all right."

Not entirely right—the pain was seeping away and the monster in Trueblood was still hard and frustrated. But he couldn't imagine doing anything gelang with an unwilling participant, so he lay still and quiet.

Lejo sighed again, slung an arm across Trueblood's body and a leg across his calf. "To tell the truth, this is the part I like best."

"What?"

"Being in bed like this." He yawned. "I mean, the *at hand* part of gelang is fine. I guess. Some of it scares me."

"What scares you?"

Lejo wound one of Trueblood's short plaits around his finger. "The feeling. It's so much. So big. I could feel my heart straining. Like it didn't have room enough for all of it. If Raj were here, I could kind of…push some of it over to him." Now Lejo's finger traced Trueblood's face. "But him being here doesn't work, does it?"

"There's no I-and-you-*with*-Raj," Trueblood murmured.

"And I don't know how to feel that much with anyone but Raj. Not yet anyway. Maybe someday." He moved closer to Trueblood, winding around him like a vine. "So *at hand* is all right, but I like the *together with* part the most. Just having someone I trust hold me this way."

Someone, Trueblood thought. *Not necessarily me. And I think the* at hand *part is more than all right.*

Raj is at the brothels filling his hands, but he's not necessarily together with someone there.

Lejo needs togetherness. He wants to belong and his hands don't have to be part of it.

His mind folded its arms and nodded, pleased all this had been worked out.

Anyway, at least I know I like to bed men.

He shifted underneath Lejo's trusting weight and bit his lip at the lingering soreness in his backside.

I think.

They had one more night alone in their cabin and spent it sleeping, curled around each other. Trueblood's young, curious body wanted more, but his father's words echoed in his head: *You can bed anyone who wants to be bedded by you.*

When the Cay set sail and Lejo was again sleeping with his twin, Trueblood didn't mind.

At least, not too much.

WAKING UP

"WHAT'S TROUBLING MY Trueblood?" Ikharus asked gently.

"Nothing."

"Ah. My mistake." The kepten draped his blue coat over a chair at the round table and sat. He took off each of his gold cuff bracelets and his silver hoop earring, setting them in a pile. Then he drew toward him the book Trueblood had been paging through. It was Abrakam's tome of horsefolk, opened to the illustration of the magnificent kheiron. His equine body the deep indigo of a night sky. Miles of skin flowing over the muscles of his chest and arms.

He looks good to me, Trueblood thought, wanting to his bones. *At least his human half. And the women in Abrakam's other book look good to me too.*

He'd had a taste of gelang and now the hungry beast was awake, moping over an empty plate.

"Did I ever tell you," Ikharus said, "what Tehvan il-Kheir did at your naming ceremony?"

Trueblood smiled sideways. "He likes to be called Fen il-Kheir now."

The mariner raised a long finger. "You are correct. My mistake again."

"What did he do?"

"It was Fen's first public appearance since being rescued. He walked into the great hall like a seasoned warrior. Nothing left of the happy little foalboy Alondra used to know. He'd built a fortress around himself. Just...untouchable. He came to the dais with il-Kheir, offered me gelango and kissed your mother's hands. He glanced at your bassinette and it was nothing more than polite. The same disinterest any fifteen-year-old would show a baby. He turned to go and then he suddenly shifted into equos."

"You mean a horse?"

True nodded, crossing his arms. "You could see the magic ripple down Fen's back as the human half of him turned equine. The hall went still and silent. Like the world was holding its breath. You made a little noise. One coo rising like a bubble from the cradle. When he heard it, Fen dipped his head and rolled one front hoof on its edge. Gods, it was something to see."

"What color is he?"

"Gray. But a silver-gray, like molten metal. His mane and tail are pure white and his eyes are blue. The equos only lasted a moment, then Fen shifted back to kheiros and walked away, aloof and untouchable again."

"But why?" Trueblood said. "Why did he shift? What did it mean?"

Ikharus's shoulders slowly raised and lowered. "Everyone wondered what it meant. I thought it was a gesture of respect, but Abrakam said Fen did it because he liked you."

"He didn't even know me."

"Exactly my thought."

Trueblood's face grimaced as he sorted through his already-sketchy childhood memories, trying to recall if he'd ever talked to Fen il-Kheir. He remembered the herd's general presence in the city and at the palace, with the epic form of Sevri il-Kheir looming above them. The kheirons were magnificent and fascinating for sure, but not the most accessible of creatures. *Untouchable* was the apt word Ikharus used. The herd was off-limits. Young

Pelippé Trueblood hadn't the courage to approach a kheiron, let alone befriend one.

Fen did it because he liked me?

"That makes no sense," he said.

The kepten was leafing through the book's pages, searching for a picture or passage. "Here. Listen. 'When a kheiron stands in equos, he stands as his purest self, with no defense or artifice or deception. He stands naked with his soul on display, with no excuses for his deeds and no apology for what he carries in his heart.'"

"I don't understand."

Ikharus smiled. "My one, sometimes you remind me of a kheiron in equos."

"I do?"

"You're a lad who keeps his soul on display. You don't make excuses for your mistakes or brag about your accomplishments." He reached to give one of Trueblood's plaits a tug. "And you should never apologize for what's in your heart."

The evening gathered father and son in its arms. Within the circle of lamplight at the table, Trueblood spoke of his discoveries about gelang. Not that he'd explored them with Lejo, but his idea that gelang was a ship with many decks and different holds.

"It's confusing," he finished. "One day I have it figured out and the next it slips through my hands and becomes a mess."

"You're waking up," his father said. "It's your time to learn of these things and be confused."

True kneaded his fingers as he spoke. Lately he was doing this on cold, wet days. Wincing as he flexed and stretched his big hands. Or getting to his feet with a tiny groan of effort or walking stiff-kneed after sitting a long time. He seemed a fraction shorter. Lines cut deep in his brow, radiated from his eyes and framed his wide mouth. When the light hit his long black plaits, they sparkled silver.

Trueblood was waking up. And the mariner was growing old.

MURDER

ONE DAY, PELIPPÉ Trueblood was going about his business on the Cay when he came across Merevhal crying. The boatswain was crying.

Arms crossed on the rail, head buried in them and *weeping*.

If Trueblood had found her butchering a puppy, he couldn't have been more taken aback.

He was a nineteen-year-old majoro now. He'd reached his full of height of six feet and ten inches, outgrowing his fear of Merevhal. Her brusque, formidable manner no longer twisted his stomach in knots, but seeing her laid-open and bawling her heart out, he didn't know what to do.

"Meré," he said, approaching on careful feet. "Are you all right?"

She lifted her head. Her face was swollen and tear-streaked, and yet lit up from within and without, glowing in a way he'd never seen before.

"What's the matter?" he asked, patting his pockets. In books, gentlemen always gave a handkerchief to a lady in distress. Trueblood had nothing in his pockets but lint. Should he offer her his sleeve?

He was growing frantic. "Merevhal, what's wrong?"

"For fuck's sake, I'm up the mast."

"What?"

She gave a shrill half-laugh, half-sob into her hands. "I'm having a baby, you twerp."

The Cay nearly capsized with shock and delight. Unbeknownst to Trueblood, Dhar and Merevhal had tried for years—*decades* to have a child. Now, at the beyond-hope age of forty-nine, the old girl was harboring a stowaway, as the salty dogs liked to say.

Dhar fainted. His mother, Osla, screamed with joy at the prospect of finally having a grandchild. Kepten True poured a tot of Altynian plonk for everyone and Merevhal strutted the decks like she'd invented procreation.

Then she started puking.

She'd never been seasick a day in her life, now she was parked permanently at the leeward rail, green to the gills.

"It's to be expected," the Sisters said, waving three hands as one. "She'll be over it soon."

Except she wasn't. The sickness only worsened, going from a shipboard joke to a serious concern and making Dhar essentially useless. Finally, Abrakam put a hoof down and told the kepten to get Merevhal off the ship.

Abrakam almost never tells my father what to do, Trueblood wrote in his most private journal. *But when he does, my father listens.*

So the wretched boatswain took shore leave and Trueblood was posted in her place.

He'd been trained well, and when taking the minoros in hand, he copied some of Merevhal's techniques, and some of his father's. Little by little, he carved out his own way of managing the crew. He knew he was doing a good job by the approving glances of the majoros. He knew the job was even better when his father had no complaints. A quiet "well done, lad," was all he needed to lay his head down at night and sleep peacefully.

He was sleeping when Murder attacked the Cay.

LONG AGO, THE earth was one. Then the stars were stolen from Nydirsil, the Tree of Life. Her branches separated from the stars and her roots tore free from the seabed. The earth cracked, splitting the land apart. Water rushed in to divide the continents and destroy the Nye forests. Mountains sank beneath the waves, or rose up where none had been before.

Monsters and demons poured from the rent ocean floor. The two most heinous creatures were the twin kraken, Murder and Misery. Ruthless hunters who destroyed ships and seafarers with their poisoned tentacles.

The history books would record Murder's attack on the Cay as happening within the South Channel. Raj Ĝemelos always insisted they were in the Horn, while Abrakam swore they were still in the Western Sea.

"*Kraken*," the night watch cried, ringing the mast bells and slicing the ship's pre-dawn quiet in two. "Kraken, to starboard! All hands on deck! Kraken!"

The Cay was not a heavily-armed ship and had never needed to be. The skilled crew could rig the sails on a moonless night in frigid weather, but they were unprepared for an ancient leviathan drawing whirlpools in the ocean with nine venomous tentacles.

Over and over the monster breached, his slimy body slicing into the water and building up the chop. The ship spun through the maelstroms, pitching and rolling. Sailors piled up as they were thrown from port to starboard, from bow to stern. A thick mist enveloped the ship. The rain blew sideways, slicking the decks.

We're going to die, Trueblood thought. Like many others, he'd been thrown out of bed when Murder hit the ship. He'd lit against the edge of the dresser and blood trickled from his clanging head. Through the pandemonium came a moment of regret for not writing in his journal the evening before. If he'd known today was the last day of his life, he would've made a better ending.

But who will tell the story?

"Longboats," Kepten True shouted from the afterdeck. Somehow he loaded his voice into the center of his chest and shot it like a harpoon through the fray. His eyes were everywhere, his orders slapping bandages on the wounds Murder tore open. He sniffed out panic like a hound and turned it into productivity.

But then the kepten went quiet.

His last order dwindled in mid-call and his eyes widened in an awed dismay.

"Da?" Trueblood followed the stupefied gaze, out beyond the roiling sea. The mist swirled and parted like a pair of curtains. The wind hushed and the rain softened. Murder bubbled beneath the water's surface and disappeared. The ship turned one more circle and settled. Everyone stared.

Later, no one would describe what they saw the same way.

It rose up like a wall of golden honey, reaching five needles into the sky.

"Da, what is that?" Trueblood said.

"The Kaleuche," Kepten True said. "Isn't that..."

"Remarkable," Rafil finished. He came close to the kepten, and with the same transfixed expression, he took Ikharus-Lippé True's hand. Years fell away from both faces and they stood like two little boys at a puppet show.

"What's for you won't pass you by, lad," the rope master said, his grizzled head on the kepten's shoulder.

It was at that moment, Pelippé Trueblood later wrote in his most private journal, *when I realized Rafil was in love with my father. The kind of impossible love that becomes a vocation. Love cloaked in a lifetime of service. An undeclared devotion that settles into your skin like a tattoo or a scar. Forever yours because it can never be his. Irrevocable because it will never be returned. Pure love that's worth more than your own life. I wonder if my father knew. But of course, he must have.*

Murder smashed a tentacle across the Cay's bow, cracking the foremast and the reverie. Sailors screamed as they tumbled from the rigging and crashed into the sea. Kepten True's face snapped back into authority and he began barking orders to offload the crew.

"Pé, see to the safe," he shouted. "Raj, get the charts."

Trueblood and Raj ran aft, bursting through the aftercastle doors. In the kepten's study, they seized charts from the rack and yanked the ship's safe from its inlaid cubby. Running back through the sitting area, Raj stopped short outside Abrakam's room.

"What are you doing," Trueblood cried. "Come on."

Raj hesitated, then his face darkened and he thrust the charts at Trueblood, tucking them between the safe and Trueblood's chin. "Take these."

"Raj, we don't have time."

"Shut up, the books are too important."

"They can be replaced."

"Not these."

Abrakam slept on a pallet on the floor of his cabin, with one long pillow instead of two short ones. Raj stripped the case off and started pulling books off the shelves. Not a careless sweep but a swift and meticulous triage, as if he'd been drilled on what were the valuable and irreplaceable tomes.

"Hurry up," Trueblood said, his arms straining under their load.

With a groan of exertion, Raj hefted the sack of books on his shoulder and the two sailors ran out of the aftercastle. Back on deck, the majoros had bridged the gap between the ships with long planks and were sending the minoros across to make a human chain. Crates and casks started passing hand to hand. Coils of rope were flung over.

"Pé, Kep wants you," Lejo said, handing the charts to a sailor and taking the safe himself. "Hurry."

Only three remained on the Cay now. Kepten True at the wheel and Abrakam at one of the harpoons. And Pelippé Trueblood, running to the afterdeck for his final orders.

"Take the wheel," Kepten True said. Trueblood put a hand on the spokes but Ikharus shook his head. "No, take the Kaleuche's wheel, Pé."

Trueblood hesitated. As the rainy wind whipped his face, he stared at his father one long, intense moment, framing the mariner in his mind, pinning him to a painted picture.

True stared back, as if doing the same. "It's time."

Their hands reached to clasp. Then slid to wrap around forearms. Each touched the other's shoulder and their foreheads came together.

"*Gelangos*," Kepten True said. *My one at hand. The one I belong to.*

"Gelangos." For an icy moment, Trueblood clutched his father, feeling he might weep.

Don't leave me, he thought. *This ship is too big. Da, I'm not ready.*

True slid both his big hands around his son's face. "You are my true blood," he said. "And I love nothing the way I love you. Do you understand?"

Trueblood waited for the follow up, *Answer your commander.*

His father held still and silent.

"Yes, Da," Trueblood said.

The mariner kissed between Trueblood's eyebrows and then stepped back. "Go," he said. "Take the helm of that ship the way I taught you. Remember what I taught you and I'll be with you until the end."

"Aye, Kep."

"Hold her broadside. I'll be right behind you."

"Aye, Kep."

"Valentos," the mariner called as Trueblood sprinted toward the gangplank spanning the two ships. *My brave one.*

It was the last thing his father said to him.

PELIPPÉ TRUEBLOOD WAS nineteen when he took the wheel of the Kaleuche at his father's order. Standing head and shoulders above the shattered crew, he held her broadside as Abrakam came across, his bow and quiver slung across his shoulder. He watched his father surrender the helm of the Cay without a backward look. Soaked and resplendent in his blue coat, he stepped onto the gangway between the two ships.

"Murder *that,* you bloated squid," Ikharus-Lippé True yelled at the water below.

Then he looked up and grinned at his son.

Trueblood's blood froze, remembering a day long ago when he first climbed the Cay's main mast.

"I've seen too many sailors achieve excellence on the open sea," True said sternly. *"Then grow careless once land is in sight. We do not strut as the end of a task is near. And when the job is done well and completed properly, no strutting is required. Excellence needs no announcement. Do you understand?"*

"Yes, Da," Trueblood said.

"Da, no!" Trueblood cried.

A single tentacle punched out of the ocean, coiled around Ikharus-Lippé True's ankle, and yanked him off the gangplank. Like bait on a hook, he flew in an elegant arc through the sky. A rainbow of blue, black and white.

"Da…" Trueblood's throat shattered around the scream. He let go the wheel and went running for the railing. He had a foot on the crossbar when Dhar and Calvo lunged and wrestled him down. He fought through their arms like an enraged bull, spitting curses and yelling for his father, now dangling upside down by an ankle.

Abrakam thundered by. "Bring him *down,*" he hollered at Seven, who'd posted up at one of the harpoons. Beniv was at the other, swinging the deadly bolt around with his feet, the trip cord tight in his teeth. Abrakam clattered up to the foredeck, bow drawn. Archers were crawling up the rigging and lowering themselves into the sheets.

"Aim for the eye, lads," the centaur cried. "A kill shot has to be in the eye."

Trueblood screamed for his father, but no sound came out. His voice moved like a soundless knife at the back of his mouth, silently howling as Murder shook the kepten like a doll. As if True had something in his pocket and the kraken wanted it badly.

Beside Trueblood, Raj made a choking noise, filling Trueblood's peripheral with blinding white light. Then Lejo started convulsing, and that side of Trueblood's vision began to sparkle like the fuse of a sunpowder bomb.

Caught up in Murder's tentacles, the kepten glowed with a strange light. It both stabbed like Raj and twinkled like Lejo. The stronger it got, the harder Murder shook him.

What is happening? Pelippé Trueblood thought, going blind with grief and terror.

Raj fell to his knees, tearing at the neck of his shirt. Light poured from between his fingers and the corners of his eyes. Lejo clawed at his own buttons, a shimmering luminescence spilling out his mouth.

Furious Kepten True wasn't giving up what he had, Murder smashed him first on the deck of the Cay, then down into the ocean. Back and forth like a vicious pendulum, trying to *break* what he wanted out of the mariner.

Within his young body, Trueblood's heart fractured into pieces. *No.*

Don't.

Give him back to me.

One final chop with three tentacles and the Cay split behind her bow. Murder flung Kepten True away, a toy he was finished playing with. Like a bluebird, Ikharus flew through the air and crashed onto the deck of the Kaleuche, limbs splayed at horrible angles, blood pouring from his mouth and ears.

Trueblood crawled to him. He gathered the mighty head into his arms and bayed like a wounded dog. Blood soaked his white clothes as he wept for his Da, his only, his one, his giantsblood, his gelangos.

Rafil came crawling to them, his wizened face pulled taut with horror. "Oh, lad," he said hoarsely. "Oh, lad, don't pass me by."

"Help him," Trueblood choked. "Rafil, help me."

The twins were sprawled on the deck now, hemorrhaging light. It filled Trueblood's eyes like the sun and moon. Through the glare burst a hot-white silhouette, winged with four legs.

The Horselord had arrived.

He promised, Trueblood remembered. *When it was my father's time, il-Kheir vowed to take his soul himself. It's a great honor.*

"No," Trueblood said, pulling his father tight against him. "No, you can't have him. It's not time. I'm not ready."

Rafil slumped on his knees, weeping inside-out. The shadow of the Horselord came closer, arms outstretched. Trueblood grabbed harder at his father, clutching at blood and bone and braids, ready to kill whoever or whatever attempted to take Ikharus from him.

"Leave him alone," he cried into the light, his voice in shreds.

He seized and clutched as the deadweight in his lap went even more dead. An orb of glinting, twinkling light rose from Kepten True's chest and floated into the kheiron's hands.

"Lad, lad," Rafil cried. "My one, don't leave me."

Trueblood's mouth moved helplessly. *No, give him back. He's mine.*

"I need you, Pelippé," il-Kheir said.

Except the voice was female. The light dimmed and it was the Horsedam, ele-Kheir, rising over him and holding his father's soul.

"You must do this for me," she said.

I can't, Trueblood screamed in his head.

"Do this for me. For your father and your twins. For my brother and his son. For the world."

You can't have him. Give him back.

"Look at me, Pelippé Trueblood."

He hated her, but he looked up into the white-hot light.

"What's for you won't pass you by."

A woman's mouth kissed his mouth.

Everything split down the center, folded back around and turned inside-out.

O wonderful, remarkable, beautiful, you are mine, my lovely, scented like spice and silvery cool like the moon that—

Then something plunged into Trueblood's chest and tore his heart apart.

Part Three
WREVOS
God of Wisdom

The Charm of Finches

THE KHEIRON FLEW west across the desert with a human boy on his back.

"Don't cry, lad," he said. "It's all over."

Little arms tightened around Fen's waist. The kheiron's war paint had turned the boy's arms and hands scarlet. "I want to go home."

"I know. You'll be there soon. Hold tight, now."

They turned south toward Zeuxis. Three kheirons flew to Fen's fivehand side, and another pair to his fourside, each with a dye-smeared child strapped to their back. Strapped *tight*. Never again would Fen il-Kheir let a rider fall.

"Why are you all red?" the boy asked when his tears subsided.

"We're redfinches," Fen said. "We deliver the souls of the damned."

"Us?"

"No. Them." Fen flipped a thumb over his shoulder. "Those men were damned."

"You got them?"

"We got them. All of them. They'll never do this again."

The last stars clung to the night sky's mantel. On the horizon, the constellation of Nyos lingered, the belt of three stars twinkling at her waist. Her mighty bow was drawn back for eternity, the arrow aimed straight at the group of stars that made Minos the Bull.

"Funny how Nyos and Minos look like they're locked in endless battle," Fen said. "When really they're a tragic love story. Do you know it?"

The bull was Nyos's beloved companion. Fierce in appearance but gentle in disposition. Dozens of tales chronicled his blunders into hilarious trouble of one kind or another. He entertained the ancient world with his dopey ways until Nyos shot him by mistake. The fool became a hero, set in the stars forever.

"Now you know," Fen said. "You tell that story to your friends when you get home. Tell them how the Charm of Finches rescued you, delivered the souls of the damned, and flew you home past the constellations. You'll be their hero."

The boys were left at a safe house in Zeuxis. The establishment could accommodate the kheirons, but Fen preferred to sleep outside the city. And where Fen went, his charm followed.

They made camp along a branch of the river. At this time of year, it was loud and frothy with mountain runoff. The roar barely masked the clings and clangs of armor dropped on the ground, but it was no match for the screaming when the kheirons waded into its icy rapids. Ululations of triumph mixed with agonized screeches. The water ran red and black as they frantically scrubbed the dye out of their hair and off their skin, howling and laughing with a manic edge.

Fen wisely hung back and built a fire before taking the plunge. He had it roaring and crackling when his charm splashed onto the bank, shaking themselves dry. Teeth chattering and hungry enough to chew their arms off. Fen went to bathe while the others wolfed down supper.

It took a lot of food to feed the demands of kheiron muscle. They didn't eat meat—their human appetites craved it but their equine digestion refused it. Standing around the fire, the Finches passed leather bags full of bread, dried fruit, cheese, tablets of butter and sugar, and dozens of little cakes made from beans and protein-rich grains.

As Fen shook the icy water off his body, his newest warrior, Lenge, came back to the stream to drink. Her cropped hair lay sleek and dark over her skull. Minute twitches beneath her chestnut coat betrayed the adrenaline hanging around her veins. A ghostly pallor in her face told Fen she was still struggling with what they saw in the slave pens and brothels today. The boy she'd flown back to Zeuxis had been in horrible shape.

"You did well," he said.

Her chin nodded curtly, lips pressed tight.

Fen let her be. He dried himself at the fire and ate. A wineskin was passed, making the loud kheirons get louder and the quieter ones more withdrawn. Jero disappeared inside his tattered copy of the *Truviad,* while Lisbel and Tomar disappeared behind some trees to fuck the last of the stress away.

Fen took the wineskin over to Lenge. "Here. Get some of that in your blood."

She coughed after the first chug, then drank deeper and drew the back of her hand across her mouth. "Thanks."

"First time is the hardest."

Again the short, tight nod before she drained the rest of the skin.

"No shame if you don't want to do this again," Fen said quietly. "I understand."

Tears spilled from Lenge's eyes and her arms crossed tight about her body.

"If this is the first and last time you fly with the charm, you have nothing but my respect."

"Oh I'll do it again," she said. "I'll do it until it doesn't have to be done anymore."

"Good girl."

"It's just...all built up inside. Like part of me is still in the air."

"I know. You need to come down now."

"Help me?"

He hesitated, plumbing the request to see if it was for short-term physical help or long-term connection. He opposed the latter. He didn't care what his charm did with each other in the dark, as long as it didn't interfere with their mission, but he had personal rules about intimacy. One rule, actually: avoid it.

He studied the quake of Lenge's shoulders, the tremble in all four knees and the obsidian hardness in her jaw. She just needed to get off and get some sleep.

He stepped closer. "Come here."

The fingers of his fourhand dug into her short hair and he gathered her sleek dark head onto his shoulder. His fivehand slid down her human stomach, past the quivering border where skin became horsehair.

"Need it bad," she said.

"Shh…" He reached the smooth, warm expanse between her forelegs. His palm opened wide and began to rub with the heel of his hand. A moan shivered out of Lenge's chest and her mouth pressed wet against Fen's skin.

"That's good," she whispered. "Right there."

He bore down harder. His hands were strong and they knew exactly where the sweet spots were. When his race was in kheiros, half-man and half-horse, sexuality divided as well. The equine procreative drive stayed between a kheiron's rear legs while the complex pleasure centers of human desire settled up here, in the thick muscles between the forelegs. Here was where you scratched when desire itched.

"Come down," he said.

A fine mist of sweat beaded along her nape. "Fuck…"

He went on whispering terse encouragement as she rubbed harder against his hand, until finally, with a little yelp, she came down. Her body softened around shivers that were luxurious with relief. Laughter as they stumbled sideways, legs colliding.

"Gods." She shook her head hard. "I needed that."

"Feel better?"

"Mm."

"Go get some sleep."

Her fivehand reached tentatively toward his stomach. "You need?"

"No," he said, catching up her fingers. "No, sister, I'm good."

"You sure?"

"Go rest, *Lengea…*" He spoke her soul name. A kheiron's true name, his *khenom,* was unpronounceable for anyone but the herd. The lengthy, sing-song appellation of sound and inflection was impossible in the mouths of men and other creatures, so kheirons kept their soul names private and used just the first syllables as an *agnom* for outsiders.

Fen had changed his agnom twenty years ago, but his khenom still began with Tehvan. Altering it would be like inhabiting someone else's body. It was the sole piece of his childhood he had left. The one part of a former self that still sounded good to him.

Lenge squeezed his hand. "Goodnight, *Tehvani…*" The old name slid into something beautiful and other-worldly in her mouth. Slightly wrong to his ear. No one but Fen could say it perfectly, because it belonged only to him.

He waited until she was out of sight before walking further down the stream. He found an ash tree with a good-sized bole and rubbed off against it. He needed no whispered coaxing. He thought of nothing and no one. A tree was a cold, disinterested lover, but it did the job.

And Fen il-Kheir didn't want lovers anyway.

TWENTY YEARS HAD passed since the Horselord's son was rescued off the harvest platform of a dead spice tree. His human legs were shattered, jagged edges of bone breaking the skin, filling his blood with infection on the voyage home and leaving little hope for survival.

Kheirons, my legantos, know the frailties and limitations of their race. A broken leg for any steed creature is life-altering. With immediate attention and skilled care, a fractured limb can heal, but the kheiron can rarely put equine weight on it again. The majority of survivors spend the rest of their lives on two human legs.

The greatest surgeon in Nyland, an unparalleled specialist in the complex and exacting care of horsefolk, had to admit to the Horselord that Tehvan il-Kheir's legs were beyond repair. The foalboy was given days to live. Maybe hours.

But he didn't die, legantos.

Two decades later, Fen walked along the stream bank on four silver hooves. The moonlight like milk along his gray coat, reflecting alabaster off his white hair and tail. One of his eyebrows was pierced with a hoop, into which had been set his moonstone. He'd foolishly given it away once, imprisoning himself in humos. In humos he was kept in captivity, sold and bought twice, branded, beaten and raped by both men and minotaurs.

Never again.

After Fen recovered, he pierced his eyebrow with his moonstone, setting it firmly under his sole, autonomous control. He'd never shift into humos, never walk on two legs again. And no one could ever make him.

He was thirty-four now. None could outrun or out-fly Fen il-Kheir. His elite legion called him Feños, *my Finch*. He led his charm on raids deep into Minosaros, to the red rock land called Arcodolori, where he'd lived as a slave. The arrow of sadness found no target in the kheiron heir. Nyland's happy foalboy had become a guarded and dangerous creature. Hard and cold like silver. An unparalleled swordsman and archer. Capable of cruel humor. He allowed no quarter to slavers, rapists and pimps, and was known for looking his prey in the eye when he killed them.

The only time Fen's demeanor softened was with the young victims of his victims. No matter how many times it happened, his warriors couldn't reconcile their cold, ruthless leader with the gentle winged soul who cradled freed slaves in his arms and flew them home.

"It's not happening to you," he said to those broken, ravished boys. "No, listen to me. I'm telling you the truth. This is nothing. None of this is real. You're a good boy and it's over now. I found you. You're safe now…"

"Feños."

Blinking back to the present, Fen turned around. Jero trotted up to him, a falcon perched on his extended forearm. The other hand held out of scrap of paper.

"It's from the queen," he said. "Dated two weeks ago."

Fen took the scrap of paper, smiling in anticipation of its bombast. Naria, the hereditary queen of Nyland, was a brilliant woman and also severely *dislekos*—her brain hopelessly mixed up numbers and letters. She possessed an eidetic memory, but she read and wrote so poorly, she delegated the skills to two full-time attendants. The pair of scribes were known as Spectacles, who read everything for Naria, and Ink, who wrote for her.

In person, Naria had a direct, engaging manner, a wicked sense of humor and a mouth like a sailor. But either she couldn't dictate her style, or Ink had too big a stick up her ass to transcribe it.

Fen suspected the latter.

As he tilted the message into dying fire's light to read, the grin around his mouth fell slack.

Lak Thennes
Hokosia

Gods keep you gelang, Fen il-Kheir. I write from the Imperial Palace where I'm a guest of Xuan-Gavriel. We received devastating news from Nyland this morning. My heart breaks to tell you our friend, Kepten Ikharus-Lippé True, has died at sea. The Cay is lost. True lies in state in the mariners' crypt and physicians fear for his son's life.

A light has gone out that will not shine again.

I ask you go home at once. I'm coming as soon as I can. Help comfort my people until I can be there.

Naria Nyland

Nine-Day Vigil

"HOLY *HORSES*," LENGE said, and the charm echoed agreement.

"Oh my Gods."

"What the fuck?"

"What *is* that?"

The air above Valtourel was cool in Fen's open mouth as he stared down at the harbor. The ship anchored there was the biggest he'd ever seen. Not just the biggest ship, but the biggest *thing* he'd seen in his life. And he'd been to the top of a gods-damned spice tree, so he knew big.

"It's not the Cay," Lenge said, hovering by Fen's side.

"No, Naria said the Cay was lost."

"It's the Kaleuche," Jero said.

"Impossible," Lisbel said. "That ship disappeared from historical record a thousand years ago."

"Looks like she's back on the record. Come on." Fen dove toward the harbor, leading his charm on a circle of the five-masted ship. All five were bare of sails and the rigging looked like a complicated, sinister spider web.

Tomar pulled in by Fen's flank. "Is it me, or is it plain creepy?"

"It's not you," Fen said. He had no love for ships. His first voyage had been on a slave galley and his last one was on the

Cay. He nearly died on both trips and never intended to set hoof on a boat again.

Spooked, the charm peeled off, flying to the kheiron pavilion while Fen touched down in the palace courtyard and took himself to the Great Hall.

The cavernous, columned room was the heart of the palace. A dais at its northern end held five thrones—a raised one for the hereditary queen of Nyland, and four lower seats for the vicreĝos, the elected regents. Each region's crest was carved into the back of the throne: a tree for Abaro, a ship for Nordater, a horse for Sudenlo and a bird for Pellandro.

Queen Naria's throne was topped with a Nye flower carved from selenite. Beneath was etched Nyland's motto: *Bonaj civitanos. Belaj koros.*

Good Citizens. Beautiful Hearts.

Joenne Windsong came down the length of the hall to greet Fen. As vicreĝo of the Nordater region, she lived in the palace at Valtourel and ran day-to-day business when Queen Naria was away. Giantsblood was in her long, lean frame and cider-bronze eyes. Rather than a multitude of braids, her black hair was twisted, wrapped and dazzlingly constructed into a crown that added a half-foot to her height.

She was a formidable woman with a penchant for kheiron lovers. The Horselord didn't like her, so Fen went out of his way to like her very much, although he tactfully declined her occasional advances.

"What happened?" Fen asked after kissing Joenne's hands. "Is the Cay really lost?"

He was far-removed from the business of House Tru, but the giantship Cay was an institution. Grasping its absence was like trying to contemplate a night sky without stars.

"She was attacked by Murder," Joenne said.

Fen felt his eyes widen. When the earth cracked apart and Nydirsil's roots torn from the ocean floor, a pack of monstrous creatures was unleashed. The worst of these were Murder and Misery, twin kraken who roamed the waters. Nobody doubted their existence, but their sightings had always been more legendary than documented.

"The kraken broke the Cay near her bow," Joenne said. "Nearly everything was lost. They managed to save a few charts and the safe. Eight crew dead, including the kepten. The rest offloaded onto the Kaleuche and came home."

"How did the Kaleuche even get to them? Where's she been all this time?"

Joenne spread her hands out. "I don't know. I'd call it a salty dog's fish tale if I didn't see proof every time I looked out the window."

"What killed Kepten True? Did he drown?"

"From what I hear, he was crossing over to the Kaleuche and Murder got him." Her arms crossed again, each hand disappearing up a sleeve. "Abrakam says the venom causes instant death. Within mere seconds of contact with the tentacles. I pray he's right. Pray that Ikharus was already dead when Murder broke him bone by bone."

"What of his son?"

Joenne told how Pelippé Trueblood was carried off the ship unconscious, his chest ringed with charred scar tissue. "As if his heart had been torn out and set on fire." His foster brothers, the Ĝemelos twins, were in the sick bay with Trueblood, both in a state of shocked delirium.

"And old Rafil is dead," the vicreĝo said.

"No." Fen would be challenged to name the crew of the Cay, but *everyone* knew old Rafil. "I don't believe it. Was he killed on the ship?"

Joenne shook her head. "He lay down next to Kepten True's bier in the crypt and just...died. In his sleep. Smiling. He went with his commander. Loyal to the end."

"Gods. When is the funeral?"

"It was already."

"That's right, I'm...late. Where's my father?"

"In the crypt. He's been keeping a nine-day vigil. It ends at sunset."

That was less than an hour from now. Fen missed it. His father wouldn't be pleased.

Story of my life.

"I'm sorry," he said. "I was up in Minosaros. The queen's falcon got to us just last night."

"I understand," Joenne said. Though her voice was soaked with sorrow, it was cool. "If you want to pay your respects, you should go now, Feños."

He went.

The nave of the mariners' crypt had alternating rows of seats for humans and rails for horsefolk. On the bier in front of the altar lay Ikharus-Lippé True. Home for good. By the bier, Sevri il-Kheir stood in equos, his ghostly white head bowed and one silver hoof poised on its edge.

A nine-day perpetual vigil, with il-Kheir taking the final watch in equos. No greater honor could be paid to the mariner.

Standing at the back of the nave, Fen drew a deep breath past the tight heat in his throat. A stab of genuine remorse in his heart. As the heir to the kheiron herd he should've taken the penultimate watch. Kepten True had rescued him. He'd always been kind to Fen in the years since and his wife, the late Noë Treeblood, was one of Fen's favorite people.

He was a good man, Fen thought. *Decent. Honest. Brave.*

A superlative mariner. A devoted husband. And a true giants-blood.

Take him into your merciful heart.

The sunset bell tolled from the Temple of Solos. Sevri il-Kheir shifted into kheiros and turned from the bier. His gaze fell on Fen. It leaned hard until it looked through him, seeing something that wasn't there. Or something il-Kheir wished were there.

Fen learned to expect this passive disappointment in his father's eyes. The anticipation didn't stop it from hurting.

He couldn't help it.

Don't you love me anymore? The thought rang like a bell in his broken heart.

Aren't I your brave one?

My Brave One

A STUDENT AT THE University of Alondra penned the sonnet "My Brave One" as word of Fen's rescue spread through Nyland. Everyone heard how the Horselord received the messenger falcon from the Cay, bringing the incredible news. Il-Kheir let go the missive and was in the air before the paper hit the floor.

The aspiring poet pounced on the anecdote and spun it into melodrama. He scratched flowery stanzas capturing the Horselord's wings, unfurled to their spectacular eighteen-foot span, cutting through the sky like knives and blowing the leaves off branches. Musicians got their hands on it next. Drummers laid down a breathless, desperate rhythm, mimicking il-Kheir's front hooves as they grabbed at the air and tossed it behind his long belly. His rear hooves seized the wind and threw it behind his tail, each seize and throw timed with the rise and fall of wings.

Verse after verse, the land fell away beneath the kheiron, replaced by indigo blue ocean, crested with white and reflecting the sun in handfuls of diamond sparkles. The Cay cut a swathe through the water, racing toward Alondra with her precious cargo. Sailors threw themselves out of the way as il-Kheir hit the deck at a gallop.

The chorus was sung in kitchens and over cradles. In taverns and markets and inns.

My brave one come home,
My only son is free.
Taken from the land, but
Returned from the sea.
Valentos, I'm here, my brave one,
Come home to me…

Fen detested the song. Merely whistling the tune in his presence warranted a death glare on his good days. A punch in the nose when he was in a bad mood. He hated gossip disguised as poetry, hated the license artists took with his pain, just to earn a coin and a quarter-hour of celebrity.

Valentos.

My brave one.

How the hell did they know il-Kheir called him *my brave one* that day? What pair of big ears on the Cay eavesdropped on the enormous yet fragile reunion of father and son, then went running to tell the tale?

That day belonged to Fen alone.

Those words were his. His father *gave* them to him.

"Valentos. I'm here."

The Horselord's voice crossed the cradle of constant pain where Fen rocked between life and death. He opened his eyes, feverish and broken and Gods, the pain. Flinging itself along his legs and coiling like a snake around his spine. His gaze wobbled over the face looming above him before a barrage of sharp coughs put knives between his ribs.

"Shh," his father said, his big hand soft on Fen's head. "Rest, my one."

"Da," Tehvan said through his burning throat.

"It's all right. I'm here."

"I'm sorry."

"No." Il-Kheir slid his arms beneath his son and gathered the hot, damp head onto his enormous shoulder. "No, no, no," he half sang. "My one, you're alive, I knew you were alive. Valentos, my heart, I'm here now. You're going home."

"Da." Tehvan's voice splintered around the most giant of giant-words.

"I'm here, *Tehvani…*"

Fen heard his khenom, his soul name, sweet and sing-song in his father's voice. More beautiful soothing words and enormous hands cradling Fen's head.

"It's over now, valentos. You're with me. I got you back. Shh. My heart, my brave one."

Fen cried and cried while his mighty father *wept* on his knees at the bedside. He held Fen in his arms the whole rest of the voyage. Hours? Days? Fen didn't know but his father *never* let him go. He told the pain it had to come through *him* before it could get to his son.

"It's over now," he said. "Everything will be all right, I promise."

In the Horselord's fierce embrace, Fen found he could stand the agony. He was going home and he was free and his father was here, he'd always be here. He'd fix everything that was broken and he'd never let Fen be taken from him again.

Valentos, I'm here…

"You're here," the Horselord said.

Fen opened his eyes and emerged from the past. A priestess was going about the nave, blowing out the candles, filling the air with swirls of smoke.

"I came as soon as I could," Fen said.

"Not soon enough." Sevri il-Kheir's silver hooves rang on the stone floor as he came along the pews and rails.

"I'm sorry, Father." He kept the emotion out of his voice, but a cold sweat gripped the back of Fen's neck and dripped from under his arms.

"You owe Kepten True your life."

"Not a day goes by where I'm not aware of that."

"Nine days passed where it seemed to everyone you forgot."

"I only got the message last night."

"If you were here in Valtourel instead of gallivanting off in Min—"

"The slave trade is a fraction of what it was thanks to my gallivanting. Maybe it means nothing to you but it's what I chose to devote my life to."

Il-Kheir crossed his arms. "Your choice, Fen, has always been to fixate on the past. It's been that way since you were born."

Sevri's pale blue eyes were cold, hard and tight, like a bowstring drawn to its apex. His voice an *arcodolori*—an arrow of sadness to Fen's heart.

Where did you go?

Fen's eyes traveled from the moonstone around the Horselord's neck, down to the wall of his crossed arms. The same arms that gathered Fen up on the Cay, rocked him and held him safe, now closed up tight and unyielding. An embrace that once sheltered Fen now shut him out.

What happened to my Da? What did I do to make you turn on me like this?

Don't you love me anymore?

Fen drew a controlled breath through his nose and counted to three. "You'd also be hard-pressed to find a day when I don't think about my birth, Father."

The air pressed hard, filled with the invisible presence of Fen's mother. Under it, Sevri's endless grief locked horns with Fen's never-ending guilt.

Fen never knew his mother. He was born breech and Zoria bled to death before he had all four feet on the ground. He'd been dragged backward into the world and a priestess predicted it would be Fen's fate to live life looking where he came from, not where he was going.

Fen closed his eyes. *When the slave trade is wiped off the face of the map, then I'll turn around,* he thought. *I'll face the future when I decide it's time and not a minute before.*

Hooves on stone again. When Fen's eyes opened, he was alone in the nave with the mariner.

He walked to the bier and gazed down at the resting kepten. Ikharus-Lippé True lay in state in white shirt and breeches, black boots and his magnificent blue coat. This garment was the blanket he tucked around Fen at the top of a spice tree before slipping Fen's lost ring back on his fivehand. The first step to making Fen whole again.

Not a day goes by when I don't remember.

Fen's wings unfurled, extending beyond the length of the bier. He plucked a single feather, one of the median coverts, and kissed it before tucking it in the inside pocket of Kepten True's coat.

"Thank you," he whispered.

As he walked back to the pavilion, he passed the palace's infirmary wing, the arched windows lit up gold from within. Somewhere behind the stained glass, the new kepten lay sick, possibly dying.

Does he even know his father's gone?

Fen walked on. Solos had slipped beneath the horizon and in the sky over Valtourel, the first stars were blinking to life. The constellation of Nyos shimmered into sight, followed by Minos. A mother drawing her bow and shooting her beloved one. An arrow of sadness into the bull's dopey heart, over and over again. A love story disguised as battle, told night after night with no happy ending.

Story of my life, Fen il-Kheir thought.

The next morning, he flew with his charm back to Minosaros, where he was needed.

Facing the Same Way

Inside the palace's infirmary wing, the nurses were beside themselves trying to care for their new patients. If they separated the Ĝemelos from Trueblood, Lejo cried out in agony, Raj thrashed with fever, and Trueblood's breath stilled to nearly nothing beneath the strange scar ringing his heart.

A giantsbed was brought in so the three sailors could lie together. Stacked on their sides, sometimes rolled toward the sunrise, other times the sunset. But always facing the same way with the mariner's son in the middle.

The healers spoke to Abrakam about giving the boys fadara for the pain. The conversation was conducted in hushed tones, as the narcotic was illegal and officially none existed in Valtourel. Its unofficial existence came with an unwritten law: fadara was so addictive, it could not be administered for medical purposes without verbal consent.

Trueblood was unconscious and the Ĝemelos nothing close to lucid. Abrakam refused on their behalf and opted to try an infusion of kyrrh.

"Kyrrh's a salve," one of the nurses said. "You don't ingest it."

"You can," the centaur said. "I've done it before."

The nurse leaned over his shoulder, fascinated as he shaved transluscent curls off the block of rare resin. "What if we put it in a *nychet?*" she asked.

A nychet was a small muslin bag, once filled with Nye and dunked in hot water to make an elixir of love and life and happiness. The spice was long gone but the tiny pouches were dried, put away and passed down for special occasions or esteemed company. It was believed the lingering Nye residue seeped into whatever tea was made in them. A miniature nyellem in a cup.

The Nylanders believed. If he were alive, Ikharus-Lippé True would say Nylanders endured because they believed.

Abrakam shaved kyrrh into one of these treasured nychets and dropped the little pouch into hot water. He stirred in honey. He added all his desperate love and devotion, all his wisdom and lore and knowledge. He held three pairs of shaking shoulders and steadied the cup at the teeth chattering within three speechless mouths. He wept as his large, wrinkled hand smoothed three brows.

Beneath his rough palm, the three young men held each other.

TRUEBLOOD LAY BETWEEN the twins. Kyrrh and honey and the love of his people coursing in his veins. The hand of a wise, wonderful centaur on his brow. A pen wrote on the inside of his eyelids in especial beautiful penmanship: *He is wise and good with problems. If I am worried and Da is busy, I talk to Abrakam and I feel better.*

"Rest, lad," Abrakam said from across an ocean. "Rest your heart."

Trueblood's teeth chattered against the rim of a cup. He swallowed and it burned like the sun down into his chest. Abrakam helped him lie down again.

Against his back, Raj smoldered like banked ash.

Within the circle of his arms, Lejo shivered like moonlight on snow.

Between them, Trueblood dreamed. First, handwriting looped across the back of his eyelids, telling long, complicated stories without end. Then, through the words burst a familiar, blue-black silhouette. Winged with four legs.

Wake up, Pelippé Trueblood.

He opened his eyes. The room was in darkness, only the merest trace of moonlight at the windows. Enough to illuminate one side of the kheirone standing by the wide bed. The silvery beams curled around the apple of her cheek, leaving the rest of her face in shadow. As he stared, Trueblood's childhood finger longed to ride along the ripples of her hair and trace the curve of her tiny waist.

A four-fingered hand reached to him. Her lips moved but no sound touched his ear.

Gods, you look terrible, ele-Kheir said to his soul.

MY SOUL'S TEETH

"**A**M I DEAD?" Trueblood said.

The Horsedam smiled. *Not yet. How do you feel?*

"Terrible. And it's all your fault."

I apologize. She didn't move from the side of the bed, yet she managed to slip into the tiny space between Trueblood and Lejo. She lay cool and dry against his body, her hand soft on his face.

"My heart hurts so bad," he whispered.

I know.

"I want my father. Please get my Da."

She put cold, soft hands on his burning chest and kissed each of his eyelids. *Your father is dead, Pelippé. My brother took his soul back to the moon. You are the kepten now.*

How she stood statue-still at the bedside yet held him in her arms was a mystery he'd contemplate later. Right now he curled into her embrace and cried a river around his already-broken heart. He sobbed until the scars ringing his chest broke open and bled, weeping along with him.

Like a child, he cried himself to sleep, and when he woke, ele-Kheir's astral presence was still beside him, gentle and immutable.

You look a little better now, she said.

Weak and devastated, Trueblood shivered against her breast. "You're il-Kheir's sister?"

Ancestral aunt is more accurate, but sister makes me feel young.

"You're so beautiful."

Her palm caressed his heart. *I ask the world of you and you pay me compliments. If only all humans were this agreeable.*

"What's happening to me?"

You're taking your father's place. In all kinds of ways.

"What's the matter with the twins? What's wrong with them?"

Their bond was broken.

"I don't understand."

It's much like Nydirsil pulling her roots free of the earth. Your father's soul was rooted in Raj and Lejo. He was literally ripped out of them when he died. She reached behind to pat Lejo's head, then ahead to tousle Raj's hair.

My poor foalboys, she murmured.

"Foalboys?" Trueblood said. "The twins are kheirons?"

Didn't you know?

"No," he said, even as a distant corner of his mind disagreed, insisting it knew, it always knew, it just didn't *know* it knew.

"But how can they be?" Trueblood said. "Where are their wings? Where is their starsilver and their moonstones?"

Serving another purpose the Horsedam said.

"And why do they have auras? Nobody else sees it, but both their light shines at the corner of my eye. My father had strange light inside him, too. I saw it when he died. What is that? What's *happening?*"

Shh. She kissed his head. *If you get upset, you'll hurt them. If you think you're strong enough to leave a little while, I'll show you everything.*

"All right."

Her presence disappeared from Trueblood's side and now her corporal form stirred next to the bed, turning its back to reveal her wings. *Will you honor me by riding, Pelippé?*

"The honor is mine." He slid down the mattress and off the foot of the bed, then mounted ele-Kheir's back. She moved silvery and cool between his thighs. It made him hard and he was embarrassed, but she laughed as if it pleased her.

"Where are we going?"

Through time, my one. Where stories live.

As she melted through the wall and launched into the sky, Trueblood felt his heart stretch arms back to the receding earth. A child wanting its mother. Somewhere back *there,* behind him, the Ĝemelos were crying. They pulled and yanked, their light clawing his heart like white-hot gold that sparkled at the edges.

"Gods, it hurts," he said.

Tell me how.

"It's two kinds of pain. Raj sort of punches and stabs me, but Lejo *aches.* Feels like he's pulling out my soul's teeth."

Lejo's always been the more sensitive of the two. It's no surprise he let your father anchor deeper into his soul. Both twins are filling the void Ikharus left behind. Filling it with their love for you. Love and memory. She glanced back at Trueblood. *Lejo has one memory with you that Raj doesn't.*

Trueblood hid his face against her feathers. "You saw us in bed?"

She laughed. *Well, I didn't watch, that would be impolite. But yes, I knew.* She shook her shoulders free of his embarrassment. *Oh, stop it. What did Lejo tell you about gelang?*

"It isn't dirty."

You were beautiful to each other. It was sweet and innocent and trusting and perfect. It meant the world to Lejo.

"Did it?"

It let him discover who he is. Now with your father gone, you're the most important person in Lejo's life. He's clawing at your soul and pulling its teeth because he loves you. Desperately.

Trueblood sighed. "Gelang never did much make sense to me."

One day it will. Hold tight now.

The kheirone rose and fell, taking them past nebulous castles carved out of the universe. Towers of pink, purple and gold clouds, stars flung across their soft walls. Single stars like diamond buttons on a coat. Fuzzy clusters of pinprick sparkles. Fat, shapeless blobs of red and blue light.

This is Os's mane, ele-Kheir said.

"Os is a horse?"

In this place, yes. In a different part of time, Os is a bird.

She flew at the dark orange eye of a fuchsia maelstrom and out the other side, into a brilliant blue sky. Below them lay the rippling carpet of the ocean, dark gray-green and streaked with white. A five-masted ship cut a wake through the center, towing a gargantuan tree behind.

"Holy horses." Trueblood's mouth gaped at the nine branches splitting from the massive trunk. One straight up and four to each side, filling the sky from horizon to horizon.

Four gods, four goddesses and Os, ele-Kheir said. *One branch for each, anchored to the sky.*

She flew him around and through each limb, naming them.

Solos, the sun god and Lunos, the moon goddess.

Truvos of the sea and his slain sister of love, Nyos.

Wrevos for wisdom. Velos, who presided over the harvest.

Meros, the terrible war god. His serene twin, Helos, balancing birth and death.

Straight overhead at the apex of the tree, the highest branch scraped against the sky, touching the face of Os, who was One.

"The anchoring stars are gone," Trueblood said. "Truvos made them into rings. Khe wears them on his fingers."

Ele-Kheir shook her head. *Not anymore. Truvos finished mourning his love and asked me to put the rings somewhere safe.*

"Why you?"

She sniffed. *Do you think I'm not worthy?*

"I'm sorry. I meant, why not put them back in Nydirsil's branches? Anchor her to the sky again and fix everything?"

Truvos declared the stars couldn't be returned until a love like he knew with Khe returned to the earth threefold. He wrote it in stone. Once you write a thing down, it becomes real. He put a destiny into motion and I can't change the course of the voyage. My job is to keep the ship safe.

"Da says when the job is done well, no strutting is required."

Oh, but strutting is the best part.

As they made one last spiral around Nydirsil, Trueblood noticed an oddly-shaped tenth branch. He leaned, squinting, and saw it was fabricated—a piece of manmade wood tied crossways where the trunk split.

"What's that?" he said, pointing. "It looks like a yard."

It's the future, ele-Kheir said.

Trueblood let out a little gasp of revelation. "The world is a ship and Nydirsil is the mast," he said.

An excellent way to look at it, Pelippé.

She flew away from the tree, crossing time and space. Neatly threading her flight between two nebulous monoliths and emerging above another ocean and another ship.

"Héjo, that's the Kaleuche," Trueblood said.

"Yes. But the Kaleuche twenty years ago."

They squeezed between a crack of the ship and passed easily through the bulkheads and decks, down to the nyellem. Ele-Kheir walked through its wall as if it were water.

"This is a better way to come in," Trueblood said. "I left the door open once and got thrashed for it."

You never make the same mistake twice.

Two babies lay on the bed. Little hands holding each other's heads. The space between their bodies twinkled.

The triumph of a mystery solved crowed in Trueblood's veins. "This is the ship in the story. This is where Da found the Ĝemelos."

Yes.

"It was you who left them here."

I never left. Not until Ikharus arrived. What kind of mother do you take me for?

"I'm sorry."

You must learn to think before you speak. Do you understand?

"Aye, Kep." It was out of his mouth before he thought.

Gods, what am I going to do with you? Ele-Kheir's hand moved in the space between the infant Raj and Lejo, drawing up gold and silver and letting it sift through her fingers. *Aren't they remark-able?*

"You did a good job."

Thank you, Pé.

He hesitated. "Do you miss them?"

To my bones.

"Do they know they're kheirons? And that you're their mother?"

No. And when you wake up, you won't remember you know. Some things aren't for you to have in the waking world, Pé. Knowing the truth when others don't puts certain destinies at a disadvantage.

Questions piling up on questions now. "Why are they always in humos? Where are their rings? And why do they have eleven fingers, not nine?"

Ele-Kheir cleared her throat. In the dim light emanating from the twins, her smile was arch. *The only question I'm addressing on this voyage is why the twins shine. Have you guessed yet?*

"Because they have Nydirsil's stars inside them?"

Yes. Raj has four. Lejo has four.

"Did you use their rings and stones to hold the stars inside them?"

Yes, but don't ask me to explain how. It was terribly compli-cated. I honestly didn't know if it would work.

Worry flickered across her luminous face, compelling Trueblood to repeat, "You did a good job."

Thank you, she said with a sigh. *Your father had the ninth star. Estelos. The star of Os.*

"What did you use to hold it inside him?"

She reached up and took Trueblood's face in her soft hands. *Nothing,* she whispered. *His love and goodness were enough. His bravery and honesty and skill. His heart was beautiful enough to hold the power of Estelos. So is yours, Pelippé. You hold the star in your heart now. You are the bond between Raj and Lejo.*

"The three of us are the threefold love in the *Truviad*?"

Raj and Lejo together are one fold. You are another. We're waiting on the third.

"Who?"

My nephew. He already senses he's part of this. Unfortunately, his heart likes to look at where it came from, not where it's going. He won't be happy about his part in the story. But that's his problem, not yours. Come along now, Pé.

"Where are we going?"

Back to your story. The twins need you.

The pain of separation had crouched in a corner all this time, fascinated by what was going on. Now it loomed up over him, jabbing on one side, straining on the other, demanding his attention.

"It hurts," Trueblood whispered.

Love often does, my one.

The need to go back and the dread of going back made him frantic. "The ship is too big for me. I'm not ready."

You have your crew. You have your pilot and your boatswain. You have your notebooks where you wrote down everything your father taught you, in your especial beautiful penmanship. It's time, Pé.

"It hurts."

I know. I'm sorry. Os's branch of the tree bears the greatest weight of the sky.

"I'm not ready."

You need to be strong, Pelippé Trueblood. Estelos, the ninth star, binds the other eight. Estelos is heaviest and only you can hold it.

"It hurts."

Hold the bond, Pé. You're the only one who can do this. You and no other.

"It hurts…"

GOOD TO BE HOME

H E WOKE, MOANING through waves of pain breaking and cresting in his heart, "It hurts."

Jabbering voices and then a cup held to his mouth. Sweet and bitter swallows down his throat. A cold bubble of water chasing after. He broke free of the pain and floated away.

He woke again, crying, "It hurts."

It burns. Burns hotter than the sun. Burns like a star in my heart but isn't it wonderful and remarkable though it burns...

Sweet and bitter again. Then cold. Followed by nothing.

Sometimes voices broke through the void. Familiar friends giving advice which he wrote down under his eyelids, in his especial beautiful penmanship.

"Live a good life," Rafil said. "Because when Truvos took Nydirsil away, it was the end of second chances."

The Sisters spoke as one: "Every copy of the *Truviad* is printed with its last page torn in half."

Beniv said, "Whatever job you're given, Troubled, be *excellent* at it. Even if you're the only one who knows. Especially if you're the only one who knows."

Abrakam tilted his wise head. "A kheiron giving you his ring would be a great honor indeed. It would mean he trusted you. Or even loved you."

The world is a ship, ele-Kheir said. *Nydirsil is her mast. The yard rigged across her trunk is the future. And Estelos is the heaviest star.*

The pen fell from Trueblood's fingers and he opened his eyes.

He lay on his side between the twins. Raj curled against his aching back, his light like a knife blade at the edge of Trueblood's sight. His arms were full of Lejo's twinkling aura and the pain—*it burns so bright*—was too much. He couldn't get on top of it, he couldn't slip beneath it. He had to lie here and figure out how to hold it.

Hold the bond, said a voice from a long-ago. Or maybe it was a line from a story.

His heart burned and he was so tired. It had been a long voyage. Land was in sight and this was the time some men became careless. They assumed the job was done and started strutting or bragging.

Pelippé Trueblood knew better.

He hooked a leg around Raj's calf and pulled him close behind. His arm tightened around Lejo's waist and drew him in. He stopped fighting their light and let it become one with his. Let it fill him until he billowed out round above an endless ocean.

My father was a flower on the Tree of Life, but I am a sail on her yard.

THE FINCHES

IT TOOK CLOSE to a month for Trueblood and the twins to recover.

Their suite in the palace had two bedrooms but they continued to sleep together. Even in the light of day, Trueblood found he couldn't bear being away from the Ĝemelos. This wasn't mere poetry—separation filled him with a choking panic, coiling around his chest until he thought his heart would shatter.

Raj slept and slept. When awake, his gaze went dead and empty, his sunny, handsome presence diminished. One moment his aura hovered quietly at the edge of Trueblood's vision, the next it jumped out with a blinding scream, upsetting both of them.

Lejo had arms locked around Trueblood's other side, his spiritual deadweight dangling and dragging. His gaze bulged into next week, taking in everyone and everything and making it his. No amount of kyrrh could get his mind to turn off and he was nearly psychotic from lack of sleep. He got so bad, some of the healers discussed offering Lejo a bead of fadara, just to get him one decent night's rest.

"Don't you fucking dare," Raj cried, snapping out of his lethargy.

"We'd fully supervise the—"

"He'd be addicted in one dose. Don't let them do it, Pé."

"Not happening," Trueblood said to the healers, making no move to check his friend or gentle him down.

"You come anywhere near him with that shit, you say the *word* fadara around him and I'll fucking kill you," Raj said.

That night, neither twin slept. On either side of Trueblood the brothers tossed and turned, tormented by the inability to drift off as a pair, yet finding no comfort in being awake together.

"Lélé, I can't find you," Raj said, the baby name dire in his deep, hoarse voice. "You're here but I don't know where you *are*."

Lejo didn't even answer. He was feeling the world and nobody, not even Raj, could siphon a bit off to lesson the strain. It was a terrible night and Trueblood didn't know whether to rejoice or despair when the sun came up.

"Gently, lads," Abrakam said. "You're in shock. You can't rush these things. It'll be like learning to walk again."

"Gently," Raj said, like a mantra. His eyes were dilated to black pearls, staring wide and deep as his hand stroked Lejo's head and repeated, "Gently, gently."

I need to hold the bond, became Trueblood's thought. He breathed to the words and timed them to his footsteps. The little phrase soothed his nerves like a familiar prayer, or a mother's platitude. Was it something Noë used to say? The words felt very female in his head. Soft and cool, like an expert, competent hand feeling your brow for fever.

Hold the bond.

Every day, the three men practiced going out of each other's sight. Stepping onto the balcony alone for a count to fifty felt ridiculous, until it started to hurt like a bitch around thirty-five. Day after day, they added seconds and feet. Building up their resistance. Stretching the bond like a muscle and then resting it.

One brave morning, after a decent night's sleep, they parted ways after breakfast to attempt an afternoon apart. The twins wanted to go into town, while Trueblood was more interested in a good scrub-down at the palace's bathing pool.

Abrakam offered to show him the way. "Will you honor me by riding, Troubled?"

Swaying on his thin, weak legs, Trueblood smiled gratefully. "The honor is mine."

"Well, I only offer because you're down ten pounds."

This Trueblood couldn't deny. His ribs showed. He tired easily. Gripping Abrakam's body with his thighs seemed a monumental effort that had him thinking about a nap before they were even to the beach.

The grotto was built to be shared by the palace and the kheiron pavilion. Separated from the public beach by a rocky outcropping, it had a grassy knoll leading down to an enclosed manmade pool, which fed into the sea at its far end. Amid the natural boulders were chunks of quarried marble, making places to sit. They'd been piled high at one side, allowing water to cascade from above.

The sun burned on the scars around Trueblood's heart but felt good on his shoulders. The day was clear as water, the air sweet through his nose and into his chest.

A rhythmic rumbling startled him. He turned to see...

Are those birds?

He blinked. A dozen kheirons were galloping down the grassy slope. The human half of each was dyed red, their hair and wings black.

"Who are they?"

"The Finches," Abrakam said.

"Oh."

The centaur pointed. "See the biggest one there? That's Fen il-Kheir."

Trueblood said nothing.

Worry crossed Abrakam's gaze. "The Horselord's son?"

"I know who he is," Trueblood said shortly.

"Forgive me. You looked confused."

"I'm fine, Abe. Just slow." His eyes followed the kheirons as they waded into the pool. The water immediately turned crimson and black around their bodies and the current pulled the dye toward the sea outlet. Attendants splashed in with soap and strigils. From the uniform flock emerged individuality. Hair streamed blond and black and gray, long and short, straight, curled, braided. The kheirons shouted and laughed, ducking and splashing and strutting.

Except Fen.

He bathed away from the herd, and while all the other attendants were young human boys, his were two older centaurides. Both of them white-haired with equine bodies of the palest gray.

"Those are the White Mares," Abrakam said. "They've been attending Fen since he was a foalboy."

"I see," Trueblood said. Indeed his eyes were stuffing themselves, unable to look away. Fen didn't shout or laugh as the Mares scraped the dye from his limbs. He sank below the surface and rose again, rinsing his body and wings. Free of its jet dye, his hair was pure white, startling and silver against his tanned skin.

The charm thundered out of the pool and shook themselves off, then went galloping along the path toward the pavilion, the human attendants running to catch up. The White Mares settled together under a rowan tree, leaving Fen alone in the pool.

"He's magnificent," Trueblood heard himself say.

"Aye, he is, lad," Abrakam said. "But his has been a difficult life and he has little love for men. Best bathe at a distance."

When Abrakam gave advice, Trueblood took it. After the centaur left, the mariner shed his clothes and waded into the cool water. An attendant brought him soap and a strigil. The scrubbing was brisk and thorough, his skin left smarting. Free at last from the residue of his sickbed, he found a place several yards from Fen, where water poured over a lip of granite, and he let the stream pound over his neck and shoulders.

All the while, Fen stayed submerged, only his head above the surface. He was fifteen when Trueblood was born, making him almost thirty-five now, yet his face was that of a man barely into his twenties. Soft with youth and hard with experience at the same time. He had a little beard growth coming in, metal gray mixed silvery white along his strong jaw.

He was beautiful. His expression far-away and thoughtful. Fingertips rubbing his chin and teeth pressed on one corner of his full bottom lip.

Trueblood sank under the water. His sore heart protested as he counted ten, then surfaced with a gasp, shaking out his braids. He counted ten again before glancing sideways.

The kheiron's glance snagged his, just long enough for Trueblood to register a startling, impossible blue.

Fen looked away.

Trueblood tried to do the same. To stay at a distance and mind his own business.

He couldn't.

He crouched near the seagate, keenly aware the current reaching his body had just touched Fen's.

I could drink you, he thought.

The sudden, intense thought made him lightheaded. He swam to shore and walked out of the pool, conscious of his body and nakedness and how he might appear in someone else's eyes. In Fen's eyes. He dried off, put on his clean breeches and shirt. Re-braided one of his short plaits that had come undone. Only then did he turn around.

Fen was coming out of the water. His equine half was gray, liquid and smooth like a mirror. Or a sword made of mercury. His hooves glittered silver. His tail was white, like the hair on his head.

He's almost as tall as me, Trueblood thought. The idea of being eye-to-eye with this sublime creature made him feel warm all over.

Fen shook himself off, head to rear feet, water scattering around him in a flurry of drops, reflecting rainbows in the last of the sunlight.

Then he shifted.

The breath stopped dead in Trueblood's lungs as Fen's head elongated and his shoulders drew into a tight column. His white hair rippled out, taking on length and falling to one side. Then he stood in equos, a perfect gray stallion. Mane and tail resplendent, hooves glaring and metallic, one of them posed on its edge.

He did that when I was a baby, Trueblood remembered. *They said he did it because he liked me.*

The horse shook off more water and shifted back to kheiros, his upper half returning to its beautiful human form. Fen turned, showing his back. From nape to waist, the outline of wings was etched in silver, lying parallel to his spine. Overlapped at the tips, making an elongated heart.

"Gods," Trueblood whispered as the silver etchings grew brighter in Fen's rippling back. He stared as the kheiron's wings lifted out of human skin and spread wide, unfolding like a magnificent flower. Four feet. Six. Could the span be ten feet? No, more. The width was immeasurable. The white, feathered planes seemed to block out the setting sun.

Fen slowly flapped those stunning wings, letting the air ruffle through them. Then, with a last shiver from head to hooves, the wings drew back in. They folded neatly, the tiered feathers pulling tight together. They dissolved back into Fen's skin and became silver etchings once more.

The kheiron stood still, his profile clean against the sky.

Do that again, Trueblood thought.

Fen turned and his gaze settled on the mariner. Something glittered in one of his eyebrows. Below it was that baffling blue.

It's the blue of my father's coat, Trueblood thought. *The coat made by giants. It was dyed from ukhor stones, which were only found at the roots of Nydirsil. When Nydirsil disappeared, so did ukhor-blue. That hue doesn't exist anymore. It isn't a color of this world anymore. You can't find that blue anywhere anymore.*

"What the fuck are you staring at?" Fen said, in a dangerously casual voice.

Trueblood felt his spine stiffen as his mind answered, *The most splendid thing I've ever seen.*

Which naturally left his mouth as, "Not much."

The ukhor gaze narrowed as the kheiron walked toward him. He stopped close enough to meet the height of Trueblood's six feet and ten inches. Close enough for Trueblood to see the fine white hairs on his forearms and want to touch them. His heart burned and the edges of the world stretched out long as he concocted the craziest idea in the whole history of the world, anywhere, ever.

We're going to kiss each other.

Fen licked his lips, teeth catching on the bottom one and slowly letting go.

Definitely, Trueblood thought. *We're about to kiss. This is happening.*

The jeweled eyebrow flicked. Then, with the tiniest jerk of his head, tossing a mane that wasn't there, the kheiron turned his back.

He shifted into equos.

And shit on Trueblood's feet.

"*Feños,*" one of the White Mares cried from beneath the rowan tree.

Her sister raised her voice in reproach as well but now both centaurides were drowned out by the rumble of Fen's silver hooves as he galloped away.

Trueblood stared after him, open-mouthed as three dung apples squelched between his toes. "That went differently in my head," he said softly.

Then he laughed. Peal after peal, it roared out of his chest and belly, until he set his hands on his knees, wheezing. He waved off the approaching mares, unable to address their concerned expressions, he was laughing so hard. He went on waving and dismissing through the guffaws. He was still chuckling as he trudged away from the pool and toward the open beach to wash his feet.

The Little Wharf Rat

FEN STOOD AT the windows of his bedchamber. They faced the sea and he could see Trueblood making his way up the grassy incline. One of the White Mares walked alongside and he had a hand on her withers. He stopped often to lean on her flank. His steps grew slower until finally the centauride knelt at his side.

"Will you honor me by riding?" she undoubtedly said.

And of course Trueblood would know to reply, "The honor is mine."

Now the mare moved briskly but smoothly up the path. Trueblood swayed a little on her back, his head bowed. Fen rested his brow and palms on the glass and watched two lilac-robed nurses hurry out to help the kepten inside.

Fen's hands curled to fists. He contemplated punching out the glass but what good would it do his pounding heart and the anger roiling his stomach? It burned his chest and throat and turned his breathing to ragged hitches. It pulsed between his ears, pressing on his eyeballs until they threatened to spill over.

"You don't get to do this to me," he said through clenched teeth. "I owed a debt to your father. Not to you."

A last flash of white from Trueblood's shirt and the door shut behind him. The wide lawn was empty now.

With the back of his fourhand, Fen wiped his brimming eyes. What the fuck was he crying about anyway? He never cried. After what he'd been through, nothing was worth his tears. No trial or tragedy could make Fen il-Kheir break down. Nobody fucked with his autonomy or his agency and no one—*no one*—made him do anything he didn't want to.

No one except Pelippé Trueblood.

FEN FIRST PUT eyes on the mariner's son when the boy was nine days old. Pelippé's naming ceremony was Fen's first public appearance since his rescue and recovery. The effort to ignore the stares and whispers in the great hall left Fen with little interest for the occasion. He offered gelango to the mariner, kissed Noë Treeblood's little hands and gave a quick glance at the baby in the bassinette. Checking off the formalities, politely doing what was expected of him so he could get the fuck out of here.

He turned to go and something, some strange urge or compulsion, as insistent as a yank on his tail, made him look back.

And he shifted.

A kheiron would have a difficult time describing the mechanics of shifting. It does, however, involve a conscious decision. If pressed, Fen would say he first moved his awareness into his moonstone, found his equos within and let it flow into his body. Intention, then visualization, then the act.

When he shifted in front of Pelippé Trueblood, it was instantaneous. No decision on his part. It just *happened*. Utterly beyond his control. He blinked twice before realizing he was staring through a horse's eyes.

The great hall receded, taking all the faces and stares far away. Fen stretched his neck further toward the bassinette. A fine, black fuzz covered the baby's delicate skull. His round eyes were open, fists waving. He cooed a little giggle, as if Fen in equos delighted him. Dozens of gifts for Pelippé Trueblood were stacked on a long table, but Fen's was the best.

Thank you, the baby's gurgling laugh said. *It's just what I wanted. How did you know?*

If he were in humos, Fen would've blushed. His silvery head dipped and he thought, *I don't know. I just did.*

Filled with a strange shyness, he rolled a hoof onto its coronet and added, *You're welcome.*

Then he was back in kheiros, dizzy at the abrupt shift and embarrassed at the hall's fixed attention. He walked out of the ceremony, which pissed off his father, but he couldn't stay one more second in that collective staring.

He avoided the mariner's family and wrote off the incident. Until it happened again.

And kept happening.

Nearly every godsdamned time he saw the brat, Fen shifted into equos. Standing as his truest self, with his heart on display. Down at the grotto this afternoon, he nearly tied his will in a knot to keep his equos under control.

I decide, he chanted through the struggle. *I decide my fate, I decide my form, I decide which direction I live my life. No one else.*

He kept his body in kheiros and kept his eyes straight ahead. Except when they were on Trueblood.

You keep looking at him like that and you're either going to shift or start rubbing against the rocks.

He looked away. For all of five seconds.

Fine. Look. Get a good eyeful and then knock it off already.

Trueblood was walking out of the pool and he was lean as rope. Whatever his strange illness had been, it consumed every bit of fat on his long frame. His ribs showed in his dark skin. A strange scar ringed the center of his chest.

"As if his heart had been torn out and set on fire," Joenne Windsong had said.

He stood naked on the beach and Fen gazed harder at Trueblood's skin than he did the scar. Smooth over all that corded muscle. Nearly hairless. In the shade it was like walnut. Beneath the direct sun, it shone mahogany. He looked like the pictures of Truvos, the sea god. Except one of his braids had come undone and the bit of freed hair bobbed by the side of his head like a clump of pollen.

Which of course, made him fucking charming.

When Trueblood was dressed and his quick strong fingers were busy braiding, Fen judged it was safe to come out. He loped up the bank and shook himself off. Fully in control, he turned to go.

And shifted.

Oh for fuck's sake.

He pulled back to kheiros. And then, for the love of Khe, he was unfurling his wings like a colt showing off for the fillies. What *was* it with this godsdamned Pelippé Trueblood?

To save face, he shit on the man's feet.

Fen's face burned hot against the window panes, knowing he'd gone a little too far. Although as he galloped from the beach, he swore he heard laughter behind him. Which was almost worse than shouted curses or threats.

Gods, his father was going to kill him.

Naturally one of the White Mares ratted Fen out. Any minute now, he'd be called on the Horselord's carpet to answer for his scatological prank. Il-Kheir used a leather tawse to discipline his warriors, but he didn't ever whip Fen. What would be the point? The slavemasters in Arcodolori used to entertain themselves by trying to flog Fen's wing markings off his back. They took turns shredding the skin bloody, but couldn't break or bend the silver tracings, which made them lash harder. A tawsing was a joke by comparison. Fen would nap through it.

While Nyland's healers had worked wonders with salves, oint-ments and unguents, little of Fen's body remained free of scars. Il-Kheir would have to be a special kind of sadistic prick to want to put his own decorative mark on such a marred canvas. When vexed with his offspring, he punched Fen instead.

Fair enough. But one of these days, Fen was going to punch back.

Meanwhile, he was still standing at the windows, fists curled, looking across to the infirmary wing and hoping Trueblood would come back out.

Why did he piss Fen off so much, yet made his soul want to show its best side? One glimpse of giantsblood and Fen shifted into equos. His head bowed, his hoof posed. It just happened.

And he hated it.

A cleared throat and a rattle of knuckles on his door. "Mysire, your father wishes to see you."

With one last glance to the courtyard, Fen went to collect his due.

THE HORSELORD'S CHAMBERS occupied one small wing of the pavilion. A few attendants and two of Sevri's generals milled about the foyer.

"Good evening, Father," Fen said. He hadn't used Da in twenty years. "To what do I owe the pleasure?"

"Leave us," il-Kheir said to the kheirons.

"Actually, I prefer this be witnessed," Fen said.

The Horselord's voice raised a fraction. "Leave us."

A hollow thumping of hooves on stone followed by the deathly click of a door closing.

Fen inspected his fingernails. *I survived a month on a slave ship,* he thought. *I endured a forced march across Arcodolori and lived on a chain for two years. I am the Finch and I'm not afraid of anything. Least of all my father.*

"From the day you entered this world, you've always preferred an audience," il-Kheir said.

"Am I here to be analyzed?"

"What you did to Trueblood was unconscionable."

"It was a joke."

"It was a disgrace. You owed Kepten True your life."

"We've had this conversation already."

"Watch your mouth," il-Kheir said.

"Oh, I'm sorry the truth coming from it hurts your tender heart. I often forget you're actually capable of feeling pain."

Fen often forgot how quickly his father could cover space. All at once he was smashed up against the wall, a rough hand covering his mouth.

"You know nothing of my pain," il-Kheir said, his voice hoarse and dangerous.

Then tell *me,* Fen thought, eyes burning above the clamp of his father's palm. *Tell me what I did. Tell me why I was your brave one on the ship coming home, but then overnight you became a stranger.*

Il-Kheir's hand pressed harder. "Kepten True lies dead in the crypt and you shit on the feet of his son. Instead of remembering who you are and acting like an heir of the Horsefolk."

His flank drove Fen further into the stones. He was one hundred and fifty years old, with the strength and power of the entire herd in his massive body. By kheiron reckoning, Fen was barely past adolescence. Still evolving and no match for the Horselord. As his temple was ground against the wall, he didn't yield or cower, but he didn't struggle either.

One of Sevri's forelegs wrapped around Fen's, hobbling him. "The priestess said you'd spend more time looking backward than ahead. If you won't take it upon yourself to face your future then it's up to me to turn your head in that direction."

Like liquid, he shifted into humos and his hand pulled away from Fen's face. It came back curled in a fist, each finger ringed in silver.

The blow hit Fen's cheekbone like a crossbolt. Pinned to the wall, he had no cushion or means to deflect. The pain burst like a bubble and flooded his entire face. He set his jaw, shook his clanging head twice and stared hard at his father.

Sevri was so angry, his body didn't know what shape to take. He shifted from humos to equos to humos again, finally settling into kheiros. Breathing hard, his pale eyes filled with murder and his voice dangerously soft.

"You will apologize to Pelippé Trueblood," he said. "Don't make me tell you twice."

"Twice you had the chance to let me die," Fen said. "I don't know why you didn't take either of them."

"Because unlike you, I finish what I start. Now get out of my sight."

"Story of my life."

Once Fen believed in happy endings and tales with a satisfying moral. But now, more than ever, he felt like a walking copy of the *Truviad*. A book cut off in the middle of a sentence, the narrative left to dangle helplessly without exposition or an arc.

And it was his own father who tore his page in half.

THIS FOR THAT

YOU MUST UNDERSTAND, legantos. Sevri il-Kheir was not always this way.

He'd been shy as a foalboy. Intense and contemplative next to his father's carefree exuberance. Given his way, Sevri would live in equos forever, giving all his ardor and passion to the pegaso mare, Zoria. She owned his heart and body and he would know no other lover but her. He never tasted a human kiss, never felt a four- or fivehand slide below his waist, and never lay between the sheets as a man. He fervently believed his soul bond with Zoria equaled anything found in a bed, even surpassed it. When she died, the warp and weft of his existence ripped down the center and left him in tatters. His sanity teetered on a precarious edge and to keep from tumbling into the abyss, he heaped all his love, all his grief, all his devotion and all his fears upon his only son.

When Tehvan was taken away, Sevri's reason for living went with him. Bereft of the last link to Zoria, the Horselord went quietly mad.

He tore the world apart looking for his foalboy. He joined his legions with Queen Nysiema's army and they swept through Minosaros in a frantic but methodical invasion called Tehvan's War.

Il-Kheir and the queen turned cities upside-down and shook them out, dislodging all manner of evil. They eviscerated the underbelly of the underworld, but Tehvan il-Kheir was never among the rescued.

Sevri died a thousand deaths in the two years Tehvan was missing. His face wore the expression of one who is constantly ripped in two. A face both slack with grief and contorted with rage. Once, his eyes had been the gold-streaked blue of lapis lazuli. Now they were hard like slate and perpetually narrowed at the world, looking for Tehvan in every corner. He strained so hard to see, his eyelashes fell out. He ground his back teeth until they cracked. He always stood cross-armed, hiding the tremor in his upper body. Palms and arms burning with the need to hold his flesh and blood.

As his desperation mounted, he consulted with people he always labeled as charlatans—oracles and soothsayers and prophets. They were no help. His contempt only increased, and even projected backward to the priestess present at Tehvan's birth. It was she who predicted the motherless, breech-born foalboy was doomed to a life of despair. Taking first steps in ground soaked with his mother's blood heralded nothing but calamity. A kheiron who didn't hear his own dam's death cries could never be a king attuned to the needs of his race.

The priestess implored Sevri to show mercy to the herd by abandoning his only son and siring another heir on another dam. Sevri insisted the priestess abandon any such idea. He pressed the point by breaking her neck.

To say this wasn't a fortuitous beginning to Tehvan il-Kheir's life is an understatement.

I swear to you, legantos, the stories and the songs are true. When the news came via falcon that Tehvan was rescued, il-Kheir was in the air before the paper reached the floor. The tenderness with which he gathered his brave one's head to his shoulder was witnessed and immortalized. It really did happen. This was the kheiron we ought to know and this is the behavior by which we should judge Sevri il-Kheir.

As I told you before, it's not always best to know the truth when others don't.

The best surgeon in Nyland declared Tehvan's broken limbs were beyond repair. For the second time, the Horselord was advised to abandon his son, this worrisome foal who'd been dragged backward into the world.

"He's suffering, mysire," the surgeon said.

"Mysire, he's in torment," the priestesses said.

They came at him from all sides, despairing and panicked and reproachful.

"This could go on for weeks."

"We can end this misery. I give you my word, with three beads of fadara, it will be quick. Painless and dignified."

"We beg you, do something. He can't go on like this, he's in *agony*."

"Mysire, even if he survives, he will never walk again. Not on two legs, not on four. His life won't be worth living."

What was a desperate father to do?

Any father would've lost his mind, but Sevri il-Kheir was both father and king. His reign was a link in an unbroken chain forged from starsilver. The chain stretched backward in time, thousands of years, to the first kheiron, the son of Khe.

But the first il-Kheir had been a twin.

His sister, ele-Kheir, was both first and last. The world had seen thousands of Horselords but only one Horsedam. She lived on the side of the moon that never showed its face to man and knew neither heir nor death.

Ele-Kheir moved in darkness but it was said she could work miracles.

Her ultimate little brother, her ancestral nephew many times removed, needed a miracle.

Sevri didn't go to the Horsedam with entreaty. He went with a bargain.

Everything has a price, legantos. The world is transactional.

This for that.

Miracles are expensive, but the Horselord was willing to pay.

On the night of a new moon, when Lunos turned away from the earth and showed her secret side, Sevri offered his soul to ele-Kheir, in return for Tehvan's fully-restored life and limbs.

This for that.

My soul for his legs.

What many people don't know is when you sell your soul, you sell what lives within it. Within the soul's deed was Sevri's connection to his son. He knew this and he signed the agreement. He signed away his compassion. He signed away his reputation and legacy as well, because ego lives in the soul. Once the deal was made, Sevri forgot it even existed. Or why it existed.

Not one song or story would recount the extraordinary and selfless lengths Sevri went to to save his son. No one, Fen most of all, would understand the Horselord's overnight change in attitude or his strange, cruel ambivalence.

Nobody would ever know what transpired beneath the new moon that night, when Lunos's back was turned on the world.

Ele-Kheir certainly would never tell the story.

And il-Kheir didn't know the story was his.

PART FOUR
VELOS
Goddess of Fertility and Harvest

Showing Off

Not wanting to poke the wasp nest of his father's temper again, Fen had his charm drill with the kheiron legions the next day. No war paint, no agenda, no stunts. They stayed synchronized and seamless within the herd mentality. Fen exhausted himself walking the fine line between showing off and not giving his best effort, knowing his father would recognize either from a mile away.

Between exercises, he had to endure Lenge's moody silence and passive-aggressive sighs. Rubbing her off back in Zeuxis had been a grave error of judgment. It broke his professional rule of not getting too intimate with his charm, and violated his personal prohibition against lovers.

The giants had a word: gelang. It meant at hand. Or together with. It described great romances, but also great friendships. A soul bond. The endearment *gelangos* meant "my one at hand," or "the one I belong to."

Fen il-Kheir had known only one gelangos in his life and that was when he was twelve and stupid. Belmiro was fourteen and not much smarter, but the most beautiful creature Fen had ever seen in his life. A head of dark waves that didn't behave and eyes the color of mint leaves. The sun rose in his wide smile and set on his sleek, thoughtful brows. A skilled archer, he drew his bow, touched the tip of his tongue to his upper lip, and Fen bared his chest for a target.

Hit me. My heart is yours so don't miss.

They started out shy and quickly became seamless. Bel finished Fen's sentences. Or he did a double-take at something Fen said and breathed, "I was *just* about to say that." Soon they could communicate with a glance, a lifted chin or arched eyebrow. They became inseparable as yolk and white in a scrambled egg. With the edges of their minds so perfectly aligned, their bodies followed easily. The first time they kissed, Fen saw new stars in the sky. The first time he slid a hand between Belmiro's forelegs, Fen lost his mind. When he came down on Belmiro's palm, his soul exploded. A single, whispered "I love you," and he was finished.

He believed it was gelang. When Belmiro left to train with the legions and asked Fen to wait for him, Fen promised. But that didn't feel gelang enough, so he slipped out of the pavilion and flew away from Alondra. He tracked the legions at a careful distance, following them to the summer encampment in Sudenlo. Here Belmiro was one among fifty first-year archers, but the only one in Fen's longing heart. He declared his love again and like a fool, he gave Belmiro his moonstone.

"I'll wait for you on two legs," he said. The sentiment was idiotic but he *meant* it. It was what he felt, it was the truth in his heart. And Belmiro was a fool for taking what was offered, but he did it because he *believed* in it.

And I spent two years as a slave for it, Fen thought.

He came home to learn his father had hobbled Belmiro and cast him out of the herd. Shunned and shamed, Fen's gelangos was living on two legs, prostituting himself in the pleasure houses along Alondra's wharves. On the rare occasions his path crossed Fen's, they had nothing to say. They weren't bitter or angry. Any concept of *them* was simply impossible now.

It felt like gelang, Fen thought, *but it made whores of both of us. So even if it was gelang, it wasn't worth it.*

IL-KHEIR RAN THE herd ragged and flew them until their feathers blanketed the ground. After cooling off at the grotto, Fen felt like a wrung-out towel. Walking through the atrium between the palace and the pavilion, his stomach rumbled, ravenous, but the thought of dinner across a table from Lenge was unbearable. He didn't often ask the White Mares for favors, but he might ask for supper in his room tonight and then topple into bed.

Mid-yawn, he stopped.

Pelippé Trueblood stood by the stone balustrade. Right where Fen would have to pass, godsdammit.

He froze, waiting for the shift into equos. Oddly, it didn't come. Either his body was too exhausted, or his soul had grown used to seeing Trueblood on a regular basis and didn't need to grandstand.

He ignored the thump in his chest. *I lived two years on a chain. I'm not afraid of a sailor.*

He started walking again, formulating a script. *Salutos* would be sufficient. Maybe a polite inquiry to Trueblood's health.

Would "sorry for shitting on your feet" be overdoing it?

Could his heart pound any harder?

"Héjo," the mariner said over his shoulder. "This is awkward."

Fen drew a deep breath. "*Salu*, Kepten."

"Salu, kheiron."

Blue thread wound around the coppery ends of Trueblood's plaits and a single silver hoop pierced his ear. His brown arms crossed on the stone rail, he stared out at the rooftops and spires of Valtourel.

Fen followed Trueblood's appreciative gaze. His heart didn't have much connection to Valtourel—like Trueblood, he was born in Alondra—but tonight, the young city tossed its head back and stood tall with accomplishment, handsome under the last of the sunset.

"What happened?" Trueblood's index finger started to reach toward Fen's face, then abruptly retreated and touched his own cheekbone instead.

"My father wasn't happy about my little farewell gift to you yesterday," Fen said. "He likes me to wear my not-so-finest moments on my face."

"I'm sorry."

"Not your fault."

"I didn't rat you out, if that's what you're thinking."

"No, the White Mares did." He shrugged, embarrassment itching his back where he couldn't scratch. "I had it coming."

Trueblood leaned further on his elbows. "So where do you wear your finest moments?"

"Good question," Fen said. "Where do you?"

"Let me get back to you when I have enough fine moments to make a garment."

The mariner laced his fingers, thumbs tapping together. One ankle crossed over the other and his hips kicked back a little. His shoulders rose and fell in slow, easy breaths.

Fen took a taste of humility and swallowed its bitterness. "I apologize."

Trueblood turned his head, eyebrows drawn down a little.

"For shitting on your feet," Fen said. "It was…uncalled for."

With a snort of air through his nose, Trueblood burst out laughing. "You think?"

"What's so funny?" Fen said.

Trueblood ducked away, trying to get himself under control, which only made him laugh harder.

Anger bubbled up in Fen's throat, then just as quickly dissolved because Trueblood's head was flung back and his smile was full of laughter. It put an arm around Fen and leaned on him, slapping his shoulders in the camaraderie of a private joke.

We own this. I and him. Like a jacket made of one fine moment.

"Sorry," Trueblood said through the fading chuckles. "I thought it was hilarious. Let's just forget it. Apology accepted."

He settled back into his crossed-ankle stance, leaning on the balcony with the tiniest smile still wreathing his chin. "Asshole," he mumbled.

"First impressions are important."

"You nailed it."

A beat of silence.

"I'm truly sorry about your father," Fen said.

"Thank you." Trueblood kept staring straight ahead, chin on his hands now.

"He was important to me. You know why."

"Of course," the mariner said softly.

"I remember when you were born."

"Do you?"

"I was fifteen. I was finally walking again."

Why are you telling him this?

"I see." Trueblood nodded, his eyes closed and chin tilted up toward the sun. "I don't remember much about living in Alondra. My memory wakes up when I was at sea with my father."

And my memory never goes to sleep, Fen thought. "It's a lot to carry in your heart," he heard himself say.

"What is?"

He shook his head. "I don't know what I meant by that."

Smiling, Trueblood turned around and put his back to the balustrade. "What I don't know would just about fill the Gulf of Pellandro."

The smile faded and Fen missed it.

He didn't like missing it.

A dark trepidation twisted in his stomach, making every hair of his coat bristle. If he were in the field with his charm, he'd pull them into a tight wedge and look for signs of an ambush. Even now his eyes were flicking around the atrium and his instincts told him to retreat. He was outnumbered here.

"Goodnight, Kepten," he said. He walked away, hooves solemn and deep on the stones.

"What, no farewell gift?" Trueblood called after.

Fen looked back over one shoulder and touched his wounded cheek. "One bruise is a statement. Two would be showing off."

Walking away again, his shoulders shook with the effort of keeping his wings retracted. They wanted to unfurl, spread and launch him into the sunset over Valtourel. For no other reason than Trueblood watching.

Look at me, he thought, reading from the story of his life.

Look at me, see me, watch me.

And when I slip out of sight, take the world apart to find me.

NARIA

"DA NEVER LIKED the way il-Kheir treated Fen," Trueblood said to Abrakam.

"Your Da wasn't alone in that opinion," the centaur said. "If Sevri didn't have as many military accomplishments in his panniers, I don't think he'd have a shred of respect from Nyland. People and creatures are loyal to him, but few admire him."

They were having a drink in the palace library. A fire crackled in the big hearth and the lamps made bubbles of gold light against the tall shelves. Abrakam was perusing a restored set of novels. Raj sat at a table surrounded by atlases. Trueblood lounged on a sofa, feet on a leather hassock and Lejo's dozing head on his thigh.

His notebook balanced on the arm of the sofa, he sketched the mast of a ship. Lately he was a little obsessed with masts, drawing them and their yards on every scrap of paper. The juncture of vertical strength and horizontal power niggled with a deeper meaning, like the sole, lingering fragment of last night's dream.

"Il-Kheir couldn't care less who admires him," Raj said, not looking up from his reading.

Trueblood smiled. The horrible dead expression had finally leeched out of Raj's eyes and he was finding more and more reasons to stay awake. Lejo, thank Gods, had escaped from the coils of insomnia. He was sleeping through the night and catnapping every other hour.

"Fen's an odd one," Trueblood said, running a slow hand through Lejo's hair.

"He's magnificent," Raj said.

Trueblood's eyes narrowed as he thought, *Back off, map boy, I saw him first.*

Lejo burrowed his head against Trueblood's leg with a small smile.

"You shut up," Trueblood mumbled.

Lejo smiled wider, showing his dimple.

"What Fen suffered would leave anyone magnificently odd," Raj said.

"It's a lot to carry in your heart," Trueblood said. His pencil doodled meandering, diagonal lines out from the mast, making it into a tree.

"Aye," Abrakam said. "For both son and father."

"But il-Kheir is… All right, Fen was out of line down at the grotto. But I thought it was funny and it didn't warrant a punch in the face."

"I agree. On the other hand, Sevri's not only raising a son, he's training an heir. And there are better ways to show your distaste for a man than shitting on his feet." Abrakam tugged Trueblood's plaits. "Your father didn't hesitate to discipline you when it was warranted."

"Yes, but he thrashed my ass, not my head."

"And never because you'd been foolish. Only disrespectful."

He and Trueblood both sighed.

"Gods, I miss him," Abrakam said.

"He misses you more," a woman's voice said behind them.

Lejo sat up and Trueblood twisted in his seat.

"Your Majesty," the centaur said, bowing. "What a surprise."

"Gods, Abrakam, do I look majestic?"

Trueblood didn't say a word as Naria, the hereditary queen of Nyland, came into the library. She was dressed in her armor, burnished bronze over green silk. Her crowned helmet in one hand, the other reaching to draw off her leather hood.

"Holy…" Lejo whispered as her hair fell down.

"Horses," Raj finished.

Like a waterfall, Naria's hair unrolled to her waist in damp tangles, unleashing an earthy, elemental scent of sweat and travel and woman.

And *metal*.

Trueblood went on staring as the twins stood up and bowed.

"Again with the bowing?" Naria said. "*Must* we? Come here, mariner."

Walking toward the fireplace, Trueblood's head floated far above his feet. Naria set down her helmet and held her hands out to him.

"Kepten Trueblood."

He kissed her palms. "General Nyland."

"I'm so sorry about your father."

"Thank you."

"You're feeling better?"

"Much."

She raised one eyebrow. "You scared the shit out of us."

"Forgive me?"

"I'll think about it. I'm in dire need of a bath right now but I'll expect you at dinner?"

He ignored the giggling vision of Naria in the bath and said, "I'll be there."

"Sit next to me. I have a hundred questions." The words were soft but around them, her smile was hungry. Like he was a meal she could devour standing up.

"I love questions." He inhaled her metallic fragrance again, wanting her to fill his mouth like a feast.

I COULD, LEGANTOS, write a separate book about Naria Nyland. If you ask nicely, maybe I will. This is Trueblood's story, but his affair with the queen, though brief, was not insignificant. So while he stands there with his mouth watering, let me tell you a little about Naria.

She was the only daughter of Queen Nysiema, who joined forces with the kheirons during Tehvan's War. Naria rode with her mother's legions, all of six years old but inherently attuned to both the glory and horror of the battlefield. She'd been groomed from birth to be queen, general, peacekeeper and statesman.

In other words, a mother to her people.

Ikharus-Lippé True was correct in saying Nyland endured thanks to the women who protected her. Her warrior queens walked with their feet deep in the earth and their fealty was to the forests.

Like Pelippé, Naria Nyland was a young commander. She headed a legion at sixteen and took the throne at twenty-five. There the similarities ended, for while Trueblood struggled with his new title of Kepten, Naria didn't know the meaning of self-doubt. Whether on the battlefield or in the bedroom, her confidence and self-assuredness was rooted like a Nye tree. A scion of an ancient, matriarchal society, she didn't have to marry to secure her place in the world, and what she wanted, she went after.

And somewhere between the first and second course of that evening's dinner, it became clear she wanted Pelippé Trueblood.

Trueblood knew nothing about pursuit and courtship. Until now, he'd only nibbled around the edges of his sexuality, and only with Lejo. They certainly hadn't *wooed* each other into bed. They never danced around a flame, or spun flirtation on a spindle, seeing how long they could draw out the thread of unfulfilled desire. Lejo folded back the covers and Trueblood got into bed. They blew out the lamp and there they went and there they were.

Trueblood remembered his complex emotions when looking at the illustrations of women in books, and he knew the uncomplicated response of his body in Lejo's hands. But he'd never felt the heat of someone's frank and immediate interest. Never knew the delicious thrill of being an apple ripe for picking. The heady rush of being unabashedly desired and the mind-blowing discovery that gratification could be instant. Or at least, lasting no longer than the length of a dinner.

Over four courses and between questions and answers, he and Naria couldn't keep their eyes off each other.

"Come see me later?" she murmured as they adjourned.

"I'll think about it."

Her hip knocked against his. "I have some boring business with horrible people. Your company can be my reward."

The notch at the base of her throat beckoned his finger, but he didn't know the etiquette of touching a queen in public. He kept his hands to himself, savoring the anticipation like dessert.

"I'll send for you," Naria said. "Don't wander off with another woman or I'll jail that fine ass of yours."

With a last smile, she swept away.

Trueblood stared after, thinking, *My ass is fine?*

The Corner of My Eye

TRUEBLOOD SPENT THE hours after dinner with the twins, filling up their reservoirs so he could leave. Overnight, he presumed. He hoped.

Raj's aura was nearly back to normal, settled down at Trueblood's periphery with only the occasional flare-up. But Lejo struggled hard tonight, his pinpricks of light spilling across Trueblood's entire field of vision, making his heart constrict and burn. The longing in Lejo stretched until it pulled, pulled until it yanked. It tightened, twisted and torqued until it *cried,* like a child for his mother. It drew Trueblood backward in time, into the locked closet of memory, until it lay dead on the floor in the smoke and blood and...

"Lé, stop," Raj said. "You're hurting him."

Lejo bunched his fists against his forehead. "I'm sorry."

"Let me go," Trueblood said, his voice fraying at the edges. "I know you're not doing it on purpose, but when you pull too hard, you tear open things I don't like to think about."

"Let go, Lé," Raj said.

"I'm trying."

"Come on. He's not leaving you forever and I'm right here."

"I *know.* Be quiet and let me do this."

Lejo's body stilled. The light cleared out of Trueblood's eyes and curled at the edges. He tried to fasten it there with something good. Something reassuring.

You kissed me and it tasted like oranges, he thought. *You said at hand was fine but you liked the together more. You slept all over me. It was what you liked best. You want someone with you all the time. You can't help it. You were left behind on a ship. Left alone in the dark but who left you together with only Raj in your hands but he was over there far away and alone and you were left on the floor in the smoke and blood and Mami wake up her dress the blood is in her dress and the smoke in my eyes and the light in my eyes and—*

"Lé," Raj cried sharply.

"Gods*dammit.*" With a grunt of frustration, Lejo stood up. "As soon as I get it quiet in my hands, it spills out."

"Hold still," Trueblood mouthed, but no sound came out.

"Settle down," Raj said, holding his brother from behind. "I'm sorry."

"It's not your fault. It's just who you are. Stop struggling."

"Why is it taking so long?"

Raj's chin moved back and forth across Lejo's crown. "Because between us, you're the better man."

Lejo's face twisted, finally filling with something that wasn't despair. "Oh, fuck off, Raj," he said

All at once, Trueblood's throat eased up and his chest relaxed. He fell back in the chair cushions, exhaling long.

"There," he said. "Stay right there."

"He will." Raj had his brother in an arm lock. "I love you."

Lejo's tear-filled eyes flashed hard as he sucked his teeth and bucked off the circle of arms. "You're so full of shit, I don't know how I can love you."

"Holy horses, you *meant* that," Trueblood said, laughing.

"Shut up."

Trueblood blinked as he swiveled his gaze to the extreme side, where Lejo's aura now crouched. Glowering, but contained. "You know, anger might be the trick, Lé. I and Raj have to piss you off more."

"Try it," Lejo said, stomping through the terrace doors to the balcony.

A polite rattle of knuckles at the open door. "Is this a lovers' quarrel or may I interrupt?"

The man in the doorway looked to be in his forties. His short hair was an iron mix of gray, white and silver. Beneath dark eyebrows, a mint-green gaze looked Trueblood slowly up and down.

A beat of silence as a sudden shyness trapped Trueblood's tongue to the roof of his mouth. His preoccupation with Naria rolled its eyes, insisting it was *quite* busy right now and had no time to wonder why this man was looking at him that way. And hope he wouldn't stop.

"Gods," Raj muttered, and stepped into the awkward silence. "I'm Raj Ĝemelos. The lad sulking outside is my brother, Lejo. This piece of sculpture is Kepten Trueblood. Take your pick, but I'm probably your best shot at good conversation."

"Alas," the man said, "I'm here for the statue."

He was tall for a human, the crown of his head on a level with Trueblood's chin. His long frame packed with muscle and both forearms tattooed from wrist to elbow with feathers.

"I'm called Belmiro," he said, one eyebrow and his upper lip arching.

Trueblood managed to pry his mouth open and extend a hand. "Pelippé. Village idiot."

"Queen Naria wishes the idiot's presence. Have you made a will?"

Trueblood turned to Raj. "I leave everything to you. Lé gets nothing."

Raj put a hand on his heart and gave a little bow. "I'll endeavor to keep him from pissing on your tomb but make no promises."

"I need friends like you two." Belmiro motioned to the door. "Shall we, Kepten?"

Trueblood hesitated, looking at the balcony where Lejo paced.

"No, don't say goodbye," Raj said. "He'll be really insulted. It might give you an extra hour." He backhanded Trueblood's ass. "To your death, sailor."

"You're looking well," Belmiro said as they headed down the long corridor. "Better than when I first saw you."

"When was that?"

"As you were being carried off the ship." His head shook slowly. "Pardon my Altynese, but you scared the shit out of us."

"So I'm told."

"I'm sorry about your father."

"Thank you."

"He was a legend of the world," Belmiro said. "I still can't take in he's gone, so I won't pretend to know how it must be for you."

"I'm still fitting a lot of things back together. I don't really feel I'm where I'm supposed to be. Or that I'm ready for what's next."

"If it's any consolation, it felt like the world was holding its breath while you were recovering. So while you're doubting yourself, don't doubt that a lot of people love you, Kepten Trueblood."

"My friends call me Pé."

Belmiro smiled. "We just met."

"And what you said consoled me. So we're friends."

They rounded a sharp corner and nearly collided with Fen il-Kheir.

Because tonight couldn't be weird enough.

"Héjo," Belmiro said.

"Salu, Bel. Kepten."

"Fen."

A glance went around the trio before Fen said, "Where are you off to?"

Belmiro tilted his head toward Trueblood. "Leading the lamb to the slaughter."

"I take back the friend thing," Trueblood said.

Another beat of silence.

"Pardon us?" Belmiro said.

Fen stepped aside. "Enjoy your evening."

Walking on, Trueblood could feel the kheiron's hard stare on his shoulder blades. Reproving and…disappointed?

What the hell does he care what I do with my time?

And why did he care if Fen cared?

OUT OF HER armor, bathed and gowned and looking every inch a woman, Naria Nyland still retained an edge of danger. This kernel of fear within arousal was a new aspect of gelang for Trueblood. In the handful of nights with Lejo, he'd felt a range of things from delirium to dumb, but he'd never felt unsafe. When the royal bedroom door closed and Naria wound arms lightly around his waist, Trueblood was instantly hard, yet his insides yapped like a provoked watchdog.

I hardly know her, he thought, as her hand wandered to the open V of his shirt. Her eyebrows furrowed as she studied the strange scar around his heart.

"Can I touch it?" she asked, and when he nodded, she reached a gentle finger. "Strange," she said, tilting her head this way and that. "Dead-on, it looks like an ordinary burn. But if I look sideways, out the corner of my eye, it almost…sparkles."

"I noticed that, too."

"You don't remember what happened?"

"No." He relaxed into both her touch and her curiosity.

"It's silvery," she said. "Almost like a kheiron's wing marks." Now her palm flattened against the thud of his heart. The coil of nerves around his stomach and chest loosened, letting him realize he was only afraid of disappointing her.

"You're shaking," she said.

"I'm a little nervous."

"A little?"

"A lot."

"Have you ever done this before?"

"I've done some of this before," Trueblood said. "But not with a woman."

Her chin rose and fell and her fingers slid soft along his neck. "I see." She drew him closer. "Just breathe with me."

Her body rose up taller and extended wider as she took a deep breath, encouraging him to match it. The mariner closed his eyes, all of him prickling and clenched, hard and melting. His teeth poised over the shiny, tight skin of an apple.

"I have two questions," he said.

"I love questions."

"Can I call you Naria while we're doing this?"

"Please do."

"And if I'm terrible at it, you won't throw me in jail?"

She shook her head. Not a trace of teasing was in her face and for that Trueblood was grateful.

Her hands slipped beneath his shirt, then slid it up over his head. His skin drew up in thousands of pinpoints and he inhaled sharp when the pads of Naria's thumbs traced each of his nipples. A sound he'd never made in his life fell out of his throat when her tongue followed. He tentatively touched the neckline of her gown. The women he lived with wore shirts, breeches and boots. This kind of clothing was a mystery to him.

"You'll need to help me with this," he said, figuring the truth was best. "And maybe some other things."

Smiling, Naria turned around, drawing her hair aside. Over her shoulder, she told him what to do with loops and buttons and laces. Naked, she took his hands and showed him what to do with her.

The lush weight of her breasts was a revelation, as was the way her nipples changed shape in his mouth. The geography of her body's planes and curves invited a lifetime of study. Bolder now, he picked her up, wanting her face-to-face with his height.

"Strong," she murmured, before her open mouth came into his. Her limbs wound around him like vines. The curves of her bottom melded perfectly to his hands. He couldn't believe none of the pages in Abrakam's book talked about the secret, satin skin behind a woman's knees, or what it felt like when a woman who'd been raised in the saddle got her legs around your waist. Their grip didn't ease up a minute, not even when he eased their tangled bodies down onto the bed.

"What do you like?" she said.

"Come on top of me." He wanted to recreate the gelang picture he'd pored over so many hours and see if he was right about it.

Naria rose up, planting a knee on either side of him. Her hands pressed down on his collarbones and as he guessed, all her weight on him didn't hurt. His hardness slid like magic into her body and he was right about that, too.

As for the soft, wet, squeezing heat, no wonder the books had nothing to say about it. No words existed.

"Good?" she whispered.

He nodded, caught up tight in the pages of this story.

"You can go harder," she said, curving over him and licking his neck. "Come on, mariner. Let me feel you."

He went harder, holding her damp waist and moving her on him. One moment he craned to watch, not wanting to miss a second of this miraculous dance, the next he was limp in the pillows, eyes rolling in his head.

"Pé," she whispered above him. "Pé, don't stop."

His name in her gasp was astonishing. The curtain of her hair swung side to side, then flew back as her throat arched to the ceiling. She slid along the slick length of him, her nails bit into his skin and she kept sing-songing, "Don't stop."

The encouragement socked him straight in his tender ego. He got harder. Hotter. He rolled over, crushed her under him and *Gods,* when a woman had you wrapped in her arms, the secrets of the universe were yours for the taking. When her legs were over your elbows, when her hair was in your fingers, when her mouth sucked on your tongue, when her eyes flashed wanton and wicked as she whispered you were *terrible* at this and she'd jail your ass if you dared stop…

This, he thought. *This is gelang.*

Sparkles at his periphery when he came into the queen, rocking hard in the cradle of her thighs and pouring like a river into her bucking, heaving body. Her nails in his shoulders, her heels in his back, she squeezed him empty, wrung him out dry. Noises he'd never made before came out of his chest and throat. They dissolved into laughing gasps as he fell off his elbows and smothered the last moans in the pillows.

"Holy Helos, you *suck,*" Naria said when their limbs stopped shaking.

He rolled off her, still laughing through heaving breaths. "That was awful."

"Gods, I love when I'm right." She crossed her forearms on Trueblood's chest and spit her hair out of her face. "In this case, my grandmother was right."

"Your grandmother?"

"She told me once, 'Girlie, if you want a good night's sleep, hang your sail on a mariner's mast.'"

"Gods," Trueblood said. "Don't tell me she meant *my* grandfather's mast."

"She did."

"I said, *don't* tell me."

The point of Naria's elbow dug into Trueblood's sternum and she set her cheek on her fist. "Come to think of it, I'm almost positive my mother and your father had a bit of a fling when—"

The kepten was positive there'd be a swift and stiff penalty for swatting a queen with a pillow. He opted to shut her mouth by kissing her instead.

"Forgive me, I have no bedside manner," she said against his lips.

"Forgiven," he said. "Can I…look at you?"

She gave him a sideways smile, then slid off his body and lay back. "Please do."

Her confidence was thrilling. As was her generosity. She lay relaxed and indulgent as the mariner sailed over the royal person with hands, mouth and curiosity. He asked questions. Paid attention to the answers. Soon, the tide came in and his majesty's sail was riding his mast, unfurling and cracking wide open, filling with the wind of their gasps, and with warm, liquid gold candlelight.

"Sweet lad," she whispered in the curve of his neck. Her fingertips drew long lines up and down his back as he came and came. "You're so fine, Trueblood."

She went almost immediately to sleep and Trueblood wasn't far behind, giving some last fleeting thoughts to the business of gelang before slipping into the twinkling peace behind his eyelids. He woke soon after, his heart aching and the watchdog snarling in his gut. An overwhelming sense of his spiritual supply lines being *stretched*.

He moved over on the mattress and put a hand on the back of Naria's neck.

"I have to go," he whispered when she stirred. "The twins need me."

He expected protest but her hand rose and the fingers gave a brief flutter. "'Night, Pé," she said, and was asleep again.

He collected his clothes from the floor, dressed and found his way through the dark, quiet corridors to his room.

"I'm sorry," Lejo said as Trueblood slipped into bed. "I held out as long as I could."

"It's all right." He nestled his back against Raj and gathered Lejo's head to his scarred chest.

"Have a good time?" Lejo said.

"Mmhm."

"What was she like?"

Trueblood's fingertips closed Lejo's eyelids. "She'd jail me if I told you."

WHILE I'M GONE

ᴍᴏsᴛ ᴋʜᴇɪʀᴏɴs sʜɪFᴛ into humos to sleep and sleep in a bed. It's far more practical and comfortable than bedding down on a floor pallet as a horse. Especially if a kheiron has overnight company.

Fen il-Kheir had no bed in his chamber. His pallet was wide, soft and sumptuous, and he never shared it.

He lay in the dark, open-eyed and staring at nothing, his fingertips playing with the moonstone that pierced his eyebrow. Such a little unassuming rock with so much power. He had no idea what he was doing when he put the tiny stone into Belmiro's hand. Belmiro had no idea what he was doing when he kept it.

They were young.

They were in love.

I'll wait for you.

Fen supposed it was a lingering trace of youthful nostalgia that kept his ears and eyes open to Belmiro's whereabouts. He didn't want Bel in his life, but something in him still cared.

Piecing together gossip with his own inquiries, Fen tracked Bel as he worked his way from the pleasure houses in Alondra to private clients in Valtourel. Somehow, the banished kheiron caught Naria Nyland's attention at a time when she needed a strong male figure in her life.

A year into her reign, Naria was negotiating the annexation of Sanpago from Minosaros. The war-torn, patriarchal culture narrowed its eyes at the independent, outspoken and unmarried queen of Nyland. Astute and ever-practical, Naria made Belmiro her official consort. A role somewhere between bodyguard and fiancé.

Whether or not sex was involved, Belmiro played his part to perfection. After the treaties were signed, he became a permanent fixture in Naria's retinue. When she was in residence at Valtourel, Belmiro lived at the palace, in a suite of rooms reserved for him. When the queen was abroad, Belmiro lived and worked in the city, the latter with the utmost discretion.

He was thirty-six now. The dark, unruly hair of his youth was cut short and invaded with gray and silver. An air of unpredictable danger in his tall, fit and tattooed physique. Mystery in his estrangement from the kheiron herd. Unquestionably easy on the eyes of Valtourel, which followed wherever he went. Society snubbed him, even as it wanted him.

I don't want you anymore, Fen thought, rubbing his moonstone between thumb and forefinger. *But I remember you.*

You're one of the few things I remember from the time of Tehvan.

Back when things were simple.

Gods, how simple. How utterly guileless and transparent first love was. He and Belmiro were so innocent and trusting in their feelings, they declared them at once.

"Come stay in my room," Bel said, the night before the legions left. "Sleep with me in my bed. I want to wake up and see you before I leave."

Behind locked doors and dimmed lamps, they shifted into humos and lay down together as men. So fearless in their heated need of each other, it was hard to say if they had no idea what they were doing, or if they knew *exactly* what they were doing.

If equos was the most honest form a kheiron could take, then humos was the most vulnerable. Succumbing to human desire left you open to attack. Making human love brought the dual drives of pleasure and procreation together, exposed between two legs that couldn't outrun danger as fast as four. Passion in humos was a hundred times more intense than kheiros because the arousal was rooted in fear. A fear that could make some kheirons go a happy lifetime without knowledge of humos intimacy.

Cocooned under the bedclothes with Belmiro, Tehvan il-Kheir realized he was doing something his own father had never dared. Holding Belmiro's naked, two-legged trust, he understood what it meant to be at someone's mercy. In their power.

"I love you, don't be afraid," Bel whispered, though his teeth were chattering.

Shaking just as badly, Fen whispered back, "Don't be afraid, I love you."

Humos tangled with humos, they went at it all night, with the inexhaustible desire of youth. Piling brick on top of stone on top of wood, making love into a ramshackle, slap-dash fortress that would've made an architect faint, yet it had its own kind of immutable beauty. It was *theirs*.

"Wait for me," Belmiro said in the morning. "My humos belongs to you. Promise me yours."

"I promise."

Bel rolled onto him, sliding and rubbing and rutting them into one last frenzy. "Wait for me, Tehvan. Don't do *this* with *anyone else* while I'm gone."

He was fierce and wild and dire and Tehvan ate it up. He promised to wait. But he failed. He was young, greedy and impatiently in love, and he followed the legions to Sudenlo. Belmiro was horrified, then livid. He insisted Tehvan go immediately home. Tehvan had to be dramatic about it, so he gave Belmiro his moonstone and said, "I'll wait for you on two legs." Then he left the compound and walked straight into an ambush.

He spent the next two years in humos, doing *this* with more *anyone elses* than he could count.

Fen il-Kheir let go his moonstone and sighed. The brief, tragic affair was long ago. It belonged to another life and another name.

But I remember it, he thought.

I remember the weight of your trust in my hands.

I remember being in the circle of your arms and wanting for nothing.

It was the last good thing I felt before everything changed.

You were the last great friend of my life. I never let anyone that close to me again.

He got up and went to the windows. On the other side of the courtyard, the palace slept. Fen couldn't see Naria's balcony, but he could imagine her tangled up with Trueblood. Their hands full. Their needs non-existent.

What's he like?

Naria Nyland was hot-blooded and unapologetically carnal. Fen wasn't at all surprised she wanted a piece of the young kepten. Who wouldn't?

But did it have to be Belmiro leading the lamb to the slaughter?

As My Father Taught Me

AT BREAKFAST THE next morning, the twins presented Trueblood with a set of pens and a new journal. It was larger than the ones he kept before.

"We guessed you'd have a lot more to say," Raj said.

With his gifts under his arm and his soul brothers at his sides, Pelippé Trueblood walked to the wharves. The top of the Kaleuche's main mast visible every step of the way, a needle growing into a spire, then into a tree trunk.

He felt more incompetent and unworthy with every step. He'd be taking the helm of this behemoth at barely twenty years old, bereft of his father and many of the maristos he'd known since childhood. Old Rafil was gone—the faithful sailor followed his beloved commander into the eternal sea, and now lay interred in the mariners' crypt. Merevhal was struggling through her difficult pregnancy. The Sisters, old and tired, were retiring together.

Abrakam, thank Gods, pledged to stay. His wise, wonderful presence laid kindling on the hearth of Trueblood's courage. As he always planned, Lejo was his boatswain and Raj his pilot. Calvo remained as quartermaster, Dhar and Beniv as the sail makers. Seven was still the cook, and with him came his younger brothers, Eleven and Sixten.

Not all was lost.

Maybe everything would be all right.

Then Trueblood remembered his father was dead and nothing would ever be right.

"Look," Lejo said, pointing to the post by the Kaleuche's gangplank. A little brown bird perched there, her expression cool, as if they'd kept her waiting.

"It's a lark," Lejo said, holding out his hand. The old familiar jealousy in Trueblood's stomach as the bird fluttered in the air and landed delicately on Lejo's finger.

"She's brought us the soul of the Kaleuche," Raj said.

"This is a sign, Pé." Lejo's smile stretched east to west as he held the lark close to Trueblood, who held out his own hopeful hand. The lark trilled a two-tone whistle, then flew away.

Trueblood led the twins to the aftercastle first. This had always been the center of his universe on the Cay, and it seemed a good place to get his bearings. It was laid out much the same, with two cabins off the foyer, a large sitting area, and the Kepten's bedroom and study spanning the width of the stern.

Kepten True's blue coat lay neatly on the giant bed, sleeves spread wide, as if ready to welcome its new owner with a hug. Lejo picked it up and held it out by the shoulders.

"No," Trueblood said.

"It's time," Raj said.

"I can't."

"It's yours now."

"It won't fit."

"Put it on, Pé," Lejo said.

He put it on. Barely holding his face together as he looked at his reflection in the cheval mirror. Behind him, the twins nodded, arms crossed and expressions sad, but satisfied.

"You look good," Raj said thickly.

"Born to wear it," Lejo said.

"Fuck me." Trueblood fumbled in the coat's inside pocket, where Ikharus always kept a handkerchief. His hand came out holding a white feather.

"Where'd that come from?" Raj said, taking it between his fingers.

"I don't know."

"Weird." Lejo took it and ran the smooth vane alone his cheek before passing it back to Trueblood.

They went into the study next, with its grand desk, inlaid shelves and cubbies, and the chart rack, which held the few rolled-up maps Raj had grabbed off the Cay. Everything else was empty—the drawers bare of even a scrap of paper.

Trueblood sat at the desk and opened his notebook. With one of his new pens, he inscribed the first page:

The Most Private Journal of Pelippé Trueblood
An especial accounting of his life
and voyages on the...

The nib faltered, smudging the ink.

"Strange to write Kaleuche now," he said. "The Cay was my life."

"Make it part of your name," Lejo said.

"I can do that?"

"Why not?" Raj said. "You're the damned kepten."

"Pelippé Trueblood Cay." It felt good on his tongue and sounded better in the air. He tore the page out of the notebook, crumpled it and started over.

"Don't forget your title," Lejo said.

*The Most Private Journal of
Kepten Pelippé Trueblood Cay
An especial accounting of his life
and voyages on the Kaleuche*

*Today, with Raj Ĝemelos as my pilot and Lejo Ĝemelos
as my boatswain, I, Kepten Pelippé Trueblood Cay take
command of the giantship Kaleuche. All I do is as my
father taught me. May he live in my heart, abide in my
coat pockets and chart my course in all the days to come.*

The new kepten took the white feather, kissed it, and used it
to mark his place before closing the notebook.

THEY LUNCHED AT Merevhal and Dhar's house, and the former
boatswain gave Lejo her key to the Cay's safe. "Take Abrakam
when you open it," she said. "He may need to explain some
things in there."

So the centaur came onboard that afternoon, bringing the sack
of books Raj had rescued from the Cay. They barely filled one
shelf in his new cabin but he hugged Raj for the hundredth time
after they were arranged, grateful beyond words.

His keen, observant eyes never missing an opportunity to
educate, Abrakam pointed out some of the Kaleuche's architec-
tural details. How the forecastle and aftercastle doors were carved
with a nine-branched tree motif, a piece of faceted glass at the
tip of each branch. The same motif was on the tiles of the sitting
room's hearth. The big round table was made from a cross-sec-

tion of a Nye tree, its surface ringed with thousands and thousands of spidery lines.

They went into the Kepten's study and sadness pierced Trueblood as they opened the safe. He knew about a few things held within, but not all. Ikharus should've been here for this rite of passage.

Raj's eyes shone as Abrakam unrolled the delicate chart for the single accessible harbor on the Altynai coast. It was the only one of its kind in the world and it belonged to House Tru.

"You can sell that and make a fortune," the centaur said. "But you'll also make a lifetime enemy of the Altyns. You decide."

A paper-wrapped object was unwrapped to reveal a small chunk of kyrrh, the rare healing resin.

"This is over twenty years old," Abrakam said. "The Altyns gave it to your father when he rescued Fen il-Kheir. Along with…"

He opened a small pouch and tipped three waxy beads onto his palm. "Fadara."

"Holy Helos," Trueblood said. "You could buy a house with that."

"Three houses."

"Get rid of it, Abe," Raj said tightly.

The centaur shook his head. "You'd be a fool to sail without it."

"But fadara's illegal," Lejo said.

"Aye, and highly addictive," Abrakam said, pulling the string of the pouch tight again. "But useful in an emergency or a dire situation. Kepten True kept it locked in the safe for twenty years but he was damn grateful to know it was there. I suggest you treat it the same way, Pé. Ah, look what we have here…"

With two hands, the centaur lifted out a stack of small leather notebooks. All of Trueblood's childhood journals. "See, Troubled? Your father taught you everything he knew and you wrote it all down. With pictures."

"You were smart to put them in the safe," Raj said.

"I wrote some things I didn't want *you* to read."

Raj reached for a notebook and Trueblood smacked his fingers.

"Oh Gods, Pé," Lejo said, as he carefully pulled from the safe a remnant of green velvet, embroidered with red and gold leaves. The treasured piece of Noë Treeblood's skirt.

On Trueblood's sixteenth birthday, when he became a majoro, he felt a need to put a symbolically childish thing away. He asked Ikharus to lock the cloth in the safe. If he hadn't, the bit of green velvet would be rotting on the ocean floor. Same with the journals, along with all his father's imparted knowledge.

"Nothing's an accident, is it, Abe?" he said.

"No, lad. Everything happens for a reason."

"For the record, I don't like this reason," Raj said.

Left in the safe were a few random trinkets—valuables given over for safekeeping. Last was a folded piece of paper with a list of cities, all crossed out save one.

"What's this?" Trueblood asked.

The centaur's face became serious. "During the sack of Alondra, the kheirons salvaged thirty casks of Nye from the vault. They flew the casks out to the Cay. Your father cached the spice in these cities, bringing them back to Valtourel a little at a time."

He smoothed the paper on the desk and pointed to the last name, Aybar—an unsavory port in the north of Minosaros.

"Three casks are still there, lads. Hidden in the basement of a House Tru hostel are the last reserves of Nye in the entire world."

THAT NIGHT, WHEN Naria sent for him, Trueblood asked if she knew about the secret caches of Nye.

"Of course," she said. "Mother told me. But not until she knew she was dying."

She stroked his head as he sighed away the last of the day's bittersweetness.

"I'll be going back to Hokosia at the end of the week," she said.

"Unfinished business with the Emperor?"

A tortured sigh. "Once a year, Xuan-Gavriel decides he wants to marry me and annex the western part of Pellandro. Not necessarily in that order."

"Do you ever want to get married?"

"Not to him."

"Ever?"

"I don't think so. No."

"Why not?"

"Never saw any need for it."

"Not even for love?"

"I have plenty of love." She stretched her chin out and kissed Trueblood. "Don't I?"

He laughed against her mouth, wondering what it was like to be so self-assured.

"If you need anything," Naria was saying, "you tell Belmiro. He'll either know what to do or who to ask."

"What's his official title?"

"Belmiro?" She shrugged. "He's my official know what to do-er."

"No really. What's his job?"

"I'd tell you, but then I'd have to jail you. And we'd have nobody who could fetch the last of the world's Nye." She moved up and onto his chest, rubbing against his cock. "How does it feel to be indispensable?"

"Hard."

"I grasped that right away," she said, grasping it.

They laughed and kissed. Then she fucked him senseless. Afterward they fell asleep and Trueblood woke to the longing pull in his heart. He kissed Naria and slipped from her bed.

Walking back to his room, it occurred to him that for the second night in a row, she didn't seem unhappy to see him go.

BELMIRO

CALVO RAN A critical eye over the ship, taking inventory and making lists. The cabins had their giant bedsteads, the aftercastle had its massive furniture. Otherwise, the Kaleuche was bare bones. Trueblood had to outfit it with *everything*. Pots, pans, dishes, mattresses, bed linens. Barrels, crates, casks, hogsheads, demijohns. Rope, canvas, candles.

"We have no godsdamned *matches*," Calvo muttered, three times as irritable and moody as he was on the Cay. Trueblood took the quartermaster's wrath in stride and was even grateful for it—without Calvo's expertise, he'd be fucked.

A stream of carts and wagons made its way to the ship and began unloading. At last the crew had something to do and they swung into action with a goodwill that made Trueblood suspicious.

"Don't get too used to this attitude," Calvo said with a rare grin. "And next time you pass the tanner's shop, I would invest in a new strap."

Trueblood didn't relish being a disciplinarian any more than when he was a boy. He left Calvo in the holds and went on deck with the twins. The Kaleuche's rigging was what concerned him next. They had the one set of sails they came home on. No extras and no supply of canvas. Beniv and Dhar were already hard at work weaving. Trueblood was more worried about what the sails hung on.

The height of the main mast was beyond comprehension. Every crew member had stood at is base and looked up, but nobody ventured higher than the futtocks shroud. Someone had to go first.

"Well," Trueblood said, sliding out of his blue coat. "Let's see if this boat likes me."

"Take a waterskin," Raj said, looking up to the crow's nest with crossed arms. "You may be away overnight."

"Or not at all," Lejo said. The lark perched on his shoulder gave a two-tone whistle of agreement.

"Then I leave everything to you, Raj." Trueblood glanced at Lejo. "You get nothing."

Lejo turned slow eyes on him. "Kiss my ass."

"I love you, too."

Loaded up with a waterskin, Trueblood drew a last breath and put a foot on the rigging.

Come with me, Da.

He didn't intend on an audience but when he reached the futtocks shroud, the entire crew was on deck. By the top of the first gallant, the wharves were getting crowded.

"I *said* just Da come with me," he mumbled.

The fear stayed healthy and under his control. He stopped to rest frequently and plan, not looking up too long nor down too long. He put arms around the mast, closed his eyes and exhaled. He nearly jumped out of his skin when a voice shouted from quite near.

"You going to climb that mast or marry it?"

Heart pounding, Trueblood looked around to see Fen il-Kheir hovering in the air.

"Kepten Trueblood."

"Fancy meeting you here."

"A kheiron always guards first-time climbers."

"I'm honored."

"And my father would geld me if I didn't keep the tradition."

Trueblood felt his eyes narrow. "You know, some things are better off in the silence of your heart." He reached for his waterskin and held the kheiron's cold, blue gaze as he took a sip.

"Just doing my job," Fen said.

"Then if you'll excuse me, I'll just do mine."

"Do you rather I fly in or out of your sight, Kepten?"

"If you're going to be a bitch, I'd rather you fly home."

Hovering between his beautiful wings, Fen glanced up at the crow's nest, then back at Trueblood. "Out, then."

He stepped off the edge of nothing, canted forward and dove into an elegant spiral, disappearing behind Trueblood. In his wake, another voice spoke, this one even closer by.

He's testing you, Ikharus-Lippé True said. *Don't show off for him. Just do your job.*

It took Trueblood nearly an hour to ascend and descend. He rested, then climbed it again, this time with the twins, in about the same time.

"Well, lads, we've got a problem," he said.

"Aye, it takes too fucking long to go aloft," Raj said.

"At this rate, we'll be living on the masts day and night. And if the wind changes suddenly, we're fucked."

Lejo's mouth twisted as he looked from crow's nest to deck. "We can learn to climb faster," he said. "But…"

"Or maybe we learn to climb better," a shy voice said behind them. They turned to see young Sixten, a book in one hand, a sheaf of papers in the other. Pencil perched behind an ear and a feverish excitement in his eyes. "I have an idea, Kep."

He spread out his materials on the big round table in the after-castle. The book was called *A History of Spice Cultivation in the Old Forest*. Sixten opened it to the center, turning it sideways to show a Nye tree illustrated across both pages. "Maybe we shouldn't treat the mast like a mast," he said. "Instead, treat it like a tree. Which, technically, it is."

They studied the system of ropes, pulleys and harnesses that got the Nye harvesters from ground to canopy, and the baskets of flowers from canopy to ground. "Something like this would let us climb the masts faster and safer," Sixten said, twirling his pencil through his fingers.

"That's how Da got Fen il-Kheir down from a tree," Trueblood said. "The pulleys were already in place. Still waiting there and ready, hundreds of years after they were last used."

"It worked before, it can work again," Raj said.

"If it isn't broken, don't fix it," Lejo said.

Trueblood took a long, considering look at Sixten. He weighed the hunch in his gut against the lad's youth, then clapped a hand on Sixten's shoulder. "Let's do it. What do you need and who do you want?"

At the end of the week, Sixten was promoted to ŝnuromastisto—the rope master.

"That's the dumbest word I ever heard," the lad said. "It sounds like I'm in charge of snoring."

"Or sneering," Eleven said, his expression sour.

I'm a bit worried about Eleven, Trueblood wrote in his most private journal. *It's obvious he feels his brothers have their specialties while he has none. It's true not every sailor has exceptional talent for a task, but those who have a basic aptitude for all tasks are just as crucial to the ship. Eleven's talent is showing up, day after day, and doing whatever job he's given with consistency. I wish we had a title for this.*

Ha. The ink is drying on those words and I realize we do have one: maristo.

The rope-and-pulley system was installed on the main mast, and Sixten and Lejo began training the crew on using it. Some of the maristos thumbed their noses at the harnesses, until one of them broke an arm falling from the futtocks shroud. Then a stubborn majoro climbed the mizzenmast without being roped in, lost his shit halfway up and had to be rescued. Trueblood waited at the bottom of the mast, his new strap doubled up in his hand. He gave the moron the traditional nine for breaking the kepten's rule, and three more for wasting everyone's time.

Da was right, he wrote. *As he usually is. Stamp disobedience and disrespect out while they're still sparks, and you won't set the ship on fire. Hidings should be brisk and business-like. I marched the lad to the bow, told him to drop breeches and bend over and I just did it. Did it fast, got it done and moved on with the day. That evening, he stood for story hour, with much teasing from his friends. But he said goodnight to me afterward and I told him to rest well. Already it feels long ago.*

While he neither relished nor regretted the whipping, he did note he was mostly annoyed by the interruption to the day's work.

Everything on the Kaleuche was on a bigger scale, including the work. Besides overseeing the sail making, Dhar and Beniv were measuring the crew for new boots and clothes, and sewing until their fingers and toes were numb. Lejo worked modest miracles with the crew, swiftly assessing skill and talent and putting apprentices where the ship needed them most.

When they stumbled to dinner, they ate around yawns. Some of the minoros nodded off in the soup. After writing in his journal and taking reports from his maristos, Trueblood fell into bed like a dead Nye tree, his jobs well done.

THEY STAYED ANCHORED in Valtourel another month, stocking the ship and taking their time getting used to the Kaleuche. Devising new ways, new rules and new traditions. Then they started short runs at sea.

"She's incredibly stable for having no ballast," Trueblood said.

Calvo was almost disturbed by the stability. "She's *too* stable for a ship with empty holds. And something about the bulkheads in the holds is off, too. Can't put my finger on it."

They made their first overnight voyage to Alondra. Once aboard, Trueblood closed the door to the bedroom in the kepten's quarters and had a bed moved into the twins' cabin.

"Why?" Raj said. "I mean, not that we mind, but…"

The reason was so elusively obvious, Trueblood couldn't articulate it beyond a shrug.

"It's because you're waiting for later," Lejo said quietly.

"Lé, shut up."

"It's not your Da's room."

"I know," he snapped. "But it's not mine either. Not yet. I haven't earned it."

The twins let it be and Trueblood was grateful. But Lejo was right—he was waiting for later. Assuming command was one thing. He could easily pretend (and often did) that his father was ill or indisposed and Trueblood was simply holding the status quo on a temporary basis. To take ownership of the kepten's giant bed was to acknowledge Ikharus wasn't coming back, anytime, ever.

His mood was irritable and his nerves jumpy as he brought the Kaleuche into the Gulf of Pellandro and turned her south. By the time they approached the Elpremi, the tricky strait between Nordater and Pellandro, the spokes of the helm's mighty wheel felt melded to every crease and line of his hands, as if it had been carved for him alone. His giantsblood sang with love for the sea. He was born for this and nothing else.

"You're doing well, Troubled," Abrakam said. It was after evening story hour and the centaur poured out two glasses of wine. "Your father would be proud."

Trueblood took a careful sip, then smiled. "This isn't Altynian plonk."

"No," Abrakam said gruffly, thumping the bottle on the table. "Gods know I love and miss Ikharus to my bones. But I'm happy never to drink liquid prunes again."

Trueblood chewed on the excellent wine, filled with an unexpected sadness.

"What is it, lad?" Abrakam said gently.

"Could you...maybe get a couple bottles of the Altynian plonk anyway? Just to have. I mean, to remember. Fuck it all, I don't know what I mean."

"I do." Beneath the bushy eyebrows, the centaur's gaze was damp and loving. "And I'll get you some."

"Thank you, Abe. We'll have a grand time not drinking it."

Next morning, the Kaleuche slipped back through the Elpremi and made a jaunt around the Gulf of Pellandro, tacking and beating. They came into Valtourel on the noon tide, just as the temple of Solos rang the zenith bell.

The stevedores had nearly completed the new wharf for the Kaleuche. A crowd gathered along it, waving and shouting as she came in. The majoros puffed out their chests as they descended the gangplank, milking the celebrity. The maristos went off in search of sustenance—both at tables and in beds. Trueblood finished logging the day in his journal and ambled down the pier. A splash of red at the end caught his eye. He smiled as the red became a shirt and its wearer became Belmiro, sitting atop a post, legs swinging.

"Salutos, Kepten," he called.

"Salu. What are you doing?"

"Waiting for you."

"Me?"

"You sound surprised."

"I am."

Bel crossed his arms and gave a lopsided smile. "I'm more than just Naria's errand boy."

He'd grown a goatee since last Trueblood had seen him. Above the bearded grin his green eyes were full of the sun. They twinkled with mischief as his foot reached to knock against Trueblood's leg. "Fancy a swim?"

"Gods, yes. Dying to get out of these clothes."

He meant it conversationally but it hung in the air like a proposition, then plopped to the ground.

Belmiro hopped off the post. "I have one or two things to do in town. Drop your clobber at the palace and meet me in the courtyard. Half an hour?"

"All right."

"See you then." He raised a hand and walked off, adding over his shoulder, "Clothing optional."

Herd Mentality

ELMIRO HELD UP a growler of ale, frosted and dripping condensation. "Fancy a drink with the swim?"

"Gimme that." Trueblood said, and drained nearly a quarter of it.

"Drinking and walking is a true talent," Belmiro said as they headed down the path toward the beach. He took a deep draught as he loped along, then coughed and sputtered half of it on his feet. "You can see I don't have it."

They skirted the grotto pool and clambered over the rocky outcropping to the public beach. The breakers were loud, frothing white on the slick sand. Trueblood found a place between two boulders to keep the ale both chilled and secure. Brushing sand off his hands, he walked toward Belmiro, who was pulling his shirt over his head.

Trueblood stopped, blinking at the silvery marks on Belmiro's back. A pair of wings, parallel to his spine, the tips overlapping.

"Bel, you're a kheiron," he said.

Slowly Belmiro looked back over his shoulder, the wind ruffling his hair. "You're pretty astute for a wharf rat."

"I had no idea."

"Of course you didn't. This is the first time I've taken my clothes off in your presence." He threw the shirt at Trueblood's face. "Close your mouth, Kepten."

Trueblood deflected the garment and walked closer, stunned at his own ignorance. "Let me see your hands."

"My, I haven't had my nails inspected since I was a foalboy." Bel dutifully held out his nine fingers and their silver rings.

"I can't believe I never noticed," Trueblood said

"To be fair, you've had a lot on your mind lately. A fellow's hands probably aren't high on your list of priorities."

"You don't ever take kheiros form?"

Belmiro shook his head. "My legs were broken when I was young. As a result it's really painful for me to stand in kheiros. So I live on two feet."

"I'm sorry."

Bel shrugged as he untied the laces of his breeches.

"I don't ever see you with the herd," Trueblood said, staring.

"For reasons too depressing to get into, I'm not really part of the herd anymore." He paused, a corner of his mouth grinning and his thumbs in the waistband of his breeches. "What, are you waiting to see if I'm hung like a horse?"

His laugh rose above the surf as Trueblood turned around.

"You're blushing, wharf rat."

"Fuck off, crow bait."

Belmiro only laughed harder as his breeches landed on Trueblood's head.

They swam for the better part of an hour, diving through the waves or bodysurfing them onto the beach. Then they stretched out on a flat rock to dry off. Belmiro held up a refusing palm to the growler. "I'm high on life. You kill it."

The sun and the ale and the day's exertions sank fingers into Trueblood's body. He dozed off, hands laced beneath his head. His grief rested as well, tired of being the driving force all this time. When he sent experimental feelers into his heart, looking for signs the twins needed him, he felt no longing yank or pull.

He sighed, perfectly content. Wanting for nothing. Melting into the gold light through his eyelids and wondering what it would be like to kiss Belmiro.

When he yawned awake, the tide was nearly out. The beautiful kheiron lay on his stomach, chin on his crossed arms. Eyes open and fixed on something far away. The sun glinted off the marks on his back, tantalizing and gorgeous.

"Can I see your wings?" Trueblood asked.

Belmiro blinked once. Then the sunlight disappeared as his wings unfurled and spread wide. They flapped once, twice, then lowered to the rock's surface, one draped over Trueblood's hips. He expected the feathers to be blood-warm, having emerged from Belmiro's body. Instead they were cool, and softer than twilight. They tickled. Beneath their caress, he started to get hard.

Belmiro closed his eyes. "Kepten, did I suddenly grow another basal phalanx or are you just glad to see me?"

AND LIKE THAT, Pelippé Trueblood went from a boy mooning over naked pictures in books to a young man bedded by two lovers in the space of a month.

"*Now* what are you giggling about," Belmiro said. Door locked, drapes drawn, they lay in Trueblood's bed, in a tangle of limbs and bedclothes.

"Naria did say if I needed anything I should ask you."

"What else did she say?"

"That you were the official know what to do-er."

"And was she right?"

"Is Naria ever wrong?"

"Often wrong," Belmiro said, rolling onto him again. "Never in doubt."

The kheiron was confident, mature and fearless in matters gelang, but his prowess hid behind an easy, self-effacing manner. He was undemanding and protective of Trueblood's inexperience with bedding men. Asking questions and being the perfect listener, he learned of the entire journey. From discovering the famous gelang book in Abrakam's library, to the strange monstrous feelings, to the clumsy but tender exploration with Lejo.

"It's good you told him to stop," Bel said. "When it comes to that kind of thing, it's enthusiastic consent or nothing."

"I was enthusiastic but it hurt."

"Of course it did. What were you using, a little spit? If that?"

Trueblood put the pillow over his head. "What do you want from my life? The book had pictures, not step-by-step directions."

Belmiro laughed and yanked the pillow away. "I think I need to see this book."

The next day, Trueblood snuck the illustrated study off the ship and that night, he discovered reading was the second-greatest thing you could do with someone in bed.

Bel's contribution to the evening was a vial of thin, gold oil. "*Algolerta*," he said. "Extracted from seaweed. Mixed with oud tree resin and saffron before being filtered through a nychet. Expensive, but worth every kheso."

Trueblood rubbed a bit of the slickness between his thumb and finger and his eyes bulged.

"I know," Bel said, tackling him. "You can thank me later."

"Thank you," Trueblood said to the ceiling later, breathing hard and blinking away the spots in his vision.

Belmiro collapsed beside him, breathing just as hard. "You're welcome."

"Where do I get more?"

"More algolerta or more of me?"

"Both."

Trueblood could hardly believe what his life had become. Kepten by day, lover by night. Working his ass off, fucking his brains out. Barely getting any sleep, yet he'd never felt so full of energy.

Maybe that was what gelang did to you.

Is this gelang?

"I can't think when I had a better time," Belmiro said, when he kissed Trueblood in the wee hours and slipped from the bed. He rarely stayed the whole night. "I'm horrible enough in the mornings without having to do a walk of shame past Raj and Lejo."

"They don't care if you sleep with me."

Bel barked a laugh as he pulled on his breeches. "Maybe Raj fucks everything and Lejo's not interested in fucking anything, but believe me, Pé. They care who shares your bed."

Trueblood sighed. "If my honor means that much to you—"

"Oh, but it does."

"Fine. Get out of here."

Alone, the mariner sprawled like a satisfied tiger in the center of the mattress, blissed-out and aching in every major muscle group. His ego stroked to a velvety purr. So what if Bel went home to his own bed? He was terrific in every other aspect. Hilarious. Sexy. Patient. The perfect lover. He guided them through night after night of exploration, yet somehow made it all seem Trueblood's idea. Best of all, he generously answered all Trueblood's questions. Even the ones about Fen il-Kheir, albeit a little more tersely.

"Were you and Fen friends growing up?"

"Yes."

Trueblood gently pushed the single syllable. "But not after he was rescued?"

Belmiro ran his fourhand through his hair. "Fen didn't want friends after he came home. He was…" The hand came out and turned over in the air.

"Untouchable."

"Good word."

"Why do you think il-Kheir treats Fen the way he does?"

Bel took a long time to answer, his mouth opening and closing as he chose words. "I was only two when Fen was born," he finally said. "But those who were older, those who were there, they all say after Zoria died, the Horselord was never the same. Not that losing your mate isn't a life-altering experience for any creature, but it left il-Kheir slightly...off. Like he constantly walked the line between life and death, and only managed to stay grounded on this side because he put everything he felt for Zoria into Fen. But then Fen was taken away from him."

He rolled on his side to face Trueblood. "I think the Horselord distracted himself from Fen's disappearance by going to war. But after Minosaros was cleaned out and Fen still wasn't found, il-Kheir had nothing to do except think about him. Spend all day wondering what became of him. Spend all night imagining what might've been done to him. Obsess over it. Be consumed by it. And finally when Fen was rescued and il-Kheir learned what the minotaurs did to him..."

Belmiro whistled softly as his index finger made a slow circle around his temple. "I think that's when he really lost his mind, Pé. He didn't just shut down what happened to Fen. He threw it out of his head, heart and soul so thoroughly that he *lost* it. And because he's king, the herd lost it, too."

"What do you mean?"

"Il-Kheir controls the herd mentality. The group mind. It looks to him for a reaction to every intense situation. If he gets fired up, we get fired up. If he shuts down, every kheiron unconsciously takes a cue and does the same."

"Holy shit. As the heir, can Fen affect the herd mentality?"

Bel nodded. "A bit, yes. He built those untouchable walls around himself, but he was still giving off soul-signals to his people. He buried what happened to him in the past, and the herd did, too. He didn't talk about how his father was behaving, and every kheiron followed suit. Nobody talked about it or acknowledged what was happening. I mean *nobody*."

"Except you."

Belmiro chuckled through his nose and his shoulder shrugged. "I'm an outcast. I can think for myself."

"You're an outcast because of your legs?"

"Sort of."

The nature of Belmiro's injury was a subject off-limits. "It would be like me asking for details of your father's death," he said. "Or even pushing you to remember your mother's murder."

Trueblood respected the boundary, but his curiosity niggled and one night, he couldn't help asking to see Belmiro in kheiros. Just once. Just for a minute.

Belmiro gave a dramatic sigh, his eyes circling the ceiling. "I'm afraid you're irresistible, Pelippé Trueblood. *One* minute."

And he shifted.

"Gods," Trueblood whispered. He didn't have time to waste rationalizing how such magic was possible or how it worked. He suspended his belief and ran his hand along Belmiro's dappled, chestnut coat.

"You like?" Bel said.

"You are one splendid stallion, my friend."

"Thank you. And could you scratch? Right between the withers. Yes. There."

"Feel good?"

"Come here, I'll show you what feels good." He took Trueblood's hand and guided it between his forelegs. "Just dig in between those two big muscles. With the heel of your hand. That's it."

"Here?" Trueblood said. "Not back there?"

Belmiro's smile was delicious. "No, back there is for making babies. Where it feels good in kheiros is here."

"Like that?"

"Mm." His body shivered, tiny bumps rashing the skin of his arms and chest. "Your hand feels amazing but my legs hurt. Time's up."

He shifted to humos, an impressive erection tenting his breeches. Trueblood stepped back and regarded it, arms crossed.

Belmiro crossed his own arms. "No doubt you noticed I'm slightly shorter when I stand in humos."

"I did notice."

"I believe you're also wondering what happens to my pants when I shift."

"Indeed I am."

"I don't know. They come with and they come back. It's a great mystery. Or maybe not. Shifting is through the moonstone, the moon is female and females think of everything."

"They do."

Belmiro's hand slid casually beneath his laces. "Are we going to talk philosophy or are we going to get naked?"

"We're going to get naked and talk philosophy."

Belmiro grabbed him with his free arm. "Come here, wharf rat."

"Crow bait."

"Fuck you."

"Oh *fine*..."

Someone's Gelangos

Sex with Belmiro reminded Trueblood of the surf down at the beach, rolling and crashing and relentless within a steady rhythm. But unlike the ocean, the tide of Belmiro's attention only moved one way. It constantly came into Trueblood. It almost never went out to Belmiro. They passed long horizontal hours talking and laughing, but about *things*, not each other. The kheiron indulged Trueblood's curiosity on any topic, but when the subject turned to himself, Belmiro subtly and gracefully tacked into the wind of conversation and brought the ship around.

We're at hand, Trueblood thought. *But we don't belong. It's definitely more connected than it was with Naria, but he's no more interested in being a gelangos than she was.*

He's just a little nicer about it.

Belmiro's fivehand raised and his palm dropped flat on Trueblood's face. "I can hear you thinking, you know."

"Oh?"

"Your deep thoughts make all the little muscles in your face twitch. And your eyebrows? They give everything away."

Trueblood smiled and moved Belmiro's hand, examining the silver rings.

"Ah, see," the kheiron said. "That's your 'I have five thousand questions' face."

"Do you always wear certain rings on certain fingers?"

Belmiro nodded. "They only fit certain fingers."

"Each one symbolizes a branch of Nydirsil?"

"Eight for the lesser gods and one for Os. Who is One."

Trueblood pushed the pillows into a stack so he could sit up better. "Which is which?"

Belmiro wiggled the last finger on his fourhand. "*Ringosol.* The ring of Solos, the sun God." He held up his fivehand pinky. "Here's the *ringolun.* Can you guess?"

"Lunos."

"This is my *ringovel. Ringomer.* So on and so on." He closed his eyes and pretended to snore. "The names aren't too imaginative. Barely anyone refers to them that way anymore. You're actually considered obnoxious if you do."

"So the individual rings don't actually do anything."

"No. This one is kind of special, though." Belmiro held up the thumb on his fivehand. Its ring was carved in the shape of two wings that wrapped around his finger. Between the feathers was the front view of a horse's head. "This is the *ringos.* The ninth. All the rings of the lesser gods can vary by design but the ringos is the same for every kheiron. The wings and the horse. Always worn on the fivehand thumb, because it's the center digit. And the only ring we actually refer to by name."

"Can I see?"

"No, I don't take this one off."

"So it does do something."

Belmiro smiled. "It definitely has the most emotional weight. It's the ring of Os. The circle of life and one-ness. The ring of the soul. A lot of kheirons engrave it on the inside. With their name or a credo. Something meaningful."

"What's engraved on yours?"

Belmiro leaned and put the bridge of his nose against Trueblood's. "That's personal," he whispered.

"Oh. So I can come in your mouth but the inside of your ringos is too personal. Thanks for clearing that up."

He was joking, but he wasn't. When Belmiro howled laughing and whacked him with a pillow, Trueblood laughed along and whacked him back. Still, the kheiron didn't answer the question. Or rather, he answered by not answering.

We're friends, but not gelangos, Trueblood thought. *And to be brutally honest, we're not even that close friends.*

An idea loitered at the edge of his mind. Enticing and elusive. He held out a hand to it, the way Lejo beckoned shy animals.

Maybe it felt different with Lejo because we were friends for fifteen years before we went to bed. Our friendship was the bed. We didn't stay lovers, but the foundation remained.

If you fall into bed with someone you don't know all that well, you really don't have much to lie down on.

"You're beautiful when you're thinking out loud," Belmiro said, moving closer, hard and intent. "In case no one ever told you before."

"You're the first," Trueblood said.

I kind of wish you weren't. It's something a gelangos should say.

Confusion and revelation filled him with his own intentions and that night, he rolled Belmiro down beneath him. Taking control of the wheel and the sails. Beating and tacking this ship where he wanted it to go. Further out to sea, where the waves undulated gentle and quiet. Someplace where the kheiron might show him what was on the inside of his rings. A haven where he could talk about himself.

"Gods, you are something," Belmiro said. The silver marks on his back fluttered under Trueblood's touch. His profile against the pillow seemed fragile and his four fingers small within Trueblood's five.

"Stay with me tonight?" Trueblood said. He held Bel's wrists pinned to the mattress, as if no choice were truly being offered.

A long exhale. "I'm afraid you're irresistible, Pé."

Trueblood moved deeper, relishing the little moan he squeezed from Bel's chest. "You're so good."

"So are you."

"I'm sorry the ones you loved hurt you." Trueblood held still within the pulsing moment and tentatively pushed at the kheiron's vulnerability.

Bel smiled and his one eye glanced up. "Someday, Pé, you're going to be someone's gelangos. And that's a lucky someone, whoever he or she is."

"Not you?"

Bel easily freed his wrists and pulled at Trueblood's arms, drawing him to lie flat against the silvery etchings.

"I'm not your one," he said softly. "I'm just your right now."

"I like right now."

"Then let it be whatever you want. Or whoever you want."

Trueblood drew back. Bel turned his head and they stared a long moment at each other.

"Go on," the kheiron whispered, as if he not only knew all Trueblood's secrets, but was asking permission to see them.

The full moon poured through the window, turning his thick, gray hair pure white. Which made it easy for Trueblood to pretend it was Fen beneath his body. All that power trembling and vulnerable as he put his trust in Trueblood. Letting him approach the walls built around Fen's past. Then scale them. Reverently touch the broken pieces within and hold them carefully. So carefully.

I'm sorry the ones you loved hurt you, Trueblood imagined saying.

In the vision, Fen's mouth trembled before whispering back, *It's why liking you so much scares me.*

Trueblood ran a hand across the white head and down along the silvery back. Fingers tracing muscle and bone, lingering on the crossed wingtips in the small of Fen's back. Beneath his touch, the kheiron's skin quivered, damp with an anxious desire.

Don't be afraid, Trueblood thought. *I won't let anything hurt you, gelangos. Not on my ship.*

He imagined that Fen took off his ringos and showed what was written within.

Now that you found me, he said, *I don't ever want to lose you again.*

The mariner saw his own name engraved in the smooth silver. *Pelippé Trueblood Cay* copied from his especial beautiful penmanship and set permanently in the underside of Fen's soul.

It was so arousing, it almost scared him.

THE TRUVIAD

THE MORNING BROUGHT loud, excited voices in the sitting room and a bump of fists on Trueblood's bedroom door.

"Pé. Pé, wake up."

The naked mariner stirred, reaching for a handful of covers. "Just a—" The door burst open. "Minute. Gods, Raj, do you mind?"

"Sorry. Salu, Belmiro."

A hand raised from beneath the blanket with a grunted, "Sal."

Lejo bustled in now. "Pé, get up. They need you down at the wharf."

"What's going on?" Noticing a handful of people crowded the doorway behind Raj, Trueblood sat up carefully, keeping the sheets swathed around his parts.

"Calvo says he's solved the ballast problem," Lejo said. "Something's hidden in the floor of the central hold."

"Something big," Raj said.

"How big?"

"Abrakam fainted when he saw it," Fen il-Kheir said.

Trueblood stopped mid-yawn and blinked at the kheiron's presence. Fen's brilliant blue eyes stared past him, over his shoulder at Belmiro, who was sitting up now.

"All right, everyone out," Trueblood said. "Give me five minutes to..." He took the breeches Lejo handed him. "Get dressed. Thank you. *Out.*"

The door closed.

"Gods, that was awkward," Belmiro said. In the pale sunlight coming in the window, he looked his age and then some. Eyes shadowed and bloodshot. His pallor could've used some calves liver for breakfast.

"Feel all right?" Trueblood asked.

"I told you I suck in the mornings."

"Go back to sleep."

"Nah, I'll clear out. Got one or two things to do in town."

"You say that frequently, you know."

"What?"

"One or two things to do in town. Is that an all-purpose expression in Valtourel? Like going to see a man about a horse?"

"Funny." Bel leaned and snagged his breeches from the floor. "Well, I'm going to see a kvartermastisto about some ballast."

"Lucky you."

They hadn't been drinking last night, yet Belmiro was the portrait of a hangover. His tone was surly and his hands trembled as they dealt with his laces. With only a quick, rubbed circle between Trueblood's shoulder blades, he slipped away.

"Where did Fen go?" Trueblood asked, stamping a foot into a boot.

"He's off sulking," Raj said.

Lejo whacked his hand against his brother's arm. "Don't be a bitch, Raj."

"What?" Trueblood said.

"Nothing. Fen just remembered something he had to do."

Raj chuckled. "Sulk."

"What are you *talking* about?" Trueblood said, stamping the other foot.

Lejo handed him his coat. "Let's go."

In the Kaleuche's cavernous central hold, a half-dozen planks had been ripped up from the floor, revealing the frame beneath.

"I knew something was wrong about the dimensions in here," Calvo kept saying. "The inside doesn't fit the outside. I knew it."

"Are you all right?" Trueblood said, crouching beside Abrakam, who had all four legs curled beneath him and his head practically within the hole in the floor.

"It's a miracle," he said, his voice hoarse. "Never in my life did I think I'd see this day."

Two massive stones lay between the floor beams. One about ten feet long, the other perhaps a third the size. Both were inscribed all over, in language Trueblood didn't recognize but felt he'd seen before.

"Abe, what are these?"

The centaur raised his head, eyes dilated to black pearls. "They're a miracle."

A book lay by Abrakam's knee. A copy of the *Truviad,* the epic of Truvos. Transcribed from the words the bereft sea god chiseled into three stones eons ago. Two of the stones preserved at the great library—one of them broken off in the middle of a sentence, the story left forever unfinished.

"Oh, Pé," the centaur said softly. "Pé, my one. What a time to be alive."

MY LEGANTOS, TO say the intellectual world went crazy at the discovery would be an understatement. Heads exploded. Within weeks, Valtourel swelled with scholars and archeologists and philosophers, all coming to get a look at the stones. Pandemonium ensued within the Printers' Guild as each tried to be first to produce a complete version of the *Truviad.* The find of the century monopolized conversation in every home, office, inn, tavern and brothel. Much argument and debate, with differences of opinion that led to cold shoulders in marital beds, friends not speaking, rude words between strangers and more than a few brawls. The uniting force echoed Abrakam's sentiments, a mix of *What a time to be alive* and *Did you ever think you'd live to see?*

But I'm getting ahead. Let's return to the more immediate aftermath, when the stones were loaded onto rollers, covered in canvas and brought up to old shipyards, which had the square footage to lay the monoliths side by side.

A council was convened so every land and every race could witness the unveiling. Queen Naria and her four vicreĝos. One of the Council of Mothers from Sanpago. Sevri il-Kheir. An ambassador from Emperor Xuan-Gavriel. Abrakam for the centaurs. Even Zornin came from Altynai, which shocked everyone. Only the pegasos were without representation, which shocked no one. It was a common joke the pegasos wouldn't bother to show up for the end of the world.

A committee from all schools of thought was also assembled. These established experts on ancient linguistics, antiquities, theology and literature circled the stones on hands and knees, peering, hemming and hawing. Consulting and conferring.

Il-Kheir leaned toward Trueblood and said quietly, "Is it me, or do they keep looking over at us?"

"One just did it again," Trueblood said.

"Odd."

"Maybe they think I forged them."

"Did you?"

Trueblood glanced at the Horselord, who gazed back deadpan for five seconds, then they both looked away chuckling.

Trueblood felt a bit more at ease in the formidable kheiron's presence, still he hesitated. "Can I ask you a question?"

"Fen's gone back to Minosaros."

Trueblood smiled at his boots. "That wasn't the question."

"I beg your pardon, it's just what everyone's asking today so I assumed. If you have a new question, ask away."

"Did you take my father's soul home?"

The ice blue eyes softened. Years fell away from the Horselord's face as he answered, "I promised."

"Did he...say anything?"

Il-Kheir had his arms crossed all this time, his thumb and fore-finger fiddling with the moonstone hanging around his neck. Now the big hand reached and the backs of his fingers pressed the center of Trueblood's chest. "That he's with you. Always." His touch thumped once, twice, then the hand retreated.

"Thank you," Trueblood said, disappointed. The answer felt forged. Generic. He wanted a private joke. Something only he and Ikharus would understand. *He said to lay off the Altynian plonk.* Or, *Remember excellence needs no announcement.* Or, better yet, *Don't leave the nyellem door open or he'll rise from the dead to thrash you.*

"Ladies," Naria called, "and gentlemen. Maybe we could have a rough idea what the stones say? At least the parts you agree on. Then we can leave you to debate the fine points."

The dean of linguistics from the University of Lak Thennes was asked to lead the tour around the plinths, starting with the broken fragment.

"As we all know," she said, "the second stone of the *Truviad* ends in the middle of a sentence. *He must begin his journey where...*" She pointed to the first inscribed line on the fragment. "It finishes here, *Khe began: as a man bound to earth.*"

The hair on Trueblood's neck stood up as the interrupted narrative was allowed to continue. *What a time to be alive,* he thought as the dean read the fragment's inscription in its entirety:

> *He must begin his journey where Khe began: as a man*
> *bound to earth.*
> *This son of Khe must begin as Khe*
> *Before he ends in the stars.*

The air tasted expectant. A little unsatisfied. Glances were exchanged among the leaders, each confirming with the other that the finished fragment didn't sound terribly significant.

"I came all the way for this?" Zornin mumbled from behind Trueblood's shoulder.

"The third stone," the dean said, "reads like a prayer. An entreaty to a future savior, if you will. It's prophetic in tone." Her gaze found Trueblood's, then moved to the Horselord. "And eerily specific."

Os who is One, take this abandoned son into your
  merciful heart.
Born in sadness.
Born beneath a dam's wings, deaf to her death rattle,
  his first steps in her blood.

The Horselord's hooves clattered on the stone floor as he took four steps back, eyes bulging.

"Mysire?" Trueblood said, reaching for the kheiron's arm.

Sevri pulled away and pointed a finger at the dean. "Read it again."

"Born beneath a dam's wings," she said. "Deaf to her death rattle, his first steps in her blood."

Abrakam said, "Sevri, it's Fen," just as the Horselord said, "Abe, it's talking about Fen's birth," at the same time Zornin said, "What in the name of fuck?"

Borne broken from the treetops.
Spirit crushed in the darkest root-pits beneath Nydirsil.
Leaving only a heart willing to give all.
A son of Khe willing to give back his gifts to a son of mariners—
a scion of Nyland who looks with giantsblood eyes.

Abrakam put a hand on Trueblood's shoulder. "A scion of Nyland who looks with giantsblood eyes," he murmured.

Now Trueblood stumbled in his boots. "Abe, is that me?"

"I don't know."

"Abe, what's it *mean*?"

"Shh."

*A son of Khe to bind his power to the truest blood of I
    and my sister.*
*His stone to the tree-tenders and his starsilver to the
    giantsblood.*
Only this can equal a love like mine.
Nay, threefold like mine.
*Starsilver unto giantsblood, the kheiron unto the
    mariner as a map unto a lost land.*

Zornin had a hand on Trueblood's shoulder now. "Steady, lad."

The kepten was feeling light-headed. "What is happening?"

"I don't know, but Gods, I wish your father were here."

Rise up, O brave son of Khe.
Stay the course charted within your wings and sails.
*Walk among giants, your fourhand in his five, your
    fivehand between six.*
*Kneel with broken heart in the roots and feast your
    eyes on Os.*
*Look up beneath starsilver and giantsblood as ripening
    fruit unto the limbs of Nydirsil.*
Look up beneath love to hang nine days for nine stars.
Rise up beneath the blood truth, brave son of Khe.

"Excuse me," Trueblood said, and sat on the floor.

"Here, lad," Zornin said, crouching down and passing a small flask. "Get some of that in your belly."

"Then pass it over here," Naria said. She tucked a leg beneath her and sat, which gave leave for most everyone to drop down a level and contemplate.

Il-Kheir did not sit. He paced. "Read it again," he said to the dean. "From the beginning."

Diplomatically, she deferred to the chancellor of the University of Sudenlo, giving him a turn with a fresh eye. He refined a word or two, questioned a phrase's context to his colleagues, but to Trueblood's buzzing ears, it sounded much the same.

Out of the stones a hand unfolded. Reached across thousands of years to point straight at Trueblood and call him by name.

The truest blood.

The mariner. Giantsblood.

Rise up beneath the blood truth.

A long silence wound around the room. Slowly, Naria Nyland rose to her feet.

"Mysire il-Kheir," she said formally. "I think it best your son come home."

Part Five

MEROS

God of War

✦AN INDISCREET QUESTION

T HE MESSAGE FROM the Horselord read, *You and your charm will come home at once.* Fen would've ignored the terse command, pretended later it never arrived, but then a second falcon came in from Naria Nyland.

I ask you come home, Fen il-Kheir. Right away. The Truviad stones have been translated. They name you and Kepten Trueblood. I can't say more and I don't under-stand everything yet, but whatever happens next, you're a part of it. Come home, please, I need you to be here.

"Well, my dear, when you ask like that," Fen said, "how can I resist?"

His sire ought to take a few lessons in diplomacy from the queen.

"What's going on?" Lenge said, peering over his shoulder.

He crumpled the paper. "They're losing their minds about those pieces of rock they found in the Kaleuche. Naria needs me to come home so she can tell me a story or some shit. Let's break camp."

"We all need to go?" Lenge said. "We came all this way. Tomar can lead the raid."

Fen glanced at the Horselord's missive. *You and your charm will come home at once.*

He sighed, deciding to be a stallion about it. "We all go," he said. "Respond to the queen's falcon that we're on our way."

"What about il-Kheir's bird?"

"Just let her go home empty-legged." Fen winked at Lenge. "Father will get the message."

He flew the charm at a leisurely pace, just to show he couldn't be ordered around. Landing in Valtourel, he made a point of going first to the kheiron burial ground, with a little bouquet of anemones.

With no memory of his dam, Fen had to be content with other people's recollections, and he'd been told anemones were Zoria's favorite flower. During their short bloom season, he always brought some to her.

He crouched and pulled the weeds from the small gravestone next to Zoria's marker. Here was buried the little slave boy who escaped Minosaros with Fen and died in the Old Forest. Fen's fingers touched the sole word chiseled into its smooth face.

Alon.

He caressed the stone as if ruffling a youth's hair. "I didn't get them all yet. Still working on it. I won't stop until they're gone."

It was a short distance from the burial ground to the mariners' crypt, so Fen paid a visit to the resting place of Kepten True and his wife.

From his bag, Fen drew an apple and laid it by Noë Treeblood's side of the tomb. He'd been doing this for years. The red-haired queen loved apples even more than Fen did, and the exchange of fruit became a secret ritual between them. When Fen was away with his charm, he stopped at orchards and markets, seeking out rare and delectable cultivars. He'd pick the most perfect apple he could find and put it on a windowsill in Noë's suites. He left it anonymously, because it was their little joke and theirs alone. Arriving in his own bedchamber, he'd find a beautiful apple on his pallet. A welcome home gift from a not-so-secret admirer.

Noë was a friend when I didn't want to have friends.

She was kind from a distance, which was the only kindness I could tolerate.

Or reciprocate.

IN THE OLD shipyards, Fen walked around the *Truviad* stones, listening to a dean and a chancellor translate and interpret.

> *Os who is One, take this abandoned son into your*
>   *merciful heart.*
> *Born in sadness.*
> *Born beneath a dam's wings, deaf to her death rattle,*
>   *his first steps in her blood.*

"*Khe l'khe,*" Fen said, stunned. He'd been born from a pegaso. Born breech, his ears never hearing Zoria's death cries. He wobbled to his feet in ground soaked with his mother's blood.

"Naria, I'm a skeptical creature by nature, but this is a little too coincidental."

"Wait," Naria said.

> *Borne broken from the treetops.*
> *Spirit crushed in the darkest root-pits beneath Nydirsil.*

Fen's heart pounded behind his eardrums and eyeballs. How was this possible? Whoever chiseled these words, how could they know, thousands of years in the future, not only the circumstances of Fen's birth but everything that came after? How he was beaten and tortured in the underworld of Minosaros, in the very place Nydirsil tore free from earth? How he was brought down from the top of a Nye tree, his legs broken beyond repair?

How? How could they know?

Anger was kindling in the pit of his stomach now, filling his throat with a choking smoke.

They knew, he thought. *It was written. It was planned and plotted and done to me on purpose. I'm a pawn in some game. They destroyed my life and left me to…*

Wait, who is they? What the fuck is this?

The flames roared higher as the dean's voice reached his ears, translating the next stanza.

> *Leaving only a heart willing to give all.*
> *A son of Khe willing to give back his gifts to a son of*
> > *mariners—*
> *a scion of Nyland who looks with giantsblood eyes.*

"We believe this indicates Pelippé Trueblood," the Chancellor said. "His mother being a descendent of the Treeblood dynasty. And of course, his father's lineage is unimpeachable."

"What do they mean by 'give back his gifts'?" Fen asked, his voice faint through the buzzing in his ears.

> *A son of Khe to bind his power to the truest blood of I*
> > *and my sister.*
> *His stone to the tree-tenders and his starsilver to the*
> > *giantsblood.*

Only this can equal a love like mine.
Nay, threefold like mine.
Starsilver unto giantsblood, the kheiron unto the
    mariner as a map unto a lost land.

"Bind his power," Fen said slowly.

Rise up, O brave son of Khe.
Go forth, voyager, stay the course charted within your
    wings and sails.
Walk among giants, your fourhand in his five, your
    fivehand between six.
Kneel with broken heart in the roots and feast your
    eyes on Os.
Look up beneath starsilver and giantsblood as ripening
    fruit unto the limbs of Nydirsil.
Look up beneath love to hang nine days for nine stars.
Rise up beneath the blood truth, brave son of Khe.

Silence in the room now. The chancellor cleared his throat and handed Fen a sheet of paper. "We wrote down the translation. In case you—"

"Thank you," Fen said. "Would you excuse us, please?"

As soon as the dean and chancellor were gone, Fen crushed the paper in a fist and lobbed it away.

"Fen," Naria said. "I know this is a lot to take in."

"Please," Fen said. "I need you to be a friend right now. Not a queen."

She wound her arms around his waist and squeezed him hard. She was his only friend right now, yet he didn't hug back. His arms stayed loose at his sides, but he let his head fall on the crown of her head.

"If I'm hearing this right," he said. "I'm supposed to hand over my moonstone and my starsilver to Kepten Trueblood."

"I don't pretend to understand it either."

"It says, 'Bind his power.' *Bind,* Naria. That means I'm a slave."

"No," she said. "No, I won't let—"

"If anyone thinks a bunch of bad poetry is grounds to give a nineteen-year-old sailor *ownership* of me, I got a few things chiseled in stone to tell them."

"I know, Fen."

Fen touched the moonstone in his brow. "This? This doesn't leave my body. Ever. You have my father's word behind that. He made a vow to me. He promised. The only way this stone comes out of my skin is if I'm dead. The only way I hand *one* of my rings to anyone is if my hand is cut off. I do *not* stand in humos and I'll kill anyone who tries to make me put a hoof on a gods-damned *ship.*"

Naria's arms were at her sides now, her dark eyes steady on his. "I know what you suffered."

"Horseshit you do," he cried. "I spent four weeks in the hold of a slave ship. I was twelve years old, chained in humos, lying in my own filth with corpses rolling over me. That's what I suffered before the real suffering started. When two slave masters had ownership of my rings. When my body was *bound* to them."

She didn't look away. Tears filled her eyes but she honored his ordeal with her attention and didn't flinch from it.

Fen gave a trembling exhale. "If you know what I suffered, then you know I put rules in place after I was rescued. You know those rules are what keep me alive."

She pointed at the long plinths on the ground. "I know these say, 'Leaving a heart willing to give.' *Willing,* Fen. That's the most important word here. Not bind, not power. Willing."

"I decide," Fen said, shaking within his skin. "It's how I survive."

"Nothing is decided. Nothing is chiseled in any future stone. We'll work this out. We'll reach a decision together. We'll find an interpretation that satisfies everyone."

Fen's shoulders deflated and finally, his hands relaxed. "All right."

She reached to him, elbow bent and fingers high, offering gelango. He clasped her palm, then her forearm. Each put a hand on the other's shoulder and their brows pressed for a shared breath.

"Thank you," Fen said softly.

Smiling, she laid her palm on his cheek. "Go process this and get drunk," she said. "Or get drunk, then process it."

"Neither is a bad idea."

"We'll talk more later. I, you and Trueblood. Just us."

"What am I, the chaperone?"

"Don't be a bitch, dear."

Fen hesitated. "How's the sun look over his yardarm?"

Her eyebrows raised. "Fen il-Kheir, what an indiscreet question."

"You love indiscreet questions."

"I know, it's terrible." A bit of color crept along her cheekbones as she tucked her hair behind her ears. "I will say he's lovely. But he's also the kind to place great significance in matters of the bedroom and as you know, I do not."

"This I know."

"He's an extraordinary young man. He's also grieving and vulnerable and in need of massive amounts of attention. Attention isn't my forte."

"Oh, I don't know about that," Fen said. "Your forte made me feel better just now."

"You'll be feeling like shit again in an hour and I'll be too busy to repeat the performance."

"You're right. As usual."

She smiled. "Anyway, I arranged for Belmiro to care of Trueblood's needs."

"Arranged?" Fen's blood turned icy. "I thought they hooked up on their own."

"You've seen them together then?"

He grunted, remembering when the Ĝemelos woke up the kepten, the morning the *Truviad* stones were found. First the flash of Trueblood's naked body in bed, then Belmiro's tousled, silver head next to him. It put Fen in a spectacularly pissy mood, which he took back to Minosaros with him.

Bel was a hire?

It ought to make Fen feel better, but it didn't.

"Why's a celebrity like Pelippé Trueblood hiring a prostitute?" he asked.

"He's not," Naria said. "*I* am hiring a skilled courtesan for Trueblood's enjoyment. I hire Bel for his time. What happens during that time depends on how he and Trueblood get along."

"It's easy to get along with people if you're paid."

"I said *don't* be a bitch."

"It's true, though. Money can buy all the goodwill you want."

Naria crossed her arms. "In that case, I'll pay you a cask of Nye to get along with your father."

Now Fen laughed. "Well-played, General Nyland."

Let Them Know It Was Sevri

LAUGHTER STILL WREATHED Fen's face as he ambled through the pavilion, settling into a smile as he headed to his room. It faded when he found the Horselord waiting for him.

"Father," he said, immediately suspicious. Fen was always sent for, not called upon. He couldn't remember the last time Il-Kheir was in here.

Not since I outgrew random inspections.

His gaze gave a quick circle around the room before scoffing at the reflex. He was thirty-four years old and his quarters were always neat. Disorder made him tense. Things in their place kept the world in place.

"Can I do something for you?" he asked when the silence stretched past awkward into ominous.

"You saw the *Truviad* stones?"

"I did." His eyes narrowed at his father's hands. They held a long, braided length of hair. Black at first glance, but on closer inspection, in the right light, it proved to be deep purple. The plait was made from hair taken from Zoria's mane and tail. It used to have a bell on it, back when Fen was a foalboy. He lost the bell, as foalboys do. As he grew up, the braid was left behind more than it was taken along. Finally it was coiled for good in a neat mat on his standing desk.

It was uncoiled now, running through and between il-Kheir's fingers. A sentimental gesture to anyone's eyes but Fen's. Just because he didn't carry it around with him didn't mean others could touch it. Least of all Sevri, who wore his own cord made from Zoria's hair around his neck, his moonstone hanging from it.

The braid was Fen's talisman. Nobody else's.

"Please put that down," he said.

The Horselord set the plait on the desk without recoiling it. "Was it you who brought the anemones today?"

"Yes." Fen crossed his arms. "Does bringing flowers to my mother displease you?"

"*Born beneath a dam's wings,*" Sevri said, "*deaf to her death rattle, his first steps in her blood.*"

Fen closed his eyes. "I know, Father. I read it."

"It's decided then."

"Nothing's decided."

"It's written in stone. You'll be bound to the mariner."

Fen opened his eyes. "What do you mean bound?"

"You'll give him your moonstone and your silver."

"Like fuck I will."

"You have no idea what's at stake here."

"If it's that urgent, why don't *you* give up your power?"

"The prophecy names you."

"Please. A charlatan carved a few lucky guesses in a rock and they matched my life."

"Don't be a fool."

"I'm not the one falling on my face before a myth."

"I won't let you deny your place in this story."

"Father, if you think I'm going to clip my own wings and live on two feet while a sailor goes looking for a tree, you—"

"You're going with him."

"Excuse me?"

"The Kaleuche sails in a week. You'll be onboard. Bound to Kepten Trueblood."

"Bound or unbound, the only way I'll put foot or hoof on a godsdamned ship is if I'm dead."

A knock on the doorjamb. "Mysire?"

It was General Fostin, il-Kheir's top aide. Without meeting Fen's eye, he handed over a little bag to the Horselord. It jingled, and the hair rose up on Fen's forearms as a sickening dread coiled in his gut.

He. Wouldn't. Dare.

Il-Kheir dismissed Fostin and dug within the bag. "I had a feeling you were going to be a stubborn ass about this," he said. His hand came out and unfolded, revealing a jumble of rings and moonstones in his palm. Fen immediately recognized a band shaped like a serpent with its tail in its mouth. It belonged to Tomar, one of his Finches. Another ring was carved in a wreath of oak leaves. It ought to have been on Lenge's hand.

"I'm sorry to bring your charm into it," il-Kheir said. "But you leave me no choice."

"You're sorry for *nothing*."

The Horselord shook his fist casually, silver clinking against polished bits of moon. "Believe me when I say this, Tehvan il-Kheir. Either you take your place on that ship exactly as it's written on those stones, or your charm lives the rest of their lives as men bound to earth." His fist tightened. "And every other charm you attempt to create."

"So you're selling me," Fen said. "Just like a slaver."

"Spare me your dramatics. You're a slave to your own self-pity."

"Does what I suffered mean nothing to you?"

"Does the fate of Nye mean nothing to you? How many times do I have to punch your head toward the future before it *stays* there?"

"You made a promise."

"I promised a frightened foalboy. Not a kheiron heir capable of facing his fears if he's going to rule one day."

"I'm old enough to know a king keeps his word. While you give and take yours as it suits you."

"This quest is bigger than the hate you carry in your heart."

"Believe me, Father," Fen said. "Nothing in this world is bigger than my hate for you."

"What an admirable accomplishment. What's your next feat going to be? Doing what's right by your race, your homeland and your gods? Or eating your heart out over the past?"

His empty hand turned up, expectant and entitled.

Fen stared back at him. *Let it be carved in stone that I was unwilling*, he thought. *Let it all fail because my consent was forfeited. Let that tree sink into the ocean and Nye disappear forever. Let them know it was Sevri il-Kheir who brought it all down.*

"All your life you've done it the hard way," the Horselord said, reaching. With a deft twist of his fingers, he tore the moonstone from his son's brow.

Fen shifted to humos, standing on two legs for the first time in twenty years.

"Now," his father said. "Was that really so hard?"

"Fuck you," Fen said through his teeth. Then his shocked limbs gave out. He sprawled on his face, naked and helpless at his father's silver hooves.

Turn around and look at me, whore, hissed a voice from the past.

"Your charm of Finches will be restored when you return," the Horselord said. "You have my word."

"Your word is worthless."

One of the silver hooves nudged at Fen, none too gently. An empty palm reached down.

"*Now* what?" Fen said, pushing up on his arms and trying to remember the mechanics of bipedal motion.

"Your ringos. You can give it over or we can do it the hard way."

His eyes pounding with anger, Fen balanced on his chest and yanked the ring from the thumb of his fivehand. He pegged it across the room and out the door. "Go find it. For once in your miserable life, go find something you care about."

The door closed and he was alone on the cold stones.

I hate your fucking guts, he thought. *I'll take the godsdamned earth apart to make sure you suffer. When I get through with you, you won't even have a soul left.*

Gritting his teeth, he pushed back onto his knees.

On your knees, whore.

Muscle memory flooded him, slimy with anxiety. His hips howled with misuse, his quadriceps cried out in agony and his hamstrings clawed his lower back. He fell onto his chest again, head buried in his arms. All the posterior and dorsal parts of his soul cowering and braced for what was coming.

Turn over, whore. Roll over and see what I have for you.

HONOR

A STORY ASKS FOR little. Really all it wants and needs is a listener.

Fen's tale is his to tell, and he has his reasons for not telling. Among them is a lack of sympathetic ears.

Naria both honored and consoled Fen with her attention. She didn't flinch or look away.

As the kheiron lies on the floor in his most vulnerable, most detested form, stripped of stone and silver, let us do the same.

This is but a fragment of Fen's story, legantos. If he can live it, we can hear it.

We can listen to learn it. Learn it to tell it. Tell it to teach it.

The Rest of His Days

"Turn around and look at me, whore," the man says.

Tehvan il-Kheir turns. He has no choice. His moonstone is gone, so he cannot outrun captivity on four legs. His owner wears his rings, so his wings are clipped.

He can choose where to put his gaze, though, and he looks nowhere but the man's eyes, envisioning his slow death at the Horselord's hands.

My father will take the world apart to find me, he thinks as he's taken apart.

As he's thrown down on floors, across beds and up against walls, he thinks, *He'll never stop searching for me.*

When he's pushed to his knees, bent over and pulled up and turned this way and that, he separates himself from the moment and thinks, *He'll spend the rest of his days making sure you suffer.*

You and your son and your son's sons.

When the needs of men are pushed inside him, forced down his throat or spilled across his face, he stands it by thinking of revenge. *You will beg my father for mercy.*

When he's struck or cuffed or beaten for not making enough noise. For making too much noise. For not following commands. For following them too fast. Too slow. For taking too long. For seeming in a rush. Or when he's beaten for no reason other than man's sadistic pleasure, Tehvan learns to separate himself from the act and to take what's given to him as belonging to someone else. All the while believing his time will come. His father will come.

Between every blow of a fist: *He'll take a week to kill you, man.*

Between every crack of a lash: *And I will watch.*

It's a brutal life and he adjusts quickly by disassociating. The collar at his neck is not his, neither are the chains, the stone cell he sleeps in, the meager food, nor the beatings. Months pass, the moon's egg cracking open and spilling across the skies five times. Seven. Then it's been a year and his mantras turn to questions.

Is my father taking the world apart?

Has he stopped searching?

Does he care if I suffer?

Will I spend the rest of my days here?

Every time Tehvan il-Kheir turns his head toward the future with the tiniest bit of hope, another man speaks behind him.

"Turn around, whore."

WILLING

RUEBLOOD LOUNGED ON a couch in Naria's sitting room, reading through a transcript of the *Truviad*. At the big desk by the windows, Naria was busy with her two scribes. Dislekos had impaired her ability to read and write so she depended on the pair of attendants to be her literary eyes and voice. Over the years, the palace had nicknamed the two women Spectacles, who read reports and correspondence to the queen, and Ink, who wrote responses and replies.

A half-dozen others were in and out of the room, needing this, delivering that or taking away the other thing. Naria's fuse got shorter and her tone more brusque, trying to get through it all before Fen arrived for their private drink-and-discuss.

Belmiro was suspiciously absent from the retinue.

Guess he has one or two things to do in town, Trueblood thought.

"There," Naria said. "Is that the last of it?"

"Seal this," Ink said, pouring wax from a tiny spoon.

"And drink this," Spectacles said, twisting the cork from a bottle of wine.

"Excellent," the queen said, sliding her signet ring from her pinky and pressing it into the wax. "Get a glass, Trueblood."

"Got one."

Naria dismissed her entourage and when the door was shut, she slumped against it. "It sucks to be the queen."

"Horseshit."

"All right, it has certain perks." She sank into a chair and put her booted feet on a hassock. Her many dogs followed, two jumping in her lap and the rest arranging themselves on the floor around her. All of them looked at Trueblood like he owed them money. Why was it animals didn't seem to like him? If he were Lejo, he'd be wearing those mutts like a blanket.

"Find any new insights?" Naria said, motioning toward the transcript.

"This sentence is bothering me: *A son of Khe to bind his power to the truest blood of I and my sister/His stone to the tree-tenders and his starsilver to the giantsblood.*"

"What's bothersome?"

"I'm the giantsblood, I get that. But I'm not a tree-tender."

"Your mother was."

"But it's not what I do. I feel this is being extremely specific about who's supposed to get what by referring to their title. Or their job. And it doesn't say one tree-tender, but *tenders*. Plural. While giantsblood is singular."

Naria's eyebrows wrinkled. "What's the plural of giantsblood?"

"Giantsbled."

She stared a long moment at him. "You just made that up."

"I did not."

"You're full of shit. Giantsbled. That's a past tense, not a plural."

"I swear," he said, laughing. "Look it up. You can jail me if I'm wrong."

Naria shook her head, chewing on her wine. "For the moment, I will take your word for it." At a knock on the door she leaned her head back on the chair. "Come in."

Il-Kheir entered. "Salutos. No, don't get up."

"I can't," Naria said, motioning to the sleeping terriers in her lap.

One of the wolfhounds sniffed around the Horselord's fore-legs before putting paws on the pale gray flank and stretching up to be greeted.

"Son of a bitch," Trueblood mumbled into his glass.

"We were expecting Fen," Naria said coolly.

"I'm here on his behalf. Down now, my beauty." He came to where Trueblood sat and pointed to the paper in his hand. "Is that the transcription? May I?"

Trueblood gave it up and the kheiron read aloud.

Borne broken from the treetops.
Spirit crushed in the darkest root-pits beneath Nydirsil.
Leaving only a heart willing to give all.

"Willing," Naria said, her voice now glacial.

The Horselord opened his big hand. "He is."

The queen and the mariner gazed at the stone and ring in the kheiron's palm. The former was teardrop-shaped, its bulb end barely bigger than a pea. Milky-white and shot through with opalescent veins. A tiny hole drilled at its narrow end, where it once hung from a hoop in Fen's eyebrow.

The ringos was carved into wings with a horse head between. Knowing what he did now about the jewelry's emotional weight and significance, Trueblood felt a twinge of revulsion. As if it were Fen's severed ear being offered to him.

I don't want it, he thought. *I won't wear it. It's beyond wrong. It would be like wearing a cloak made of Fen's skin.*

"When the Kaleuche sets sail," il-Kheir said, "Fen will be with you. As is written."

Naria tapped her teeth together before speaking. "Mysire, I'd feel a little more confident if Fen himself were here to show his willingness."

"Understandable. But this has all been a shock to him and right now he's…"

"He's what?" Trueblood said.

The Horselord's pale blue gaze turned on him. Soft. Youthful. The way it had been when Sevri spoke about Trueblood's father. "He hasn't walked on two legs in twenty years," he said. "Certain muscles atrophy if not used and he's in quite a bit of discomfort now."

"He's in pain?" Naria said. "Who's with him? Should I send a healer?"

"The White Mares are with him," il-Kheir said. "As usual in his times of trouble, Fen does best in their company alone." He smiled at Trueblood. "Lad, I've never wished your mother were still alive more than I do right now. She'd be good company for Fen as well."

"My mother?"

The Horselord nodded. "She was dear to him." The mighty chest expanded and contracted in a sigh. "I've asked a priestess to come to the pavilion. While my son masters some crucial physical skills, I'm sure he'll need spiritual guidance as well. What he wants right now is privacy. Hence…"

He leaned and placed the stone and ring on the little table between Naria and Trueblood.

"It's settled then."

"So it appears," Naria said. "Thank you, mysire."

The kheiron departed, leaving Trueblood and Naria. And Fen, in spirit.

"I don't feel good about this," Trueblood said. "At all."

"Me neither."

"Am I supposed to *wear* the ring?"

"I don't know."

"What do we do?"

Naria had unconsciously pulled one of the dogs against her chest, holding it like a barrier between herself and the kheiron's talismans. "Pé, I don't know," she said.

Trueblood stood up. "I think we should go see Fen. See for ourselves what his situation is."

The queen gulped the rest of her wine and shooed the dogs from her lap. They hurried to the pavilion but the doors to Fen's room were closed tight. One of the White Mares emerged to graciously but firmly deny entry.

"He'll see no one," she said. "Please, Your Majesty. Kepten. Not tonight. Not when he's like this. Leave him in peace."

"Mydam," Naria said, "you and your sister know him best. Was this his choice?"

"He says he'll go," the centauride said.

"Willingly?" Trueblood said. "That's the word in stone."

A beat. "He says he'll go," the mare said again. "Please excuse me now."

Frustrated, they took the *Truviad* back to Naria's chambers and invited in Abrakam and the Ĝemelos to hash it out. Nobody, not even Lejo and his moral compass that only pointed one way, had a satisfying revelation. Although they were in agreement about the distinction between *tree-tender* and *giantsblood*.

"If it were me deciding," Lejo said, "which it isn't..."

"Pretend it is," Naria said dully.

"I would *place* the moonstone in the joint guardianship of the vicreĝos of Nyland, who are technically the tree-tenders."

"I agree with the spirit of that," Naria said. "But four women in four cities can't hold one stone. Someone has to take literal guardianship."

"Then no question, give it to Torenn Treeblood. She's Pé's cousin as well as Noë's successor. The last Nye trees are in Arbaro, so Fen's moonstone should be placed in the care of Arbaro's vicreĝo. While his ringos is *placed* under the singular protection of Kepten Trueblood."

"Emphasis yours," Raj said.

"Do I wear the ring?" Trueblood asked. "Because that doesn't feel right to me. At all."

"Put it in the ship's safe," Lejo said.

"*Place* it in the safe," Raj said.

"Give Fen a key."

"Godsdammit," Trueblood said. "He of all people should be here making these decisions."

"Nothing's in stone yet," Naria said.

"I swear I'm going to drop a rock on the next person who says nothing's in stone."

A collective sigh.

"Why don't we sleep on it," Abrakam said. "Let's call it a night and go to bed."

"Did someone say bed?" a voice called.

They all turned to see Belmiro lounging on the doorframe.

"Is this a lovers' quarrel?" he said. "Or may I interrupt?"

"It's what I pay you for," Naria said.

"Official interrupter, is that your title?" Trueblood said.

"More or less," Belmiro said, his eyes up to no good as they raked down Trueblood's body.

"Oh," Naria said, sitting up a little. "Abrakam, what's the plural of giantsblood?"

"Giantsbled."

Trueblood smiled.

"Shut up," Naria said. "One word and I'll jail your smug ass."

"One giantsblood, two giantsbled," Lejo said.

Raj nodded, puzzled. "Everyone knows that."

"Even I know that," Belmiro said.

"Get out of here," Naria said. "All of you."

"Now I know why they call you Troubled," Belmiro said later.

"Do you?"

"You've sighed eight times in ten minutes. And not the good kind of sigh."

"Sorry."

"It's all right, you've got a lot on your mind. It's just I'm really good at easing troubled minds."

"You are."

"See? You sighed again. I'm not doing a good job here."

"Is loving me a job?"

He pulled one of Trueblood's braids. "Joke? Ha ha?"

"Do you love me?"

"Héjo, here we go," Belmiro mumbled, closing his eyes.

"Joke?" Trueblood said. "Ha ha?"

Belmiro tightened the arm slung over Trueblood's chest and bit his ear. "I like you passionately."

"Mm."

"Up for another round?"

"No, I'm tired out." He wasn't. He just wanted to lie quiet in bed, sigh over his troubles and pretend Fen's ears were open and eager to hear them. Pretend the weight of Fen's arm lay on him. And pretend he wasn't pretending.

"Goodnight then," Belmiro said, yawning as he punched a pillow into place. "Wake me up if the need arises."

"You're staying?"

"If you'll have me."

"You going to be a bitch in the morning?"

"Probably."

Trueblood both envied and resented Bel's ability to turn his mind off. The kheiron lay down, took four deep breaths and the fifth was a snore. Naria was the same. Except for the snoring.

He imagined Fen's voice in the dark. *I'm so damn tired, but I miss you when I close my eyes.*

"You're ridiculous," Trueblood mouthed soundlessly.

I know. Fen moved up closer to Trueblood, bit his ear and whispered, *Who knew gelang turns you into an idiot?*

Trueblood's hand pretended to slip beneath the covers and make the brave son of Khe rise up. "Look at you all full of truest blood."

A rustle behind him. "Did you say something?" Bel mumbled. "No. Goodnight."

Gods, the invisible Fen said. *Do people in love get anything done, or do they just lie around being idiotic?*

Trueblood tossed and turned through the dark hours, not so much sleeping as chaining together a few catnaps. Finally, a little before dawn, he slipped out of bed and pulled on clothes. He headed down to the beach. Maybe the water would have some answers.

Or he could just drown himself.

The Boundary

THE GODS, LEGANTOS, have a terrible sense of humor. Often their idea of solving a problem is putting the problem directly in your path, then laughing as you deal with it.

Trueblood stripped down and was about to wade into the pool when he realized Fen il-Kheir was there. Submerged to his chin and looking like he could strangle a kitten and feel nothing.

Fuck my life, Trueblood thought. The thing he dreamed of all night was the last thing he wanted to see this morning. But it was too late now, his balls were literally out.

"How's the water?" he asked.

"Wet."

"Good one." He stepped into the cool depths and dove deep. He rolled and floated, letting the drink flow through body and mind. Turn a page and start fresh. He emerged with a gasp and swam toward a pile of marble, keeping his distance from the kheiron.

Think before you speak, a wise voice within said. *Not speaking is also an option.*

The hoop in Fen's eyebrow was gone. Where it once hung was a healing gash, bisecting his eyebrow.

Without moving his head, Fen's gaze swiveled to Trueblood, then looked away again. "Did you come to gloat?"

"No. Rather the opposite."

"Can't see why. You got the happy ending in the *Truviad*."

"You think?"

"Spare me your wide-eyed charity."

"Look, I—"

"Spare me your thoughts as well. I'm not interested in anything you have to say right now."

"If you think this is easy—"

"Oh *fuck* you," Fen said. "Easy is your middle name. You just sit there and look cute while the world arranges itself around you. You got my moonstone and my ringos. You got a brand new ship and a crew who adores you. You got to fuck a queen and now she's paying the top whore in Valtourel to keep your cock wet."

"Excuse me?"

Fen stared at him a beat, then chuckled out his nose. "Gods, you are stupid," he said. "They want you to find a colossal tree when you can barely see past the end of your nose."

"What are you talking about?"

"Belmiro's a prostitute. Oh wait, sorry, I believe courtesan is the polite term. A top-tier, extremely expensive courtesan, but let's be real. He's a whore. He used to turn tricks on the wharves in Alondra, now he's being paid to fuck you."

Trueblood stared. Then he sliced his hand through the water, sending a wave of it in Fen's direction. "You are so full of shit."

"Naria told me herself. She thinks you're a great lay but she doesn't have time or energy for the amount of attention you need. So she delegated the job to Bel. Both jobs."

"Get the fuck out of here."

"Better grow up, wharf rat. You can't shelter under the queen's skirts forever. Although right now, they fit you better than Ikharus's pretty blue coat."

The skirt comment didn't bother Trueblood, but his father was off limits. His fingers closed around a loose hunk of marble and fired it at the kheiron. He wasn't angry enough to aim for Fen's head. He wanted to put the kheiron back in his place, not kill him. He popped the rock on the meaty ball of Fen's shoulder, hard enough to break the skin.

"Son of a *bitch*," Fen cried.

"Your face was getting crowded with your finest moments," Trueblood said. "Thought I'd spread them out a little."

Sparks were in Fen's blue eyes. "Try that again and you won't have a face left."

"Wrap your mouth around my father's name again and you can kiss your pretty silver ring goodbye."

Oh fuck I'm dead, he thought as the kheiron lunged at him. He flexed his knees, pushed off and dove out of the way. He kicked hard as he headed for shore, expecting a hand to close around his ankle at any second.

He'll kill me and throw my body over the seawall. No, first he'll break every bone in my body, then throw me over the seawall to drown.

And he'll enjoy it.

When the sand of the shallows scraped his chest, Trueblood came up, braced for attack but also considering running for his life.

From the deep water, Fen stared, his malevolent gaze a strung bow, the arrow pointing straight at Trueblood.

Fire away, the kepten thought, letting the narrow escape make him cocky.

The kheiron slowly shook his head. "Go back to your whore, Kepten. Wasting the queen's money has to be some kind of capital offense."

Shaken, stunned, and more pissed off than he could remember being in his life, Trueblood seized his breeches, turned his back and dragged them onto his wet legs. He needed to get to the bottom of this whore shit.

"This whore shit is horseshit," he mumbled.

It had to be horseshit, right?

He'd find out.

"How do you even initiate that conversation?" he said, untangling the sleeves of his shirt. "Héjo, Bel, can I ask you something? Are you a prostitute? Oh, no reason, just wondering."

Chaotic splashing made him turn around. Fen was pulling himself out of the pool, muscles standing out in long cords on his arms. With a final grunt, he toppled on the grass.

"Oh," Trueblood said, stupidity putting an arm around his brain. "You have your legs on."

Fen shook the water off his head, then glared at him. "My legs *on*?"

"Sorry, I meant... Sorry."

"You really are too stupid to live." He dragged his hands over his face, then he stood up. Blood dripped from his shoulder wound and water sluiced down his skin. One of the art books in Abrakam's library couldn't have constructed a more perfect specimen of man, down to the last pubic hair.

Trueblood quickly dropped his gaze to Fen's legs. Mighty and mythic and immutable. Then they buckled beneath him and he crashed forward into the grass.

"Careful," Trueblood said. "You need help?"

"I don't need anything from you." Fen stood slowly, took one wobbling step and halted. His long legs rippled as he locked his knees. The muscles in his jaw bulged even tighter.

Is it painful for him to walk? Trueblood thought. *Or just difficult?*

His eyes widened then, locking onto Fen's waist where a silvery line traced. Fainter than the etchings of his retracted wings. A pale demarcation line across the small of his back, hugging each hip and curving along the iliac lines that framed his abdomen. The boundary where man and horse met.

Trueblood's fingertips itched and his mouth watered. Belmiro didn't have a line like that. Or maybe he did, but his pale skin made it indiscernible. Fen's skin was the warm, pale brown of an eggshell and through it, the silvery belt glistened like magic.

"What the fuck are you staring at?" Fen said through his teeth.

"Nothing," Trueblood said, noting that like Belmiro, Fen was shorter when he was in humos.

"Want me to hold still while you make an oil painting?"

"Sure. You can hang it in your cabin and then you won't have to talk to anyone you don't like."

Fen's hands went to fists. "Let's get a few things straight, sailor. I'll get on your ship but don't expect a damn thing else. My father's got my charm hostage and I'm doing it for them. You're not my kepten, I'm not your subordinate. We're nothing close to friends and just so it's *crystal* clear, I don't bed men. So close your fucking mouth and get that idea out of your head."

"Don't flatter yourself it was ever in my head."

"Good. Because bottom line, I hate your guts."

"The feeling's mutual."

"Glad we agree on something, man."

Man was spit out like the vilest of insults, landing wet and contemptuous on Trueblood's face. He yanked his shirt on and started up the path toward the palace, kicking rocks out of his way and muttering under his breath.

It took all of twenty steps for him to start feeling like shit. He stopped in his tracks and sighed, painfully aware of Fen's situation and the kind of man his father raised him to be.

I should help him.

No. Right now, doing the right thing will only make things worse. Leave him be.

His neck ached with the effort not to look around and see if Fen was all right.

Don't look back. You can help him by not watching him stumble and fall. Don't fucking look at him when he's like this.

Because he'd rather die.

He walked on, conscious of every step. The precise physics of locomotion he normally gave zero thought. He imagined every heel-to-toe roll feeling like broken glass or knives in his soles. Every foot fall costing a monumental effort.

He walked on, pondering all these things in his heart, where anger and confusion battled with compassion. His pride smarted and sulked, licking its wounded feelings. Yet each footfall was a kick to Fen's pride. He had suffered injuries Trueblood couldn't even imagine.

He was pissed off enough to throw another rock at the kheiron, and at the same time, he felt compelled to protect him.

And when he thought about the pale silver line circling Fen's waist, he desperately wanted to touch it.

In My Bed by Choice

B ELMIRO WAS AWAKE and sitting up when Trueblood returned to his room.

"Where'd you go?" he said through a yawn.

"Oh, down to the grotto to have a swim and get in a fight with Fen."

"For real?"

"Yeah. It was epic."

Belmiro scratched his stubble. "No offense to your masculinity, but I'm shocked you got out of it unscathed. He's one sick stallion when he's pissed off."

"He's also at a slight disadvantage right now."

"Oh." Belmiro drew the word out long, nodding. "You're right."

"Still, he's got interesting psychological warfare skills."

"Yes, our Fen does know how to find a person's weakness."

"Mm." Trueblood dug in his dresser drawer for a dry shirt.

"He get under your skin?"

"Sort of."

"You want to talk about it?"

Trueblood turned around to face him. "How much does Naria pay you?"

"Pardon?"

"How much do you get paid to sleep with me?"

Belmiro's mouth hung poised above his chin, then slowly closed. "Fen, you unbelievable bastard," he murmured.

Trueblood stared. "He was telling the truth?"

The kheiron exhaled roughly. "For the first time in my life I'm speechless."

"That makes two of us." He picked up Belmiro's breeches from the floor and handed them to him.

"Are you throwing me out?"

"No, I just think this is a conversation better had with pants on."

"Fair enough."

Watching Bel dress, Trueblood's mind flipped backward through the affair. The fun, the laughs, the questions and answers. The rare serious moments and the rarer tender ones. And the sex.

All for money? Only for the money?

"It's not like I thought we were in love," he said. "But Khe, I did think you were in my bed by choice."

"I was," Belmiro said.

"Then what the fuck was the money for?"

"Because... Gods, how do I even explain this?"

"This? You mean the job?"

"It wasn't a job."

"You can argue semantics all you want, but sleeping with me had a price. You were paid." Trueblood motioned to the bed. "This was paid for. You joked about not doing a good job the other night but it wasn't a joke. I was a job."

Belmiro scrubbed his hands through his hair. "I don't know what to say. I'm sorry."

Trueblood felt both sorry and sick. All the decadent sex sat in his gut like a rich dessert eaten too fast. Washed down with money and giving him indigestion. "Thanks a fucking lot," he said.

Belmiro was fidgeting foot to foot and glancing repeatedly at the door. "I should go," he said. "You probably want to think about this and I have one—"

"One or two things to do in town," Trueblood said. "Does that mean customers?"

Bel's chin raised a hair. "Clients," he said, the S crisp behind his teeth. "And if you want to shit on my profession to make yourself feel better, I suggest you save your breath." He crossed his arms, fingertips drumming on his bicep.

"Why do you do it?" Trueblood asked.

"For the money."

"You have no other way of making money?"

"Not the amount I need."

Trueblood shook his head a little. "Need for what? What are you buying?"

"Fadara."

A long, swollen silence.

"Do you get it now?" Belmiro said quietly.

"I..."

"I'm addicted to fadara. I've been addicted since I was sixteen."

"I see."

"Good. Do you *see* I fuck for a living so I can buy the shit that helps me live?"

"I do now," Trueblood said.

"Then know I'm in some kind of pain all the time. When I say all the time, I mean every minute of every day."

"From your legs?"

"Yes. Doesn't matter if equos, humos, kheiros. It hurts all the time. It's not your fault, I'm just explaining my situation. If I'm on fadara, I can function in polite society and play nicely with others. If I'm coming off it, I become extremely unpleasant. If I'm not on it, you don't want to know me. My life is pain management on a really desperate scale. The kind of scale where selling myself is a viable option. Plus I have no problem admitting I'm good at it."

"Have you ever tried to stop?"

"Oh Gods, Pé, grow up."

Stung at being told twice in the space of an hour, Trueblood walked away to the window.

"Sorry," Belmiro said. "That was harsh and I'm between doses."

"I wondered why you were always so surly in the mornings."

"It's a mean withdrawal."

"Apparently."

"Pé." Belmiro's hands settled on Trueblood's shoulders. "I'm sorry. I meant it when I said you were something. I meant everything I said to you."

"When you were high and fucking me for money."

A long sigh against the back of Trueblood's neck. "I...truly regret it ended up this way."

"Did you ever plan on telling me?"

"No."

"How much did Naria pay you? No, don't answer that. Forget I asked. I don't want to know."

He drew a deep breath, flicked off Bel's hands and turned around. "Look, I don't know much about addiction but is there anything that can help you?"

"Think I haven't looked?"

"I *said* I don't know a lot about this, all right? Don't rub my face in my ignorance and then kick me when I'm trying to get informed."

Belmiro squeezed his eyes shut. "Sorry. I'm coming down into unpleasantness and starting to crave. To answer your question, what could help me is Nye. But as you know, not much of it is in the world."

"Despite being the village idiot, I do know this."

"I stole some once," Belmiro said, drawing his toe along the carpet.

Trueblood's eyes widened. "You stole Nye?"

"Yeah. I lifted Torenn Treeblood's keys to the vault."

A sudden anger surged behind the kepten's eyeballs. "My mother used to wear those keys. I was hiding in her wardrobe when the minotaurs killed her to get them. Then they set the palace on fire. I was seven years —"

"I don't need a history lesson, Pé."

"Those were my *mother's* keys."

Belmiro stepped back, palms in the air. "I'm sorry. I returned them and didn't kill anyone."

"Doesn't make it right."

"I know. I'm not making excuses. It's a capital offense and if I got caught, we wouldn't be having this conversation. The point is, I was clean for a month. Best month of my life. At that point, I hadn't been pain-free in ten years. I took one grain of Nye and it was like a war ending. I forgot what peace was. I cried every day because everything was so beautiful. No withdrawal. No craving. No fixing. No pain. I tried to make it last. I held onto the last grain until I was foaming at the mouth, I hurt so much. Then it was gone and I had to go back to fadara."

"Oh fuck everything everywhere," Trueblood said. He sat on the bed, feeling like holy horseshit.

"I know. So." The kheiron took a deep breath and made a vague gesture toward the window. "While you're out there, if you find all this woo-woo prophecy written in stone actually has some weight, and you find nine stars to reattach a tree to the sky and make Nye grow again... I'd be grateful."

His tone began sardonic but trembled with a simple sincerity at the end. It was a quiet entreaty, and Trueblood's soul wrapped around it. Here was a task for him. Maybe not the most lofty or noble, but it was a purpose. A job that could be done well.

Even excellently.

"What are you smiling about?" Belmiro said.

"I'm the kind of lad who does best when he has a set goal," Trueblood said, standing up. "I think you just gave me one."

A beat, then Belmiro offered gelango. Their hands clasped, then forearms. A hand on each shoulder and their brows pressed.

"Take care of yourself," Trueblood said. "In all the ways you can."

"I will. I'm really sorry, Pé."

"I'll get past this. I mean, I'm pissed off right now but at the same time, I don't want you to suffer."

"Well." Belmiro picked up his head. Tears rimmed his eyes. "That might be the nicest thing anyone ever said to me."

FATHERLESS SON

WITH ALL HIS heart, Trueblood wished he were a minoro again. He wanted to be ordered around. Wanted a list of back-breaking, labor-intensive tasks as long as his arm and an authoritative presence breathing down his neck, keeping him focused on the ship instead of his problems.

Well, he was the damn kepten. His crew could give him the side-eye if he threw off his coat, rolled up his sleeves and picked up a hammer or mop, but they couldn't tell him no.

"I have things on my mind," he said to anyone who ventured to ask what he was doing. "I just want to *work*."

Everyone kept their distance. Except the lark, who swooped around, warbling and chattering at him. Pecking holes in the woodwork, which made Trueblood even more irritable.

When he wasn't shooing the bird, he mumbled under his breath, having it out with Naria Nyland. The imaginary confrontation was orderly and articulate, with well-argued points and eloquent conclusions, but he was sure when he came face to face with her, he'd go blank. Be reduced to toddler insults and kicking dirt on her shoes. Then end up in jail.

Who the fuck does she think she is?

Naria was in Hokosia, so he couldn't even see her to find out. Instead he walked along the waterfront that night, wondering who he thought he was. He looked up at the hull of the Kaleuche.

Neat, trim, shipshape, ready to set sail with an imposter at her helm. A monster trying to sort out the business of gods.

"I wish you were here, Da," he said softly.

Grief like a waterfall in his throat and chest. He squeezed his jaw tight, sucking air through his nose. He started walking again. His heels hit the ground hard, each long leg thrown from the hip, eating up the distance between the wharves and the mariners' crypt.

I wish you were here.

Why aren't you here?

You didn't finish the job. You showed off at the end when things are most likely to go wrong. This is all wrong. It's not supposed to be this way.

The stones howled cold beneath his knees as he kneeled in front of his parents' tomb. Noë's mysterious devotee had been here—an apple lay beneath her inscription. The letters of her name were dulled with time while the chiseled edges of *Ikharus-Lippé True* were sharp against Trueblood's fingertips. Nothing lay beneath his father's name. His devotee had brought nothing but troubles.

"Da," he whispered. The most giant of giantwords. A noun meaning both father, and the steel-hearted courage it took to be a father.

Why was there no giantword for fatherless son?

He pressed his forehead and palms against the one he loved most.

"I wish you were here," he said. "I need you here. I don't know what I'm doing. I can't remember what you taught me about this. You just said it was my time to learn of such things. I don't like what I'm learning and I need to talk to you about it."

He breathed deep, over and over, trying to take it in and let it go. His damp eyes rested on the apple. Left by someone who knew Noë well.

"Who's going to know me well?" he said. "Who's going to bring me what I need?"

Grow up, Pé.

Everything happens for a reason.

"This reason can go fuck itself." He sat still a moment, then he swiped the apple and sent it flying. Both of his hands smacked down on his father. Flat palms at first. Then fists.

"You *said* you'd be with me until the end," he cried, pounding his rage on the one he loved most.

He let rip, yelling at Ikharus this wasn't *fair.* This was all *his* fault. *He* did this to him. It was a tantrum but he didn't care. Nobody was here but ghosts, so he let it out and let it echo off the marble in a spectacular lament to growing up. Until the lament doubled back in an admonishment that ricocheted in his ears.

Grow up, Pé.

Grow up, Pé.

Grow up...

The night broke open and grief spilled down like rain.

And because nobody could see, Pelippé Trueblood sank over his knees and wept.

He cried his heart in two. He reached inside his shirt and rubbed a palm in a circle over his scarred chest. The tender skin broke open and bled, which made him rub harder. The pain was something to sink his teeth into. The pain was pulling him out the other side. And not gently either.

Enough.

The silvery voice in his head was female. The same voice that chanted *hold the bond* when Trueblood was learning to separate from the twins. Back then, the words touched him like a mother's gentle hand. Now, it was still a maternal hand, but it was having none of his horseshit.

I said, enough.

His face stung as she, whoever she was, gave him a good yank and a shake and another slap.

Put your ass on that ship, put that ring on your finger and GROW UP.

"All right," he said. "All right. I will. Just give me a fucking min—"

A sudden noise made his bones jump in his skin and his breath suck back into his throat. He flicked his narrowed gaze hard from side to side.

Fen il-Kheir stood in the shadows of the crypt, holding the flung apple.

No telling how long he'd been there but his expression—somewhere between contempt and horror—told Trueblood he saw the whole spectacle.

Breathing hard, drawing the bloody heel of his hand across his eyes, Trueblood got to his feet. Instead of a rock, he threw his words. And this time, he aimed for the heart.

"What the fuck are you staring at, *man?*"

Between Two Columns

SINCE HIS MOONSTONE was confiscated, Fen had been coming to the crypt to practice walking. The pews and rails and columns gave him plenty to lean on. The late hour ensured privacy.

When Trueblood came in, Fen's first reaction was to be annoyed at the interruption. He was in no shape to quickly skulk away, so he backed into a recessed alcove and went statue-still. This wouldn't be long. The kepten would light a candle, leave a flower, pass a moment of silence and leave.

But he stayed. This wasn't a token payment of respects, this was a man trying to withdraw emotional currency from a vault forever closed to him. At first, Fen was embarrassed by the feverish muttering. But as it grew in volume and despair, the chagrin morphed to a strange affinity. When an apple went flying between two columns and Trueblood's voice echoed off tombs—"You said you'd always be with me!"—Fen nearly died. He recognized the lament. He had one just like it in his heart. Wearing slightly different clothes but the same bones beneath flayed skin:

Where did you go?

Why did you forsake me?

Why did you abandon me?

Don't you love me anymore?

A seed of revelation put a tentative root in the rocky soil of Fen's heart.

He and Trueblood weren't so different.

The Horselord was accurate in saying Fen had always done things the hard way.

He could try another way.

He could pay witness to Trueblood's grief and show he understood. He could give something to the future instead of taking revenge on the past.

He could if he wanted to.

If he were willing.

He took a few slow, silent steps. He braced a shoulder against a column and bent to pick up the apple. Righting himself, his rings clattered against stone. Trueblood whipped his head around and saw him.

Shit.

As they stared, Fen frantically tried to take the tiny root and its one fragile leaf and put it into an overture. *I'm sorry* seemed a good place to start, and he was about to say it when Trueblood spoke first.

"What the fuck are you staring at, *man?*"

The emphasized word cut deep. After Trueblood stormed out, Fen dropped the apple, picked up the implied insult and used its sharp edge to sever all his fascination to this fucking *sailor.*

The fascination was back as soon as he saw Trueblood smile at breakfast.

Part Six

Nyos

Goddess of Love

⟡ABOARD

From the Most Private Journal of Kepten Pelippé Trueblood Cay

These are things I know.

My father raised me to be the goodness in the world that the Nye trees no longer make.

Sex can be bought and sold, but gelang has no price. And I want something priceless.

I am still angry and disappointed in Naria. She came home last night, and I went to her and told her how I felt. She apologized and I accepted. This morning, I went back and forgave her. I have to. I don't want that unsettled business on my ship because I don't know if this is my first voyage or my last.

Voyages that begin on ill-will rarely improve. Arguments unsettled or grudges held get tossed into the hold and spoil.

My father pressed the point not to leave port angry. "When Truvos sailed off with Nydirsil chained behind, he was pissed. And look what happened."

I and Fen il-Kheir are the next chapter in the Truviad. Fen il-Kheir suffered horribly, and suffered on a ship. He dreads this voyage.

He is viciously proud and will never admit his dread.

Loss of pride can make or break a man. I'm sure it's the same with half-men.

The kheiron is beautiful to me. His face and body in my eyes, his story in my heart—these are beautiful things.

I don't hate him. I don't particularly like him right now. I must tell the truth and say I'm a little afraid of him.

I will not be cruel to him.

This ship does not punish mistakes. It only punishes disrespect. If I disrespect Fen il-Kheir, the entire voyage will be punished.

I don't have to like him to be decent to him.

I will do my part. I'll wear Fen's ringos, but I will not flaunt the wearing in Fen's face nor permit any sailor on the Kaleuche to do so.

If Fen wishes to be one of the crew, he is welcome. If he wishes to do nothing, I'll continue doing my job and doing it well. Not announcing my excellence. Not strutting afterward.

This, I know, is what my father would've done.

This, I know, is the True Way.

But here is one more thing I know: when I sleep in the kepten's bed on the Kaleuche, it will be with someone I love. I will sleep there with a gelangos or not sleep there at all.

If this wasn't the True Way before, it is now.

ONE LINGERING PROBLEM nagged at the Kaleuche's new kepten: the *Truviad* gave them no map, no directions, route or clues as to what they were supposed to actually do now.

"We just put a kheiron onboard and…go?" he asked.

"Why are you asking me?" Raj said.

"You're the pilot."

"You need a geographical destination, I'm your lad." Raj pointed at his brother. "Prophetic and philosophical journeys are his department."

"The kheiron unto the mariner as a map unto a lost land," Lejo said.

"Thank you. That's helpful." Trueblood pulled at a plait. He had stubbornly slow-growing hair, but his braids finally reached his shoulders now. He'd started tying the front ones behind his head, the way his father had. One or two always fell out and got in his eyes.

"I say business as usual," he said. "We have contracts to honor, cargo is waiting for us and our partners have been incredibly patient and gracious. We take the usual route." His finger touched down on the map spread on the table. "Up to Minosaros. Around Hokosia. Up to Altynai, weather permitting. Then home."

Abrakam nodded agreement. "Will you open the ship to new crew before we leave?"

Trueblood chewed his bottom lip. He'd forgotten the age-old tradition of inviting youngsters to climb the Cay's main mast and, if successful, join the crew.

"I'm leaning toward no," he said. "Not this year. First, we're still learning to safely handle the rigging. Second, to have a guarding kheiron for the climbers is insensitive to our guest." He held up the finger that bore Fen's ring and raised his eyebrows. "Am I right?"

"For sure," Raj said.

"Agreed," Lejo said.

"Don't kiss my ass," Trueblood said. "If I'm wrong, say so."

"It's fine to be wrong," Lejo said. "Just never be in doubt."

"Will you be keeping the Minosaros leg to just Zeuxis?" Abrakam asked.

"Yes," Trueblood said.

The centaur grunted.

"What's on your mind, Abe?"

Abrakam set a finger on the city of Aybar. "You have other cargo you could pick up here," he said, his gaze intent on Trueblood.

The gaze traveled around the circle, thoughts of the last cache of Nye within each pair of eyes.

"I'll fetch that cargo when Nyland asks me to," Trueblood said. "Let me get one voyage under my belt and see what happens with the kheiron."

"Fair enough, lad."

"It's a month to Zeuxis. I and Fen could end up killing each other before we even get there."

"Or bedding each other," Raj said.

Trueblood turned to Abrakam. "When was the last time a mariner keel-hauled one of his crew?"

The centaur pulled his beard gravely. "I'd have to look it up, lad."

"Please do."

THE DAY THEY set sail, Trueblood could taste Fen's fear.

The kheiron feared the open water. The ship itself. The motion. The unknown and the memory.

All who sailed feared these things. They'd be unwise not to.

But what Fen feared most, Trueblood realized, was having to walk aboard the ship.

In front of the gathered multitudes, including his charm and his father, the queen and her vicreĝos, Fen il-Kheir would walk in humos to board the Kaleuche.

"I have an idea," Trueblood said to Abrakam. "If you're willing."

The crew had all boarded. Fen stood with his charm, a casual shoulder leaning into a stack of crates and his body held stiller than a statue. He'd dressed in the whites of the Kaleuche without protest and his calves were shod in new black boots. Hands thrust in the pockets of his breeches and chin lifted, he was splendid.

And scared shitless.

A cheer went up and the throng parted, letting Abrakam through. Trueblood rode on the centaur's back, hands resting easy on his thighs, or reaching down to touch hands of children and women. Abrakam made his easy way through the crowd to where the Finches gathered around their leader.

"Will you honor me by riding, Feños?" the centaur asked.

Fen blinked slowly. His deep blue gaze swiveled to Trueblood, who inched forward on Abrakam's broad back, then looked away to wave at the cheering citizenry of Valtourel.

"The honor is mine," Fen said quietly. He turned one last time to his flock, offering gelango and pressing his brow to theirs. Abrakam took that time to tuck three of his legs beneath him and brake one foreleg on its hoof. Now Fen had only to take two steps, which were disguised by the length and breadth of the centaur. He put a hand on Trueblood's shoulder and swung a leg over.

"Thank you," he said gruffly.

"Smile, for fuck's sake," Trueblood said through his grinning teeth. "No one will notice your legs if you get that pissy look off your face."

Fen closed a quick hand around Trueblood's coat as Abrakam rocked up to four hooves. "You know, I shit on your feet once. I'll do it again."

"I laughed it off once. I'll do it again."

So Pelippé Trueblood Cay and Fen il-Kheir boarded the Kaleuche as equals, riding on the back of Abrakam Centauros.

The mariner wasn't certain all the ill-will was left behind on the wharf, but whatever came onboard was wrapped in the cloak of one shitty joke, cushioning the sharpest edges.

It was the best job he could do.

The Motion That Bothers You

THE IMMENSITY OF the Kaleuche made Fen dizzy.

"I know giants built it," he said to Abrakam. "But it's so… big."

Every word he knew for big, plus the words than meant bigger than big, all shook their heads and declared they weren't up to the task of describing the Kaleuche.

Gazing up at the main mast, wider around than the arms of five men could reach and stretching to the sky until it blurred, Fen felt a little sick. Thinking of the impending launch, that horrible rock, roll, pitch and yaw, the sickness swelled into a panic.

I can't do this. Within his skull, the frantic thought ran around in circles, clawing at the walls and banging fists on closed doors. Ready to chew a limb off to get out of the trap.

I can't do this. Not again. I can't. I swore never again. Don't make me do this.

Abrakam put a hand on Fen's shoulder. "Feños, may I speak frankly?"

Fen clenched his teeth and nodded.

"I'll never know half of what you suffered when you were a foalboy," Abrakam said. "But I do know some of it took place on a ship."

Fen bit the inside of his lower lip to keep the nausea back. He nodded again.

"Nobody wants you to suffer," the centaur said. "Not I, not the kepten, not the crew."

Fen tried a shaking breath. Then another. He had no reason to doubt the centaur's word, but all he could believe was the dark, filthy hold where he'd been chained up with hundreds of others. The constant up and down, side to side movement filling the cramped space with screaming and vomit and shit and more screaming.

Until it filled with dead bodies.

He still had time to make a run for it. Trueblood could keep the fucking ring and Fen could throw himself over the side. Swim to shore and screw the consequences.

"The kepten doesn't want you to suffer," Abrakam said. "But he won't be able to prevent your suffering if he doesn't know what's causing it."

"Pardon us," a crew member said, approaching the main mast. He and a mate both wore a harness of straps around their waist and legs and had massive coils of rope criss-crossed on their chests. Fen backed away, bumping into Abrakam and nearly toppling onto his ass. He stared, open mouthed as the two sailors hooked their harnesses onto the rigging and began to shimmy up the impossible vertical danger.

I wouldn't be afraid to fly up there, he thought. *Why can't I stand to…stand and look up there?*

Because I fly no more.

And neither do they.

"They're crazy," he whispered, shielding his eyes to follow the ascent.

Abrakam chuckled. "Many are called to sail on the giant-ships," he said. "But only those who prove they can handle its size are chosen. So." He patted Fen's wingless back. "You weren't chosen, but you were called. Let's find the kepten and find your place onboard."

As Fen followed Abrakam toward the back of the ship, a little bird swooped in circles around their heads.

"Good morning, my beauty," Abrakam said. "Yes, I see you. You're lovely. Out of the way, please." He looked back at Fen. "We seem to have acquired a mascot."

"She's a lark," Fen said.

"Lejo believes it's a sign. She's the newborn soul of the Kaleuche." The centaur chuckled. "If you ask me, Lejo's just thrilled to finally have a pet of some kind."

The lark landed on Abrakam's withers and tilted her head at Fen, her expression curious.

One wonders why you are not happy. One cannot be happy until you are. Please be happy.

"I'll work on it," Fen mumbled.

They found Trueblood in his study, writing in a large notebook.

"Kepten, our friend is not enamored of sea voyages," Abrakam said. "Where's the best place for him to sleep?"

Trueblood looked up, blinking a moment, as if he forgot who Abrakam was. His mouth set in a straight, tired line as he marked his place with a small white feather and closed the book. "Come with me," he said.

Fen followed the mariner on deck, straight into the lark's aerial antics again.

"Khe l'khe," Trueblood said. "You have a whole sky to fly in. Get out of my way."

Fen dodged the enthusiastic bird and skirted the flurry of furious activity as they made their way below.

"Is it the motion that bothers you?" Trueblood asked.

"A little," Fen said.

Trueblood stopped on a tread. "A little or a lot?" he asked, not looking back. "Plenty of the crew get seasick, even I do. You won't be thought less of or made fun of. Not on my ship. Just say what it is."

"A lot," Fen said.

"All right then." Trueblood set off again at a brisk pace, leading them down further and further into the belly of the vessel. "You'll want to be below the waterline and near the center of the ship. Next to the main mast is the most stable place. Problem is…" He opened a door to a cabin. The light from the corridor revealed a trim, neat room with a bed, chest of drawers, a small desk and a chair. "You have no window," Trueblood said. "So it's dark and it can feel tight and closed-in. Some sailors like that. Others not so much."

Or not at all, Fen thought.

Trueblood looked back at him. His eyes were shadowed, but direct. "You?"

Every cell in Fen's body screamed *No* as he stepped into the dim cabin and pretended to take an appraising look around. "Well, I…" His hands closed over the chair back as he cleared his throat. "The dark kind of bothers me, too."

Trueblood's gaze fell on the white, strained clench of nine knuckles. "I see."

Fen let go and put his hands behind his back. Already the walls were inching closer to him. Breathing on him. In the dark, it would only get worse. Too small and tight and filled with vomit and screaming and dead bodies, all of it heaving and rolling in the pitch black…

"How long were you on the slave ship?" Trueblood said, pulling the corner of a pillow straight.

Fen pried his tongue from the dry roof of his mouth. "Month."

"And they had you down in the hold." His voice was extraordinary around the words. Factual. Dry. Yet wrapping them in silken respect. Honoring the horrible ordeal in the spaces between.

Fen drew his breath in and let forth a confession. "I've been afraid of the dark since."

Trueblood nodded, tight-mouthed again. "Then we won't have you sleep here."

Like many Alondrans, Trueblood sometimes tacked a tiny, breathy E before words that started with S. *We won't have you esleep here.*

"Come on," he said. "Let's see where we can put you."

We, Fen thought, following him out.

Filled With Silver in the Dark

Valtourel and Zeuxis lay two thumb widths apart on a map. What looked like a week's journey would take a month.

"A month?" Fen said, blanching. It was as long as he'd been on the slave ship.

"Where the North Channel meets the Gulf is a graveyard," Abrakam said. "Full of shoals and rock formations and undertows. Sailors say whatever gets chewed up in the Teeth is swallowed by the Gullet and spit out between Sanpago and Nyland."

"In other words, the Channel is the asshole of the ocean?"

The centaur's laugh bellowed across the decks. "Well-played, lad. Indeed it is. Passage straight across is too dangerous. Instead, Trueblood will sail toward Pellandro, hug the edges of the Gulf and come into Zeuxis from the Northwest."

The geography lesson was lost on the miserable kheiron. He was sure he'd be dead of seasickness before they reached Zeuxis. In his first week, he slept in four different cabins, trying to acclimate to the ship. Nobody made fun of him. In fact, everyone did their best to be helpful.

"Try sleeping on the floor," one sailor said. "You'll feel the roll less."

"Keep the curtains drawn," another said. "You want the light to come in but you don't want to see the horizon going up and down out the window. That'll make you puke like nobody's business."

"Always puke on the leeward side," a minoro named Melki said. He took a green-faced Fen by the hand and led him to the opposite side of the ship. "Upchucking into the wind only makes you twice as miserable."

Miserable had a new definition and Fen wouldn't have been surprised if he saw his boots tumbling out of his mouth and falling over the lee side. He was going to put a permanent dent in the rail from leaning his arms on it, trying to hang onto his stomach.

"Here," someone said, handing him a cloth bag filled with squares of ginger root dusted with sugar. "Keep one of those tucked in your cheek."

"Here." Another bag was pressed in his hand. "Preserved lemon peel. The sour keeps your mouth wet."

"Mint leaves. Here. Chew on these after you eat."

"No, chew them before."

"Both. Before and after."

"Drink, lad. Even if you can't get a morsel in your stomach, keep drinking water. You're better off pissing all the time than barfing."

"Barf off the lee side," Melki reminded him.

Fen tried anything anyone suggested. He chewed the mint leaves before attempting to eat, and afterward, but nothing stayed down. He was sick day after interminable day and sick long into the night. He kept drinking. Cold water, warm water and hot water. Water poured over the mint leaves, or steeped with the lemon peel. Or the ginger. Or both. If someone suggested drinking tepid piss, he'd stand outside the privy stalls with a cup, soliciting donations.

What if I die?

The foreboding thought was soon followed by a worse one.

What if I don't die?

"Fen, come with me," Trueblood said. It was the evening of a particularly crippling day and Fen was starting to wish he were dead. His head floated far above his body and Death's presence trudged behind as he followed Trueblood to the aftercastle. They passed the lark, who perched upside down on the mizzenmast, industriously pecking at it.

"*Ŝuo*," Trueblood said, flicking his hand at her. "Shoo. Quit poking holes in my ship."

She ignored him.

They went through the small foyer into the grand sitting room with its giant-sized chairs and couches. Fen knew the crew gathered here each evening to tell stories. He hadn't attended because he was always busy puking.

Trueblood's study was at the rear. It glowed honey-warm with polished wood and a dark orange rug. A large desk with cubbies to keep objects and instruments from rolling away. A rack of charts. A separate table with two chairs, where the Ĝemelos sat waiting.

"You look like shit, my friend," Raj said, not unkindly.

"I look better than I feel."

"Sit down," Lejo said, getting up.

"If you don't mind, I'm less nauseous on my feet."

"Stand then," Raj and Trueblood said together.

"I'd hate to ruin your nice rug."

"Have you gotten one decent night's sleep since we left Valtourel?" Trueblood said.

"No."

"You need to," Raj said.

"Here are the options," Lejo said.

Trueblood crossed his arms. "We have fadara on the ship. It's—"

"Illegal," Fen said.

"Yes." The kepten glanced at the twins before looking at Fen again. "The Altyns gave it to us. Or rather, they gave it to my father when he rescued you." Trueblood smiled. "In a manner of speaking, it belongs to you."

"Oh," Fen said, not knowing what else to think.

"It's kept locked up and for obvious reasons, it's not administered without consent."

Fen drew a shaky breath. "Did they actually give me fadara on the Cay? Or they had it just in case?"

"My father gave you one bead while you were still up in the tree," Trueblood said. "I don't know if that was the only dose."

"Well, this is the first I'm learning of it. So for the record, I didn't give consent."

"This is true," the kepten said.

"But I was dying and none of you were born and I'm grateful. So it's a moot point."

"Not really," Trueblood said. "The record should reflect what happened."

"I don't consent now," Fen said. "It's tempting as fuck, but I've seen the addiction first-hand. And the withdrawal. No thank you."

Remembering those wretched addicts in Arcodolori made the gorge rise up in his throat. Death chuckled at the back of his neck, a gang of Fen's worst nightmares laughing along.

Make this easy. Just come with us. No more suffering. You'll love it.

"So, the alternative," Trueblood said. He pushed a paper-wrapped object toward the center of the table. "This is kyrrh. Also given to you by the Altyns. Typically you don't ingest it. It's a salve for gashes and burns. Or grotesquely broken bones."

"Take a bow, Fen il-Kheir," Raj said.

"After projectile vomiting, broken bones are my specialty." Fen didn't know how he was making jokes right now, but it seemed to have something to do with Trueblood smiling at them.

"When the three of us were sick," Raj said, "Abrakam shaved kyrrh into a nychet and made a tea out of it. Seemed to help us."

"The point is it certainly didn't hurt," Lejo said.

"It might do something for the seasickness," Raj said. "Or it might not. It could help you sleep, or not. But unlike fadara, it's not going to fuck your life. Best case you feel better. Worst case you feel the same."

"It's up to you," Trueblood said. "You've tried all the tricks and home remedies. This is what we have left."

"I'll try it," Fen said. "Thank you. For offering and for asking my consent."

"I'll put the kettle on," Raj said, getting up.

Trueblood went to his desk. "While the water's heating up, I have one last trick." He came back with a length of linen bandage and a small stone. He pressed it below the heel of Fen's fourhand and wrapped the cloth around and around to hold it there.

"What's this do?" Fen said.

"I'm not sure what it does or how it works, but sometimes the pressure on the inside of your wrist takes the edge off seasickness. Sometimes. No guarantees."

"I'll cut my nose off if it helps."

"Well, don't do that," the kepten said softly. "It's a nice nose."

It is? Fen thought. A sudden desire to shift into equos flickered through his soul, but of course without his moonstone, it had nowhere to go. It simply choked and died.

And it hurt.

When Trueblood was finished, Fen obediently held out his fivehand. The moons of his fingernails were blue-gray. He was so cold inside his skin. Ice in his bones and in his heart and stomach.

"Too tight?" Trueblood said, his touch deft and gentle.

"No."

"Come here, Fen," Raj called. Crouched by the hearth, he swung the hook back from the embers, wrapped a cloth around the handle of the kettle and poured hot water into a large mug.

Fen sank into a corner of the large couch, tired to the point of slight psychosis and his pride in shreds. Death took a step back but left his malevolent offer on the table.

I could make this go away. Come with me and it will all be over.

Fen's teeth chattered on the rim of the cup. A warm swallow, bitter at first and then a sweet aftertaste and a lingering heat in the corners of his mouth. His trembling stomach wrapped curiously around it, then asked for more. He took another sip, closing his eyes as the tea slid down his throat.

I want to go home, he thought. He was twelve again. Chained up in the dark hold, being taken farther and farther from his home, his people, his land and his father.

He'll take the world apart to find me.

He'll find me and then he'll kill you.

You'll beg my father for mercy when he gets his hands on you...

"Drink it all," Trueblood said, in a father's firm tone.

"I don't want to dream."

"You won't. I give my word."

But words were so easily given and taken back. The proof was on Fen's face. In the healing gash of his eyebrow where his moonstone once hung. More proof in the smooth, whitened skin of his thumb where his ringos should've been. It shone on Trueblood's index finger now. He sat opposite Fen, leaning forward with his forearms on his knees, hands interlaced, the silver horse head peeking from between.

Give it back to me, Fen thought. *Let me fly from here. I'm begging for mercy, put your hands on me and give me back what I left in the dark...*

"I think he's nodding," Trueblood said from far away.

A second voice murmured from even further off. "We'll carry him down?"

"No, leave him be. If sleep finds him here, let him stay."

He'll find me, Fen thought, drifting. *He'll take the world apart and beg me for mercy when his hands find me all filled with silver in the dark...*

...In the dark...

...All filled with silver...

...His hands will find me...

HIS BROTHER'S HEART

H E WOKE.

The great sitting room of the aftercastle was empty and dark. A tiny lamp burned on the table by the long couch where Fen lay, covered with a quilt.

Did I find me? he thought stupidly.

Beneath the quilt, his body was warm and relaxed. His stomach smooth and his chest wide-open for air to pass through unobstructed.

I found it.

He folded back the blanket and sat up carefully. A little light-headed but the crippling nausea was gone. Or it was still asleep. He noticed the mug on the table, covered with a small plate. A note lay on the plate, in beautiful, precise penmanship:

Drink the rest if you wake up. Even if it's cold. Sleep here if it's comfortable. Amatos.

—Kpt. P.T. Cay

Fen didn't drink yet. He got up and walked around, holding onto the backs of chairs and the edges of tables until the stiffness was out of his legs. He peeked through the half-open door to the kepten's bedroom. It was empty, the giant bed still crisply made. Not even a dent in the blankets.

Is he still awake?

He left the aftercastle, stepping onto the deck and drawing the cold, taut air into his body. He remembered to judge the wind and pick the leeward side to take a long, vigorous piss, one hand on the railing and the other aiming carefully. His stride was a little more confident as he walked the length of the Kaleuche. As the deck leaned and draped beneath his feet, his stomach adjusted. He played with the newborn courage to lean into the motion instead of fighting it.

I'm getting better at this.

The silence of the night was magical. He passed a few crew members on night watch, who only smiled or nodded, unwilling to break the holy quiet.

Fen was almost sorry to go back within, but he was cold now, and the cold was waking up the nausea again. He needed to drink the rest of the tea.

He walked around the aftercastle with his mug, looking at things. Two bedrooms lay within the foyer. Abrakam's on one side, its door firmly closed. The other belonged to the Ĝemelos. This door stood ajar and Fen, being human, peeked inside.

All the beds on the Kaleuche were big. Some minoros could comfortably sleep feet-to-feet along their length. The twins' room had two beds. One was empty. In the other, Raj sprawled on his back. Trueblood lay beside, arms crossed over his middle and forehead pressed to Raj's shoulder. Lejo curled against Trueblood's back, his arm slung across the mariner's waist and his hand on his brother's heart.

Three chests expanded and contracted in unison, perfectly timed with the rise and fall of the ship beneath Fen's feet.

It was a painfully intimate scene. Flirting with the boundary of something sexual. But all three men were clothed. The door was open. They weren't hiding. Their sleep was blameless.

Pelippé Trueblood sighed in his dreams.

Easy is your middle name, Fen thought. *Your mother died but you had the arms of your father. Your father died but your crew is your family. Raj and Lejo would kill for you. Naria toyed with your desire and I bet she feels like shit about it. Even if you were nothing but a job to Belmiro, I bet he misses you.*

Going below to his cabin, the kheiron wondered, *Who misses me?*

His charm? Sure. Sitting around in humos, hobbled and wing-clipped. Both missing and resenting him.

His father? Imagining Sevri looking out a window of the pavilion and wondering about Fen was something from a child's storybook. Idealistic and beautiful, but fiction.

He sat on his long bed, staring at the smooth pillow. Remembering apples once left for him by a slim, red-haired queen in an embroidered dress of green velvet.

"Feños," Noë Treeblood said. *"You're home. We missed you."*

He gulped down the last bit of kyrrh tea. It was stone-cold and bitter but he needed every drop of its oblivion.

WHERE I CAN'T FIND YOU

FEN'S SHAKY CONSTITUTION finally picked a cabin it could tolerate. The hunk of precious kyrrh now lived on his little bedside table.

"It's yours," Trueblood said when the kheiron protested. "The Altyns gave it to you. Besides, a little goes a long way."

This was true. You didn't cut kyrrh with a knife, you shaved it with a razor. Fen experimented and found a flake in a mug of hot water, first thing in the morning, got him through the day. So did rubbing a bit of the resin beneath the heels of his hands, then binding the little stones tight to his wrists. Repeating the remedies at night allowed him a thin but restful sleep.

He would never like being at sea. He gradually got used to the rise and fall of the horizon before him but it was never *pleasant*. As he felt better, his eyes opened to the ship and saw she was magnificent. From the Tree of Life motifs carved on her doors to the star finials on every curtain rod. The choreography of sailing had a majestic beauty. The crew worked as seamlessly as any kheiron legion. Discipline was tight and Fen admired Lejo's handling of the minoros. These under-sixteens were a rambunctious but lovable gang. Especially Melki, who appointed himself Fen's aide-de-camp and brought a mug of hot water to his cabin every morning and evening.

Stomach primed with kyrrh, Fen joined the crew in their daily workout—a torturous circuit around the ship that would've made Sevri il-Kheir's eyes glitter.

Fen held even in upper body strength, but his legs weren't up for sprinting the Kaleuche's miles of stairwells. Yet. His pride set its teeth and narrowed its gaze on the sailor called Sixten. That lad was *fast*. He was the guy to beat.

Walking the Kaleuche from top to bottom was an arduous journey, both physically and mentally. By the time Fen made his way down to the ship's lowest level and did his self-assigned laps up and down the keel line, he forgot the way back to the top.

Lost for the umpteenth time, he asked a minoro which way to go.

"It's quickest if you take the shortcut through this hold," the boy said. "Straight through, out the other side and you'll see a staircase. It'll take you to the half-deck, then you can take the starboard stairs to the weatherdeck."

"Starboard is left?"

"Right."

"Got it. What's your name again?"

"Niro." He headed off, calling back over his shoulder, "Straight through the hold and up."

"What do you think you're doing?" a voice called out. So authoritative and commanding, Fen whipped around and nearly saluted.

Trueblood?

He'd only seen the mariner this angry twice before—once in the grotto when he threw a rock at Fen, and then in the crypt when he threw an apple. Now the formidable Kepten Trueblood came striding down the long corridor, throwing each leg out from the hip. Eating up the length of the ship in four loping steps, reminding Fen this was a man descended from giants.

"What did you just tell him?" Trueblood said, walking straight past Fen and backing Niro against the wall.

"The way to go, Kep."

"Which way?"

Niro gulped. "D-down there, around and up the—"

"Don't lie to me."

The boy balked, as if to make a run for it. Trueblood was faster.

"No, you don't. Hold still. Look me in the eye. Which way did you tell him to go?"

"I forgot, Kep. Honest, I forgot."

"Which way?"

Fen's insides caved in, as if under the weight of the dressing-down. "Kepten, it's all right, he just—"

Without turning around, Trueblood held up a silencing hand and Fen's voice backed off.

"Answer your commander."

"I told him to go through the hold," Niro said between gulping breaths.

"And then you walked away."

Niro was crying now. "Aye, Kep."

"What's the rule about that? Look at me."

"You don't cut through the holds alone. You make sure someone sees you come out the other side."

"Why?"

"Be… Because… I forgot."

"We're in the Gullet. What's it full of?"

"Rogue waves, Kep."

"And what can happen when the ship catches a rogue wave?"

"The hold doors can slide shut and bolt from the outside."

"And if you're in there alone?"

"No one would know."

Trueblood crossed his arms. "I thought you forgot."

"Kep, I'm sorry. I didn't…" Niro bit his lip, balled his fists and stared down at his boots.

"You did. Go wait in my study."

The boy's answer was practically invisible. "Aye, Kep."

Only when the sound of his footsteps faded off did Fen speak. "I'm sorry."

"You did nothing wrong."

"What will you do to him?"

"Refresh his memory." A wry smile played around his mouth. "Second hiding I've doled out this week. My command lasted all of a month before I had to start thrashing people. I don't know if that's good or bad."

"You don't have to," Fen said.

Trueblood sucked his teeth and the smile faded. "What did you do when one of your charm disobeyed an order? Give them sweets?"

Fen felt his temper flare. "My finches don't disobey orders."

"Because you recruit them right out of the legions," Trueblood said. "You get them pre-disciplined. I'm training boys, and if I don't discipline the little things, I can't control the big things. This was a little thing that could've been a big problem."

"Why?"

"Because you were about to walk through the longest hold in the ship on rough seas," Trueblood said, his voice rising. "Trapped inside is the last fucking place I want you. I've got eight thousand things to do and it might be hours before anyone noticed you were missing. Another couple hours before I could find you."

He stopped, his expression confused, as if the words had leaped out without permission. He shook his head hard. "The rule is, don't cut through the holds unless someone can watch you out the other side. Especially on the rough seas. Do you understand?"

Fen flicked his eyes to the ceiling and muttered, "Aye, Kep." He was half a head shorter than Trueblood, but he wouldn't be talked down to. He'd been liberating slave markets in Sanpago before this wharf rat was out of diapers.

The rat stepped closer, his gaze dangerously benign. "I don't consider you a friend, but I wouldn't wish what happened to you on my worst enemy. And if you were trapped somewhere onboard, I'd take the ship apart to find you."

"Is this where I give thanks?"

"I don't want your thanks but I want it clear. You can mouth off when it's just I and you alone, but don't ever disrespect me in front of my crew. I know where to put your not-so-finest moments."

Teeth set tight and eyes narrowed, Fen raised and lowered his chin a hair.

"Now if you'll excuse me, I have to hand someone their ass." Trueblood took only a few steps before turning back. "And one other thing you need to get straight. Starboard is right. *Port* is left."

"Right."

Shaking his head again, Trueblood walked off.

FEN'S BATTLE WITH seasickness made remembering windward and leeward easy. Other terms went in his port ear and out the starboard. Every shipboard direction had its own name and gods-damn, sailors were *touchy* about their correct usage. Forward was toward the bow. Aft meant toward the stern. You didn't go downstairs, you went below deck. The sails and rigging weren't up there, they were aloft. Sailors under the age of sixteen were called minoros. Those sixteen to twenty-one were majoros. At twenty-one, you became maristo—a mariner.

A few specialized roles had their own giantword title. Calvo, for example, was kvartermastisto, the quartermaster. Young Sixten was the ŝnuromastisto, the rope master.

"Ŝnuromastisto," Fen said, laughing. "Sounds like you're in charge of sneering."

"I prefer master of snoring," Sixten said. "After rope, I'm an expert sleeper."

The sailors fell into bed at night. The days started early and were crammed with work. Fen learned the Kaleuche ran so efficiently because her crew was given a *ripozo,* an hour's rest after midday dinner. Sometimes two hours after a particularly arduous morning, or if the crew were being rewarded. If the crew fucked up, ripozo was forfeited. Those were bad days.

In good weather, the sailors rested on deck. In rain or cold, cabin doors closed, or crew ambled into the aftercastle to grab a chair in the great sitting room.

The literacy onboard astounded Fen. The majority of crew could read and write, or were learning how. Books were everywhere on the ship and the evening story hour was the highlight of the long day.

While the shelves in Abrakam's cabin appealed to Fen, his stomach wasn't a fan of reading at sea. He spent the ripozo doing nothing, off in one of the little secret places on the ship he was staking out. He took some bits of stale bread and fed the lark, trying to get her to eat from his hand, the way Lejo could. She'd come close to Fen to peck at the crumbs, but shied away from his extended fingers.

His hideouts never stayed secret long.

"Here you are," Trueblood said, out of nowhere, making Fen jump in his skin.

"Shit," he said, breadcrumbs flying out of his hand.

"Sorry."

"You're always sneaking up on me."

"I don't sneak." Trueblood waved an irritated hand at the lark, who was pecking at the wall. "Héjo, knock off putting holes in my ship. Ŝuo. Go see Fen, he has food."

The bird flew out of his range and landed on the toe of Fen's boot. He brushed the crumbs off his shirt toward her. "What do you want?"

"Me or the bird?"

"You."

"Nothing."

"Well, do you mind?"

"What?"

"Every time I go somewhere to be alone, you turn up."

Trueblood leaned down a little. "Kheiron, there's nowhere on this ship you can hide where I won't find you."

Fen stared back a long moment. "Challenge accepted."

The game was on and soon it was the entire crew versus the kepten, as everyone tipped Fen off to good hiding places. When the kheiron vanished at ripozo, every sailor went mum and Trueblood was on his own to track Fen down.

He never failed.

"Fuck you," Fen muttered when Trueblood peeked around the foremast.

"You suck," when he was located behind the rain barrels.

"Come *on*, man," he said, laughing as Trueblood pulled him out of a longboat.

The kepten admitted Fen had stealth and declared the contest a draw. When the novelty wore off, Fen continued to seek out his favorite hideaways during ripozo. Engrossed and anticipatory, he fed the lark or the gulls, always listening for the distinctive cadence of boots on the decking and a three-word greeting.

"Here you are."

You found me, Fen thought.

One Word and Its Sequel

Trueblood took the helm to bring the Kaleuche into port at Zeuxis. The harbor was deep enough to accommodate her hull, but navigating the rocky shoreline was tricky. If something went wrong, the responsibility lay with the kepten.

This, Fen learned, was the True Way.

"The place has vastly improved since we were kids," Raj said.

"You should've seen it when I was a kid," Fen said.

Lejo Ĝemelos could pack a novel into one word and its sequel into his eyes. He glanced at Fen and said, "Here?"

His expression went on to ask, *This is the place you were brought to by slave ship when you were a foalboy of twelve? This is the place you were sold?*

Fen nodded. "Here."

The city, once a mangy feral den of drugs, prostitution and slavery, now hummed with industry, law and order. She proudly wore her seal as the administrative seat of Sanpago, the region annexed by Nyland after Tehvan's War. She had no elected vicreĝo yet, but one day, one of their burgeoning Council of Mothers would have a throne in the great hall at Valtourel.

Raj chuckled under his breath. "Remember the breakneck schedule we'd have here?"

"It's kind of unforgettable," Trueblood said. To Fen, he continued, "My father got in and out as fast as humanly possible. The minoros were curfewed to the teeth. Everyone hauled ass offloading and loading cargo, racing against the tide."

"Calvo was especially enchanting in Zeuxis," Raj said.

"What do you mean, was?" Trueblood said. "Bit of advice, Fen: stay out of the quartermaster's way today."

"I do that every day, but thanks. What's the curfew situation like now?"

"Minoros need to be accompanied. Majoros are free to come and go but all the same, sticking with a mate isn't a bad idea."

Fen hesitated. "I have one or two things to do in the city, and…" He trailed off because Trueblood was looking like Fen announced he had an orgy to attend. "What are you staring at?"

The kepten shook his head. "Nothing."

"Anyway, I'll be going alone."

"Suit yourself."

A beat of silence where Fen felt more explanation was needed. Trueblood had a funny little habit of looking for him and the convoluted streets of Zeuxis were a far cry from the ship's bolt holes.

"I'm going to the orphanage west of the marketplace," he said. "It's the safe house my charm used when we went on raids. Since I'm here, I'd like to say hello to some people, see the children and explain what's happening."

"For sure." The kepten's expression was narrow and intent as they approached the harbor, the spin of the wheel in his large hands deft and confident.

"So that's where I'll be."

"All right."

Feeling dismissed, Fen turned to go. He was halfway down the stairs of the afterdeck when the kepten called to him.

"Héjo, Fen, one thing? You've been at sea a month. It'll feel strange walking on land. If you keep stumbling for no reason, or it seems like the ground is moving, that's normal."

"Thanks."

"Stupid question, but do you have a knife or something?"

"Two."

"Good. Your boots have an inside sheath for blades."

"How handy."

Trueblood smiled, eclipsing the sun. "We think of everything."

THE GROUND WAS not only *moving*, it seemed to deliberately dodge Fen's footsteps. He cursed under his breath as he stumbled for the third time, colliding with a cheerful cheese vendor.

"Héjo, sailor," she said, laughing and shoving him off her. "Bring me flowers first."

He made it to the orphanage without falling on his face, barely. In the scrap of muddy grass, a giantsblood romped with a half-dozen children hanging from his limbs.

"Feños," he bellowed. "Save me."

Fen grinned. "You're on your own, Boru."

The giant planted a foot and dragged his other leg with its two clutching passengers. Step and drag, step and drag to the gate, where he thrust an immense hand toward Fen. "Salu, salu, my one."

Unlike Trueblood's neat plaits, Boru's hair had been left alone to wind into rough, tangled ropes that reached the backs of his knees. His gold eyes were streaked with black and their tiger-like gaze swept from Fen's head to his boots.

"This is a new look for you," he finally said.

"It's a long sad story," Fen said. "And don't you have enough of those here?"

Boru freed a hand to flip the gate's latch. "You're always beautiful to me, kheiron. Come in, come in."

More of the orphanage's staff were traipsing out the front doors, calling Fen's name. A mixed bag of men, centaurs and giantsbled, they'd started the operation with a single tent and built it into a sprawling, two-story haven. Fen shook hands and let his cheeks be kissed silly, glad to see his constituents but saddened to note familiar faces in the crowd of children. Some of them were rescued by his charm years ago, yet they were still here. No family to contact, connect or claim them.

The laughing chatter faded to the edges of Fen's mind. Through the middle, Alon fell away from him, down into the gnarled, bony hands of the dead Nye trees.

What if they don't want me anymore?

Fen shook his head hard and now his gaze fell on another familiar face. A little boy far from the crush, sitting alone in the muddy yard.

Instead of falling away, memory now came rushing at Fen like an enraged bull. He'd rescued this lad on the charm's last raid into Arcodolori. Busting through the upstairs window of a brothel, taking part of the wall with him, Fen scared the life out of a customer. Literally. The bastard's throat was slashed before the broken glass stopped tinkling to the floor.

Fen felt nothing as his knife swiped through flesh and veins, leaving death in its wake. Why should he? His next act was to free the child impaled on the dead man's cock. If you could feel that and not lose your sanity, a severed jugular was nothing.

He swallowed hard and approached the boy on careful feet, stumbling once as the ground shifted.

"Not a word out of him all this time," Boru said, trailing behind. "Not even his name. We put down Sennoma in the register and it's stuck."

Sennoma—*no name.*

"Héjo," Fen said gently, stopping several feet away. The youngster kept his eyes on the ground where he was drawing circles with a stick.

"Functional catatonia is the only way I can describe it," Boru said. "He's here. He's present. He understands. But his mind is somewhere far, far away. No social engagement. He doesn't connect."

Fen crouched down on his heels, tilting his head to get under Sennoma's thousand-mile gaze. "Salu," he said. "Do you remember me?"

Sennoma looked up, then down again. With no more interest than if Fen were a rock.

"You came flying with me. You rode on my back. But I had four legs then."

He closed his ringless thumb within a fist. If he could release his wings, maybe it would trigger the boy's memory. Then again, maybe all memory of that day was better off where it was. Far away and forgotten.

Godsdamn this fucking place.

"It's good to see you, lad." he said. "I think about you all the time. I didn't forget."

Sennoma's stick drew another circle in the dirt. Fen got up slowly, backing away with no sudden movements.

"You tried," Boru said.

Sighing, Fen turned around. "He's safe. I guess you can't ask for m—"

The breath exploded out of him as Sennoma crashed into his back. "What the...?" His knees buckled and his arms flew out for balance as the boy skittered around him and reached for Fen's hands. Huge blue eyes looked wildly at his rings.

"It's me," Fen said, wiggling them. "You remember these?"

His hands were flung away and now the boy was behind him again, digging under Fen's shirt.

"I think he remembers," Boru said.

"Héjo," Fen said, laughing as he peered over his shoulder. "Yes, it's me."

Sennoma patted his palms against Fen's back over and over. Pointed at the sky and patted him again, harder now.

"No, they're put away," Fen said. "I'm sorry, I don't have them right now. They're... No, don't cry. It's all right."

The boy was slapping Fen's legs, tugging at the fabric of his breeches and kicking the toes of his black boots. Pointing to the sky, over and over. *Up, let's go, let's get out of here, what are you waiting for?*

"I can't," Fen said. "I'm sorry, I'm...different now. I won't be able to fly for a little while."

Sennoma flung himself into Fen's arms and Fen picked him up. Draped on Fen's shoulder, he kept hitting Fen's back and pointing to the sky.

"I know. I want to be up there, too. I'll get them back. I'll take you to fly again, I promise." He set Sennoma down, took the handkerchief Boru passed and wiped the boy's tears. "How about we go for a walk in the meantime? I and you. Walking's good." He glanced at Boru. "Is that all right?"

"I don't know, kheiron. You're awful young." Boru leveled his golden gaze at Sennoma. "Lad, can I count on you to bring Fen back here safe?"

The boy took Fen's hand and nodded vigorously, thin shoulders squaring into a line. They made an odd little couple as they set off for the market: a kheiron still getting his sea legs and a survivor in charge of his return.

ME's Just Saying

"Pé, stop fucking him with your eyes," Raj said.

Trueblood pulled his eyes off Fen and sucked his teeth. "Shut up."

"Are we going to trail him through the market all afternoon? Or meet up and have a drink like civilized people?"

"I'm not trailing him, we just happen to be here at the same time. And he's got a kid with him so the time isn't conducive to drinking."

Shaking his head above a knowing smile, Raj turned back to a vendor's long table, cluttered with old sea instruments, charts and maps.

"Shut up," Trueblood said, moving toward a booth with leather notebooks. His fingers trailed over the soft covers while his eyes followed the kheiron's path. He watched Fen buy squares of sugared ginger here, a bag of preserved lemon peel there. Dried fruit and nuts. At a grain vendor, he bought a couple bags of something and Trueblood made a mental note to tell Calvo that if the kheiron was buying his own foodstuffs, he needed to be reimbursed.

"You going to buy that, dearie?" the vendor said. "Or just make love to it? Me can turn my back if you're shy."

Smiling, Trueblood held out the notebook and asked its price. The Zeuxis market was always entertaining because Gods, they talked so *weird* here. Nobody could say when, how or why the speech pattern developed, but denizens of the city deliberately swapped their subject and object pronouns.

"You want a book that size, Kepten?" the vendor said. "Because me has others, bigger or smaller. Just tell I what you like."

"I like this one," Trueblood said, mindful not to mimic her. "How much?"

"Because it's you, me asks only five khescs."

"Because it's you, I'll give four."

The vendor scowled. "Don't insult I, Kepten. Feel the quality of the leather."

As he haggled, Trueblood's eyes kept track of Fen. He was at a toy booth now, buying something for his companion, a scruffy little boy of perhaps eight or nine. Plainly dressed. Barefoot. Purchases tucked in one thin arm while his other hand stayed firmly in Fen's. Something about those linked hands made Trueblood's chest fill up with longing admiration.

He's good with the young ones, he thought. *More than good. Devoted to them. They're the work he does best.*

"Look, Pé," Lejo said.

Trueblood turned back to see his friend beaming above the stray cat held in his arms.

"Isn't she beautiful?"

"No."

"She's been following me for an hour."

"No."

"Come on, she has no home and I could give her a great life."

"You already have three cats, which is three more than my father allowed you. Say thank you and be happy."

"Pé, who's that with Fen," Raj said.

Trueblood looked toward the toy vendor but Fen and the boy were gone. He followed Raj's pointing finger. Fen was by a produce cart now, talking to a man. Something about the fellow's greasy appearance and tense demeanor made Trueblood abruptly hand over five khesos to the vendor and thank her. "Let's go say hello," he said to the twins.

As they approached, the little boy shrank behind Fen's body, squeezing between the kheiron and the vegetables.

"Héjo, Fen," Raj said, the eternal ambassador. Fearless at joining a crowd, ready with a sunny smile and extended hand. Able to take the social temperature of any situation and act accordingly. "Salu, I'm Raj Ĝemelos."

"This is Penton," Fen said. "An old friend of mine." He looked back at the child who'd practically climbed into a stack of pumpkins to disappear. "That's Sennoma. A newer friend who chooses his acquaintances with caution."

"Nice to meet you," Trueblood said, with a handshake for Penton and a quick smile for the boy. The latter was Lejo's own specialty. He stepped up to the cart to look at the display of fruit, keeping the stray cat at his hip, casual and accessible.

"Me knew your father," Penton said to Trueblood.

"Did you?"

The wiry little man shrugged. "Everyone did. So, Fen, me's got a bit of news about Haize. That is, if me can speak freely in present company."

"Speak away."

"Who's Haize?" Trueblood said.

Fen paused, drawing a deep breath. "My former owner," he finally said. "With whom I have some unfinished business."

"Me hears him is doing business in Aybar now," Penton said. "Built heself a big house in the city and a bigger brothel outside the no-fucking zone." His eyes darted sheepishly to Sennoma. "Excuse my Altynese."

Fen cracked his knuckles one at a time beneath his thumbs. "Who works for him?"

"Officially, about a dozen men and women *work* for he. Him's got his license posted by the door and never gives inspectors a hard time. Still, if you ask I…" Penton turned palms up to the sky and left the question dangling. Something about the gesture was a touch too dramatic. So deliberate, it was a signal. The extended palms trembled in the air, each finger making minute twitches. A small jingle in Fen's pocket and some coins passed.

He's an addict, Trueblood thought. *Between doses. Starting to crave. Soon to slip into unpleasantness. His information comes at a price.*

"If you ask I," Penton said, pocketing the khesos, "the inside dimensions of the brothel don't match the outside."

"Sounds familiar," Trueblood said.

"Pardon?"

"I had the same problem with a hold in my ship. But go on."

"Me's just saying. The building's got enough missing space to conduct some illegal trade. Me has no proof of course, but Haize's reputation does precede he."

"That it does," Fen said.

"So, me doesn't know if you have business in Aybar?"

"We might," Trueblood said, and Fen looked at him.

"We might?"

"Mm." He glanced up at the sun. "Anyway, I'm heading back to the ship now."

"I need to get Sennoma back to the orphanage," Fen said.

"I'll go with you," Lejo said. He had the little boy on his hip and Sennoma's arms were full of the cat.

Hands shook around, and Penton lingered a moment in True-blood's grip.

"I'm sorry about your Da," he said. "He was decent."

The correct pronouns made the simple words sound like a royal commendation. "Thank you," Trueblood said, trying to imagine what kind of precarious existence it took to make bare minimum decency your highest praise.

Penton gave Fen a vigorous back thumping. "When you find Haize, flay that cocksucker alive. Save a piece of his hide for I."

"Me will deliver it personally," Fen said.

"FEN, WHAT WERE you buying at the market?" Trueblood put up a quick hand. "Sorry, that came out wrong. I meant at the granary booth, were you buying something you need to be eating?"

That didn't sound quite right either. Gods, it was like he was thirteen again and the monster was doing the talking.

"Well, yes," Fen said. "I don't eat meat so I get protein from things like farro and amaranth. I was going to show Seven how to make it. Or I could make it myself, if it's too much trouble for him to—"

"He'll make it," Trueblood said. "Just show him. Then go see Calvo and get reimbursed for the cost."

"I don't need to be reimbursed."

"Whenever you buy foodstuffs, you should get a receipt."

"It's not a problem for me to buy my own."

"I know, but you're our guest and feeding you is the ship's responsibility."

"All right."

"I kept my eyes out for kyrrh in the market," Trueblood said. "But I didn't see any."

"Neither did I, but I've got enough to last me a good while. Loaded up on ginger and lemon in the meantime. Oh, and I bought this." Fen fumbled in his pocket and came up with a shark tooth. "For Seven to add to his necklace. A little token to make up for my picky eating."

"He'll love it." Trueblood hesitated, fanning the edges of his new notebook. "Lejo told me about the orphanage. For an hour."

Fen smiled. "He left the cat there."

"I had a feeling he would. Is Sennoma someone you rescued?"

"During our last raid." He exhaled roughly and drummed his fingers on the back of a chair. "Weird mix of feelings whenever I go to visit the kids. If I see a face I recognize, it's both joyful and disappointing. I don't want them to be there anymore."

Trueblood nodded. "Is there anything the orphanage needs?"

"What they don't need is a shorter list."

"Lejo wants to help," Trueblood said. "And so do I. So make the longer list and we'll see what we can do after we leave Aybar."

"Aybar?" Fen said. "We're going?"

"I didn't mention it?"

"Um, no. Why are we going?"

"Three reasons. I have something to fetch and you have unfinished business."

"What's the third reason?"

"Because Lejo said so."

Fen fixed him with a sideways stare. "Lejo."

"Raj is my directional pilot while Lejo is more of a spiritual compass. His needle only points one way, toward the right thing to do. Sometimes it yanks him in that direction, hard enough to pull on me."

His hand rubbed an absent circle around his heart. Even after he said yes, Lejo's insistence was a stubborn drag in his chest. His peripheral hadn't sparkled this furiously since they left Valtourel.

"Interesting," Fen said slowly.

"You can say weird."

Fen laughed. "It is a little weird, Kepten."

"I know. Lejo doesn't often tell me what to do, but when he does, I listen."

A Young Leader

THE KALEUCHE COMMUNICATED with Nyland by messenger bird. Usually falcons, although it was a pure white pigeon that brought the news that their former boatswain had had a baby boy and was naming him Ikharus. Fen watched as the new father, Dhar, first staggered backward and sank onto a bulkhead, weeping into his hands. Then he and Trueblood threw arms around each other, yelling, crowing and laughing. The day's ripozo was extended and that night, Dhar sat next to the kepten at dinner.

Another morning, a raven arrived at the ship, heralding bad news: a majoro's father had died. Everyone went about their business in subdued quiet while the bereaved sailor sat with Trueblood on the afterdeck. For a long time, he talked and the kepten listened. They stood and offered gelango, holding still with their foreheads pressed until the sailor let go. That night, he sat next to the kepten at dinner.

He treats them like family, Fen thought, quietly observing how Trueblood handled the mood of his crew as a whole, as well as the individual caprices and crotchets. Constantly available and approachable without ever letting them take his solicitous nature for granted.

How much of that is him? Fen wondered. *And how much is his training?*

One afternoon, Fen went to the aftercastle to work on the charts. While he tried his hand at all the jobs onboard, assisting the pilot was fast becoming one of his favorites, both the task itself and the company. Raj drew first in pencil and Fen went over with ink. The work was challenging, but incredibly relaxing. They spent long hours at the big round table and sometimes at ripozo, Trueblood sat down with them, writing or sketching in one of his notebooks.

The kepten's study door opened and a red-faced minoro emerged, running the back of his hand across his eyes as he left.

Fen moved toward the doorway. Trueblood was coiling up a length of leather and laying it in a drawer.

"What was that hiding about?" Fen asked.

"None of your business." Trueblood shut the drawer and went to his desk. Gathering some papers into a neat pile, he looked up to see the kheiron studying him.

"What are you staring at?" he said, the little Alondran E sneaking in front of *staring*.

"A very young leader."

The kepten's eyes rolled. "Is it true kheirons age twice as fast as humans?"

"Twice as slow, actually."

"Which makes you, what, sixteen in human years?"

"Can we start over?" Fen said. "What I meant was you handle your crew well."

"Meaning the way you would if one of your pre-disciplined charm got out of line."

So much for starting over, Fen thought. "Well, no," he said. "One of my charm shoots his mouth off to me, he gets a fist in it."

"We do things a little differently at sea."

"Apparently." Fen hesitated, then tilted his head in the direction of the bedroom. "I notice you don't sleep in there."

Trueblood looked up, his brows tight together. "Strange observation."

The heat rose along Fen's neck. "Only because I don't sleep much. And once or twice I've been up. Walking around. And passed by..." Now his head inclined in the direction of the twins' cabin.

Trueblood's forehead went soft and his hand made slow circles on his heart as he weighed his words. "What's between I and the Ĝemelos doesn't have a name," he said. "I've slept in the same room as them since I went to sea. I sleep best between them."

"I don't want you to explain," Fen said, lying.

"You're right, I'm too young to be commanding this ship," the mariner said, as if he hadn't heard. "My father died before he could teach me everything he knows. Half the time I feel like an imposter. A fraud. The other half I'm just making shit up and copying what I remember and pretending I'm him. Pretending this is just temporary and he'll be coming back later."

He got up and walked past Fen, over to the bedroom door where he rested his arm on the jamb. "Lejo says I don't sleep in here because I'm waiting for later. He's right." He dropped his arm and turned around, pulling the door closed. "What I do during the day is what's important. Where I lie down at night is none of anyone's business. This is still my father's bedroom and I don't belong in it. Not yet. Not until…"

"What?"

"Never mind." Trueblood strode briskly back to his desk. He sat, moved the feather marking the page and started to write. "Anyway, was there something you needed?"

"No, I'm waiting for Raj to…" Fen's voice trailed off as he focused in on the feather. Small, crisp and white. He guessed a median covert.

He stepped closer to the desk, knowing it was a median covert.

"Gods, what do you *want*?" Trueblood said.

"Where did you get that?"

"Get what?"

Fen picked up the feather and twirled the thin calamus in his fingers. "This."

"I found it in my coat pocket. Why?"

Fen looked back at the wall hook where the kepten's blue coat hung. "This is mine."

"Pardon?"

"I put this in the… During the vigil for your father, I pulled a feather from my wing and put it in his pocket." He looked back at Trueblood. "I thought he'd be interred in his coat. I assumed yours was a new one they made."

"It's the only one."

"Huh."

A beat of silence. "Do you want it back?" Trueblood asked.

"No. No, it's yours. His. I was just surprised you had it." He put the feather on the desk and backed away. "I'm just waiting for Raj. I'll—"

"You know something?" Trueblood said. "I got no closure with my father's death. I didn't get to take a watch during the vigil or see him interred. One minute I was holding his broken body in my arms, then I woke up and it was weeks later and he was gone. I didn't get any kind of good-bye, I just never saw him again. He…disappeared. You know?"

"I know."

"The same thing happened to him though. With my mother. She disappeared from his life. He said it was the cruelest thing that ever happened to him."

"For sure," Fen said, thinking of his own sire and dam. It was exceedingly difficult to envision Sevri and Zoria as a couple. As lovers. He'd never seen them together, only heard stories.

She disappeared, he thought. *Leaving only me. Dragged out backward. Taking my first steps in her blood…*

Trueblood picked up the feather. "Thank you for this. When I found it in my coat pocket, it seemed random. Kind of odd and mystical, but that was probably me being scared and stupid and looking for signs from the gods. I like knowing you put it there."

"Your father saved my life."

"Your father saved mine." Trueblood twirled the feather until it pointed at Fen. "I'm sure in some cultures, it means we're brothers. But just so we're *crystal* clear, I still hate your guts."

The words smiled at the edges, landing like a friendly punch on Fen's shoulder.

Which was better than a rock thrown at him.

"Feeling's mutual, wharf rat," he said.

"Good. Now get lost, crow bait."

His Most Vulnerable Side

"Fen, you tell a story," Dhar said that evening.

All eyes turned to the kheiron.

"I don't know any stories," Fen said.

"Everyone knows one story," Beniv said.

"It doesn't have to be made up," Melki said. "Tell a true story."

The eyes pressed on Fen, growing hopeful. "Well," he said. "Do you know the legend of the finches?"

A bit of silence and Melki tugged at Fen's breeches. "We do, but you're supposed to pretend we don't."

Fen glanced toward the large couch where Trueblood was sketching in his notebook. Raj and Lejo lounged on either side of him and minoros squeezed in wherever they could, sitting at Trueblood's feet and perched on the arms of the couch. Or standing behind and leaning over his shoulder to watch him draw.

"Niro, if you're going to breathe down my neck, close your mouth," he said.

The boy grinned.

Unbelievable, Fen thought. *The other day, Trueblood thrashed his bare ass for giving me wrong directions. Tonight, the lad smiles at Trueblood like he makes the sun rise and set.*

He lets them get away with nothing and they fucking adore him for it.

"Heed the rakontistos, lads," Lejo said, nodding at the kheiron.

"What does that mean?"

"Rakontistos is the storyteller," Melki said. "All of us are legantos. The readers."

"Aŭskultantos, lad," Abrakam said. "The listeners."

"I know, but I can't pronounce that."

"Heed," Raj called loudly. "Go ahead, Fen."

"Well, larks bring souls to the newborn," Fen said. "And finches bring souls of the dead back to the moon. The souls of the righteous live on the moon's bright side. The side we can see. But the damned live on the side that never shows its face to man.

"Kheirons are creatures of the moon. The moon goes through phases of showing and hiding her face, and kheirons can do the same. We wax and wane between man and horse. Or rest as half of each. And it's said…" He glanced around but found he couldn't meet anyone's eyes. He looked back at his hands, twisting one of his eight rings.

"It's said when a kheiron is in equos, his pure horse form, it's like he's the full moon. He's showing his best side. He shows all of himself, without fear or excuses or apologies. But when he stands as a man, in humos, he's turned away. Showing his…"

He almost said *worst side,* before realizing it would insult everyone in the room. But he didn't know how else to put it.

"His most vulnerable side," Lejo said quietly.

"Yes," Fen said. "A kheiron in humos doesn't have four legs to run or silver hooves to kick. He's never more afraid than when he stands as a man. And he wants to hide it."

Melki looked up at him. "I thought you said it was a true story?"

Laughter filled the room. Pleased with himself, Melki leaned crossed arms on Fen's legs. "We never met anyone who was *in* one of the stories," he said. "Most of them are about dead people from a thousand years ago. But we tell *The Kepten and The Kheiron* all the time."

"Is that so?" Fen said.

"Who was the boy they found you with?"

Fen's stomach squeezed and his heart startled into thudding. "What?"

"In the story," Melki said patiently. "The Altyns found you in the Old Forest and a boy was with you. But he was already dead."

Sweat dripped down the back of Fen's neck. His insides screamed but he kept his face bland as he swallowed and said, "Well." Then he could say no more.

If I tell them, he thought, *will they want me anymore? Gods, what would Trueblood do if he knew who Alon was and what I did to him?*

"Melki, leave him be," Lejo said. "We only want his story if he's telling it."

Trueblood stood up, scattering the minoros around his feet. "Thank you for the tale, Fen," he said. "Now hit your bunks, sailors."

In the days that came, Fen braced himself for questions from the crew. Wanting first-hand details of the story and asking who was with him.

None came.

He didn't know if they lost interest or if Trueblood or Lejo had a firm talk with them about nosiness. If it was the latter, he was grateful, and he ought to say so. But he'd rather barf over the windward side of the ship than talk about how he escaped.

Or who was with him.

ALIVE SOMEWHERE

IN A LITTLE house in southern Minosaros, a broken mother keeps a chair empty at her table and a candle of hope lit in her heart.

She believes her son is alive somewhere.

He'd be thirty-one now, but he's stayed in his mother's mind as a boy of eleven. He's frozen in her memory, dazzling blond and gentle, waving back to her before he goes out into the world and never returns.

This lad was called Jindo when he walked away from home for the last time.

He was sold into slavery.

He escaped on the back of a kheiron.

He fell out the sky as a boy renamed Alon.

The Altyns found his corpse at the foot of a spice tree.

Now he lies buried next to a pegaso in Nyland.

One day, legantos, his story will be told, but not today. For now, know you must breathe gently when you hear it. Don't upset the inner flame within this brave mother who still waits for her boy. You have the privilege of knowing what she doesn't and it comes with awesome responsibility.

Simply listen.

Listen to learn it. Learn it to tell it. Tell it to teach it.

ANYTHING BETWEEN US

THE MORE COMFORTABLE Fen appeared on the ship, the heavier the ringos weighed on Trueblood's finger. Other than the hoop in his ear, he'd never worn jewelry. His father's marvelous gold cuffs were his for the taking, but the few times he tried to wear them, he found them a hindrance. They got in his way. So did the ring, but in another of his ways.

This isn't mine. I have no right to wear this.

What the hell was keeping him from just giving it back to Fen? Saying, "I'm not wearing it anymore. End of story."

Would the ship sink if he gave it back?

Would the sun fall out of the sky?

This is horseshit, he thought several times a day, keeping his hands in his pockets or behind his back whenever the kheiron was around. He went on thinking it was horseshit, but he kept the godsdamned thing on. In this, his maiden voyage, he needed all the supernatural and superstitious help he could get.

He was brooding over the ring's grip when he came across Fen at the base of the main mast. The kheiron had a morbid fascination with this monster. He stared up at the sailors in the rigging, his expression somewhere between horror and envy. He wanted to be *up there.* Badly. It would be the closest thing he had to flying right now. But without the security of his wings, he'd be terrified to be up there.

Inside his pocket, Trueblood picked at the ring with his thumbnail. Thinking. And finally asking, he hoped casually, "You want to climb it?"

He expected a swift refusal, but Fen's eyes stayed on the crow's nest as he drew in a long, considering breath.

"Kind of," he said.

"I'll teach you how."

Fen nodded a little. "Can you teach me without there being an audience?"

"Why?"

Still looking up, the kheiron smiled. "My father said I don't do anything without an audience. True in some aspects. However, if I'm going to plunge to my death, I'd rather it be witnessed by as few people as possible."

"I won't let you die," Trueblood said, laughing. "But I know what you mean about having all eyes staring when you attempt something new. Tell you what. Two more nights and the moon will be full. We'll do a midnight summit. I can't guarantee no one will be watching, but it won't be everyone."

AFTER A SHORT lesson about the harness system, Fen started up the main mast. Trueblood coached and directed from below Fen's feet, the memory of his father's voice in his ears.

That's it. No, don't worry, you're smart to rest. Rest as long as you need. Ah ah, don't look up. Don't look up, don't look down, just look where you are.

"All right?" he called at the gallant arm.

"Yeah," Fen said, breathing hard.

"You know," Trueblood said. "The mast likes when you give it a hug."

"Say what?"

"Everyone spends so much time being afraid of her or cursing at her. Every now and then she wants to be complimented." Trueblood put his arms around the mast, embracing it close and turning an angelic face up to Fen. Eyelashes batting. "Nice mast. Thank you for being the spine of the ship. You work so hard and no one appreciates you."

"You are weird, Kepten Trueblood," Fen said.

"Telling you. Be nice to the main mast and she's nice to you."

"Gods." Fen put a single arm around the mast and leaned his head on it. "Good mast. Nice needle of death. Thank you for not killing me."

The two majoros keeping watch in the crow's nest reached down for Fen's arms as he approached the hatch. Trueblood heard shouts and laughter as the kheiron was hauled up. The three were in a pile on the floor, slapping shoulders as Trueblood ascended.

"He's one of us now, Kep."

"Holy *horses*," Fen said, getting to his feet and looking around. "Gods, look at that…"

Trueblood caught his men's eyes and jerked his head toward the deck, indicating, *Get lost a little while. I got this.*

"Khe l'khe," Fen said. "This is…"

Pleased, Trueblood put his back to the mast, shut up and let Fen enjoy the panorama.

"This is great," Fen said. "Thanks for doing this."

"My pleasure."

"Being up here, I feel like…" Fen's hands rose in the air, then fell to his sides.

"Like what?"

"I don't know. I keep thinking *I feel young*. I don't even know what that means."

"As long as you don't feel nauseous."

Fen leaned over the rail of the nest and faked an exaggerated barf.

"It's been done before," Trueblood said, laughing. "Worst cleanup job on the ship. It fucking goes *everywhere*."

"I feel young," Fen said again. "Kind of…how I felt before I was…taken. Which is odd because I don't have much memory from then."

"Mm," Trueblood said, cautiously regarding this bit of dropped bait. "It's funny. My memory runs into a wall when I'm seven. Almost everything before my mother died, including the day she died, is gone. I only have a handful of distinct recollections, and the rest is just isolated feelings here and there."

"My memory does the same," Fen said, his gaze deliberately forward. He said no more and Trueblood let it drop.

A long interlude of quiet passed and Trueblood started to think about the descent. What would be best—if he climbed above Fen or below him? Probably below. He'd be in the way of Fen's temptation to look down and—

"I'm sorry about Belmiro."

Trueblood blinked. "What?"

"I mean, how I blew that whole thing open. It was shitty of me."

"Huh," Trueblood said. "Didn't see that coming."

"Belmiro or my apology?"

He laughed. "Well, both, now that you mention it." He slid his back down the mast to sit on the floor.

"I guess while I was losing my stomach for a month, I heaved a lot of my petty vindictiveness over the side," Fen said. "I feel bad about it. And I'm sorry."

"It ended up being for the best."

"How so?"

"You were right about *easy* being my middle name, and learning about Belmiro opened my eyes to a lot of things. Made me do some fast growing up. Newfound appreciation for my own lot in life. So on and so forth. Life lesson learned. But it did kind of suck."

"Mm."

"But at least I have a better idea of what I want when it comes to gelang."

"You ever been in love?"

"No."

Fen leaned his arms on the rail. "I was. Once." A deep breath in and a long shiver out. "You know I was abducted outside the kheiron training grounds in Sudenlo. I wasn't supposed to be there. I had two years to go until I'd be old enough to join the legions. But I was in love with one of the archers, so I sneaked after them."

"I see," Trueblood said. "Who was she?"

"He."

Trueblood's eyebrows raised. *You said you didn't bed men* poised on the tip of his tongue, then he bit it back. Maybe Fen just meant human men. He didn't say anything about males of his own race. Fuck it, anything Fen lobbed during the fight in the grotto was long heaved over the side of the ship.

Just start over, Trueblood thought.

"We were young," Fen was saying. "He was fourteen, I was twelve. But it felt real."

"Was he happy to see you?"

"Yes and no. I think he was thrilled for thirty seconds, then horrified at the trouble he could get in. He didn't hug or kiss me or anything. He just told me to go home."

"Ouch."

"Yeah. And being young and stupid, I gave him my moonstone before I left the encampment. Which turned out to be a huge disadvantage when I got ambushed."

"Fuck."

"Yeah. I walked right into the shit. They had my rings off me in no time and I couldn't gallop away."

"That's…" Trueblood's voice stuck helplessly in his throat. "I can't even… I'm sorry, I don't know what to say."

Fen shrugged. "Point being, and coming back to the subject of memory, pretty much everything before that day is gone." He tucked a leg under and sat on the floor. "And I hate it. I mean, what the fuck? Why doesn't my memory erase what happened *after* that day and leave me the good shit from when I was nine, ten, eleven? Holy horses, I can't do anything right."

"Anything right, what are you talking about?" Trueblood said. "You were a foalboy. None of it's your fault. Not how you were taken and not how your mind handled it."

"I chose to follow him."

"Then the people who were supposed to keep an eye on you failed. Whoever let you slip past them out of Alondra holds responsibility here. And what about the watch on the perimeter of the training grounds? There's a memory lapse that needs refreshing. You know, Fen, when we get through with all this *Truviad* horseshit, I want names. Clearly I need to hand a few people their ass."

Fen was laughing under his breath. "My father kicked more than a few asses."

"I'll bet."

Fen paused, biting on his bottom lip. "The kheiron I followed to the camp? My father broke his legs."

"Say again?"

"Broke his legs. I don't mean Father threw him aside and he landed badly. I mean Father took a maul and one at a time, he broke each leg."

Trueblood pulled breath in with a hiss, screwing up his eyes. "Why? I mean, it wasn't his fault you came after him."

"No. But he waited a week before he told anyone I'd been at the training grounds in the first place, and that he had my moonstone. A week Father wasted searching in all the wrong places."

"Gods. All four legs?"

"Yeah."

Trueblood swallowed. "Did he live? He couldn't have."

"He did. You've met."

"Met?" The moment the word left his mouth, the pieces crashed together. "Wait. Are you talking about Belmiro?"

Fen nodded.

"Belmiro was your..."

More nodding.

Trueblood's stomach caved in. "Oh, *shit*."

"Mmhm."

"Well, this isn't excruciatingly awkward. At all."

"No, it's fine," Fen said.

"Fine?"

"I mean, I and Bel... After I came back, we..."

"You don't have to tell me."

"See, he'd built a new life on two legs. And because of everything I'd been through, it was a life I had a hard time dealing with. Plus it was my father who put Bel into *his* shitty situation. How do you tiptoe around that?"

"What a fucking mess."

"Yeah. Basically anything between us was impossible. Each was a reminder to the other of things best forgotten."

"Khe l'khe," Trueblood said, rubbing his face. "No wonder he ended up hooked so bad."

"Hooked?"

"Great, now it's my turn to blow Bel's cover."

"What are you talking about?"

"He's in his line of business because he's a fadara addict. He started using it to manage the pain in his legs and couldn't stop."

"Shut up," the kheiron said.

"Telling you, Fen, for a long time, nothing in the *Truviad* made sense to me. Leave all that cryptic prophecy shit to a philosopher. I like clear directions. I like a purpose. When I found out about Belmiro's addiction..." He snapped his fingers. "There it was. Purpose. I need to find that tree so Nye can start growing again so I can bring a little back to Bel and turn that shitty situation around."

"Right," Fen said, nodding.

"So, like I said, you blew it out in the open but it did some good. It got my head out of my ass and helped me discover I don't like gelang that comes at a price."

"Kepten Trueblood," Fen said, "neither do I."

Trueblood pulled Fen's ringos off his finger and held it out to him. "Here."

"What?"

"Take it. It's yours."

Fen looked hard at it. "Why?"

"Because you were a slave once and—"

Fen drew back, eyes narrowed. "You don't know shit about that."

"You're right, I don't. Only that you were taken away and sold. That's all the information I need to give this back to you. You're not my slave, you're not my servant, you're not my subordinate. I want you here, because everything in the world points to I and you being the last chance. But it's no good if you have no choice in the matter. You come on this quest because you want to. Because you're willing, the way it was chiseled in stone. Come because you have something to offer. Because you care about it. Or else take this, fly back to your home and keep doing the work you do best, which is saving other boys from slavery. I won't think less of you. But me wearing this is stupid symbolism. I don't need to think I have some kind of power over you. It insults both of us. Here. Take it. You're free. You always were."

Fen took the ringos and slid it on the empty thumb of his fivehand. He stood up and leaned on the rail of the nest again. Trueblood expected flashes of lightning at most, Fen's wings to immediately unfurl at least.

Neither happened.

Fen just looked out at the world. His face was a stone, although his shoulders trembled a little.

"You all right?" Trueblood said.

"Mm."

Gods, I really am an idiot, he thought miserably. Aloud, he said, "I'm going down now."

Fen didn't answer or move.

Trueblood climbed down the mighty mast alone. Taking his time and resting often, the way his father taught him. Staying on the rigging the whole time and finishing the job.

He walked along the deck, not strutting. Feeling small and foolish and fraudulent. Missing his father badly.

He felt the kheiron before he saw him. A wind that wasn't of the earth ruffled his hair. Silvery, cool and sweet. Then something dropped over his head and face. He yanked at it, saw it was Fen's shirt.

He looked up.

Fen arced across the skies, wings spread, circling the ship, spiraling up into the night.

PART SEVEN
TRUVOS
God of the Sea

AMONG THE STARS AND SKIES

"K HE L'KHE," TRUEBLOOD whispered. He raced forward, thundering up the steps of the forecastle and out to the bow of the ship. Eyes locked on the rise and fall of Fen's wingspan. Awed by the strength it must've taken to control them, all the while holding his human body tight and pointed and compact, streamlining himself into the perfect shape for flight.

Impossible flight, he thought. Scholars hated kheirons because they made no scientific sense. Everything about their bodies was wrong. Their wings defied math, broke the laws of nature and laughed in the face of anatomical physics.

It's magic, Trueblood thought. *The world needs magic, impossible things that have no price. And it needs those things to be free.*

He wrapped one of the rigging lines around his wrist, put a foot on the bow of the Kaleuche and leaned far out, following the kheiron's flight. Watching him turn into an inky shadow and grow smaller and smaller against the night sky. The kepten raised an arm, waving Fen's shirt like a victory flag.

You're free, he thought. *Free to leave, free to stay. Free to fly. Fly home, kheiron.*

MORE THAN A few crew members were horrified. None would say it to Trueblood's face, but it was obvious they thought it was a foolish move. All that long next day, eyes searched the skies, looking for the kheiron. When not inspecting the horizon, every sailor studied the Ĝemelos nervously, wondering if Raj knew which way Fen went and if Lejo knew what the right thing to do was.

Sundown and Fen didn't return.

"It's no good if he's here under duress," Trueblood said to his crew's pinched faces. "There's nothing worse than a sailor who doesn't want to be at sea. If he's gone, there's nothing for it. He's not the one to be here anyway."

"Do you believe that?" Abrakam said privately.

"No. Yes. I don't know. Knowing what I know about him, it felt like the right thing to do."

"That's what matters."

"Lejo hasn't cornered the market on moral compasses, you know."

"Aye, lad, I know."

Night fell over the Cay. The egg of the moon rolled bright and beautiful across the sky. The ship quieted and cabin doors shut one by one. Holding Fen's discarded shirt, Trueblood walked the decks alone, bow to stern, port to starboard, looking between the sky's diamonds for a winged shadow.

"I'm reminded of when you first went to sea, Troubled," Abrakam said. "You'd pace the Cay like this. Holding a piece of your mother's skirt."

Trueblood said nothing as he rubbed the material between his fingers, the same way he would rub beaded red-and-gold leaves on an embroidered tree.

Sensing Trueblood wanted to be alone, the centaur went away. Trueblood sat with his back against the foremast, arms around his knees. The lark flew down and perched on his shoulder, her serious little face studying the stars. It grew colder, and she puffed herself out into a ball. When Trueblood put his hand over her, she didn't shy away. She let him slip her in his coat pocket.

He stayed there, looking up at the sky, chilled to his bones. He imagined Sevri il-Kheir twenty years ago, straining eyes around the world, looking for his lost son.

"Foalboy, come back to me," Trueblood whispered.

He was no father, but it felt real. It took his breath and spilled down his face in icy wet streams as he murmured again, "Foalboy. Where are you, my one. Come back to me…"

His cheeks were still damp and numb when Lejo appeared in front of him and held out a hand. Trueblood took it and let himself be led to bed. He draped his coat on the back of a chair, careful not to disturb the sleeping lark. Then he lay down between the twins until his blood warmed again.

"Do you know where he is?" he whispered once to Raj. "Can you find him?"

"Shh." Raj's hand dropped heavy on the crown of Trueblood's head. "He has to find himself."

"It's all right," Lejo murmured, drawing tighter against Trueblood's back.

Trueblood knew the sound of his friends' slumber. He waited for that distinctive double cadence of breath, then slipped out and into the other bed. He spread Fen's shirt across his pillow and lay his head on it, breathing in the last bits of Fen's skin. His hand crept beneath the pillow and closed around the folded remnant of green velvet.

Come back, he thought. *I can't find you among the stars and skies. Come back here, where I can look for you.*

Come back because you want to.

Come back because you're free.

Foalboy, come back to me…

WORTHY OF LOVE

FEN REACHED LAND at daybreak but didn't know exactly where he was.

He settled by a stream in a glade of birch trees and withdrew his wings. He drank deeply then sat down to rest.

He was free.

He flexed his ringed fingers and thought about what he could do.

Get his bearings somehow, and fly back to Valtourel. Hide somewhere until he could figure out how to get his moonstone back.

He could steal it.

Or, he could simply ask Naria for it, and if she refused, then steal it.

Maybe Belmiro could get it for me.

He was cold, even in the sunshine. He didn't tolerate heat and cold well when he was in humos.

He was hungry, too.

And I'm tired.

The thought pressed on him, simple and sudden.

I am really tired of doing this.

He found a mossy spot by the stream where flat rocks had soaked up the sun's warmth. Wrapped in his wings, he slept the day away.

When he woke, he was still cold, hungry and tired.

And lonely.

Solos was sliding behind the trees. The Kaleuche would be thinking about dinner now.

Were they thinking about him?

Was Trueblood searching the skies, watching for Fen's return?

Do you miss me?

He lay watching the sky darken to lavender, then indigo. Lunos rose, stately as a woman ascending a staircase, a tiny sliver shaved from her perfect circle. She was starting to wane and turn her face away. Showing her most vulnerable self.

Fen stared at the play of moonlight on the water, his eyes blurring and focusing. The silvery shadows turned into wings. Wings attached to a pure white horse's body. A human female torso rising from its withers.

They had never met. But Fen knew her at once. He felt no surprise at her arrival, right here and right now. The Horsedam's presence seemed as ordinary and inevitable as his own reflection in a mirror.

Oh look, his mind said casually. *It's her.*

Salutos, Tehvani... She spoke his khenom, his soul name. Almost perfectly. Slightly off to his ear, because it belonged to no one but him.

"Salu, sister," Fen said.

Have I ever told you I adore when you call me sister?

"It hasn't come up. Then again, this is the first time we've met."

You know, your humor is quite like your father's.

"Knowing that doesn't make me feel better."

How do you feel right now?

"Lost," he said. "Twenty years since I was found, and I still feel lost."

Ele-Kheir shifted into humos. Clothed in a gown of moonbeams, she sank down on the moss beside him. *Come here*, she said, gathering his head onto her lap. He turned his face against her stomach and let her hold him. Her hand was soft in his hair and her wings were warm on top of his.

Little brother, you're one of the bravest souls I know.

"My soul is tired of being brave."

He waited for a reproachful sigh. Platitudes. A harangue about duty and destiny.

She went on holding him, her hand stroking his head. *Some-one's here to see you,* she finally said. soft as a feather floating on water.

"Who?"

Sit up. Look. Just beyond those trees.

Night had fallen like a black blanket and it took a moment for Fen's eyes to pick out a darker shadow in the grove and identify its outline. A horse stood among the trees.

Fen got to his feet, peering at the silhouette. Inky-black but transparent at the same time. Here, but not here. He walked closer, blinking under furrowed eyebrows. The horse stepped out as well, and now Fen saw it was a mare. And she wasn't black, but a deep purple.

Zoria.

The mare tossed her head and a swathe of the night sky dimmed behind the colossal wings that spread from her back. Between that magnificent span, her eyes shone deep gold.

"Mother," Fen whispered. He walked toward the pegaso, arms outstretched, wanting to fling them around her neck so he could bury his face in her coat.

"Mami," he cried.

He passed straight through her. She was only shadow, no sub-stance.

Hold still, Zoria said.

Fen sank on his knees, wanting nothing more than to remain standing and shift into equos. Show his mother his best side. His purest, most unapologetic self.

Hold still, my one.

He looked up into the gold eyes as Zoria's head came closer, then moved over his shoulder. Her wings circled him as one of her ebony hooves rolled on its edge.

"I'm sorry," he whispered, his entire life bound up in the two words. *I'm sorry I was born, I'm sorry I made you die, I'm sorry I didn't hear you, I'm sorry, I'm sorry, I'm sorry…*

It wasn't your fault, she thought to him. *Shhh, my son, my love, my foalboy. None of it is your fault. All of it is meant. It isn't easy to bear but I promise, one day you'll see why it all happened.*

A shimmering moment of pure love held his heart in gentle hands.

Valentos, believe I'm here. I'm always here.

Her love embraced him again, then she was gone.

She sees you, ele-Kheir said. *You may think no one misses you but believe me, Tehvan, she does.*

"I believe you."

Your father loves you.

Fen looked back. "Now you're asking a little too much."

I suppose I am.

He got up and walked toward his ancestral aunt. "He did love me once. I remember it. But something happened. Something changed him. Was it me? Was it what happened to me, or something I did? Or didn't do?"

The kheirone stood motionless in the moonlight, eyes closed.

"If you know, please tell me," Fen said.

Some things aren't for the waking world, Tehvan il-Kheir.

"Some things nobody should have to suffer."

Fair point, little brother. I'll tell you. But you can't remember I told.

She raised her hands.

And she broke Fen's legs.

At least, that's what it felt like. All at once, Fen was on his back, writhing and screaming at the jagged edges of bone punching out of his bloody skin. The stream and the moss and the trees vanished. The night vanished. It was day and he was in the sky, hundreds of feet in the air at the top of a Nye tree. Sprawled broken on an old harvest platform and the caracaros were adding their wails to his.

Above him, ele-Kheir hovered. Between her hands pulsed a nebulous cloud of pale blue light.

Do you know what this is?

"Please," Fen cried. "Stop. I'm sorry. I won't ask anymore, just make it stop."

Look here, Tehvan. Look at what I hold.

"Please. Don't do this to me again. I can't. I can't do it again. Please."

This, Tehvan. Do you see?

"Yes," he screamed, weeping, fingernails dragging in the rough planks of the platform.

This is your father's soul. This is the price he paid. This is what happened and what changed him. Not you or anything you did. Your only crime was being the thing he loved most in the world.

"Please…"

This is your father's soul. He gave it to me. For you. Everything for you. His love, his compassion, his ego, his memory, his reputation. All of it. This for that.

Her arms reared back and she flung the light at Fen. It crackled from the soles of his feet to his waist, bone sinking beneath skin and skin mending together, leaving Fen standing by a stream in the moonlight. His expression dazed. As if he'd fallen asleep standing up and was waking from a complicated dream.

"I'm sorry," he said slowly, shaking his head. "What was I just saying?"

That you've suffered greatly.

"Yes."

You play a profound part in everything coming to pass right now, Tehvan. Still, you are but one part. Things happen for a reason. The reason doesn't always make itself known and if it does, it's not always a reason you feel was worthwhile.

"Mami said the same thing," Fen said. "But in a much nicer way."

It's what mothers do. Aunts are a little more direct. And I am a busy dam.

They sat down on the moss and he put his head in her lap once more. Her hand fell soft on his head and her feathers lay warm on top of his. *Things are happening in the world right now,* she said. *And the world needs you.*

"I hate that reason," he said. "I have so much hate in my heart and I can't let go of it."

You're worthy of love, little brother.

"I try to believe that," he said. "But part of me is always just so fucking scared. Part of me is still a foalboy wondering if anyone is coming to find me. If anyone will rescue me out of my own body. If anyone will ever understand what they did…" His voice cracked open and he fought to finish. "And if someone does come, does find me and rescue me, will they even want me? Because part of me is Alon, too. Part of me believes nobody's going to want me, not ever. The Alon in me wants to slide off my own back and fall away and…die."

My mother felt the same way, ele-Kheir said.

"Your mother?"

I and my twin were children of rape.

Fen rolled in her lap and looked up at her. The thread of the *Truviad* unwound in his mind, retelling how Khe pursued the pegaso who lived at the top of Nydirsil.

He gave chase and forced himself upon her, ele-Kheir said. *Siring twins, male and female. The first kheirons.*

"But that's all it says," Fen said.

All?

"The *Truviad* just glosses over the rape part of it. The pegaso, your mother, isn't even mentioned again. Ever again. Did she even have a name?" He sat up. "She doesn't. She's never named in any of the stories."

Ele-kheir touched his face. *She didn't think anyone would want to know it.*

"She thought nobody wanted her."

She hid herself on the other side of the moon. Watched Truvos tow her home away and thought everyone would forget her name. Forget she was part of the story.

"Tell me her name. Please."

You already know it. She kissed his face. *Every kheiron knows it.*

She shifted into kheiros, unfurled her wings and flew away between moonbeams. Fen sat on the bank of the stream, stunned and staring. The moon had traveled far across the sky now, hovering between the constellations of Nyos and Minos. Showing her face. Reflecting a kheiron's best side.

No, he thought. *No, that's wrong. We got it backward. The best side is home to the pegaso. And it never shows its face because it's afraid.*

When a kheiron stands in humos, he's most like his ancestral mother. Vulnerable to attack. Scared and shamed, thinking nobody wants him.

To stand in humos is to honor that nameless pegaso.

"Her name *is* Humos," he said.

He stood up on his two sound legs. He flexed his ringed fingers and willed his wings to release.

Trueblood likes a simple purpose. A reason. He's not going on this voyage for destiny or prophecy, he's doing it to bring Nye back to someone who's suffering. That's the job he wants to do well.

My job can be showing Humos she's wanted. I can go on this voyage to bring her home.

I can if I'm willing.

Fen il-Kheir looked up at the waning edge of the moon.

And he decided.

Coming Off
the Kheiron

T RUEBLOOD SWAM UP to consciousness. He was warm beneath the blankets, yet a chill lingered in the air.

He opened his eyes.

Fen sat astride a chair, arms folded on its back, chin on top. His wings filled the cabin, blocking out the bed where the twins lay sleeping. The tiers of feathers, white and silver and perfect, rose and fell gently with Fen's breath and Trueblood wanted them on his skin.

"Salu, foalboy," he whispered.

Fen's head tilted a little. He blinked thoughtfully, then answered, "Salu, lad."

They stared a long, long time at each other.

The cold coming off the kheiron smelled delicious.

Fen lifted his head and unfolded his arms. He slid the ringos from the thumb of his fivehand. His eyes closed once as his wings retracted, melding back into his body. Without a word, he held out the circle of silver.

"No, you're free," Trueblood whispered.

"I know." His finger extended further, the ringos dangling from its tip. "I'm free and I'm onboard now. I'm part of this now. Part of the quest and part of your crew. If you'll have me, I'm willing to stay."

Trueblood freed an arm from the blankets and started to reach. Then he hesitated. "It's yours."

"I want you to wear it," Fen said. "My choice this time. It means something different now."

Their hands touched, closing around the bit of silver for a breath in. A breath out.

Fen looked away, biting at his lip. "Did you look for me while I was gone?"

Trueblood nodded. "I didn't like not being able to find you."

Fen smiled. Then he swung his leg over, got up and put the chair neatly and quietly against the wall. "Amatos, Kepten."

Until the morning.

"Amatos."

Trueblood slid the ringos onto his finger. He closed his eyes and breathed in the cold, delicious scent of a kheiron onboard his ship. The scent of choice. Of freedom.

If you'll have me, he thought. *I'm willing.*

STRAP OVER THE SPOON

THE LARK FLEW away and didn't return for three days. Lejo was beside himself. When she finally swooped in, the tender-hearted boatswain gave her a glare that could sour milk. The capricious bird went meek. She flew toward Lejo, but he turned his back. Her chirp cajoled, but when he refused to speak to her, the warble grew contrite. Then she cried.

"Holy Helos, I didn't know birds cried," Fen said.

Trueblood looked slightly horrified. "That's the worst sound I've ever heard."

"Lé, for fuck's sake, forgive her," Raj said. "Before everyone's heart breaks."

Apologies were made and though the lark continued to take short, mysterious journeys, apparently she and Lejo reached an understanding and the ship didn't suffer through any more avian weeping.

The Kaleuche arrived in Aybar, one of the few natural harbors on the continent's east coast that could accommodate her hull.

Trueblood took a page straight from his father's rulebook and put the ship under a strict curfew. Minoros under thirteen did not leave the ship. Period. Majoros did not go anywhere alone, and the maristos who accompanied them were to be armed.

Reading from another page of the True Way, the kepten declared those with business to conduct in Aybar would do so briskly. Preferably before sunset.

"Here." Trueblood pulled the ringos off his finger and held it out to Fen. "I know you work alone. I won't follow you. What happens in Aybar stays in Aybar. Just be careful."

"I'm always careful."

"While you're being careful, try not to get yourself killed."

"Is that an order?"

"A strenuous request."

"Kepten, I think you're starting to like me."

"I hate your guts but the crew enjoys having you around. They won't get any work done if they're moping over your corpse."

"Imagine that."

"Fly in, do what you have to do and fly the fuck out." Trueblood bit his tongue around the advice not to strut before the job was done. He wasn't Fen's minder.

"You be careful as well," the kheiron said. "I notice the crew likes having you around."

"Most of the time."

Fen threw up a farewell palm, then loped down the gangplank. He turned back at the bottom and called, "Up the whale's ass, Kep."

Trueblood laughed at the sailors' expression for good luck. "Who taught you that?"

"Melki."

"I should've known."

"It's my new favorite phrase." Fen waved again. "Up the whale's ass."

Trueblood raised a hand with the traditional comeback: "Hope it doesn't fart."

Walking back to the aftercastle, he noted the mixed dynamic on the anchored ship. Most maristos and majoros had zero interest in sightseeing in the armpit of the world. Meanwhile, the under-thirteen minoros lined the rails, salivating at the forbidden fruit of Aybar. Nothing made a boy yearn for something like making it off limits.

Eleven was going into the city and taking Sixten with him. On a leash, he half-joked.

"You both mind your Ps and Qs," Seven said.

"I take Qs," Sixten said.

Eleven scowled at his older brother. "You know, I've been out of diapers some time now."

"I mean it, Lev. Get into trouble and you'll be answering to me *and* Mami."

This was no empty threat. Even when these brothers were thousands of miles from home, their mother's presence loomed large. A woman who'd borne and raised nineteen children did not suffer horseshit gladly. One message falcon reporting bad behavior and her grown boys would get the business end of her wooden spoon when they arrived back home.

"Give me the strap over the spoon any day," Seven said.

Ikharus-Lippé True had always brought this famous matriarch a small gift from his travels. Now Trueblood knew why. He'd have to find a little something for her before they returned to Valtourel.

Accompanied by Raj, he left the ship and made his way through the teeming city.

I-and-you-without-Lejo is a very different feeling than I-and-you-without-Raj, he once wrote in his most private journal. *Alone with Raj, there's always the possibility of finding incredible fun, but also the possibility of getting into trouble.*

Raj stopped short and put a cautionary forearm across Trueblood's path. Mumbling, "Careful," as a horse-drawn wagon thundered by, ignoring the dismayed cries of pedestrians.

As they moved on, Raj's eyes were everywhere at once, consulting the map, memorizing the route, pinpointing not only their location but the whereabouts of every person in a ten-foot radius.

Watching for hazards. And always keeping Trueblood at the center of his gaze.

The kepten had never walked along holding hands with Raj. Not once in any city, anywhere, ever. Still, he'd never not felt the pilot's solid and dependable presence, exactly where he needed it to be. Whether at Trueblood's side, or a step ahead or behind, Raj was always and reliably *there*. And in a place like Aybar, Trueblood preferred his hands to be free.

"Gods, it stinks," Raj said, skirting piles of trash, offal, human and animal refuse. Rats were everywhere, walking down the middle of streets like they owned the place and giving you dirty looks for being in their way. Stray cats and dogs were in the hundreds and it was a good thing Lejo was behind on the Kaleuche. Trueblood would never get him out of here empty-handed and Gods knew what kind of dirt and disease the creatures would track onto the ship. They'd barely made it past the wharves and already he felt filthy.

Get in and get out, he thought, lengthening his stride and shouldering his way through the crowd. "What's this place we're going to?" he asked.

"One of the House Tru hostels. The giantword is *loĝigos*." Raj looked back and grinned. "I only know because Abrakam never misses an opportunity to educate."

"Wouldn't it be an egregiously obvious place to hide Nye?" Trueblood said.

"Sometimes things hidden in plain sight are overlooked."

"Thank you, I feel much better now." Trueblood tightened his grip on the sword at his belt and flexed both calves to feel the knives sheathed in his boots. Raj was similarly armed.

No heroics, no trouble. Get in and get out.

The map's route led them further into the city. Along streets where the houses on either side leaned precariously forward, turning the thoroughfares into pens. Little statues of Minos were built on corners and stoops and bovine faces were carved into any malleable surface.

"I haven't see any minotaurs," Trueblood said.

"Over there," Raj said. "Just past that tavern on the left."

Trueblood tried to keep it to a glance and not stare. He'd gone his whole life in the presence of horsefolk, taking their existence for blind granted. But his mind refused to process a human body with a bull's head. Looking at this impossible and revolting hybrid, he finally understood the scholars who lost their minds trying to fathom kheirons.

One of your kind killed my mother, he thought. *Killed her for the keys to the Nye vault. We had to divide up what was left of the spice and hide it all over the world. Now here I am to get the last of it. But I could kill you while I'm in the neighborhood. Exact a little revenge of my own. I have the right.*

The thought filled his mouth with metallic relish and for a twisted moment, he imagined the bull's head mounted on the wall of his study.

"Easy, Pé," Raj said. "Get in and get out, remember?"

Almost regretfully, Trueblood shook his thoughts free of the vendetta. "Let's go," he said.

"It's down this way. At the end of this street."

But nothing was at the end of the street.

Except a crater in the ground and a few charred beams.

"Hold my fucking horses," Raj said.

As if approaching a dead kraken, they walked toward the remains of the loĝigos and peered down into what used to be the foundation. A group of wretched individuals in rags looked back up at them.

"Salu," Raj said. "What happened here?"

The band of unfortunates slinked back into a corner, shaking their heads and mumbling.

Trueblood took his hand off his sword and showed both empty palms. "We're strangers to the city but we know this was a loĝigos. House Tru owned it." Given his appearance, it was pointless to pretend he wasn't a member of the dynasty in question. "I had people here. What happened?"

"Giantsbled went away long time ago," one fellow said.

"Went where?"

The man shrugged. "Them just left."

"Maybe ten years," a toothless woman said. "And not gradual. Them all left at once and the loĝigos sat empty."

Ten years. Trueblood was seven-almost-eight when Alondra was sacked and the kheirons loaded as many casks of Nye as they could onto the Cay. Surely by the time he was ten, some of those casks were here in Aybar.

The giantsbled left. Did they take the Nye with them?

"What happened then?" Raj said. "Who came to live here?"

"Was a brothel for a time," the first man said. "Then one night it blew up. Big fireball straight up into the sky. Us watched it burn. Destroyed everything and everyone inside."

"You need sunpowder for that kind of explosion," the pilot said.

"Some say minotaurs were trying to make a new kind of fadara," the toothless woman said. "Us heard about new things going on in the drug trade. Them's been trying to heat up the poppy sap and get it to combine with kyrrh."

"Kyrrh doesn't combine with anything, sister."

The woman's mouth was dark and vast as she laughed. "It will if you get it hot enough. If you got iron nerves and a deft touch with sunpowder."

Raj looked at Trueblood and quietly asked, "What happens when a clumsy touch with sunpowder meets some hidden casks of Nye?"

"You blow a hole in the ground and destroy a street." The kepten sighed. "The casks either left with the giantsbled or went up in smoke."

"Fuck me," Raj said.

"Give them something for their time and let's go back to the ship."

Raj handed down some khesos. Walking away from the pit in the ground, he put a hand between Trueblood's shoulder blades. Two rubbed circles, a pat, then it dropped.

"Nothing for it," he said.

"It wasn't for us, so it passed us by."

The rest of their walk back to the wharves was silent and sober.

"Well, I hope Fen had better luck on his errand," Trueblood said.

No sooner had the words left his mouth than a collective exclamation ran down the street. Heads tilted up and fingers pointed.

"Khe l'khe," Trueblood said, shading his eyes. "Is that what I think it is?"

Above the city a pegaso hovered. Copper-red with a black mane and tail. The sunrays burst through her snowy wings. Off one rear leg dangled a rope, which she was attempting to shake free.

"Looks like a thwarted pego-napping," Raj said.

"Oh, that's too bad." Trueblood grinned. "Not."

Another communal gasp, louder this time. Fen was in the sky, shirtless and splendid. Racing after the pegasos, he looked like a giant dove.

"Well, I'll be damned," Raj said slowly. "Fen's getting laid."

Future Horsefolk

Penton was right: something about the architecture of Haize's new brothel was off. Fen stood back from the two-story building, examining and mentally measuring its front façade. All the right-hand windows were aligned a good four feet from the outside edge. Fen moved over and noted the right side of the brothel had no windows at all. Whatever business was going on in that narrow space, it wasn't for public knowledge.

Fen rubbed his fingertips against his palm, trying to come up with a plan and wishing his charm were with him. Herd mentality was never more useful than when strategizing.

Access to that space is hidden, he thought. *It wouldn't be on the ground floor, which is open to the public. A door kept closed and off limits raises suspicion. It's upstairs in one of the bedrooms. Maybe it's a trap in the floor. To get into that space you have to be in the know, or you have to pay.*

He jingled the coins in his pocket. He could pay. Money wasn't an issue. It was the logistics of doing this alone.

This isn't a job for one, he thought, exhaling the bitter resignation. *Not today. Go find Haize. That's the unfinished business.*

Behind him, the air split with the neigh of a horse.

Kheirons, legantos, have only a small affinity with common equines. They share no language, rather the connection is at an elemental, instinctive level. This shrieking whinny chilled Fen's blood, but it was the words within it that grabbed him by the soul.

Help me.

This was no workhorse.

Fen whirled around and nearly unfurled his wings before fully assessing the situation. Across the cobbled plaza, his eyes locked onto a copper pegaso mare. Her wings strained against the air, dragging against the ropes around three of her legs. Three men were holding onto her bonds while a fourth dodged the kicks of the mare's free limb.

She screamed again in Fen's head. Her terror was contagious, triggering something deeper than herd mentality. This bond was cellular. It was the *folk* in horsefolk.

"Mydam," he called, hustling through the crowd.

"Get back, you idiot," one of the men cried.

"Watch that hoof, sailor, she'll kick a hole right in your chest."

Fen shut his mouth and spoke from his equos.

Mydam. It's all right, I'm coming.

He threw both his body and thoughts through the chaos. Hands grabbed at him, yanking him from certain danger.

"Look out, you fool."

"Lad, get back, you don't know what you're doing."

A desperate whinny of words poured out of the mare. Fen saw she was young and far from home. And growing hysterical.

"Ease off," he said, putting a commander's authority into his voice. "This isn't the way you catch a pegaso. Give me that." He hipped one of the foreleg men out of the way and caught up his rope. "Come here, my beauty."

Look at me, mydam, Fen thought. *Pretend to come to me. I won't let them hurt you.*

Fen filled his eyes with greed and gave a complicit glance at one of the captors. "She's gorgeous."

The man grunted. "Tell me something I don't know."

"How'd you boys lure her in?"

"We didn't. She wandered into town on her own. Like she was lost."

"Finders keepers," another sang.

You're far from home, little sister, Fen thought. *This is no place for you.*

Her wings shuddered as her three bound hooves came nearer the ground.

Look only at me. That's it. I'm going to put my hands on you. Don't be afraid.

She tossed her head as his hand slid along her neck and the crowd gasped.

"Don't yank on her," Fen said to the men on the rear leg ropes. "Ease up. You're terrifying her. Break a mare's spirit and she'll fetch half the price she should."

The word price made the mare buck and rear. She was terrified but she wasn't stupid.

It's all right. Fen had a firm hand in her mane. *I won't let them take you. Come down now. Pretend I'm taming you. Good.*

Her rear hooves touched down and stayed there. The front ones refused to stand still. She wasn't rearing, but she was ready to kick.

That's it. As if giving gelango, Fen carefully rested his forehead against the mare's long nose. *Breathe with me now. I'm here and I won't let them hurt you.*

A murmur went through the crowd.

"You have to woo her, lads," Fen said. "Sweet words and a gentle touch. Just like you'd seduce a woman."

"Well, it was Kenji's idea." One of the louts flipped a thumb at his friend. "And he beds men."

"Then no wonder your technique with fillies is terrible," Fen said.

Louder laughter now and Fen ran a firm but gentle hand between the pegaso's ears.

Don't struggle. Stay with me now.

She huffed a breath out her nostrils and her eyes circled the sky. *What is wrong with these assholes?*

Fen had to fold his mouth around his own guffaw and cough into an elbow to swallow it down.

The mare's ears twisted. *Are you all right, mysire?*

I'm fine, Fen thought. *Play along now.* "Give her a little slack," he said to the fellows holding the ropes. "Not too much. Just let her take a few steps."

He walked backward and the mare followed, tugging a little at her bonds.

"Holy fuck, lad, she's eating out of your hand," Kenji said. "Let go her legs."

"No, don't," Fen called, putting fear in his voice. "She's still too wild."

"Horseshit. Look at her. She adores you."

"Too soon," the kheiron said, covertly assessing the men's grip on the ropes. "She could bolt. Or knock my teeth out. Keep some slack but keep holding tight, lads."

Stay close to me, he thought to the mare.

She gave a little snort. *Humans are easily entertained, aren't they?*

They are. Can you shake a leg free?

Almost, she said. *I need more distraction.*

Put your head over my shoulder. Close your eyes. Look tame.

He put his arms around the mare's neck and stroked her mane. A spattering of applause went through the crowd.

"Incredible," Kenji said. "Lads, she's going to make us a fortune."

I've got a leg free, mysire, the mare thought.

All right. On three you fly. Straight up and don't stop. Don't look back. One. Two. Three.

"Fuck, she *bit* me," he yelled, and threw himself aside. The pegaso's wings opened with a crack as she barreled into the throng. Five steps and she was in the air. The unfortunate fellow on her leg rope flew with her a few feet, then let go and toppled into the crowd of people.

"Son of a bitch," Kenji yelled.

"Women," Fen said. "Who can understand them?"

"You fucking *moron.*"

Now Fen was at the center of an angry mob, all intent on killing him.

Easily entertained, easily disappointed, he thought, throwing punches and elbows. Kicking ribs and groins until he managed to get back on his feet. A sound of tearing linen as his wings burst through the back of his shirt, sending more people flying. Screams of wonder and frustration as he took to the skies. The pegaso was far ahead of him, getting out of Aybar without a backward look.

"You're welcome, crazy filly," he called after. "Good Gods, fly down to Nyland if you want to see humans in their natural habitat."

He chuckled the whole flight back to Aybar. A little way before the wharves, he made out the unmistakable tall form of Trueblood in his blue coat, walking with Raj. Fen touched down and caught up to them.

"What did they want?" Raj said, looking Fen up and down. "The shirt off your back?"

"It's a kheiron's occupational hazard." Fen looked from one to the other, noting the empty hands. "Did you find the...thing? The stuff?"

"No," Trueblood said. "Building is in ruins and the cache is long gone."

"Shit, you're kidding."

"Do I look like I'm kidding?"

Trueblood looked like he'd eaten an entire bag of preserved lemon peel. Meanwhile, Raj looked like a dog who'd stolen the cook's soup bones. "And how was *your* morning?" he asked with a broad grin.

"It was eventful."

"No shit. We saw you pursuing a frisky pegaso across the roof-tops." His elbow pressed Fen's side. "*Someone* likes redheads."

"You saw her? Holy shit, you wouldn't believe what happened."

"Try us."

Fen told a condensed, modest version of the story. "Poor thing, she was scared out of her eyeballs."

"Scared but grateful," Raj said. "It's a good combination."

"I guess," Fen said.

"Did she recognize you?"

"Me? Why would she?"

"Don't all horsefolk know the son of il-Kheir on sight?"

Fen laughed. "No."

"What's her name?"

"I don't know."

"You didn't get her name?" Raj said. "Have I taught you nothing?"

"Why would I want her name?"

"Héjo." The pilot rapped knuckles on Fen's head. "You kheiron prince? She dam in distress? Together you make future horsefolk?"

"Raj, shut up," Trueblood said.

"Yeah, shut up." Fen turned to the mariner. "And what's up *your* ass?"

"Nothing. Let's get out of…"

Trueblood trailed off, looking toward the waterfront. Fen followed the stare. Seven and Eleven were running up the street toward them. Sprinting like their hair was on fire.

"This is not good," Raj said.

Now Fen could see the cook was white as death. His brother was wild-eyed and frantic as a captive pegaso.

Trueblood held up a palm, both to greet and stop them cold. His voice boomed deep and terrible as he demanded, "Where's Sixten?"

ALL MY BEST MEN

"WE WERE WATCHING the dancers," Eleven said. His voice had the shrill edge of one who knows he's fucked up badly. "He was *right* next to me."

"Until he wasn't," Seven said.

"Kep, I swear, I turned my head a minute."

"That's all it takes," Fen said under his breath.

"Kep," Eleven said. "I'm sorry."

Trueblood held up a finger and his voice was calm and emotionless. "Be sorry later. Right now we go to where you last saw him and fan out from there. Seven, go back onboard. Send Dhar out. Fen, go get your bow. And a shirt."

The cook swallowed hard. "Kep, shouldn't I go with?"

"I need you with Lejo and Calvo." Trueblood gave a quick smile. "I can't have all my best men ashore."

Fen was a mix of dread and bloodlust as they headed back toward the center of the city. He itched for a fight even as he worried about Sixten. The lost bounty of Haize sulked in his gut. Taking out an unsavory citizen or two would be a decent consolation prize.

"Don't get punchy on me," Trueblood said, as if he'd heard Fen's thoughts.

"I'm not punchy."

"You are. Don't bring your emotions into the situation. We lost something. We will find it."

They came to the square where Eleven said the dancers had been. In a loose phalanx, they started circling, moving outward street by street.

"Think like your brother, Lev," Trueblood said. "You know him best. Be fifteen again. You're in a forbidden place. Watching girls dance."

"Half-naked girls," Eleven mumbled.

"Your mother's going to kill you," Dhar said.

Trueblood's voice raised. "Knock it off."

"Was it a troupe?" Fen asked. "Was someone passing a hat for money? Who was working the crowd?"

Eleven rubbed the back of his neck and kicked at the ground. "It was hard to see anything but the girls." At the rolling eyes, he threw up his hands. "For fuck's sake, I'm a *sailor*," he cried. "After two months of being at hand with yourself, naked females are distracting."

"I'm a sailor two months away from my wife," Dhar said. "My hand is my mistress but I can still sew a straight seam."

The voices grew thin in Fen's ears. He was thinking about the dancers and remembering what he knew about Aybar. Girls weren't a commodity here. Boys were.

Sixten was a handsome lad. He wasn't a fool, but he was a young, sex-starved and distracted sailor who was tired of his hand. In other words, a sucker.

Girls weren't goods in Aybar. They were sucker bait.

Aybar didn't want Sixten's khesos. It wanted Sixten.

"Fen," Trueblood said. "What are you thinking. Tell me."

"I think he's in trouble. But..." Fen drew a deep breath. "I might be looking through the punchy prism of my own experience and projecting the trouble."

"I won't dismiss the gut reaction," Trueblood said. "Given where we are."

"Sixten's also a little old for the trade. Aybar likes the young ones. If he's been picked up by a pimp or a slaver, it's not as a long-term investment."

"Gods, kheiron." Eleven dragged hands through his hair until the whites of his eyes bulged. "I respect your knowledge of this place, but please, stop talking."

"Steady, lad," Dhar said.

"My mother's going to *kill* me."

"Old Rafil always said to look for the simplest solution first," Trueblood said. "In this case, that's Sixten being led by the cock back to one of the brothels."

Raj nodded. "And where are brothels always built?"

"Near the wharves. For convenience."

"Let's go."

Heading back to the waterfront, Dhar kept a hearty arm around Eleven. "He's probably right under our nose. He can look out the window of the establishment and see the Kaleuche's mast."

"He knows he's in the shit," Raj said. "No doubt he's putting off the inevitable."

"Not Sixten," Eleven said. "He always went out to meet a hiding. When he was in the shit, he wanted it over with. If Mami was really pissed, she'd make him wait until Da got home. Sixten would die a thousand deaths. The buildup was worse than the beating." His voice frayed around the edges. "He wouldn't run away. I know him."

"So he decided a romp in the sheets was worth a beating," Raj said. "Since he already has it coming, why not two romps? You're only young once."

Gods, I hope you're right, Raj, Fen thought. *Please, let it be the simplest solution. Trueblood lost the cache of Nye. I got waylaid by a pegaso and lost a chance to kill Haize. So be it. Let it all be the price for Sixten.*

This for that.

Between the fervent entreaty was a nauseating certainty the lad was either chained up in the hold of a slave ship or marching into the desert. It curdled in his stomach as Raj, the ambassador, went door to door among the houses of love, applying his fearless charm and bottomless pockets to the downstairs madams and their patrons.

"He'll find him," Trueblood said. "The Compass never worries."

"For sure," Dhar said. "I don't panic until Raj panics."

Fen was eating his panic. When Raj came out of a doorway, his arm around Sixten, all the blood rushed out of the kheiron's head.

"Lad, I am going to kill you," Trueblood said quietly.

"I think I just lost ten years off my life," Dhar said.

"Same here." Fen's laugh sounded like the bray of a donkey as he sank onto a crumbling stone wall, shaking all over. "Good thing my hair's already white," he said, watching Eleven go running toward his brother.

PIES IN THE OVEN

"THE KEPTEN'S GOING to beat your ass to a pulp and I'm going to *watch*," Eleven yelled. "Then I'll watch while Seven thrashes your hide. Then I'm sending a message bird to Mami so she knows. The next time we're home, she's going to beat your ass again and I'll watch *that,* too."

"This is a rather perverted side of you. Lev," Sixten said, earning a slap upside the head.

Trueblood lengthened his stride, putting the fraternal justice system behind him. Unfortunately, Fen had long legs.

"You all right?" he said.

"Splendid. Please stop talking."

"...Because you're a fucking *moron*," Eleven cried, followed by another slapping sound.

A smack back now. "How about we pretend I already feel like shit and don't need assistance, huh?"

"Settle down, lads," Raj said. The tone was barely past conversational yet both brothers went quiet. They walked the rest of the way in silence.

"Sixten, ready the sails," Trueblood said as they went up the gangway. "When we're tacked, go to your cabin and stay there."

"Fine."

Trueblood stopped dead and looked back over his shoulder. "Excuse me?"

Sixten blanched. "I mean, aye. Kep. Kepten." He flinched as Eleven backhanded his upper arm.

Trueblood pointed a long finger at the maristo. "Don't. Hit him. Again."

"Sorry, Kep," Eleven said, elbowing his brother and not looking sorry.

Trueblood took a step and let the finger press Eleven's chest. "You were the accompanying guardian today, were you not?"

Eleven's gaze dropped to his boots, his mouth pressed tight.

"Look at me when I'm talking to you, maristo."

Eleven looked up. "Aye, Kep, I took him into town. He was my responsibility."

"And you let him out of your sight."

"I did."

"You have shit to eat here, and I have both a strap to lay over your hide *and* message birds of my own I can send to your mother. You will own what you own and I will handle your brother without assistance. Do you understand? Answer your commander."

Now he had Eleven's full attention. "Aye, Kep."

"Go to your cabin. If I see you on deck before you're sent for, you'll be sorry. More so if you put a finger on Sixten. Do you need me to repeat any of this?"

"No, Kep."

Trueblood turned on his heel and walked away. Behind him, he heard Raj tell the brothers, "Hop it now. Both of you."

Trueblood banged open the aftercastle doors, shrugged out of his blue coat and threw it across the table in his study. He sank into the large chair at his desk and dropped his aching head in his hands. He imagined in a week, if he was lucky, his heart would stop pounding.

"Well, that was unpleasant," Raj said in a shaky voice. "Is it too early to get drunk?"

"Let's just weigh anchor and get the fuck out of here," Trueblood said, drawing in a massive, fortifying breath before he lifted his head. "Where's Lejo?"

"Right here." The boatswain's arms were crossed so tight, it looked like he was trying squeeze himself out of existence. "You'll deal with Sixten tonight?"

"I'll deal with him when I'm not so angry," Trueblood said. "Otherwise I'll be beating him with my emotions, which isn't a good thing."

Lejo nodded. "I forget how young he really is."

"We all do," Trueblood said. "Even me. He's exceptional. He's mature beyond his years, he's intelligent and talented. All of which makes it easy to forget he's fifteen and technically still a minoro."

"Until he does something stupid."

"I don't punish mistakes, I punish disobedience and disrespect. This was both. If he were a majoro, then possibly I'd give him the mother of all dressing-downs and a month of swabbing the decks."

"Is that what you have in store for Eleven?" Raj said.

"Not after his shitty attitude just now." Trueblood sighed. "Fuck me, tonight is going to *suck*."

"I'll handle Sixten," Lejo said. "I'm the damn boatswain."

"And I'm the kepten," Trueblood said. "Thank you, Lé, but it's my sucky job. I do it. And I'll do it when I've calmed down. Just keep Sixten away from his brothers. If either of them rough him up, I want to know about it."

"You will."

"Raj, please weigh the fucking anchor and get us out of here."

"Where to?"

The blood roared behind Trueblood's eyeballs as he counted five. "Out of port and away from the coastline will be sufficient. Thank you. Everyone."

He rubbed his face hard, then dug fingers between his plaits and pulled until the bite in his scalp cleared his head. When he looked up, Fen was there. He'd been in the room the whole time, but silent.

Trueblood counted five again. "When I said 'thank you everyone,' did you not catch the subtext of *get out*?"

"No," Fen said. "I'm kind of stupid that way."

"You don't want to be standing between me and my bad mood."

Fen stepped a few feet to the side.

Trueblood smiled weakly. "Gods, I may go hide in the galley and peel potatoes to calm down."

"You peel potatoes to calm down?"

"Well, I'd rub one out but I'm not feeling particularly sexy right now so potatoes are next best, may I help you?"

Fen's brow lifted while his mouth twitched sideways.

"Sorry," Trueblood said. "That was crass."

"No, it was funny. Good one."

"Yeah. Well. Get your laughs now because later you'll be seeing your first public flogging onboard."

"You don't typically thrash crew in front of everyone."

"Only for certain offenses."

"Are those offenses written down somewhere?" Fen asked.

"Written down?"

"I don't know, in the giantship rule book?"

"No. It's just the way things are done."

The kheiron's head tilted. "Who's way?"

"My father's way."

"Ah." Fen nodded slowly. "It was his way, but this is your ship."

He smiled then. A real smile that reached to the corners of his eyes. It had both a friend's good-natured tease and an elder's wise counsel.

"I'll leave you alone," he said, and left, closing the door quietly behind him.

Trueblood counted to twenty before answering, "Please stay."

He sighed, caught between the True Way and his way. He should whip Sixten in front of his peers to make an example, to drive the consequence home, but he couldn't.

I can, he thought. *I can also choose not to.*

Because my ship, my rules.

I don't have to do everything *the way Da did.*

He'd discipline Sixten privately in his study. Of course, he wasn't obligated to communicate the decision. Especially since he now knew Sixten preferred to go meet a hiding. The lad could have the whole rest of the afternoon, plus the evening through supper, to think he was getting it in front of the crew. A good long stretch to stew in anticipation, reflect on his actions and die a thousand deaths.

What to do about Eleven remained a conundrum, but Trueblood elected to put faith in hard work and trust the solution would present itself. He inspected the holds and settled the ledgers with Calvo. He entered the day's events in his journal, taking especial pains with his especial penmanship, because writing beautifully soothed him. Numbers and words filed down the rough edges of his mood, and he was calm when Seven rattled knuckles on his door and asked for a word.

"I'm not here to beg clemency for either brother," he said. "Both deserve what they got coming. I hope you won't take offense if I ask how you feel about giving Eleven his due. Him being ten years older than you."

"I'm ten inches taller," Trueblood said.

Seven fiddled with the string of shark teeth he wore around his neck. "Aye, Kepten, you are."

"I know how to put age out of the picture. Rank is only relevant here."

"This is true. And I meant no offense. Or to imply you weren't capable of the job."

Trueblood leaned back in his chair, lacing hands behind his head. "Say what's on your mind, Sev."

"Eleven gets arrogant when his pride is wounded. He hates being in the wrong, and rather than be graceful about it, he makes his fuck-up into someone else's character flaw. He'll use the age difference as a barrier between the strap and his ass. If you need…" Seven paused and tapped his fingers on his chin. "If you need, say, a witness," he said carefully. "Or a sergeant-at-arms to keep him in line, I'll be happy to oblige."

"I appreciate the offer and the counsel," Trueblood said. "More than you know."

"The counsel is yours whenever you want, la—" The cook laughed, knuckling his mouth. "Did you hear what I almost did?"

Trueblood had to laugh as well. "Rafil called my father lad."

"Well, maybe when I'm seventy, I'll have the privilege. For now, I'll take my thirty-three years where they belong. You know where to find me, Kep."

"Thank you, Seven. And when you send that bird, give my regards to your mother."

He squared away some last bits of business, then had the steward bring him supper in his study. Chewing over the day, he made up his mind and when the steward cleared the tray, Trueblood asked him to send both Seven and Eleven to the aftercastle.

"What's *he* here for?" Eleven said.

"At last count, you planned on attending three of Sixten's thrashings," Trueblood said. "You object to a witness at your own?"

Seven leaned against the door with a bored expression. "I have pies in the oven, Lev. Can we get on with it?"

Eleven scowled, backed into a corner of his own device. "Fine," he said, undoing his laces. "You can be in here but you can't *watch*."

Seven graciously turned around and justice was served. Eleven took his due in silence, save for one or two bumpy grunts at the last strokes. He was red to the hairline and sweating when it ended, and as the brothers walked out through the sitting room,

Trueblood heard Eleven say, "Godsdamn, he swings a lot harder than True did."

"Because he's younger," Seven said.

"I think I pissed myself a little."

"Because you're getting old."

Lejo brought Sixten in, but left the study and closed the door. With no witnesses, the lad bent over and got twelve of the best. Trueblood swung hard and while Sixten was stoic at the outset, he was a snotty wreck at the last stripe, bawling from much more than the pain.

The job sucked. If any task was worse than whipping a fifteen-year-old boy until he cried, someone would have to tell Pelippé Trueblood what it was.

He opened the study door. Lejo stood up, expression both grim and relieved.

"Take him back to his cabin," Trueblood said. "And tell the crew no story hour tonight."

The boatswain's eyes widened a hair. Then he nodded briskly and took his charge away.

Trueblood coiled the strap and put it back in the drawer. Then slammed it.

"That's done," he said. "Today is *done.*"

Taking away the evening tales punished everyone. But fuck it. His ship. His rules. The loss of the beloved privilege was another thing Eleven and Sixten could think about when they lay face-down in their beds tonight. And the rest of the week.

The heels of Trueblood's boots hit the floor hard as he went to the liquor cabinet in the sitting room. He crouched, pushed aside vintages and wrestled out the Altynian plonk that Abrakam had so kindly procured.

"Liquid prunes," Trueblood mumbled. "Just what the evening requires."

He regarded the goblets only a moment, then pulled the cork with his teeth, spit it aside and chugged straight from the bottle.

Our Favorite Bedtime Story

"THERE YOU ARE," Raj said.

"Me?" Fen said.

The pilot had two bottles of rum in his sixhand and another in the crook of his elbow. His free hand reached for Fen's wrist. "I need you. Come on."

"Where are we going?"

"To get the kepten drunk."

"I'm not sure he wants company," Fen said.

"He does, he just doesn't know he does. Lejo. *Lé.* Let's go."

"Go where?" the boatswain said, looking like he wanted to go nowhere but bed.

"To drown Troubled's troubles."

"That's a terrible idea."

"I know. Possibly my worst ever. You definitely don't want to miss it."

"No one can say you don't have balls, Raj," Fen said.

"They better not," the pilot said. He paused at the aftercastle doors. "Lads, if you're going to talk me out of it, now's the time."

"Like you'd listen," Lejo said.

Raj opened the door and breezed into the sitting area. "Salu," he called, clanking the rum on the table. "My name's Raj and I'll be your steward this evening."

"Go away," Trueblood said. An empty bottle of wine was at his elbow. His notebook lay open on the table, the pages blank.

"We're here to cheer you up," Lejo said.

"I don't want to be cheered up."

"Too bad," Fen said.

"Would you all kindly fuck off, I don't feel like talking."

"We're not talking, we're drinking."

The kepten gave a martyred sigh. "Get a glass."

Raj clapped his hands together. "That's my boy. Fen, get some glasses."

"Please," Trueblood said quietly.

"Pardon me. Fen, *please* get some glasses."

They pulled up chairs and Raj poured generous tots of rum around. They toasted and bolted them down. Then an awkward silence fell.

Fingers drummed on glass. A little small talk went back and forth. Raj poured more rum. Trueblood bent over his book and sketched a tree. The roots fell off the bottom of the page and the branches spread from spine to edge. Fen's eyebrows wrinkled as the mariner drew two straight lines across the tree, right where the branches forked from the trunk. He rounded their ends, making it into a pole. Like a yard across a mast.

"What's that?" Fen said.

"What?"

"The part going sideways."

Trueblood scowled and his pen slashed carelessly across the sketch. "Something from a dream I had once. It's nothing."

"This is a terrible party," Lejo said. "I blame you, Raj."

Raj put down his glass and wiped the back of his hand across his mouth. "I know how to spice things up."

"This can't end well," Trueblood mumbled.

Raj got up and went into the foyer. He put hands and an ear against Abrakam's closed door.

"Raj, what are you *doing*?" Lejo hissed, sounding ten years old.

The pilot put a finger to his lips and slipped into the centaur's room.

Fen felt a decidedly juvenile thrill of getting caught and he didn't even know what was going on. He glanced at Trueblood, who had his face in his palm, but beneath the fold of his fingers, he was smiling.

Gods, that smile.

Raj slipped out again, a book under his arm. "Look, Pé. It's your favorite."

Trueblood looked up and his face did ten thousand different things. "What the—oh for fuck's *sake,* Raj."

Lejo put his face in both palms, shaking his head. "I could've been asleep by now."

"What is it?" Fen said, trying to see the cover of the book.

"This is the *best* bedtime story," Raj said, sitting down at the table. "Actually, the story is pretty boring, but the illustrations are out of this world."

"Gods, how many times did we sneak this out of Abrakam's library?" Trueblood said, leaning forward to drag a corner of the book toward him. "Gimme that."

Raj slapped his fingers. "Wait your turn."

"What it's about?" Fen said, craning his neck.

"Sex," the three men said.

"This tome taught us everything we know," Raj said.

Trueblood and Lejo exchanged a glance.

"Shut up," Trueblood said.

Lejo's cheekbones flamed. "I didn't say anything."

"You thought it."

"So did you."

"You thought it out loud."

"You wish."

Fen felt his eyebrows knit. *I'm no expert on gelang,* he thought. *But that little exchange was a thing.*

"You been to bed since then?" Raj asked, turning pages.

"Me?" Fen said.

"No." Raj flipped a thumb across the table. "These two."

"No," Trueblood and Lejo said.

"Don't be so touchy, lads. I think it's adorable you were each other's firsts."

"I'm going to kill you," Lejo said quietly.

"When was this?" Fen said to Raj.

"When I and Lé were sixteen. Old enough to go into brothels. I couldn't wait, but my brother has certain ideas about matters gelang—"

"I'm sitting right here," Lejo said.

"—and Trueblood was still a baby."

"I was fifteen and taller than you," Trueblood said, his arms crossed.

"You're a giantsblood, you're taller than everyone. Anyway, we anchored somewhere in Pellandro—"

"Denkos," Trueblood and Lejo said, then looked at each other. "Shut up."

"I couldn't get down the gangplank fast enough to learn the ways of the world," Raj said. "These two stayed behind and…" His hand circled in the air. "Educated each other."

"Did Abrakam and Rafil do this to my father?" Trueblood said to the ceiling. "Is this torture some kind of shipboard ritual I didn't know about?"

Raj reached and pinched Trueblood's cheek. "You love it."

"Unfortunately, I do."

"You ruined my brother for anyone else."

"He did not," Lejo said.

Trueblood looked at him. "I didn't?"

"No. I mean, you were fine but—"

"*Fine?*"

Raj's laughter filled the room as he filled glasses around the table. "Drink up, lovers. You, too, Fen. You know all our secrets now."

Fen drank, enjoying himself, but wary. *Don't think you're getting any of mine,* he thought.

The bottles drained away as the book and the laughter went around the table.

"Feel better?" Raj said to Trueblood.

"No."

"Liar."

Trueblood smiled and glanced at Fen. Woozy with fatigue and rum, Fen was slow to disengage. Reluctant, if he were being honest. Trueblood's eyes were gold with lamplight. His skin smooth over his smiling cheeks and strong brow. His top teeth were white and straight, but the incisors and canines were slightly different lengths. His grin was like the foothills of a mountain chain.

And he peels potatoes to calm down, Fen thought dreamily. *When rubbing one out isn't an option.*

His slurry thoughts drifted beneath the table, constructing more imagery that triggered a delayed jealousy.

Lejo and Trueblood were lovers?

Long ago. They were kids. Obviously not since.

But still. The way they laughed over a few of the illustrations in the contraband book had the intimacy of a private joke. The exchanged glances and *shut ups* were laced with complicity.

They were lovers. They peeled potatoes together.

Fen's brow tightened as he studied the twins. Both were mouth-wateringly handsome, but Lejo definitely had an edge with those dimples. Tight hard body beneath the white linen shirt. One of the ship's cats had jumped in his lap, and was now nosing and purring along Lejo's neck. His hand moved in long strokes down its back. Fen easily imagined the cat was the long flat plain of Trueblood's thigh. Lejo's hand running up and down, pressing and kneading the muscle and...

Holy horses, what is wrong *with you?*

The neck of the rum bottle clinked against Raj's glass. A single drop fell.

"All gone," the pilot said sadly.

Lejo stifled a yawn against his fist. The party was winding down. Fen waited for Trueblood to say, "well, goodnight, lads" and then they'd clear out.

Then he remembered Trueblood didn't sleep in the quarters' big bedroom. He slept in the foyer cabin. Between the twins. Or maybe with just Lejo.

Either way, Fen was the one who needed to clear out.

He rose on swaying legs. "Well, this was delightful. We should never do it again."

"Goodnight, Fen," Trueblood said. "And thank you for sharing my misery."

"Amatos," Lejo said, his chest hitching over a hiccup. He was so utterly likable that Fen hated him a little.

Raj raised a hand. "Rest well."

And it's all your fault for going to brothels, Fen thought. *Leaving those two alone to educate each other. Your worst idea ever. Glad I missed it.*

"Goodnight," Fen said, and left the aftercastle feeling both befriended and lonely.

OLD ENOUGH TO KNOW

*From the Most Private Journal of Pelippé Trueblood
An especial accounting of his life
and voyages on the Cay.
As written by Pelippé Trueblood
(Me)*

"PELIPPÉ," FEN SAID. It rolled over his tongue as his thumb fanned the pages of the notebook, admiring the beautiful, precise handwriting and the childish sentiments.

These are the people I love.

Raj and Lejo are my brothers.

They are my friends.

We are gelang.

I love Raj and Lejo.

The ink swerved away from the O in Lejo, in a curve that looked harsh and angry. Written below, once more in the calm, perfect penmanship: *My love is bigger than the sun.*

Fen replaced the little leather book on the shelf. Trueblood had dozens of them, lined up in shades of brown, from honey-gold to cinnamon to walnut, like a cross-section of layer cake. His finger hovered over another, then paused.

He shouldn't be snooping.

He shouldn't even be *in* Trueblood's study.

A dark umber notebook opened in his hungry hands. The entries were more mature in this one. No grand, prequel announcement. Just the date at the top, followed by a block of neat writing, and ending with *P. Trueblood.*

The writing was serious, but little drawings filled the margins and the spaces between paragraphs. Sometimes repetitive designs. Ocean wave motifs. Compass roses. A ship's wheel. A centaur. One page had an astonishing sketch of Kepten True in his blue coat.

Details don't scare Trueblood, Fen thought, his fingertip marveling across every button on the coat, every kink in each braided plait, even dotted lines along the seams of True's boots.

Da, Trueblood had written beneath his father's wide-legged stance. And then, like an outpouring of grief, he wrote it again and again in a slither across the paper *Da Da Da Da Da...* Until it fell off.

Fen skimmed long stretches of writing. Tall masts were drawn in the margins, some half-morphed into trees, gnarled branches sprouting between the yards, twigs and leaves tangled in the rigging. He turned a page and the breath caught in his throat.

A winged man, his suntanned torso rising out of breeches and boots. Hands on hips, looking to the side. His hair left white and a stab of blue in each eye. The wings spread from the spine of the book to the edge of the page, every feather precisely outlined.

That's me.

He licked his lips, feeling his gaze grow wider. Trueblood drew the breeches low on Fen's hips, the top grommets unlaced. At his waist, the line where his equine torso would've begun was meticulously shaded with cross-hatched marks. A little arrow pointed toward it, with tiny, secret words: *I love this.*

A hand yanked the book away and Abrakam looked sternly at him. "That's private."

"I'm sorry."

"Don't abuse the privileges you've been given. You know better."

"I... I do. You're right. I'm sorry."

Abrakam smoothed the book shut and slid it back on the shelf. "If you want to know what's in Trueblood's heart, ask him. He's not your father. What he wants you to know, he'll tell you. What he keeps guarded, he'll give you the reason why."

Fen nodded, miserable.

"Go on now. This isn't your place."

Fen left, mortified to be caught with his hand in the sugar sack. Sucking on the sweetness of what he found.

He drew me in his book.

He put a hand on his hip, thinking about the silvery line that ran low around his waist. The border of human and equine when he was in kheiros. Every kheiron had one. Fen's was especially visible because of his dark skin. At some point, Trueblood saw it. He drew it.

He loved it.

If you want to know what's in Trueblood's heart, ask him.

"Was it hard being the son of your commander?" Fen asked.

Trueblood laughed. "You're the heir to the kheiron herd and you're asking me if it was hard?"

"This is called making pleasant conversation. I can insult you if you prefer."

"It was hard," Trueblood said. "I had to learn to call my father Da and call my commander Kep. And keep them separate."

"How did you know which one you were talking to?"

Trueblood shrugged. "By his voice. Or the subject matter. Sometimes he'd ask a question and I'd answer, 'Yes, Da.' Other times, he'd ask something and add on, 'Answer your commander.'"

He was beautiful in the moonlight.

"Khe, I miss that," he said. "When he'd be formidable. Pressing a point home by saying, 'Do you understand? Answer your commander.' It was intimidating but it was simple. The answer was simple. *Aye, Kep. I understand. You have my word.*"

"What else do you miss?"

"Him saying my name."

"Pelippé."

"Just Pé." Trueblood set his chin on his hands. "Go to sleep, Pé. Don't worry so much, Pé."

"Abrakam calls you Troubled."

Trueblood smiled. "That's me."

Gods, that smile.

Fen wished he had a similar tale to share. For his sake as well as Trueblood's. Something to keep Trueblood smiling. Questions to make him shrug the moon off his shoulders. Secrets he'd keep tucked in the pages of his little leather books.

Soft laughter caught his ear from further down the deck, where Beniv and Calvo were sitting on one of the bulkheads.

"How long have they been together?" Fen asked, inclining his head.

"Gods, twenty years at least. I mean, I've never known a time when they weren't gelang."

"Want to hear something idiotic?"

"What?"

"I think I was twenty-five when I realized the ritual handshake is called gelango because gelang means at hand. Like I never put that together."

"Don't feel bad. I once saw a kheiron in humos and said, 'Oh, you have your legs on.'"

Fen pointed a finger. "*That* was pretty idiotic."

"Thank you. I put a lot of effort into saying stupid things."

He smiled and Fen died a little inside. He liked Trueblood so much it hurt. It hurt so purely and simply and beautifully, it made Fen feel young.

Young and free.

He looked away, staring at Calvo's easy, muscular sprawl. Beniv between his knees, wrapped in a blanket, his head on the quartermaster's chest.

"Your father never had another mate after your mother died," Trueblood said. "Did he?"

"No. She was his one and only."

"You say that like it's unusual."

"It is, actually. Stories I've heard about past Horselords, they all had multiple lovers. My great-grandfather was a notorious stud. He'd mount anything on four legs. But my father loved only my mother. After she died, he had no more need for any kind of companionship."

"Something beautiful about a love like that, yet it's sad at the same time."

"Did your father have anyone else?"

Trueblood took a long time to answer. "He had his… I'll say his *favorites* when we came ashore."

"Courtesans?"

Trueblood's mouth twisted. "I don't want to idealize him, but no, I don't think they were. It doesn't seem his way. Then again, you never really know somebody, do you?"

"Mm."

"I've never told anyone this, but I think old Rafil loved my Da."

"You mean in love with him?"

"Yeah. It's something I didn't figure out until the end of his life, and it's only a guess. But I think Rafil adored my father in every way possible. Kept it secret and un-acted upon. Then when Da died, Rafil willed himself out of life and followed. With him until the end."

Fen nodded. "I don't think I ever heard a bad word spoken about your father in my life." He laughed softly. "I'd actually be shocked if Rafil were the only mariner in love with him."

"Oh, there were others."

"Really?"

"Once... I must've been thirteen or fourteen. Old enough to know about such things. One of the majoros developed an infatuation with my father. I walked in on an embarrassing situation where Da was... I guess rejecting him. Or letting him know it was impossible. Putting him back in his place. You know what I mean."

"Did your father bed men?"

"Not to my knowledge. Anyway, he came to see me later. To put me in *my* place, so to speak. I asked if the majoro would stay aboard. Da said, 'No, he'll be put ashore. It's a distraction.' Then his face got all stern and he said, 'I'll not have you hold this against him.'

"'No, Da,' I said.

"'I mean it,' he said. 'One smart remark or one side-eye in his direction and you'll be up against the mizzen mast. I'll thrash you myself. Am I clear?'"

"I bet you answered your commander," Fen said.

"Oh I did," Trueblood said. "But I was hurt."

"Hurt?"

"Hurt that Da would think I was capable of that kind of cruelty."

"You don't have a cruel bone in your body."

"Sure. I throw rocks at you because I'm nice."

"You threw it because I was being an asshole."

"And I didn't aim at your head."

"Which I appreciate."

Fen tapped his thumbs together. "You know, your mother was one of my favorite people."

"Oh?"

"My stunning personality doesn't lend itself to having a lot of friends. But Noë was always kind to me."

"I didn't know you had a relationship with her."

"Well, I didn't spend a whole lot of time in her company but whenever I did, it felt easy and relaxed. I liked being around her. Liked the way she smiled at me or said, 'Oh, Feños, you're home, we missed you.' She made me feel good. And she liked apples as much as I did. You can't not like someone who appreciates a good apple."

Trueblood laughed, and it seemed a good place to end the chat and the evening.

"Goodnight, Kepten," Fen said.

"Goodnight. Sleep well."

The kheiron whistled through his teeth as he went below. Closing the door of his cabin, he was struck by how at home he felt. Contentment and belonging infused all the little nighttime rituals he'd cultivated on this journey. Binding the small stones on the insides of his wrists. Shaving a bit of kyrrh for the mug of hot water Melki left him. His bow and quiver hung from pegs on the wall, his boots lined up underneath. The braided rope of his mother's hair coiled neatly on his night table, next to his knives and a little horse Eleven carved for him. Incredible how a ham-fisted brute like Eleven could pull such tiny, detailed beauty out of wood.

He was pulling his shirt over his head when a brisk knock came at the door. "Come in."

Trueblood stood in the doorway, a long finger pointing at Fen's face.

"It was you," he said.

"I'm sorry?"

"You were the one leaving apples at my mother's tomb all these years."

Fen opened his mouth, then shut it and nodded.

"Huh." Trueblood crossed his arms, shaking his head a little. "You got a mighty sweet side for an asshole."

"Well, keep that to yourself or my reputation won't precede me." Fen tossed his shirt aside and was immediately conscious of the kepten's eyes on his skin.

I think I want him.

The fear was electric in his veins. This was the same delicious trepidation that quaked through his limbs when he and Belmiro were in bed and in humos together. But a thousand times more intense. Primed with knowledge. Keen with memory.

Ruined by all the men who used to fuck with him.

"Seriously," Trueblood said. "I always wondered who was bringing the apples. Both I and my father did."

"I thought for sure he knew," Fen said. "I mean, it was my and Noë's little thing. I brought her an apple when I came home and she left one for me in my room." He shrugged. "I missed her bad after she died. So I kept doing it."

"I love that you did."

What else do you love? Fen thought. He almost dared to ask, but balked at the last second and said, "Good. And I still hate your guts."

"Glad you cleared that up. I was about to invite you back to my cabin."

Fen laughed and Trueblood put up a farewell hand before backing into the corridor and closing the door. Fen stared for five heart-pounding seconds, then yanked it open again.

"Were you really?" he called to Trueblood's back.

The kepten turned. "What?"

"About to invite me."

"No."

Relief and disappointment ran down Fen's back. "Oh. Good-night."

"Amatos."

Fen closed the door, leaned against it and exhaled.

What just happened?

Speak Your Name

"Pegasos," came the cry from the crow's nest one morning.

Far out to sea was a flight of winged horses, their silhouettes blurred but unmistakable. The crew came pouring on deck, leaning bellies and arms against the starboard rail. Hands reached for telescopes and necks craned to the sky.

"They're real," Melki said, sitting on Fen's shoulders.

"Of course they're real," Fen said. "You've never seen one before?"

All around him, heads shook and eyes shone wide in incredulous faces.

"How many?" Calvo said, a hand shading his eyes and the other arm around Beniv.

"I count nine," the sail maker said.

"Lucky nine," Dhar agreed.

"Feels like a sign," Sixten said.

"I was just about to say the same," Seven said. "What do you think, Kepten?"

Trueblood lowered his telescope. "It feels like seeing something beautiful."

"I think we should follow them."

Now all heads turned to Raj. Rather than wide-open and wondering, his expression was narrowed tight, cold and calculating.

"You think?" Trueblood said carefully.

Raj nodded several times. "Follow them."

"Why?" The kepten moved closer to his pilot. "I'm not questioning your compass, Raj, I just want to know what it's telling you."

Raj's mouth hesitated before he spoke. "Something's happening. Or starting to happen."

Fen swung Melki down and moved closer as well. "I don't know a lot about pegasos," he said. "But I can count on one hand the number of times I've seen them on the move in broad daylight. And I'm already down a finger so..."

Trueblood nodded, tapping his teeth together. "Lejo, where's your needle pointing?"

"Toward Raj."

"All right then." Trueblood clapped Raj's shoulder and motioned toward the helm. "Pilot, change course."

"Aye, Kep."

Fen moved back to the rail to watch and Trueblood followed.

"You're the son of a pegaso yet you know little about them," he said.

Fen smiled. "They are notoriously elusive creatures."

"But heirs to the kheiron herd are always born from a pegaso, right?"

"Mmhm. It's a wonder the lineage lasted this long when the impression is pegasos don't hold still long enough to mate."

Trueblood laughed. "I guess you'll find out someday."

The kheiron nodded slowly. "I'll have to, if the line is going to continue."

"Do you want to sire children?"

"I guess so."

"Sounds like you haven't given it much thought."

"Think again, Kepten," Fen said. "My dam is dead and my sire is an asshole. So I wonder all the time what kind of parent I'm going to be."

Trueblood smiled to himself. Lately, when Fen labeled his father in choice terms, he sounded a lot like Lejo—like he didn't mean it.

Trueblood squinted, but the pegasos were only a smudge now. He turned back to Raj, who caught his eye from the helm and raised a reassuring hand. He should go back in his study, but Fen's presence had invisible hooks in him, holding him right here to talk more.

"Did you call your father Da?" he asked.

Fen shook his head. "Not since I was a foalboy. It was Father to his face. Less flattering names in private."

"What's his khenom?"

"Why?"

"Because I'm nosy and curious."

Fen twisted the ring on his fourhand thumb.

Truvosol, Trueblood remembered. *The ring of Truvos. But it's obnoxious to refer to it that way.*

"I don't like to say his khenom," Fen finally said. "It's an intimate thing and I'm just not close enough to him anymore. Truth is, I've kind of forgotten how."

"I'm sorry, I shouldn't have asked."

"I'll say another if you want."

"Who?"

Fen spoke a multi-syllabic invocation, more like a phrase of music than a word.

Trueblood blinked. "What?"

Fen smiled. "That's Belmiro's khenom." He said it again. It began as the recognizable *Belmiro,* then slid into something not of this world. If Trueblood had a knife to his throat, he couldn't have repeated it. His tongue hesitated in his mouth, not knowing where to even *start.*

"Khenoms are all like that," Fen said. "When I say Bel's, I get it a little wrong. He's the only one who can say his soul name perfectly. I'm the only one who can say mine. Every other kheiron gets it slightly wrong."

"And men get it completely wrong."

"That's why we have agnoms."

"On behalf of man, I thank you for being so considerate."

Fen smiled. "Here's a funny thing. If I were in a pitch-dark room with Belmiro and twenty other kheirons, and all of them said Bel's khenom at the same time, I could immediately tell which one was him. I can't say his khenom properly, but I know it instantly when I hear it."

"Huh."

"So when I was young, really little, if I was separated from my father, I wouldn't call his khenom. I'd call Da, then say *my* khenom. He could find me much faster."

"Faster than I can?"

Fen touched his teeth to his bottom lip and smiled, his nose wrinkling. "Maybe."

Kheiron and giantsblood stood poised on the edge of affinity, the moment shimmering between them. "Say your name," Trueblood said.

His ears were prepared for the name to start *Fen,* but it didn't. Of course it didn't.

"*Tehvani…*" Fen began, and the rest slid across Trueblood's skin like a kiss. Before he could ask, Fen said it again.

When the hair settled back down on his arms, Trueblood said, "Sometimes I forget your agnom used to be Tehvan."

"That's fine. I left it behind a long time ago."

"Could you change your khenom?"

"No. It would be like changing my eye color."

Well don't do that, Trueblood thought. *Your eyes match my coat. Which is only slightly less significant than nine pegasos in a daytime sky.*

"Now what are you staring at?" Fen said.

"Nothing."

The kheiron smoothed his hair and struck an affected pose against the railing. "Want me to hold still while you get your oil paints?"

"Get over yourself."

"Hey, look who's back."

Trueblood followed Fen's pointing finger toward a shape in the sky. The lark, missing for days now, flew over their heads. She fluttered down to perch on the rigging, wet and bedraggled, her crest pointing in all directions.

"And where have *you* been?" Trueblood said.

She gave her two-tone whistle and pecked at the mast.

"Looks like she got laid last night," Fen said.

"Lucky her," Trueblood said.

The little bird's eyes seemed to roll as she turned her back on them, preening her feathers back in place. She pecked at the mast a few more times and looked at Trueblood as if daring him to say anything. He held his finger out to her and almost dropped dead when she hopped onto it.

"Holy shit," he said, laughing. His other finger approached her head, shy and cautious. She allowed him to pet her. "Pegasos in the sky and a lark being nice to me. What's next?"

He glanced at Fen, who looked back. The clear azure gaze was soft, like a careful fingertip stroking a bird's head. Not believing its own good luck.

I'm in love with you, Trueblood thought. Quietly. As if noticing the weather. Surely this was supposed to be a thunderous epiphany. Not ordinary and banal. Yet there it was. The next thing.

Pegasos in the sky, a lark being nice to me and I'm in love.

He half-expected to see sides constructed around him. Love was a box and he was in it. Something was no longer happening to him. It happened. The tense was past.

And here I am.

Glad we got this cleared up.

"I have work to do," he said. "Hold the baby?"

Fen snorted. "Gods, you're weird." But he reached out his hand and set his finger next to Trueblood's, smiling as the bird came to him.

A Whisper Apart

Faint lines etched the corners of Raj's eyes, products of his constant squint toward the horizon, following the smudge of the pegasos flight. It often disappeared, making the pilot's shoulders rise up around his ears, but it always appeared again. The flying herd backtracked a little, hovering as the Kaleuche caught up, then they raced toward the earth's curved finish line.

"They want us to follow," Raj said.

The lark whistled, and from her perch on Lejo's shoulder she took to the air, little wings pumping vigorously as she followed the steeds.

As they sailed further north, hugging the coast of Minosaros, the days lengthened. Aybar was far behind them and the land changed from scrub to the stark red rocks of Arcodolori.

One warm night, they moved the story hour on deck, gathering under the last of the long day's light and watching the stars emerge. Fen told the story of Minos the Bull, the beloved bovine dope who was slain by the one who loved him most.

"Love does nothing but get you killed," Eleven said over his woodcarving.

"Don't be a bitch," Dhar said.

Eleven laughed as he spun his knife in clever fingers. "Well?"

"Love gets you laid," the sail maker said.

"What's laid?" Melki asked.

Silence on deck. Trueblood chuckled in his chest. "Do tell, Dhar."

Dhar turned a hand in the air, looking for divine intervention. Finally he said, "Laid is another word for happiness."

"Like Nye?" Melki said. "Love gets you Nye?"

"The feeling you would get from Nye. You make that by being with someone you love. That's why it's called making love."

"You make the goodness in the world that the Nye trees used to make," Trueblood said.

Melki looked around the crew, sitting or leaning against bulkheads and barrels and masts. Beniv with his head in Calvo's lap. Sixten dozing on Seven's shoulder. Trueblood's legs stretched out long and stacked like logs with the Ĝemelos' legs.

"So are we all making love right now?"

Throats cleared and adult mouths folded around stifled laughter.

"In a manner of speaking, lad," Abrakam said.

"Will we ever have a new goddess of love?" Melki asked, looking up at the constellation of Nyos.

"I don't think Nyos is really dead," Trueblood said.

"The stories say Truvos killed her."

"How do you kill a god, though? I think he just killed the thing that let her walk around on earth. Now she's up in the stars but her spirit, her presence…" Trueblood stretched his arms to encompass the ship, the ocean and the world. "Is still here. I don't think Truvos could destroy that without destroying himself in the process. That's what I believe, anyway."

"She just shoots him," Fen said absently. "Over and over, every night, Nyos shoots an arrow into the thing she loves most. Whoever put her in the stars that way was cruel."

All eyes turned up, contemplating the drama playing out in the constellations, except for Trueblood. His eyes were fixed on Fen's throat, stretched long and tender from the V of his shirt.

"Arrow of sadness," Fen said. "They say Nyos fletched her arrows with peacock feathers, because they contained the eyes of the stars and gave her impeccable aim. She never missed a shot. Her perfect vision ended up being her undoing."

Melki got up and put arms around Fen from behind, laying his head on the kheiron's shoulder. Fen looked back, startled, then patted the boy's crossed wrists.

You're so beautiful, Trueblood thought.

"The arrow of sadness wounded Minos so badly, his blood splashed all over the land, coloring the rock formations red," Fen said.

"Really?" Melki said.

"Well. No. The rocks are red because they have a lot of iron in them."

"Don't ruin it, Fen," Seven said. "If I wanted scientific explanations, I would've become a scholar. The face value of stories is enough for me."

"You've been saying that since you were a minoro at old Rafil's feet," Abrakam said.

"Gods, I miss him," the cook said.

Hands thumped horizontal surfaces in appreciation.

"The Cult of the Bull believes the red soil has ears to hear and secrets to tell," Fen said.

"The what of the bull?" Melki said.

The kheiron sighed. "Long ago, a small group of people in Minosaros started twisting the legends around. Instead of Minos being simple-minded, they believed he possessed unparalleled wisdom. Instead of his death being an accident, they interpreted it as intentional. Nyos wanted his power for herself so she killed him, and all the wisdom and secrets and magic in Minos's blood went into the soil of Arcodolori."

"Then what happened?"

"The small group got bigger. The belief in the bull's superiority became a religion. The religion infiltrated the government.

And then…" Fen trailed off and looked at Abrakam. "I'm not too good converting that into history," he said.

"The Cult of the Bull's foundation was hatred for Nyos," the centaur said. "She was gone, so the hatred was directed at her children, who tended the trees. Nyland became the enemy. The minotaurs felt the trees belonged to them. And for a long time, lads, the world saw nothing but war between the nations."

"Is that the war named after you, Fen?" Melki asked.

Fen's smile was edged with sadness. "More like the last battle in a centuries-old conflict."

"So it's over now?"

"Not quite," Fen said. "Still some fighting left to do."

THE DAYS LENGTHENED. The pegasos beckoned, turning them away from the coast. The ship sailed. Stories were told.

And Trueblood longed.

Fen lived in his head now, morning, noon and night. He looked through Trueblood's eyes, experiencing the world with him. Sometimes offering his thoughts and counsel, other times just his presence.

What is happening to me?

Outwardly, Trueblood was composed, quiet, confident and in command. Within, he was thirteen and monstrous. His skin ached, his heart stretched in all directions until it turned transparent. All of him was a window to the howling need inside, until he was sure it was written across his forehead in sloppy penmanship.

"What's troubling Trueblood?" Fen said during ripozo.

You, Trueblood thought. "Nothing," he said.

"My mistake." Fen raised his telescope to the last visible scrap of Arcodolori, lips moving faintly under his breath. Even at this safe distance, his posture was tense. Braced to run at the slightest provocation.

"Will you feel better when it's out of sight?" Trueblood asked.

"I don't know if I'll ever feel better about it."

"Still some fighting left to do."

The scope came down and Fen gave a tight smile. "You know, I really love how the crew comes together to tell stories at night."

"The lads like the ones you tell."

"Do they?"

"Mm."

"I have so many tales about Arcodolori, but they're not... I can't tell them in front of the young ones."

"Tell me."

"You don't want to hear."

"If you can live it, I can hear it."

Fen shrugged and leaned his crossed arms on the railing.

"I'm listening," Trueblood said softly.

Saying it felt like the biggest gamble of his life. But his ears were the only thing he could offer the kheiron. As he waited in the quiet, listening to the creak of the ship and the lap of the waves against her hull, he ached with hope and longing.

I want to know you, Fen il-Kheir. I want to hear all your stories. Tell me, and I'll be so careful with them, I promise.

"When I got sold to a second master," Fen said. "I was force-marched from Aybar to a region called Danysh. It's one of the few green places in the north of Minosaros. They grow a little food and a lot of fadara. Fadara and slaves, that's Danysh's economy. Slaves are either laborers on plantations, or they're whores at the brothels. I was the latter."

He glanced at Trueblood, who kept a placid, attentive face.

"I'm listening," he said.

"Fifteen slaves left Aybar. I was the only one who reached Danysh alive."

"Tell me."

"The fadara addicts were the first to go. They went mad from withdrawal." He shuddered. "Gods, the way they would scream. Think of a baby having a fit, how their voice builds and builds until it cracks open and rattles. That's what it was like. They'd beg the minotaurs to kill them. Cut their throats and end it. But those bastards were either deaf or had hearts of stone. The screaming didn't phase them, but we were all clawing our ears off to get away from the sound."

He steepled his hands over his mouth and nose and drew a long, deep breath. "One night," he said, muffled, "I saw a slave smother one of the addicts to death."

"Gods."

"Instead of being horrified, I was grateful."

"He probably was, too," Trueblood said quietly.

Fen took his hands down from his face. "Once the addicts were gone, slaves started dropping dead of dehydration. The arid environment literally *drinks* you and they didn't bring water for us on the march. We'd only drink when we made camp for the night. I learned to save my spit. Talking was a waste of moisture. All day long I kept my mouth shut and let the saliva pool up in my mouth and I'd swallow it a little at a time. I basically survived by drinking myself.

"At night, the minotaurs would chain us up and eat around the fire, then throw us the scraps."

"What did they eat?"

"Rabbits, squirrels, birds. Sometimes a big lizard. Whatever they could skin and roast over the fire."

Trueblood's brow knitted. "You're vegetarian, though. What did you eat?"

"I had to eat what was there, which was meat. It made me sick as shit, but I had no choice." He gave a bitter chuckle. "Once, when it was down to me and two other slaves, the minotaurs spitted these giant grasshoppers and put them in the fire. We each got one. A *whole* grasshopper each. It was a feast."

"Would it be stupid to ask if they were tasty?"

"I don't really remember the taste, but I ate all of it. Antenna. Feelers. The charred exoskeleton. Everything. The desert is no place for picky eaters."

"Gods."

"After eating, the minotaurs would sit around and drink and tell their own stories. That's how I heard about the red soil having ears to hear and secrets to tell. The ancient people would mix the soil with water and whisper wishes into the clay. Then make the clay into little statues which they'd pray to. I thought maybe if it worked for wishes, it could work for names."

"Names?"

"Remember I told you, the other day, when I was separated from my father, I'd call my khenom to help him find me?"

"I remember."

"Well, I… Gods, I never told this to anyone."

Trueblood sat still. He could barely breathe, he wanted to be told so badly.

"At night I'd spit in the ground until it made a clay," Fen said. "I said my khenom into the clay and rolled it into little balls. They dried overnight and as we marched the next day, I'd drop them along the way. Leaving a trail of my name for the gods to hear and my father to follow. But it didn't work."

His shoulders rose up high, then he exhaled slowly. "My stories don't have happy endings," he said. "Another reason I don't tell them."

"Mm."

"It's so beautiful," Fen said. "Arcodolori is so impossibly beautiful. And violent and ugly and terrible at the same time. Horrible days when I'd look out on this breathtaking scenery and wonder how I could be living such a miserable life in such a gorgeous place. How such inhumane cruelty could be sustained in a land that looked like the gods' nursery. All those rock formations looked like forgotten playthings to me. Toys the gods left behind after they grew up. It was literally a gods-forsaken place."

Trueblood got up and went to stand by Fen at the railing. "One day," he said. "I don't know, one idealistic, happily-ever-after day when that part of the world is a better place, would you ever go back?"

Fen thought a long time. "Maybe. Someday when I'm in a better place. And when I have someone who could go with me."

"Who do you see that being?"

A faint smile lifted a corner of the kheiron's mouth. "Once, when I was little, I asked my father how he knew my dam was the one for him. He said she came the closest to saying his khenom perfectly. It made sense to me. Still does. I guess if I ever went back to Arcodolori, it would be with someone who can call me by name." He glanced at Trueblood. "Let the record show I'll follow my father's lead on something."

"That's a good story," Trueblood said.

"Still no happy ending."

"Because it's still being written."

Fen's elbow dug in Trueblood's side. "You've got a soft spot for an asshole."

"Shut up." He hipped back and after their sides bumped once, then again, they settled a whisper apart. "You don't have to answer this, but who was the boy the Altyns found with you?" He moved a hair, enough to close the gap and feel Fen's body through his clothes.

Fen's touch moved away. Then it came back. "His name was Alon," he said.

"Alon, like...lark?"

"Yes. When we escaped, we decided to take new names. We named each other. I choose Alon for him because he was delivering his own newborn soul. He chose Fen for me, because whoever crossed my path would be damned."

"*He* named you Fen," Trueblood said softly.

"Yes." Fen wiggled one of his rings, turning it round and round. "We escaped together. But when we got over the Altyn mountains, he fell off my back and…"

"I'm so sorry."

"He's buried next to my mother. I asked Father and he did it for me. It was the last promise he made and kept."

"I see."

"I don't like to talk about it." Fen's body moved a little closer.

"You're talking about it now."

"Because it's easy to tell you things."

"My listening doesn't come at a price," Trueblood said.

And I want to kiss you, he thought.

LATER

ELLING TRUEBLOOD HIS stories, Fen felt utterly naked. Shedding not only his clothes but his skin, leaving all of his bones on display. A roasted grasshopper ready to be eaten. Antenna, feelers and all.

"My listening doesn't come at a price," Trueblood said.

Fen stared at him. For a stunned moment, he wondered how the kepten could possibly know how transactional Fen's life was. How he learned at a painfully young age never to do anything without getting something in return. This for that. He learned to be wary of kindness, sympathy and compassion because they always seemed to have a hidden cost.

Only a moment he wondered.

Because in the next moment, he saw it was no wonder at all.

"I don't know a lot about gelang," he said slowly. "But I imagine listening is one of the best parts about it."

That and kissing, he thought

Gods, Pelippé Trueblood, I want to kiss you. I want to tell all my stories into your open mouth and ask for nothing in return.

His legs swayed a little and he swallowed hard. "I still hate your guts but right now, I'm rather glad to be onboard."

Trueblood drew a long, deep breath. "Come with me."

"What?"

"I want to show you something."

"Your cabin?"

"You wish. Come on."

Fen followed down the great stairwell, then down littler, winding ones to the holds. "What, you mean I still haven't seen everything there is to see on this boat?"

"No. And still no place you can hide where I can't find you."

Fuck, I love when you say that, Fen thought.

Trueblood paused outside a door. You had to look hard to discern it was a door. It lay flush with the interior wall of the ship, only the knob and the latch giving away its function.

"It's a step up," Trueblood said. "And the lintel is low. Watch your head."

Fen ducked as he entered the room, while Trueblood snapped a match on his heel and lit the lantern.

A scent not of this world embraced Fen like a surprise. It *flung* arms around him and held him close, weeping, *You're here. Here you are. You're back.*

"Khe l'khe," he whispered, his eyes and nose and throat full of that smell, holy horses, what *was* it? It seeped into his pores, filled his veins and danced over the roof of his mouth until he could taste the air because he *was* the air. He was life and youth and purity and truth and love and it was all, everything was so beautiful and could he stay here forever, could it all be his, please let it all stay this way, just like this so perfect and smelling so good...

"Where's it coming from?" he said hoarsely. His words sparkled as they left his tongue and he was so sad to see them go, yet they hung in the air like soap bubbles and wasn't it beautiful, wasn't it all just *splendid*...

"The walls," Trueblood said, his face dreamy. "Decades and centuries of transporting Nye. The scent got into the walls and it never leaves. To me, this is the most especial place on the ship."

Fen carefully and happily gathered the edges of his blown mind together, pulling them back into some kind of order. He inhaled to the tips of his ribs. "I've never smelled it so intense."

"Growing up, I'd always watch when new crew members went down to the Cay's nyellem for the first time. They'd only heard stories about spice. It was nothing but legend to them. They never saw it. Or smelled it. They'd walk in the first time and Gods... They'd cry. Say it was the best thing to ever happen to them in their lives. It was magic."

You're so beautiful, Fen thought.

"Watch," Trueblood said. "If you rub the wood..." He did so and held his fingertips to his nose. "It sticks to your skin for a little while." His hand danced past Fen's face. Fen inhaled spice and skin and his mouth watered. His eyes followed the hand's trail through the thick, heady air, sparkles in its wake that drifted slowly to the floor.

He shook his head hard. "Can't believe you kept this from me."

Trueblood smiled and his tongue touched the edges of his upper teeth. "It's a magical place, but it's also the darkest place on the ship. The ceiling is low and... I didn't want you to be afraid."

Fen swallowed. "Who's the bed for?"

Khe, but his mouth was so *juicy* right now.

Trueblood moved a few inches toward it, hands on hips. "Anyone. Sleeping down here is a privilege you earn. A reward. Rest of the time it's shut up tight. The one time my father whipped me in front of the crew was when I was in the Cay's nyellem without permission."

"Uh-oh."

"Unlawful entry *and* I didn't shut the latch properly."

"You told me he only punished disrespect," Fen said, looking at Trueblood's broad back.

"I disrespected the nyellem and the kepten's rule."

"Double trouble."

"Almost. Nine is a typical beating. I got twelve that time. Bare-assed over a barrel with the whole crew watching."

Fen's eyes followed a shiver of memory as it made Trueblood's shirt ripple from nape to waist. He easily could've blamed the residual Nye in the walls for what happened next. He knew what he was doing. But he had no idea *why* he did it.

Other than he wanted to.

And every scented board in the walls nodded, saying, *Yes, yes, go ahead. By all means. We insist.*

He reached out his fivehand. Stretched his ringed fingers and rested them gently on the hard curve of Kepten Trueblood's backside. And said, "That must've hurt."

The room went quiet as dust. Then Trueblood's back and shoulders expanded in a huge intake of breath. They hitched with a single chuckle, then deflated. "Hurt my pride more than my ass."

"Still…" Fen's fingertips wandered up a little. Then down. "Tastes like shit when you disappoint someone."

"Yeah. A beating basically makes your outsides sting more than your insides."

A long, spicy moment of silence. "I know you miss your father so bad."

The kepten's coiled locks shook as he glanced over his shoulder and down his back. "Every day."

Fen took his hand away. "Sorry."

Trueblood looked up. "Don't be sorry for touching me."

Their eyes held. Trueblood turned more. Fen stepped backward. They turned. And stepped. The wall bumped Fen's shoulders and told him it was far enough. Trueblood came the rest of the way. Lips slightly parted and eyes full of bewildered curiosity. He put one hand on the wall by Fen's head. Then the other.

Their eyes reached through bubbling sparkles to touch.

What do you see? Fen thought, which left his mouth as, "What the fuck are you staring at?"

"You," Trueblood said. "All day long, all I do is stare at you."

"Why?"

The kepten ran his hands up and down the wall. Once. Again. A third time. Then his fingertips pressed lightly on Fen's face, lined up along each cheekbone.

"Because I want you so bad," he whispered.

Fen closed his eyes and inhaled the scent that had no name. His own fingers plucked at the hem of Trueblood's shirt, gathering it into his fists, working up the courage to slide beneath.

Trueblood shook as his hands found the wall again. His head lowered and he put his forehead on Fen's shoulder. His breath drew in with a hiss when Fen touched his back. Tentative at first. A few shy fingertips. Then his full, brave palm. Then both hands.

"Khe, man," Fen whispered.

Trueblood turned his head a little. The apple of his smiling cheek swelled round against Fen's shoulder. "Usually 'man' sounds like an insult from you."

"Does it?"

"Mm."

"What about now, man?"

"Not so much."

Fen shrugged his shoulder and caught Trueblood's head in his hands. He drew in a long, shaky breath. "This is crazy."

"I know."

"I can't breathe."

The kepten's finger touched his mouth. "I know." He drew along Fen's bottom lip. "Me neither."

They kissed. The walls of the nyellem folded together, turned inside-out, splintered apart in sparkles and soap bubbles that popped in Fen's ears and danced behind his eyelids in orange and yellow and pink and purple.

"Fen." Trueblood breathed the name like a song. Moaned it like soft music. His tongue tasted of truth and life and home and a long search finally ended.

You're here. Here you are.

No place I can go where you can't find me.

The mariner's mouth kissed down his neck and a sound squeezed through Fen's throat. The blood flowed hot in his veins, swelling hard between his legs, writhing and wanting, he wanted so bad, he wanted so much. It was right in his hands, everything he longed for in his arms, but so many things had been cruelly snatched away from him before. Even as his embrace grabbed and clutched, it was full of hesitation.

Was this for him? Could this be his?

Breathing hard, Trueblood's head lolled on Fen's shoulder again. "Feels like I've been falling in love with you for a long time."

Fen's ears touched the incredible words and shivered. "I loved you the first time I saw you."

Trueblood's head came up and his smile broke open like an egg. "You shit on my feet the first time you saw me."

Fen laughed, fingers closing in fists in Trueblood's clothes. "No, you moron. I mean the first time. When you were a baby. At your naming ceremony, when I shifted into equos without thinking about it. Because something in you makes me want to show my good side."

"All your sides are good," Trueblood said, his hands sliding warm and strong around Fen's face, pressing their brows together.

"You make me want to be better." Fen turned them, putting Trueblood's back to the wall now. They kissed. Harder this time. Yanking arms from their shirts and putting hands on bare skin. Wrestling and rocking, weaving one arm on top of the other, over and through and across and pulling tight like a knot. Fastening each other down. Holding it there tight.

"It's so much," Trueblood whispered.

"It's not enough." Fen ran his hand down Trueblood's stomach. Hesitated. Then took one lace in his precise fingers and pulled it loose.

"Kepten," someone called from another universe.

Their mouths startled around the kiss, drew away gasping and panting.

The call came stronger. *"Kepten!"*

"I'm in the middle of something, lads," Trueblood mumbled, his fists tight in the kheiron's hair.

"No place on the ship where they can't find you."

"I know." He kissed Fen again. "We should talk more about this later."

"We should." Fen ran a hand along Trueblood's jaw. "It's long overdue."

Trueblood turned his mouth into Fen's palm for a warm, damp instant. "Wait for me. I'll go deal with whatever they're carrying on about. And then I'll meet you. Back here. Later."

"Later." Fen had never known such a beautiful word.

"And we'll talk about it."

"In depth. And when we're done talking, you can fuck me on that bed."

It slipped right out of his mouth. Savage and simple. Tinged with fear, only because he wanted it. For the first time since he was twelve years old, he wanted it desperately.

Trueblood's fingers pressed Fen's skin. Eyes wild in the dark. An open mouth with words piling up in the back of his throat, but unable to get any of them to come forward.

His speechlessness was intoxicating.

"It's a reward, right?" Fen said, closing his teeth around the mariner's bottom lip. Relishing this power coursing through his body. This foreign joy in being a man so he could lie with another man.

"I'll tell you what the reward is," Trueblood said. "It's not fucking you on that bed. It's taking you to the bed in the kepten's quarters. I've been keeping it empty all this time because I made a promise I'd only lie down there with someone I love. And just so we're *crystal* clear, I'm so in love with you, I can't sleep at night. Neither will you. Do you understand?"

"I do."

"You sure?"

"Perfectly."

"That bed is so big, you could get lost in it. But believe me, I'll find you." His mouth crushed down. All of his body pressed Fen, hot and tight and hard. "If I don't sleep, you don't sleep. All night long, I want to find you in my bed and wake you up."

Groaning, Fen took one last taste of his kiss and then shoved him away. "Go. Your crew needs you."

"All right." Shirt slung over a shoulder, he stepped back and tied his breeches. "Dammit, I'm pitching a tent. This is going to be embarrassing."

"Sorry."

"Horseshit, you're sorry." Trueblood opened the door and stood silhouetted an aching moment. His finger raised and pointed. "Shut the door when you leave."

"I will."

"Shut it *tight*. Understand? Answer your commander."

His heart exploding in his chest, Fen answered. "Aye, Kep."

A smile more brilliant than the sunrise stretched Trueblood's face and at that instant, Fen would have killed for him.

The smile snuffed out like a candle flame when the shouts of the crew above rose up.

"Kepten," they wailed. *"Kraken! Off the port side! It's Misery!"*

"Fuck," Trueblood cried, and bolted for the stairs, his shirt falling to the floor.

Shirtless as well, Fen took the extra second to make sure the door of the hold was shut tight, then ran after.

Behind him, the nyellem hugged itself, shivering in joy, joy, joy, joy…

Part Eight

HELOS

Goddess of Birth and Death

BRING HER DOWN

THE FIGHT AGAINST Misery was glorious in its terror.

In later years, the crew would tell the story, and speak of how Kepten Trueblood had bravely commanded the ship that terrible day. Calling battle stations and strategy, barking orders right and left, all the while standing shirtless at the helm and keeping the Kaleuche under his strict control.

"Fen," he cried, like a song. "Bring her down."

One hand holding the mighty wheel, he brought the other to his mouth and his teeth scraped Fen's ring from his finger. Fen caught it in one hand as he reached for his bow with the other.

A crack like a cloth shaken out as his wings unfolded.

"The eye," Abrakam cried after him. "Feños, the shot must be in her *eye*."

"*Bring her down, Fen!*" the crew called.

"Get back, lads," Trueblood hollered from the helm.

Misery breached, a forest of tentacles snarling in the air, one just missing Fen's leg. Her swollen body slapped down and the ocean caved in on top of it. Water bucked and heaved under the port side, knocking crew into a pile against the opposite railing.

Archers clung to the rigging with shins and toes as they fired their bows out to sea. Finding an assault rhythm of riddling the depths to make Misery come to the surface, where Fen would be waiting.

"Keep her angry," Fen called, flying by to snatch a full quiver from Melki. He swooped past the helm and called to Trueblood, "Turn starboard. Bring us ar—"

A splintering crash as one of Misery's tentacles busted through the port railing. Crew scattered like wet rats. A bone-cracking howl as Sixten was dragged across the deck, his ankle trapped in Misery's grip.

"*Six!*" Eleven came barreling out of the melee, a double-headed axe in both hands, ready to chop.

"No," Abrakam cried, running down the sailor and trying to wrestle the axe free. "You cut that tentacle, you'll kill us all."

Eleven screamed as his brother was dragged over the side, fingernails leaving gashes in the wood. The axe clattered down. Footsteps pounded.

"No."

"Lev."

"Don't."

"Eleven, *stop.*"

One last cry of despair and Eleven threw himself into the frothing waves, following Sixten to death.

Fen froze in the air, heart in his mouth. Arrow nocked, wings fluttering, he looked back over his shoulder. His eyes met Trueblood's and their combined horror and anger was a tangible thing, electric and sharp and sinister.

"No, Fen," Trueblood cried. "Let him go. *Bring her down.*"

Fen turned back as Misery breached, tentacles unfurling in a shower of droplets, a tatter of white cloth clinging to one sucker.

Fen saw red. Then redder. His fury sharpened to a point and his skill narrowed to the tip. Through the gap in the railing Misery reached. She got one slimy leg curled around the mizzen mast.

"Fen, do it," Trueblood screamed behind him. "Fucking take her *down.*"

Fen waited. Patient and courteous. Eyes unblinking.

Misery reached further, her head emerging from the chop. Her tentacles whipped through the air, gray-green and slick, water sluicing off the iridescent scales. A cracking of timber, the groan of splitting beam, shouting and cursing and screaming. Fen heard it all, but didn't take his eyes off the kraken.

"Turn around and look at me, whore," he said. "Roll over and see what I have for you."

Misery froze. Her grotesque head turned and she looked up at the kheiron.

"From one whore to another…" Fen's fingers let go, poised delicately in the air as the taut string collapsed against the notch of the arrow.

It flew.

The aim was true.

Not a sound as the bronze tip pierced Misery's upturned eye.

It shuddered as it lodged in the skull.

An elegant, economical and gorgeous shot.

Father should've seen that, Fen thought. *Maybe they'll tell him one day, how—*

"No," Abrakam cried. And his terrible call echoed behind Fen.

"No."

"Kepten."

"Trueblood."

"No. Trueblood, no…"

Fen il-Kheir hovered on the steaming air, his back to the ship.

If I don't turn around, everything stays the same, he thought. *The priestess said I'd live my life looking behind me. My father punched my head to get it to face the right direction. I mustn't turn around. Don't make me. Let me stay here. Let me keep looking ahead. That way. Toward my future. With him.*

"Pelippé," Lejo screamed.

No looking back, Fen thought. *I must face the future.*

"Pé, no!" Raj cried.

Weeping rolled over the waves as the last bit of Misery slipped below the surface.

Fen turned around.

DEAD CALM

L ONG AGO THE earth was one.

Then Nydirsil, the Tree of Life, tore her roots free from the seabed, unleashing the unspeakable evils imprisoned in the bowels of the earth. The two most heinous creatures to break free were the twin kraken, Murder and Misery.

Murder's venom was instantaneous. Misery's was far more sadistic. Victims of her poison lay in torment, reliving their worst moments. Suffering their harshest pain and grief and shame and devastation. Misery worked its way into their hearts until they broke. It took over their minds until they were lost. It killed slowly. Excruciatingly. And enjoyed every minute.

Misery lay dead on the bottom of the ocean floor now, one of Fen's arrows through her eye and lodged in her soft skull. Her venom continued to pump out in the cold depths, creating a noxious patch that glowed sickly yellow and violet, rising in red steam off the waves. The Kaleuche managed to catch the wind's death rattle and sail clear of the poisoned air. Then the wind dwindled to a breeze. Then to nothing.

The ship bobbed in a dead calm.

The crew sat about the decks. Listening to Seven weep for his brothers, staring at their hands and waiting for Trueblood to die.

MISERY'S TENTACLE HAD left deep gashes across Trueblood's back, their edges bubbling with a green foam. The bleeding had stopped, which Abrakam said was a bad thing. Flowing blood might get some of the venom out.

The crew held him down so the centaur could cut the wounds deeper. Trueblood bucked and writhed. He screamed. He begged. He bawled. He panted through his teeth, sputtering and hissing. Eyes and nose dripping and fingers clawing the air.

The crew was disintegrating under his agony. Breaking down and weeping as they grabbed and clutched and sat on Trueblood's furious body. Fen made a stone of his heart, going deliberately blind, deaf and mute. Thinking only of Eleven, who threw himself overboard so he could die with his little brother.

When this was over, Fen planned to do the same.

I'm done, he thought. *I've done all I can do. My life has been good enough. I can do no more.*

Finally Abrakam stepped back. "It's the best I can do."

The Ĝemelos washed Trueblood's back and bound it. Their twinned expression was gray and stunned, but their strength and tenderness were absolute as they carried the kepten down to the nyellem.

"It might comfort him," the centaur said. "It may even help."

"Can anything help?" Dhar asked, his face swollen.

Abrakam turned away, shaking his head. "Let him rest, lad," he said. "Let Fen be with him."

ONCE THE KALEUCHE'S nyellem was stacked floor to ceiling with casks of spice. Now it only contained the memory of kisses and a bed, where Kepten Trueblood lay facedown, dying.

"I'm with you to the end," Fen said. "As soon as you go, I'm coming after you. There's no place you can hide where I won't find you. Not in this life or the next."

He sat, a courteous and patient witness. Dying with Trueblood every miserable step of the way. Watching as the venom worked its way through Trueblood's soul, eating all the joy and pleasure and happiness and leaving only the razor-sharp bones of wretchedness behind.

Over and over, the mariner watched his mother die. He always claimed he didn't remember the day but Misery found it, hidden away in the folds of his brain. Misery pried it free and scrapped with it like a dog with a bone. Gnawing on the minotaurs killing Noë Treeblood and her unborn child while little Pelippé watched from his hiding place in a wardrobe.

"Mami," Trueblood cried. He wept it, screamed it, called for her incessantly, *Mami, Mami.*

Misery finally tired of toying with Noë and went looking for something else to chew. Trueblood's body began to shake in an odd, rhythmic pattern. A measured tremble through his limbs with a thudding grunt in his chest. As if he were being...

Beaten, Fen realized, helpless to do anything but watch as Trueblood bent over bare-assed in the looping fugue of his mind, taking the blows from his commander's strap. Punished for disrespect in front of his crew. Tasting the shitty tang of his father's disappointment. Over and over and over...

When that memory doubled back on itself, it curled around Kepten True's death. Then it seemed the entire ship's heart would break, that every joint and board and nail and peg would lose its mind.

Fen agonized over his ringos, first wanting it on Trueblood's hand because Fen belonged to him. "I'm yours," the kheiron whispered. "Not your slave, not your subordinate, not your possession but *yours.*"

Then the desperation would reverse and Fen put the ringos back on his own finger, needing to spread his wings and cover Trueblood's body because he belonged to Fen and no one else. The whisper swelled into an angry lament: "He's mine. You can't have him. You took everything else from me. My dam. My youth. My body. My father. I let you have all of it now leave me alone with him. You don't get to have this, don't you fucking dare, *please…*"

The ringos went back and forth. His voice rose and fell. He didn't move from his spot next to the bed. He didn't know if the Kaleuche was sailing or still caught in a dead calm. He had no idea what was going on above deck. A steward brought trays and set them down without speaking. Fen put things in his mouth and chewed but had no awareness of what he was eating. Melki loyally brought mugs of hot water and kyhrr and Fen drank them because he could do nothing else. He dipped a finger in the tea and brushed it over Trueblood's lips. He rubbed his hands along the walls of the nyellem, then brought them to Trueblood's face.

Take this cure.

Take this reward.

"Take him into your merciful heart," he begged the scented darkness. "But don't take him away from me. Please."

Day after long day, Trueblood witnessed murder and mayhem. Bent over for the lash and disappointed his father, then watched him die. Fen rubbed the walls until his fingers were raw and brought the scent of spice to his kepten, because it was all he could do.

And I'll do it until the end.

I'm with you until the end.

"Maybe we should take him out of here," Dhar said.

"It seems to help him," Fen said.

"That's what I mean." Dhar stared at his feet. "It would make it go quicker."

Fen seized the first thing he saw and threw it at Dhar's head, roaring at him to get out. Later, he broke his vigil at Trueblood's bedside, went above and found the sail master.

"I'm sorry," he whispered, legs trembling so badly they buckled. "I'm so sorry."

"Lad, my heart's breaking for you." Dhar caught him up tight, pulling Fen's head on his shoulder. Raj moved in on one side, Lejo on the other. The minoros crowded in. Beniv and Calvo. Galley boys and coopers and carpenters and stewards and sail makers. Until the entire crew sprawled on the deck, weeping, apologizing and forgiving. Praying and pleading and begging one another, the gods, the ocean, the sky, anything.

Give him back to us.

Only Abrakam wasn't there. He was holed up in his cabin, combing every book, every scroll and tome and volume, searching for answers. Taking the world's knowledge apart to see if anything had come even close to the power of Nye to cure the bite of Misery.

Fen knelt with a hand on the main mast, then put both arms around it and hugged its immutable, ironbound strength. The lark flew in to perch on Fen's arm, give one sad peck at the mast, then raise her voice in a mournful dirge.

Fen looked up at the moon and prayed to its secret side.

Please, he thought. *Humos, take my kepien into your merciful heart.*

Give him back to me.

Something You Hold Dear

"Fen," Abrakam cried across the deck. "Feños, come here now."

Fen stirred at the base of the main mast. He'd fallen asleep against it, a prayer half-finished in his mouth. Cold and cramped, he got up and followed the centaur back down to the nyellem.

"Look," Abrakam said. He peeled a square of linen off one of the wounds on Trueblood's back. The mariner cried out as it pulled free, bringing with it a chunk of…

Flesh? Fen thought, swallowing hard against the gorge in his throat. No. It was solid and opaque, like weathered glass. Brown-gold closest to the linen, then tapering down into delicate, yellow-green tendrils. As if Abrakam had somehow cast a little sculpture from the mold of the wound.

"What is that?" Fen said.

"Kyrrh. Last night, I packed a wound full of it, to see what would happen. When I went to look under the dressing, it all came out like this. Rock-hard with the poison solidified. So I tried it again. It works, Fen. The misery adheres to the kyrrh. *Bonds* to it. Look at the wound."

The other lacerations on Trueblood's back bubbled, but the kyrrh-treated gash was quiet at the edges and clean within.

"Gods," Fen said, already moving toward the door. "I've got more in my cabin. I'll get it."

"No, Fen," the centaur said. "This was yours."

Fen stared. "All of it?"

"All of it."

Fen closed his eyes. A chunk of kyrrh the length and width of his thumb. Shaved with a razor, it could last a lifetime. It took the entire thing to cleanse two small wounds. Dozens still remained.

"We need more," he said.

"A lot more."

Silence as both he and the centaur visualized their predicament. The ship bobbed in a dead calm somewhere in the Northeast Sea. An entire continent lay between them and the one place on earth kyrrh was found.

Fen had flown across that continent once before. Weak and malnourished with a human child on his back. Sheltering from the desert suns in crumbling caravanserais. Living off stagnant well water and figs.

Twenty years had passed. The memory should've long faded away.

But some things you never forgot.

And everything happens for a reason, Fen thought.

"I'll go," he said. "I'll fly to Altynai and get more." He ran a hand through his hair, thinking what he'd need to bring with him this time. "Get the twins. Dhar, Beniv and Calvo, too. I'll be up in a minute."

Abrakam left the nyellem. Fen knelt down and slid his ringos off Trueblood's finger.

"You hold on, hear me? I'm coming back. And when I do, we're talking about this." He pressed his lips to the kepten's damp brow. "I'll see you later." He kissed him again. "I'll talk to you later."

As he straightened up, he felt a tug at his leg. Trueblood's fingers closed around a bit of his breeches, holding on. His knuckles flashed white with effort, then his hand went limp again.

"A MOONSTONE WOULD come in handy here," Fen said. "You can carry more as a horse."

"Hold still," Dhar said. He and Beniv were furiously sewing, constructing a sack to ride on Fen's chest, without its straps getting in the way of his wings. Calvo and Seven were packing it with provisions. Fen craned his neck past them to look at the map Raj was drawing at the table. His fingers shook around the pen, his entire body clenched with the effort. Lejo sat close by, his side wedged tight against Raj's, trying to hold them together.

Their strength always lay in the space between them, Fen thought. *I can picture Raj without Lejo. Or Lejo without Raj. But there's no Ĝemelos without Trueblood.*

His eyes slid around the dark concentration on each crew member. Seven, red-eyed and determined as he packed food for Fen. Somewhere back in Nyland, a mother was cooking dinner, not knowing two of her sons were dead.

Trueblood has no son. If he dies, this giantship has no kepten at the helm. House Tru dies with him and the Kaleuche has no giantsblood to sail her.

I have to come back.

A tiny clatter as the pen fell from Raj's fingers. He and Lejo stared at nothing, their twinned gaze empty and lethargic.

"Raj." Fen reached past Lejo and took the pilot by the shoulders. "*Raj.* Look at me." He shook the pilot hard, until he pulled from Fen's grip with a sharp inhale through his nose.

"We'd go with you if we could," he said, with so much strange regret in his voice, Fen prickled with dread.

"I know," Fen said. "But you need to go down to the nyellem and lie with him while I'm gone. You understand? Put him between you and keep him there. Don't follow where he goes this time. You and Lejo make him stay. You're the only ones who can."

Lejo lifted up his head then. "Kyrrh comes at a price."

"It didn't when Kepten True rescued me."

"That was before the *Truviad* stones were found," Lejo said. "Things are happening, Fen."

"Happening for a reason," Raj said. "Falling into place the way they're supposed to."

"I have a feeling kyrrh won't be gifted this time. Not for all the love in the world."

"What price, then?" Fen said. "How much?"

"The Altyns will ask for what you love," Lejo said. "Their currency is something you hold dear."

"Then we'll all pay," Beniv said behind them.

Fen turned. Beniv and Calvo were pulling off their matching rings, given by each to the other and worn for over twenty-five years. With a delicate clink they were set in Fen's palm, gold against silver.

Dhar was next. He'd been born encauled—emerging within an intact birth sac. Since ancient times, the dried caul was believed to protect sailors from drowning. Dhar always had it near him. Now he gave it up.

Seven gave over his necklace of shark teeth. Then he added Eleven's carving knife with the mother of pearl handle, and Sixten's fingerless gloves that protected his hands from rope burn. "I think it's what they would've given," he said.

"I know it is," Fen said. "You knew them best."

Word spread quickly, and one by one, every crew member gave up a little treasure. Even Abrakam, who offered the book full of gelang illustrations.

"What?" he said to the twins' stunned look. "You think you were the first to discover the world's greatest bectime story?" Shaking his head, he smoothed the book's cover and added it to Fen's sack. "Gods, it hurts to let it go. But maybe Zornin will enjoy it."

Melki threw arms around Fen, his young body nearly contorting to hold the tears in. "You're my most treasured thing," he said. "I don't have anything else."

Fen had to fight hard to keep it together. "I'm coming back," he said, a hand spread wide on the boy's head. "I'm coming back and you're going to tell this tale to your grandchildren. I promise."

The Ĝemelos were likewise empty-handed. Their greatest treasure lay dying in the nyellem. They offered Fen gelango and the friends held each other tight, three heads pressed in a triangle.

"You can do this," Raj said. "Only you can do this."

"Follow your heart," Lejo said. "Your heart knows what to do and the way to go."

The boatswain, the pilot and the kheiron walked out of the aftercastle on deck, where they stopped short. The Kaleuche was surrounded by the pegasos flight, nine steeds circling the masts. Or rather, eight. The ninth was a mare's shadow. The sun shone through her, refracting from black into shades of dark purple. She touched soundlessly down on the afterdeck and her aubergine wings shuddered to stillness.

"Salu, Mami," Fen said, going up the stairs. "Are you coming with me?"

My one, I've always been with you.

He held still as she bent her head toward and through his shoulder, and her love flowed into him.

"Mysire," a new voice said behind him. Fen turned and the copper mare from Aybar tossed her black mane.

"You again," he said.

Her golden eyes blinked. "I wanted to see a kheiron in his natural habitat."

Fen had to laugh. It was either that or go horseshit crazy. "My friend Raj will kill me if I don't get your name this time."

"Darea."

"It's good to see you again."

Are you ready, Tehvani... The way Zoria said his khenom was nearly perfect. Which was why il-Kheir had loved her so.

"I'm ready," he said.

IN HER LEE

I COULD, LEGANTOS, WRITE a separate book about Fen's second flight across the desert. If you ask nicely, maybe I will. For this story, the destination is more important than the journey, although certain things beg mentioning.

The pegasos formed a loose phalanx with four on a side. Darea flew immediately to Fen's fivehand, where he was struck by her colors. She was the exact shade of copper as the tips of Trueblood's plaits. When she turned her sleek head and looked directly at Fen, her gaze was the same giantsblood topaz.

Zoria flew in front of Fen. The stars twinkled straight through her body and wings, yet her spectral presence blocked the strong headwinds and let Fen draft in the lee of her love. When he stopped to sleep through the heat of day, it was her wings shading him from the punishing sun.

Night fell and he took to the skies again, flying like a small treasure in the cupped palm made by nine winged horses. In their slipstream he crossed the Altyn range, at which point the eight flanking steeds peeled off. Darea made an extra spiral around Fen. Her golden gaze seemed to be memorizing him.

"Thank you for coming with me," Fen said.

"It's an honor." She flew away, leaving just the kheiron and his mother's spirit over the Old Forest.

Caracaros circled them at a distance as they flew past the tree where Fen crashed two decades ago. The ropes and pulleys set up by Kepten True still in place.

One day, I'll bring Pé here, Fen thought. *I'll show him what his father did for me. Stories with pictures are the ones Pé likes best.*

THE ALTYN RANGE was a trove of gold and gemstones, but one particular peak pulsed with a vein of garnets. The cave within was called Koromontos, the heart of the mountain, and here lived the Altyn headman, Zornin, with his clan.

The firelight bounced off facets, splashed back cherry and dazzled ruby. The cave squeezed Fen tight in its fist, making the blood pound hard at his temples. Every time he glanced up at the polished walls, he saw his own distorted reflection, bathed red like he was doused in wine.

Beside him sat Sorĉi, the Altyn witch. She was thin as a husk, more wrinkles than flesh. Her eyes were milky white and sightless, yet her voice cut like a newly-honed sword when she ran her hands over Fen and declared he looked better than the last time she saw him.

"Thank you for what you did that day," Fen said.

The old woman snorted. "You didn't come here to show gratitude for past deeds, kheiron."

"I came for Kepten True's son. But I'd be remiss if I didn't at least acknowledge that I owe you my life."

"You were needed," she said, but before Fen could push at the cryptic statement, Zornin asked for his story.

Fen told of Misery's attack on the Kaleuche and how Trueblood's life now hinged on kyrrh.

"We gave it willingly when you were a foalboy," Zornin said. "But kyrrh can only be gifted once. What you need today comes at a price."

"As expected," Fen said. "I and the crew are willing to trade."

He watched as the Altyns picked through his treasure. A ship's ransom for the life of their kepten.

"A pretty trove," one of them said. "Much that is dear. But little that has power."

Zornin grunted, turning the pages of the gelang book.

"That comes with Abrakam's compliments," Fen said.

The Altyn closed the book and slid it inside his tunic. "Is this all?"

"No," Sorĉi said. "He's got much more."

Fen drew in a breath. He was ready.

"I'll give you my moonstone," he said. "I don't have it with me and Zornin can attest to why. He was there when the *Truviad* was translated. He knows the moonstone is in the hands of the tree-tenders. If you'll take it in trade for enough kyrrh to save Trueblood, I'll send a falcon immediately to my father and Naria Nyland, telling them it's yours when all this is done."

The silence screamed in his ears. Nobody moved a sinew. Even the fire was quiet.

"And if your price includes my ringos," Fen said, "you can have that, too. The stones said I'd have to begin and end as Khe did. As a man bound to earth." He swallowed and tried to smile as he met Zornin's gaze. "I'll be at peace if it ends up on an Altyn's hand. Because you all saved my life."

Glances went around the circle, each eventually landing on the witch.

"Come closer, foalboy," she said. "Let me look at you again."

Her gnarled hands swept over his head and face. Her fingertips touched his brows and held still, caressing the scar where his moonstone once hung. Then they continued on, thorough and frank.

"Just as I thought," she said. "You're holding back the real treasure."

"I'm sorry?"

"You have a secret."

A murmur from the tribe. Bodies leaned forward in interest and the flames of the fire stood up tall.

"Secrets are expensive," Sorĉi said. "Such a price to pay if they're discovered. Which is why we guard them so close. Once given, you never get them back."

Fen's breath, already shallow, quickened. His heartbeat pounded behind his eyes now, garnet sparks dancing through his gaze like a radiance of cardinals.

The witch's grip on his wrist tightened. "Not one," she whispered. "Many. Oh, so many secrets in your bones. I can smell them. I can hear them between your heartbeats. You are rich, kheiron. You can afford the best."

She spoke to Zornin in a tongue Fen couldn't understand. The headman went away and came back with a paper-wrapped object. Sorĉi unwrapped it to reveal an obscene hunk of kyrrh. It had to contain decades, maybe centuries of collected sap.

"This for your secrets, Tehvan il-Kheir," she said. "All of them." She set the kyrrh between their seated bodies and rolled her hands up to the cave's ceiling. "Put them in my hands. And believe me, I'll know if you keep any back."

Fen stared into the witch's palms. They were strangely smooth and soft, puddled red as the firelight bounced off ruby facets and collected in the creases and lines.

"Tell me," Sorĉi said. "Tell me everything that happened in Arcodolori."

The words beckoned seductively. A siren's call within the wrinkled crone. Aspida, the horrible turtle disguised as an island oasis, luring travelers to death. Or Kharbidis, the gentle eddy that morphed into a whirlpool of razor teeth, reducing ships to slivers.

Mesmerized and tempted by this poisoned candy, Fen still clutched at his trove, desperately hoarding the precious stash.

It wasn't me. It was him. He did all those things. I just watched. It was another life. It was long ago. None of it matters anymore.

The witch's foot bumped the hunk of kyrrh, moving it closer to Fen. "Tell me."

He began to talk.

And once he started, he could not stop.

XEROMI

WHEN THE NEEDS of men are pushed inside Tehvan il-Kheir, forced down his throat or spilled across his face, he stands it by thinking of revenge.

You will beg my father for mercy.

Between every blow of a fist: *He'll take a week to kill you, man.*

Between every crack of a lash: *And I will watch.*

Months pass, the moon's egg cracking open and spilling across the skies. Then it's been a year and Tehvan's mantras turn to questions.

Is my father taking the world apart?

Has he stopped searching?

Does he care if I suffer?

Will I spend the rest of my days here?

IN THE CITY of Aybar, boys fetch higher prices than girls. Young boys are more expensive than older ones. At thirteen, Tehvan is considered old. He and a dozen other past-their-prime slaves are sold north, where the fadara plantations need labor and brothels need prostitutes. The buyer is a grotesquely corpulent man named

Haize. He has glittering black eyes and a soft, prissy little mouth that grows wet at the corners as he inspects Tehvan top to bottom.

Tehvan keeps his expression impervious as he's poked, prodded and fondled. It's not as difficult as it used to be. Most slaves detach from reality with fadara, which eventually makes them captive to two masters. Tehvan disconnects by dividing his tripartite nature. The humos slave being used and abused is not him and has nothing to do with him. *He,* Tehvan il-Kheir, lives safe in a private fortress of the mind, existing in either kheiros or equos. Here in his head, Tehvan walks on four legs, watching everything that happens to his two-legged aspect with cold detachment.

That's him, he thinks. *All that's happening to the human. It's his problem to deal with. Yes, I am forced to share space with him, but he's nothing to do with me.*

He fortifies his castle with future scenarios. One day, when the ordeal is over and Sevri has broken open this godsforsaken land and killed every last person in it, he'll take Tehvan home, but leave the humos behind.

"I don't believe we'll be needing that anymore," Sevri will say. "What do you think?"

Tehvan will pretend to ponder the matter. "No," he'll say. "It's nothing that belongs to me. I have no use for it."

Pleased, Sevri will nonchalantly kick humos aside with a hoof and put a proud hand on Tehvan's head. "I'm in awe of you. Such strength and fortitude of mind. It's no wonder you survived when so many others surrendered."

A shy love fills Tehvan's veins as he crafts his reply. "I survived because I knew you'd find me."

A lash across the back of his calves yanks him back to the present. He's been sold. His now former owner looks decidedly sulky as he strips Tehvan's rings off his fingers and hands them to the obese man, who looks about to rub off on them. All men get a ridiculous rise from wearing the rings. As if wearing a kheiron's silver while fucking him will make wings of their own sprout.

Men aren't my concern, Fen remembers as he's rounded up with the others. Once more the sickening stench of burned flesh and his own scream echoing in his skull as he's re-branded.

No, it's not me it's him. Him. It's all happening to him. Not my pain but his.

He's marched through the desert. He learns to save his spit and not be picky about food, but it's hard learning to ignore the incessant wailing of the fadara addicts in withdrawal. One night he can stand it no longer. He slips through the dark, presses his hand over a screaming mouth and pinches the nose shut. The wretch writhes and struggles, yet his eyes are filled with grateful relief. Slowly they empty until he stares past Tehvan into nothing.

The kheiron goes to sleep, unfazed by murder.

It wasn't me who did it. It was him.

In years to come, during rare tellings of his time in captivity, Tehvan will say he witnessed the appalling incident and was powerless to stop it. It's not like anyone can verify the story—Tehvan was the only one who survived.

It wasn't me. It was him.

HAIZE OWNS TWO fadara plantations and a brothel in Danysh. The armpit of the world, where evil lives in the open and goodness ekes out a miserable existence on its knees underground.

Or on four legs in one's head.

Haize is a brutal, hedonistic master, and his brothel slaves have an unusual hierarchy. Status is assigned by price. The expensive higher-ups are allowed to turn tricks on the side to make money. A few make enough coin to buy a slave of their own.

Xeromo. Slave of a slave. The lowest of the low. Someone who has to buy their freedom twice. Their price comes with knowing the master owns everything, and slaves who own slaves must acknowledge where the bread is buttered. The master has a turn with your xeromo before you do. The master can take a piece of your property for free. If he tells you to beat your possession, starve it, torture it, kill it, you obey. Or die.

Xeromi are the worse in "well, it could be worse."

Other than death, xeromi have no worse.

Tehvan il-Kheir, with his hard good looks and exotic wing marks, fetches top prices at Haize's establishment. He knows how to play the game now, and soon he's running a discreet but lucrative side business. He's not saving for a xeromo. Not yet. First he buys back eight of his rings from Haize.

On my face. On my knees. I bought them back with my mouth and my body. I whored out my humos to buy back what was mine.

Not daring to wear the rings openly and not trusting any hiding place, he cuts tiny slits in his arms and legs and sews the rings beneath his skin.

The ringos, his ninth ring, will never be won back. Never earned or bought. But if he can steal it, he'll be free. Haize knows this, too, which means Fen's best chance at freedom lies with someone else stealing the ring for him.

Haize knows this as well.

Tehvan's position is complicated. He needs a third party for his escape plan, but Haize is watching him. Any whiff of a friendship, partnership, cahoots, complicity, accessory or accomplice will be immediately suspect.

The foalboy is now old beyond his years. His intelligence and cunning hone a desperate plan to a lethal edge. The plan has no allowance for morals, no contingency for compassion.

He's fourteen when he has enough to buy a slave. A boy called Jindo.

"Before the sun goes down tonight, you'll think I'm your enemy," Fen tells him. "But I'm the only ally you have right now. I'm your one chance to get out of this place."

Jindo is eleven. Golden-haired and soft-skinned, with a crooked front tooth. His wide, gray eyes are trusting, though they narrow slightly at Tehvan as he listens.

"Forget who you are," Tehvan says. "Forget how you were raised, forget everything you know about how the world works. By morning you're going to hate me, but never forget this: I didn't buy you for me. I bought you for freedom."

Tehvan delivers Jindo to the master's house. Haize's mouth grows wet, just as Tehvan planned. He knows Haize's weaknesses. He knows Haize's type.

When Jindo returns to the slave quarters, trialed and tested, childhood has left his eyes. His gaze is a bow sighted on Tehvan, bitter and loathing.

"Wait," Tehvan says. "Learn to ration the hatred because things are going to get worse."

He plays his part to cruel perfection, managing not only Haize's perception but the other slaves' as well. He berates and belittles Jindo and makes sure enough people see how he treats his property. He's prepared to be tested by the master. If Haize takes the boy for a night, Tehvan looks jealous, but not *too* jealous. If Haize makes him beat or humiliate Jindo, Tehvan looks sorry, but not *too* sorry.

"I don't care if you hate me," he says to Jindo. "I said we were allies. I never said we were friends. Do what I tell you and you'll get your freedom. You'll never have to see me again. You want to hunt me down later in life and settle the score, I'll meet you. I'll honor that fight, I'll even admire you for it. Just know that I never lose."

"How do you fucking stand yourself?" Jindo says.

"I don't," Tehvan says. "It's not me. And it's not you, either. This isn't us, we're not here. None of this is happening."

It takes a while for Jindo to hate being a xeromo more than he hates Tehvan. A little while longer for the irrational loathing to clear from his eyes, for his gaze to settle cold and calculating on Fen and order, "Tell me what to do."

"It's the ring on his left forefinger," Tehvan says. "But you can't let him know you're after it. Start to get interested in all his rings. Ask for their stories. Ask to see one and give it back immediately. Gain his trust. The idea is to get him to take *all* of them off. You have to get him by the ego. Tell him you want nothing between you and his hands."

Every time Jindo returns from a performance in Haize's bed, he throws up. Tehvan can't blame him. For the first few months in this corner of hell, he did nothing but get fucked and throw up.

He has to keep up his end of the charade. Put forth the precise amount of brooding sulk when Jindo's up at the master's house, then be convincing when he makes the boy pay for being so desirable. He keeps their private conversations short, unemotional and infrequent, but he makes a point of using a certain word in all of them:

Us.

"It's freedom," Tehvan says. "For both of us. The ring can get us out of here. You can do this."

"It hurts so much," Jindo says.

"I know. Look at me."

"I don't know who I am anymore."

"Look at me, Jindo. Believe what I say. If I can survive it, you can. It's not happening to you. No, look at me. I'm telling you the truth. This is nothing. None of this is real, we're not living the lives we were born to live. This is all a mistake and it doesn't *count*. You can do this. I can get us both out of here but I need that ring and you're the only one who can get it."

Long tense days pile up into longer anxious nights. When no one is looking, Jindo murmurs, "Us." out the side of his mouth and Tehvan replies, "Us," from between tight teeth. The kheiron fights to keep his demeanor bland, passive and submissive while on the inside he is screaming, clenched, writhing in frustration.

When he retreats into the furthest equos cave in his mind, he rears up shrieking, tearing holes in the sky with his hooves.

"It's done." Bruised, scraped and dazed, Jindo stumbles into Tehvan's cell one morning. "I got it."

"Where is it?"

Jindo puts a finger down his throat.

Tehvan stares at the puddle of bile on the stone floor, his ring glittering at the center of it.

"He was starting to wake up. So I swallowed it." Jindo's stunned eyes fill with tears. "Did I fuck up?"

"No," Tehvan said, a bubble of hysteria in his throat. "No, that was…smart. You're smart. Good thinking." He's laughing by the end. Falling to one knee, then the other. He reaches out to Jindo and pulls him close. "Good boy," he says. "You did it. It's all right now. No, don't cry. You did a great thing."

As if remembering all at once who he is, and how old he is, and what he's been made to suffer, Jindo crumples into Tehvan's chest, crying his mind out. He wraps arms around Tehvan's shoulders, legs around Tehvan's waist, clutches on tight, crying and crying. Unabashedly weeping like Tehvan didn't dare to all these years, once he realized no one was coming for him.

"It's all right," he tells Jindo. And himself. "You're safe. It's over now. Just a little while longer and we'll get out of here. Don't cry. I'm here. I won't leave without you, I promise."

He slits the skin over the little bulges in his arms and legs, tip of his tongue held in his teeth in a quiet relish because this pain is *good*. In contrast, the escape from captivity is almost anti-climactic. Tehvan il-Kheir simply puts on his rings, straps Jindo to his back, walks outside and flies away.

TEHVAN FLIES AS far from Danysh as he can before the heat of the desert drives them to take shelter. Hidden among the old caravan ruins, Jindo can't stop crying. Tehvan makes no reproach, only a soft counsel not to cry too much—tears are best conserved inside than out in the desert. When Solos charges behind the horizon on his winged steed, the boy is asleep in Tehvan's arms. Once on Tehvan's back, he stays asleep, his body limp and trusting, yet his arms wound tight and immutable around the kheiron's waist.

It's time for Tehvan to be himself again, but after two years of living outside his own experience, he doesn't know how to reconnect. He's not sure he even wants to. A slimy unease is creeping up the walls of his stomach and reaching fingers into his chest. A worry that if he died today and his soul were laid on the scale of righteous-to-damned, it wouldn't be a goldfinch who came for him.

You did terrible things. You killed. You whored. You bought and sold human suffering. You beat and abused and humiliated a little boy.

You can pretend it was someone else but it was you all along.

They sleep a second broiling day away and in the late afternoon, Tehvan wakes to the boy's hands fumbling at the laces of Tehvan's breeches. Anger and revulsion gallop over his own horizon. It takes every ounce of his exhausted wherewithal to grab his emotions by the mane, gentle them down and realize Jindo is trying to *thank* him. To pay Tehvan for freedom with the only currency he knows.

"No," Tehvan whispers, catching the boy's hands in his wrists. "No. You owe me nothing. This doesn't come at a price."

"Don't leave me," the boy says, sobbing. "I'll do anything. You can do whatever you want to me. Whenever you want. Just keep me with you."

"No one will ever do anything to you again," Tehvan says fiercely. He rolls and pulls the boy's back against his chest. He releases his wings and folds one over both their bodies. "There. You're safe under here. No one can see you. No one will touch you while you sleep."

"You can fuck me if you want. I mean it. I'll do it for real. Not pretending."

"Stop."

"I'll do anything you wan—"

"Shh," Tehvan says. "No more of that. You're not my slave and you're not my whore. You never were. It wasn't *you* back there, remember? You're free. Do you understand?"

He goes on murmuring as the broken boy cries himself to sleep.

"You owe me nothing, Jindo. It's over and it was another life."

You're fooling no one. It was you. You who did things to him.

"This is now," he says through chattering teeth. "Nobody will ever touch you again, I promise. You're free."

He clutches the sleeping boy, trying to punch through to Jindo's experience, be held in a circle of impenetrable arms and be told everything was all right.

I'm him. I am small and safe in my father's grasp and his wings cover me up. Nobody can see me or touch me anymore. It's nothing I am anymore. I don't need it. I survived because I knew he'd come and now he's here and he's holding me. I'm Jindo and my father is me.

The reassurances work as well as walls built of dry sand. One blown away by the laughing wind before another can be erected.

It was you all along, Tehvan il-Kheir. You can't hide.

As they make their way across the desert that night, Jindo shyly asks Tehvan, "Can I give myself a new name?"

"Good idea," Tehvan says immediately. "New names for our new life."

And this isn't me anyway.

IN ANY LANGUAGE

"I SOLD MYSELF TO buy that little boy." Fen said to the Altyn witch. "Then I sold him to get my freedom. Everything that was done to me, I did to him. It let us escape but it doesn't make it right. Nothing will ever make it right.

"Night after night, I baited a trap with my xeromo. My mouth watered while waiting for it to spring, not caring that each night was killing Jindo. He was the price of freedom and he paid for everything in the end. He was still trapped when we escaped. He was still inside that cage of shame, believing no one would ever want him again.

"I tried," Fen said. "I talked to him. On the ground and in the air. I gave us new names. I told him he was the lark bringing his own soul. I told him all kinds of stories, trying to erase all the shit I said and did in Arcodolori. I thought I got through to his heart. It seemed he was free, but the trap had him by one last finger. Being out in the world again was too much for him, he didn't know who he was or if anyone would want him. His alternatives were to stay trapped or die."

He extended the thumb of his fivehand. "He let go. So I took his place in the cage and I've been imprisoned inside for twenty years. The door's been open but I chose to stay within. It was easier. But now…"

A log on the fire belched out a pocket of air, scattering sparks around the circle of attentive ears. All listening to learn and learning to tell.

"Once," Fen said, "I told my father nothing in this world is bigger than my hate for him. But that's not true. Not anymore. What I feel in my heart now is bigger than hate. It's a secret that's bigger than the sun."

Sorĉi's sightless eyes closed. Her ear tilted. Her palms rose, hungry and ready to eat.

"I love Pelippé Trueblood," Fen said. "I love him more than I hate everything that happened to me. Because now I know it happened so I could be with him. Knowing doesn't make it better. It doesn't make it go away. It doesn't make me forget it or forgive my captors. But it gives me a place to put it. Loving Trueblood gives me both peace and purpose. I survived so I could be with him. I want to keep surviving so I can keep being with him."

The witch was glowing now, her people clutching each other, awed and weeping as Fen poured every last secret he owned into the old woman's hands.

"I've spent my life looking backward and hating my father for not finding me. I spit my name into the dirt and left a trail for him to follow. He didn't come. I cried for him while men and minotaurs raped me, hoping the wind would carry my khenom to his ears. He didn't come.

"I did things in Arcodolori I can never take back. I killed a boy in the desert. I killed a mother's son and felt nothing. I sold myself so I could buy another mother's son and groom him for my purposes. I gained his trust by treating him like shit. I convinced him I was both enemy and ally. He got me my freedom and I got him killed."

A shiver crossed the old woman's shoulders. The air around her crackled in a hundred shades of red.

"My father buried Alon next to my mother and let me forswear humos, but he never again listened to the things I needed to tell him. Then he took my charm hostage and gave me no choice but to take the form of what I hated most in the world. He took my moonstone. He took my wings. I went onboard the Kaleuche on two unwilling legs and with my mind made up. I closed my heart and vowed I wanted no part of the voyage. I wanted nothing and no one. But I do. I want Pelippé Trueblood."

The tears streamed down his proud face. "Please. You took pity on me when I landed broken in your trees. Show me that kindness again. I've found my gelangos. I love Pelippé Trueblood. Loving him helps me stop hating. Loving him lets me be myself. For the first time in twenty years, I believe I'm worthy of love. Please, Sorĉi, take my secrets into your merciful heart and let me keep Trueblood in my hands."

The old woman settled back on her cushions, eyes still closed. "A fair trade," she whispered. "Such beautiful secrets, Tehvan il-Kheir. I'll keep them forever. They'll never be sold. They'll be buried with me in the earth when I die."

She took her hands in his and ran her thumbs over his palms for a long time.

"Your father loves you," she said.

Fen, exhausted, could only shake his head.

"Not a word exists in any language for how much your father loves you. He's written all over you. I can feel him in your fingers."

She leaned and kissed his scarred eyebrow. "Rest here a while, kheiron. Eat and drink. You'll need all your strength for the mariner."

THE KINDEST THING

FEN PRACTICALLY CRASH-LANDED on the deck of the
Kaleuche, delirious with exhaustion and dread.

"Am I too late," he said hoarsely. "Is he alive?"

"Yes," a half-dozen voices replied. "He's alive, lad. Only just."

Fen had strength enough to retrieve the kyrrh from his bag
and give it to Abrakam. He meant to follow the centaur down
to the nyellem, managed three steps, then collapsed into Lejo
and Raj's arms.

The flight of pegasos reared back from the Kaleuche, their
wings thundering. The limp sails stirred, shook themselves out
and filled up with the breeze. They stayed full when the winged
steeds retreated.

They were sailing again.

That night Fen slept between the twins in their cabin. Raj was
a solid and immutable presence to lean on, while Lejo rested soft
and pliant against Fen's back. The kheiron's sleep was deep and
dreamless, filled only with shades of red, shadows of purple, and
the occasional flash of copper or gold.

He woke alone the next morning, aching in every major muscle
group. He was touched when Calvo brought him breakfast, but
sad news came with the meal.

"While you were gone, we lost Seven," the quartermaster said.

The fork paused midway to Fen's mouth, then he set it down. His mind ran a gamut of illness and freak accidents, while his heart knew the cook had taken his own life.

"What did he do?"

"Waited until Lejo was asleep and lifted his key to the kepten's safe."

"What's in the…" Fen's eyes closed as he raised a finger. "The fadara."

"He took all three beads of it. Abrakam said it would've been quick. Painless."

"Gods."

Calvo ran a hand through his thinning hair. "Tell you, lad, their poor mother. It won't be painless for her."

Fen folded his napkin and pushed the plate away. "Thanks for bringing it, Cal, but I'm not hungry now."

"Don't give it a thought. Let's go see Trueblood." Calvo patted Fen's back. "He called for you while you were gone."

"He did?"

"Aye, lad. He wanted you awful."

Fen followed Calvo down the stairs to the nyellem. Last night, Abrakam had packed Trueblood's wounds with kyrrh and pressed a clean linen cloth on top. Now he peeled the fabric back, drawing out the hard, jagged molds of the resin and the yellow-green poison clinging to the edges. Trueblood moaned as the misery tore free from his flesh. Fen crouched down and held both his hands tight.

"I'm here, valentos," he said softly.

The smell was appalling. Calvo pressed his face into the crook of an elbow and Fen buried mouth and nose against the mattress, swallowing hard. The old centaur's face was an impervious mask as he dropped the soiled linen into a canvas bag.

"Burn it on deck," he said to Calvo. "Far from the others. Keep the minoros below."

"Aye, Abe."

"Be careful," the centaur said. "Burn it off the lee side, sack and all. Judge the wind and do not breathe the smoke."

Fen rested his cheek lightly on Trueblood's temple. The fingers twined in his fluttered, squeezed once, then went still.

"He's not running as hot as I remember," Fen said.

"Fever's definitely breaking." With a knife, Abrakam cut generous, decadent chunks from the block of kyrrh to pack the wounds again. "This is several lifetimes worth," he said. "It must have cost a pretty price."

"From where I stand, I got the better bargain," Fen said. "But Sorĉi seemed content."

"One day you'll understand the value of secrets."

Fen gathered Trueblood's plaits into a neat rope. He knew what miseries he'd relive over and over if their places were switched, but wondered what secrets Trueblood might trade to save Fen.

"Abrakam."

"Aye, lad?"

"What would be your misery?"

The centaur laid clean linen on Trueblood's glistening back and his large hands smoothed it from shoulders to waist. "Watching your father lose his mind after your mother died. Then lose it again after you were taken."

Once, such words would pierce Fen's pride like arrows, making him volley his entire arsenal in rabid defense. Now they thudded on him like a soft rain, sliding down his skin to rest thoughtfully in his lap.

"Did you know my mother?" he asked.

"Gods, lad, of course. I mean, as well as any creature can know a pegaso."

"What do you remember?"

The centaur carefully wrapped up the kyrrh in its paper. "When she and your father were together, they wanted for nothing. They walked in their own little world, Fen. Their love was something extraordinary. No one had ever seen anything like it. Except in stories."

Abrakam pulled the sheet and blanket up around Trueblood's lower body and smoothed the linen bandage one more time. "Keep an eye out for fever," he said. "And don't let him get cold."

He left, closing the door carefully.

Fen sat, turning Trueblood's large hand over and back. Contemplating how the skin was dustier over the knuckles. The rich rose-brown of his palms and the delicate pink half-moons at the base of his nails.

The scent of the nyellem made time slide out of meaning. Fen had no idea how long had passed before he heard a rustle of bedclothes and a long sigh. Trueblood blinked his eyes open. Slowly they focused on Fen.

"You look different," he murmured.

"Do I?"

"Mm."

Fen set his thumb between the smooth, black brows. "Thinner, maybe?"

"A little."

"I went on a small trip. A side quest. I left some shit behind."

"Left what?"

"Things I didn't need anymore."

Trueblood closed his eyes, turning his face into Fen's palm. "I missed you."

Fen went on stroking his head, feeling it was the kindest thing anyone had ever said to him.

"Don't think this little stunt has gotten you out of the conversation we're having later," he finally said.

Trueblood's eyes didn't open but the corners crinkled. "Told you I'd meet you back here."

"You're late."

"Sorry."

"Horseshit, you are."

Trueblood lifted his chin a bit. "Come here."

Fen leaned and they kissed. Just once. Soft and quick.

"Later?" the mariner said.

"Later."

GREAT WAS THE day when Kepten Trueblood rose from his sickbed. He was thin. He walked on shaky legs, pausing frequently to regain his balance or his breath. Or to lose his stomach over the leeward rail.

"Well this is an odd role-reversal," Fen said.

Even Trueblood's laugh was weak. He took a bath in the galley, then sat in the sunshine of the afterdeck to shave his beard and rebraid his plaits. The simple tasks exhausted him and he went back to the nyellem to lie down, claiming the bright light hurt his eyes.

Fen went with him. In the dark hold, his head resting on the mariner's chest, he told Trueblood everything. He thought the secrets would be easier to divulge, now that they were sold to Sorĉi. He was wrong. He didn't care what the witch thought of his deeds, but he gave a frighteningly large damn what Trueblood thought.

"I smothered that boy in the desert," he said, the words like boulders in his mouth. "It was me."

"All right," the kepten said softly.

"I killed him."

"I know."

"I didn't feel horror or relief. I felt nothing."

Fen's muscles seized, terrified, ready to bolt and flee, but Trueblood's arms tightened around him.

"I got you," he said. "No, stay here. Tell me all of it."

Fen's fist clutched the back of the kepten's shirt. "Sometimes, Haize would make me rape Jindo." Then he was shaking so bad, the bedstead rattled against the walls. "Let me go."

"No, you stay with me," Trueblood said. "If you can live it, I can hear it."

"After a while... When we were...on the same page. I mean..."

"When you were working together?"

"Right. We figured out how to kind of fake it. Stage it. Make it look convincing. But the first couple times... Shit."

"It's all right."

"No, don't," Fen said. "Don't say it's all right because it isn't."

Trueblood's hand moved soft and steady through Fen's hair. "No," he finally said. "No, it wasn't right. But nothing about Arcodolori was right. And you weren't at an age where it was your job to make things right. You were trying to survive. It was your job."

Fen's entire life sat in a wadded-up ball in his throat. He lay still and let it go however it wanted to. A little through tears. Some in sighs. A bit of shaking. The rest in silence.

"I'll never pretend to know half the horrible shit you went through," Trueblood said. "I'm not going to dwell on the horrible because I think you have that covered. You're with me now and it's my job to point out the excellent things you did."

"Good luck."

"For starters, you took Jindo with you. You gave him your word and you kept it. You didn't leave him behind." His heartbeat kicked up beneath Fen's ear. "You were with him until the end and he died free."

"He died alone," Fen said, his mouth thick with anguish. "The fall didn't kill him. That's how tough he was. He suffered alone at the roots of the tree. He was still alive when the vultures came to feed. I heard him crying while they…"

"I'm so sorry."

"The Altyns found him with my ringos still clutched in his hand."

"You did everything you could."

"I wanted to bring him home. Rescuing him would've been like rescuing myself."

"I know. You rescued him. He died free. And you did bring him home. You brought him back to Nyland and buried him next to your mother. He's your little brother. You visit his grave and you kept the name he gave you. You made rescuing boys like him your life's work."

"I'm sorry."

"It's forgiven." He held Fen tight. "It all happened so you could be with me. Which means I need to be fucking worth it."

Everything was pouring out of Fen's eyes and he couldn't answer.

Trueblood went on talking. "It also means what happened is mine to protect. You have a door inside you that reads *Arcodolori*. I stand in front of it now. I forgive you everything that happened inside and if anyone else wants to go in there and judge, they have to come through me first."

Fen cried hard. A short but violent storm that left a damp patch on the kepten's shirt.

"Do something for me," Trueblood said after.

"What?"

"The room where Arcodolori lives? Try to make it a nyellem. A special place. A sacred place. A memorial to when you had to be at your worst so you could live to be your best. All right?"

"I'll try."

His lips grazed Fen's head. "But keep the door closed."

Fen laughed against where his tears had soaked. "Gods, I hate your guts."

"I'm sorry," Trueblood said, rocking him. "I'm so sorry about everything that happened, valentos."

Fen chose silence as a reply, allowing the sympathy to cloak him. Letting Trueblood witness how deeply he hurt.

"It wasn't right then but it's right now," the mariner said. "You're with me and this is now."

"Right now," Fen whispered, exhausted. "This."

"Right now. Only this."

RIGHT NOW

THAT EVENING, THE Ĝemelos moved all Trueblood's things out of their cabin and into the great bedroom.

"It's time," Lejo said.

"Are you sure?"

With an exasperated sigh, Lejo's eyes circled the ceiling. "Honestly, Pé, if you're this reluctant, maybe I'll just bed Fen myself."

"Queue up, Lélé," Raj said.

Trueblood drew his aching body to its full height. "I'll keelhaul the both of you."

"You wouldn't even know how."

"I'm a smart lad, I can figure it out."

Laughing, they left him to arrange his new accommodations. His old journals were lined up on a shelf, shades of brown leather from dun to dirt. The remnant of his mother's skirt was folded under a pillow, then after a second thought, moved to the top of the handsome dresser. He took his time, contemplating all the possessions, objects and treasures that made up a life story.

"I love what you've done with the place," Fen said from the doorway.

"Thanks."

They stared a long moment.

"Holy horses, you two." Raj pushed Fen into the cabin. "See you at breakfast," he said before closing the door.

Moonlight trickled through the windows, pouring over Fen's body, stark against the door with his tow hair and white clothes.

"Can I ask you a question?" he said.

Trueblood nodded.

"When in your life were you most afraid?"

"Right now."

"Me too."

Trueblood's heart thudded in his ears while Fen rubbed a slow circle on his chest.

"Gods, I can barely breathe here."

"Tell me something," Trueblood said. "All these years. Was there anyone who came even close to being gelang with you?"

"I had a few encounters within my charm. After a raid when we'd be on a sick adrenaline high and getting off fast and hard was the only way to come down."

"I see."

"Funny how I had rules about not getting intimate with the Finches, but they ended up being the only ones I had any kind of sexual contact with." He smiled at his feet. "The rest of the time I'd take my frustration out on a tree."

"Always in kheiros though."

"Always."

"No one you let past your skin."

"No one like you." The breath stuttered in Fen's chest as he inhaled deep. "Man, I'm so fucking nervous."

"It's all right, so am I."

"Look, I'm not sure how this is going to go."

"Fen—"

"I want it. My body wants to take its skin off and let you close to me, but I'm not sure if my head is going to be onboard. My head might still be stuck behind a wall or even stuck in Arcod-olori."

"Fen, I get it."

"Apologies in advance if I break down for no reason."

"You have ten thousand legitimate reasons to break down. I don't want you to apologize for any of them."

"Tell my head."

"You had rules with your charm," Trueblood said. "If you have rules now, anything off limits or out of the question, anything you *don't* want me to do, you can tell me."

"Well." Fen rubbed the back of his neck. "I was thinking we could start with everything and use process of elimination?"

Trueblood had no idea how he was smiling this hard when his nerves were screaming this loud. Every emotion in the world was in his veins. His heart on the verge of exploding and they hadn't even kissed. Four feet of space separated them yet it felt like Fen was in his soul.

"What the fuck are you staring at?" Fen said, smiling back.

"You. Breaking down."

"It's what I do."

The kepten took a step closer. "All I want you to do is tell me things. All right? Don't keep the breakdown in your head. The second we do something that doesn't feel good, we stop. We do something else. Or we stop altogether. You're not going to disappoint me."

Fen exhaled. "I think that's what was scaring me the most."

"Disappointing me?"

"Yeah."

"You can't. It's impossible. It doesn't matter if you're not all right with sex. I only want you to be all right with me. Whatever else happens is...extra right."

Fen took a bit of his shirt lapel and wiped his eyes. "Didn't know gelang involved so much crying."

"You're so beautiful," Trueblood said.

"Gods, man, nothing's going to happen if you keep telling me shit like this."

"I wanted to get the talking out of the way."

"You're lucky that listening to you feels like making love."

"It's all making love to me," Trueblood said. "All of it. If we lie down and go to sleep, it'll feel like making love. If we stand here and stare at each other all night, it's making love."

"If you throw a rock at my head, making love?"

"If you shit on my feet, making love."

Their eyes held and they breathed together. Then, one by one, Fen slid each of his rings off his fingers, collecting them in a palm.

"This is what right now means to me," he said, setting the bands on the dresser.

His throat warm, Trueblood regarded the little pile of starsilver. For the kheiron to come to him bare-handed was an honor most men wouldn't realize, let alone experience.

I am not most men.

"Right now," he said. "This."

"Right now," Fen said, holding out his empty hands. "Only this."

Valentos.
Gelangos.

Trueblood's mouth on Fen's neck. His mouth on Fen's heart. He put a knee down, then the other. His mouth on Fen's stomach. Biting his sides as fingers pulled at the strings of Fen's breeches. Light as birds, his fingertips danced at Fen's waist.

"What is this?" he whispered.

"What is what?"

Trueblood touched, then kissed the silvery line arcing down from Fen's hipbones. "This. I love this. Does it have a name?"

Fen drew in breath after shaking breath as Trueblood's tongue drew along the border where man and horse met. "No," he said.

His laces were undone and his pants clung by a prayer. He could exhale them down. He held his breath and stood still, poised on the edge of letting Trueblood see him. Trueblood on his knees, face turned against Fen's stomach. The coils of his hair soft and springy through Fen's fingers.

"This," Fen whispered. "Does this have a name?"

Trueblood's eyes shone in the dark as he looked up. "What?"

Fen opened his hands, encompassing the room, their bodies, their heaving chests.

And Trueblood said, "This is gelang."

Trueblood's hands. His mouth. His tongue. All dragging along Fen's skin. Scraping his clothes off. Stripping him down. Laying him bare.

"I need to know you're all right," he said, drawing Fen toward his bed. "We won't do anything you don't want."

Fen fell to his back, pulling Trueblood all along his body. "Am I yours?"

"Yes."

"Then I'm all right. And this is everything I want."

Under Trueblood's hands, the plumage of Fen's heart went from red to gold. Damned to righteous. Trueblood delivered and brought his soul. He stopped when Fen said to. Started when Fen could breathe again. All through the night, his bold, unapologetic passion stayed careful and attentive, taking all the time in the world to do whatever Fen wanted.

"Just this is enough," he kept saying. "Whatever you want is enough for me."

"I want more," Fen said.

Trueblood had the utter patience of an expert trainer gentling a nervous colt. His constant stream of reassurance wound around Fen's anxiety like a silk scarf, smoothing out all his rough edges, until the kheiron couldn't remember what he'd ever been worried about or why.

"You're so fucking beautiful," Trueblood said, kissing along the humos-equos boundary. "I've been out of my godsdamned mind thinking about you in my bed. You have no idea…"

Fen had all the ideas tonight. His hands full of the mariner's plaits, his back bent like a bow, heels digging down and hips pushing up into the wet heat of Trueblood's mouth.

"Gods, Pé." Fen's voice bounced off the ceiling, then careened off each wall before toppling beside him on the tangled covers again.

"All right?" the mariner said softly.

"Everything right. Don't you fucking stop."

Trueblood reached long for a little vial on his nightstand. His grip on Fen turned slick and slippery. Slowly he took Fen apart, opened him up, unfolded him like a love note with endless pages. Story after story told. Layer after layer of skin shed. All the laughing curses and growling praise and murmured encouragement coaxed Fen to bigger acts and braver deeds. The kheiron was steeled with desire and limp with trust when he fell to his back and pulled Trueblood onto him. "Come in me now."

"Are you sure?"

"I am nothing but sure." His hands drew Trueblood's head down and he whispered in his mouth, "It's you and I want it. I want this, Pé. I want it from you. Nobody else."

Trueblood drew back tall, gathering up Fen's knees on his forearms. A shiver ran down the length of his body as he slowly pushed inside.

Time closed its eyes and held its breath.

Each lover gasped the other's name.

The mattress swelled like a wave as Trueblood fell on his hands. The crown of his damp head curled into Fen's shoulder, mouth open in a wordless groan, teeth closing on Fen's fingertips.

"Right now," he whispered. "This."

Then Fen's mouth filled with Trueblood. Kisses like the sea, watery and liquid and deep. His knee curled around Trueblood's waist, a heel grabbing the opposite hip. He pulled hard, pinning the kepten into him, unable to get him close enough.

"Right now. Only this."

"Look at me," Trueblood said, holding Fen's head in his big hands. "Look at me the whole time. Look at me when you come."

It hit them fast. Fen flung himself over the edge and Trueblood dove after him. The kepten poured into the kheiron, who came back hard, starsilver colliding against giantsblood. Hands clenched numb, eyes still locked but no longer seeing anything.

Trueblood held him afterward, wrapped around Fen's back, arms crossed tight.

"Valentos, I love you," he said.

Fen couldn't speak. To lie here naked and unafraid, to feel a man against his back in a way that was nothing but beautiful and caring and careful, was beyond any words.

I'm free, he thought over and over. *I'm stone-less and bare-handed and I am finally, finally free.*

"Tell me what you feel," Trueblood said. "I need to know you're all right."

"I'm so all right," Fen said. "I'll tell you when it's not."

"Promise me."

"I promise."

Trueblood got up to get them water. He stumbled a little, and had to pause with his hand on the wall, taking slow breaths, but his smile was a beautiful thing.

"One of us is bleeding," Fen said, running a hand through the rumpled sheets and finding tiny streaks of red.

They lifted limbs and craned over shoulders. "It's me," Trueblood said. A healing scar on his side had torn open a little. Fen shaved off a bit of kyrrh and pressed it to the raw edges. Trueblood lay down again and wrapped Fen's arms around him like a cape.

"I can feel your heart beating on my back," he said.

"My heart is feeling so many things."

"Tell me one."

"I want to be with you. Wherever you go the rest of your life, I want to be somewhere near."

"I want that, too."

"Can it work?"

"We'll make it work."

Fen gathered up a handful of the mariner's plaits and held them to his face. "What about our heirs?"

Trueblood glanced back, chuckling. "Is this a biological question?"

Fen lightly smashed his palm against the laughter. "Dynastic, you moron."

"Talk to me. What are you thinking?"

"That I love you but we both have certain…procreative obligations and godsdammit, Pé, stop laughing."

"I'm not laughing at you, I just smiled."

"You know what I mean."

"Yes, I know what you mean. One of these days, both of us are going to father children. We won't pretend it's not going to happen. At least, I won't."

"I won't either but will it bother you?"

"You mean will I be jealous if you have sex with a pegaso?"

"Well, when you put it that way…"

"I have no idea. If it happens, I'll talk about it. All right? We can do anything as long as we're honest with each other."

"All right. I know I'm being stupid—"

"You're not."

"—But I've never felt like this. Never in my life. This is more feeling than I ever had in my life."

"Me too." Trueblood held Fen's head, smoothing a thumb over his bottom lip. "My heart's pounding right now and I'm so in love with you, I can barely contemplate being with anyone else. For any purpose."

"You have more of me than anyone else ever has."

"I know. I'll be really careful with it."

"Promise?"

Trueblood held his lips against Fen's, breathing. "It's safe with me. All of it."

His skin burned under Fen's hands, but not with desire. His teeth chattered within their kiss.

"Damn, kheiron, you made me come so hard I spiked a fever."

"You're welcome," Fen said. Then he got up and went out to the hearth to heat up the kettle and find a mug.

So this is what it's like, he thought, pouring hot water over a flake of kyrrh, stirring in honey and taking it back to bed.

Our bed. I'm part of an us now.

We are gelang.

At hand to offer his lover a cup of what he needed. Then lying down together, scooping up the covers and tucking them in tight around their naked bodies.

"Rest now," he said, his fingertips gently closing Trueblood's eyes. "You're tired."

"If I sleep, I'll miss you."

"I'm right here. I'll be at hand."

They slept quickly and dreamlessly. Woke in the night again, hard and hungry.

"Again," one pleaded.

"More," the other demanded.

"Don't stop," they promised.

The kepten's room was full of heat. Steam curled from the walls, redolent with sex and spice. Through the night, the flame of the mariner and the finch burned, burned, burned.

"Again."

"Come to me."

"This."

"Tell me its name."

"Show me it's yours."

"Valentos."

"Gelangos."

WHEN YOU LOOK FOR ME

TRUEBLOOD TOOK THE ship's wheel an hour the next morning, still following the course set by the pegasos. He passed the helm to Raj, then walked the Kaleuche from top to bottom, bow to stern. He stopped to talk to everyone. Or listen. He praised jobs well done. Pointed out the things allowed to slip and firmly demanded they be put back to rights. He spent the most time with the carpenters. Misery had done significant damage to the port hull and while the temporary repairs were sound, they weren't made of wood from Nye trees. They'd have to be watched carefully.

Calvo needed Trueblood's ear next. The food provisions were starting to dwindle. Without Seven's guidance, the galley cooks were being a little too lavish at mealtimes. Some belt-tightening would have to be done. If it didn't rain soon, they might have to ration water. Something else to watch carefully.

Everyone needed a piece of him and he took the time to give his full attention, even as his thoughts kept wandering off to Fen. Trueblood wanted him. Again. Right now.

Soon, he thought. *Tonight. He's with me now. We're together and it can wait.*

He almost couldn't bear sitting through the evening story hour. The minoros fought for the floor space at his feet, crowded the back of the sofa to lean on his shoulders. Their love was a blanket, but Fen's gaze kept snagging on his and flooding him with impatient heat.

I can't wait to get you alone in bed, the ukhor-blue stare said.

We won't even make it to the bed, Trueblood replied with his eyes.

Sighing, he crossed one knee over the other. Fen looked away, the color up high in his face.

When the minoros finally—*finally*—said goodnight and left the aftercastle, Fen went with them. A few of the young ones were still processing everything that happened. Lejo had his hands full with silent anxiety, out-loud homesickness and a lot of night terrors. Fen tried to help with some extra time and reassurances. It was work he did best.

Trueblood wrote in his journal. He was several entries behind.

One by one, his majoros and his maristos said goodnight. The ship downshifted into quiet. Trueblood marked his place with Fen's feather, blew out the lamp in his study and went into the bedroom.

Fen wasn't there.

For a moment, the kepten didn't know what to think, then a smile pulled his mouth sideways.

Oh, I see. The game is on again.

He was tired though. And Fen should know. Odd that he'd throw the old hide-and-seek gauntlet on this first day, at this hour. More than odd. A little thoughtless.

The smile inverted to a frown. Where was he?

Doesn't he want me?

He batted the thought away like a fly, but it buzzed around, worrying at him as he left the aftercastle. He looked in a few of Fen's old hideouts on the main and halfdeck, but the thrill of the search stopped there. He went below another level and stood for a lost moment in the corridor, outside Fen's old cabin door.

Were you about to invite me?

He touched fingertips to the door, then pushed it open.

The lamp was out and Fen was in bed. Lying on his stomach, covers pulled high and face turned to the wall.

Bewildered, Trueblood crept in and knelt down.

"Héjo," he whispered.

The kheiron's back rose and fell in long breaths.

"Fen."

"Mm?"

Trueblood slid a hand into the white hair, rubbing the soft skin behind Fen's ear. "What are you doing here?"

"Sleeping."

"I want you to sleep in my bed."

"I know."

Trueblood leaned elbows on the mattress and stretched to look over Fen's far shoulder. "So why are you here?"

Fen's eyes opened. "Because I like when you look for me."

I Know Who I Am

EN BARELY RECOGNIZED his gentle hands that night. Couldn't believe such tender ardor wrapped in this kind of volcanic passion was anything he was capable of. It came bubbling out of him in words without beginning or end.

"I want to be with you," he whispered against Trueblood's smile. "When I'm with you, I know who I am."

"You're mine."

"I want to be where you are and I want us to be together."

"It's done. You don't have to want that. You have it." Trueblood rolled on his stomach, hands sliding through the tangle of bedclothes. "Now have me."

Fen moved against him, careful of the healing cuts on the mariner's back. The cool, piney scent of kyrrh shivered up from his skin.

"Hurt?" Fen whispered.

"No."

"Good?"

"Mmhm."

"You like this?"

"Gods, I'll follow you anywhere for that."

"Promise you'll always look for me," Fen said, cresting the wave of the mariner's body.

"I promise. I'll take the world apart to find you."

"Say my name."

"Fen."

"Say my khenom."

"I don't know how."

"Try. I want to hear it in your voice."

"You say it first."

"I said it to you once. Just say what you remember. Please."

Trueblood turned his face on the pillow and spoke Fen's soul name. Slowly. Tongue to the roof of his mouth, then bottom lip curling under his top teeth and exhaling *Tehvani...* His lips and tongue and teeth around the string of sounds. Carefully. As if every syllable were fire or ice.

"Say it again," Fen said, head tilted and listening.

"Tehvani..."

He came close. He almost got it. Not quite. As if he'd said Fan instead of Fen. Troubled instead of Trueblood.

But it was close. Oh, so close.

Closer than any other human came to recognizing the kheiron's soul and calling it by name.

It sounded beautiful and flawed, floating over the plain of a bed built for giants.

You found me. You looked for me and you found me and you called me by name. Brought me back home, brought me to your bed and called me by name. Because I am yours and there is no place on this ship or in this world I can hide that you won't find me.

"Pé, I love you." Fen was unstoppable now. "I love you."

My friend, my kepten, my mate.

He rose up on his knees with the broad plain of Trueblood's scarred back heaving beneath his cheek.

My love, my life, my man.

His hands spread like another pair of wings, alabaster in the moonlight, outlined stark against Trueblood's black skin.

My one.

"Fen, I can't even do but..." The mariner's fists crawled up the wall above the bed's headboard, flattening and then curling, scratching, looking for purchase. Looking for the wheel of this ship they sailed over the night. "I can't even do but want you so good like this."

Fen's ego howled with power and prowess as the rambling words kept falling out of Trueblood's throat, babbling and sing-song.

"It's so good, so much good when you're all up in me, I can't do but even want you like this."

"Let go," Fen whispered, running his palms along Trueblood's arms, taking them down. "Come here now."

"Can't do but want you like this."

"Do what I tell you. Come down on me now. Give all of it to me."

Give me the helm. I sail this ship tonight. I'm at hand and you can trust me.

"Want you like this." Trueblood sank into his lap, fingers laced behind Fen's neck as they rocked over the waves on their knees. "Don't stop. Don't ever fucking stop being like this."

"I can't. I belong to you like this."

Trueblood slid the ringos off his finger and pushed it onto Fen's. "Fly, gelangos."

A warm shudder flew down Fen's back. Nape to waist. His wings lifted from his skin, unfolded and unfurled to stretch from one side of the mattress to the other, light spilling from between each feather.

"It was put in stone," he said. "When the *Truviad* said starsilver would be bound to giantsblood, it meant *this*. The rings have nothing to do with it. They never did. It's us, Pé. I and you."

The bond was love. Not servitude but soul mates. Not ownership but...

One-ship, Fen thought. *One ship.*

One love.

One story.

Fen covered Trueblood's mouth with his. The wings folded forward and wrapped around the kepten, drawing him tight against Fen's body. Fen kissed him and kissed him again. He used his wings like another pair of limbs, extending and retracting them as they fell off their knees and onto their faces. Rolling to one side, then the other. Twisting and turning and giving and taking through the long night. Then resting deep, the finch curled around the mariner, one wing folded over their bodies.

"Like this," Trueblood said. "Everything ever again, only like this."

"I'm so happy," Fen murmured. He'd never in his life said such a thing. It filled his mouth and heart and veins with a fragile sweetness. Filled his hands like an unexpected gift.

For me? Can this be mine?

"I love your happiness," Trueblood said, each drowsy word threaded onto a string.

They slept, nine fingers twined between ten. Together and at hand.

"FEN. FEN, WAKE up."

"Mm?"

"Oh my Gods."

"What?"

"Holy shit." Trueblood lay on one elbow, face wide with panic as a hand ran up and down Fen's back. "Fen, what the fuck is…"

Still half-asleep, Fen pushed up, trying to look down his own back. "What are you talking about?"

"Get up. Come here."

Yanked by the wrist, Fen stumbled toward the cheval mirror.

"Stand here," Trueblood said. "Can you see?"

Fen turned this way and that. "No."

"Wait." The kepten grabbed the smaller mirror he used to shave and held it front of Fen, tilting it to catch the reflection of the kheiron's back. "Now look."

Fen felt his eyes bulge. His wings were retracted, but the silver markings had changed overnight. Before they lay parallel to his spine, tips crossed. Now they spread horizontal, out across his shoulder blades. Parting like a pair of curtains to reveal a new set of markings etched in his skin.

"Holy shit," Fen said, craning as he stepped back, closer to the big mirror. "What *is* that?"

Trueblood leaned to look, his breath warm on Fen's skin. "I think it's a map."

Part Nine

Os

Who is One

FOR THE WORLD

The kheiron unto the mariner as a map unto a lost land.

TRUEBLOOD STOOD AT the wheel of the Kaleuche and Fen stood close by. From now on, Fen would always be near him.

"Terribly sorry to torture you again, Kepten," Raj said. "But may I see the map?"

Dopey grins and rolled eyes as Fen slid his shirt up his back for the fifth time. He knew Raj didn't need to see the map. He was just being Raj.

And he noticed Trueblood wasn't complaining.

The flight of pegasos surrounded the ship, Zoria at the bow and the copper Darea on her starboard. Eighteen wings synchronized in an elegant escort.

"Your mother is so beautiful," Trueblood said.

Fen felt odd saying thank you. Zoria's beauty was none of his doing. He really meant he was grateful Trueblood could see her at all. Grateful the braided rope of Zoria's hair was coiled on the dresser in the kepten's bedroom, along with all of Fen's little possessions. Because it was their room now and they were gelang.

Fen remembered one of the earnest entries in Trueblood's childhood notebooks: *They are gelang. That means they are together and love each other and sleep in the same cabin.*

Not much sleeping was going on in the kepten's cabin. They were making love every night like the world was ending. Sometimes soundless and soft, other times like they were trying to fuck each other out of existence. They went at it until the wee hours, finally collapsing in a pile of spent, boneless limbs. Barely enough time to dream before it was daybreak and Melki, now an apprentice steward, was knocking at the door, bearing a tray with two plates of breakfast.

"Good morning, Kepten," he said, unfazed and cheerful as he opened the curtains. "Good morning, Fen."

Remarking on the weather, he took Trueblood's strewn clothes from the floor, folded them and laid them in a drawer, then folded Fen's clothes and laid them in another. Sometimes he collected a stray feather or two. Once he spotted Trueblood's hoop earring on the rug and set it discreetly on the dresser by Fen's pile of starsilver. He took both pairs of boots to be shined and came back with two jugs of hot water for shaving.

Two of everything now.

Because they were gelang.

From the helm, Trueblood smiled at Fen. "Come here, you moron."

Humming with happiness, the kheiron slid arms around Trueblood's shoulders from behind and slid a hand into the V of his shirt. They stood together, the sun on their faces, hair rippling in the wind.

"I love my life," Trueblood said.

Fen exhaled slowly and closed his eyes. "I love mine, too."

Rise up, O brave son of Khe.
Stay the course charted within your wings and sails.

A new smudge appeared on the horizon. As it grew in size and shape, a hush filled the sails of the Kaleuche and laid fingers on the mouth of every crew member. Later, those who were there would describe the silence as awed, holy and humbling. Nobody spoke a syllable. Many claimed they barely thought as the ship approached Nydirsil. No word, no expression, no simile or metaphor or idiom, no rationalization or theory could capture the spiritual massiveness of the Tree of Life.

"It filled up the sky," young Melki would tell his grandchildren one day. "It took nine days from first sighting to reach her."

Nine days of gelang.

Nine nights of lovemaking.

The earth that clung to Nydirsil's roots after she was uprooted made an island. The Kaleuche approached the shoreline and when the sounding line said she could go no further, her anchor was dropped.

Still cloaked in a solemn quiet, the large, masted longboat was lowered with Trueblood, the Ĝemelos and Fen. If any of the crew wept as they watched the four sail toward the inlet, they kept it in the silence of their hearts.

When the wind dropped and the sails sighed against the mast, the four friends rowed. Together as equals. Beached at the base of the tree, between bumpy roots, they walked toward her. Fen's fourhand in Trueblood's and on his other side, his fivehand fingers twined between Lejo's.

Walk among giants, your fourhand in his five, your fivehand between six.

They stopped as one and gazed up at the incomprehensible height of the tree. The mast of the world.

"We've been training our whole lives for this," Trueblood said. "We outgrew the Cay and got the Kaleuche to practice on. Getting us ready for this."

"So we hang for nine days," Fen said. "Starsilver and giantsblood."

He took a deep, easy breath, ready to play his part in the story. *I am the Finch,* he thought. *I'm not afraid of anything.*
Except living without Pé.

"All right," he said. "All right, let's do this."

"Not you, Fen," Lejo said.

"What?"

"I and Lejo take him," Raj said. "Not you."

"Horseshit," Fen said. "Starsilver and giantsblood. I've got the starsilver. I'm the…"

His voice died away as Raj and Lejo took their shirts off and turned from him to look up at the tree. Etched on each of their backs were distinctive and familiar markings.

"What the…" His fingertips reached to touch. "You're kheirons?"

Lejo smiled and nodded. "The marks showed up on our backs the same morning yours changed."

"But where are your rings?"

"The stars," Trueblood said. His eyes had gone far away.

Raj had the same distant expression, rubbing a little circle on his chest. "I guess that's how she held them inside us."

"She who?" Fen said. "Held what inside you?"

"I thought it was a dream," Trueblood said. "But I remember now. She showed me everything."

Fen was feeling far too left out of this conversation. "Pé, what are you talking about?"

Not taking his eyes off the tree, Trueblood took Fen's hand. "Truvos gave Khe's rings to Ele-Kheir to keep safe. She split them up. Raj has four. Lejo has four. My father had the ninth until he died. Now I have it."

"Funny she didn't divide them three, three and three," Raj said.

"Of course not," Lejo said, with one of his rare, disgusted expressions. "Four gods, four goddesses and Os, who is One."

"I'm the ringos," Trueblood said. "The ninth that binds the eight. A sail on the yard of the world's mast. I remember."

"*That's* what you've been drawing all this time," Lejo said.

"Now it makes sense," Raj said. "Come on, Lé."

Bewildered, Fen watched the twins walk back toward the boat. "What the fuck is going on? Where are they going?"

Trueblood let go Fen's hand and pulled his shirt off, his eyes narrowed on the tree. Beautiful enough to stop Fen's thoughts cold and let joy in his lover's presence wind around his head like smoke.

Mine, he thought.

You're mine and we are gelang. Where you go I follow.

A clatter of wood on wood from the boat. Raj was breaking down the mast.

A wall broke down in Fen's heart and all at once, he understood.

The mast would be set crosswise against Nydirsil's trunk. Exactly like the pictures Trueblood doodled in his notebook.

Masts that turn into trees, Fen thought. *Trees that turn into masts. Pages and pages of them. All with a tenth, sideways branch. Straight across.*

Lejo was coiling rope to tie Trueblood like a sail to that improvised yard. They'd leave him to hang in the tree.

Threefold love times three to make nine days.

"And what do I do," Fen said. "Just stand here and watch?"

*Kneel with broken heart in the roots and feast your
   eyes on Os.
Look up beneath starsilver and giantsblood as ripening
   fruit unto the limbs of Nydirsil.
Look up beneath love to hang nine days for nine stars.
Rise up beneath the blood truth, brave son of Khe.*

Kneel. Look. Rise.

This was Fen's job.

This is what I was trained for in Arcodolori, he thought. *To do nothing. Just stay on my knees, look up and see what the world has for me.*

This was his epic tale, chiseled in stone. Be born in sadness, oblivious to death. Step in his mother's blood while his head stayed turned toward the past. Be willing at twelve years old to give up his power for love, only to be enslaved for it. Endure being bought and sold and abused in the root-pits before being flung broken-legged into a tree. Survive all that *and* the loss of his father's love so he could be willing, again, at age thirty-five, to give up his gifts for love. Real love. Love he sold his secrets for. Love that freed his own body. Love that broke down his barriers of shame and made him feel worthy. Love both at hand and together with. A love that belonged to him, finally in his hands and he believed it was real and believed it was for him.

Without a price. Finally a *this* which hadn't cost him *that.*

And now I give it up. I kneel down and watch it all be taken away again. Then rise. Because I'm the whore in the story and my job is to take shit the gods dole out.

Anger surged in his chest as he formally withdrew his consent.

"Fuck. This."

Trueblood looked at him then. It was a look Fen knew well. He'd seen the same penetrative expression on his father far too many times. The stare that *pierced,* until its owner looked straight through you, only seeing what they wished was there.

"You're not doing this," Fen said. "I'm not letting you do this."

"I'm sorry," Trueblood said. "I didn't know until now what it all meant. How both of us fit into..." His hand gestured toward the tree. "This part."

"What do you mean, this part?"

"I have to do this. And you have to survive it. You have to rise up when—"

"How much do the gods think I can take?" Fen cried, seizing Trueblood's arms and shaking him a little. "Pé, look at me. You do this and I'm dead. You understand? There's no rising after this. No happy, brave ending. If you go, I'm going with you. That's how it is. There is no me without you."

"If you don't live, the story doesn't get told."

"I don't care about any story but ours. We lay in your bed and wrote it, remember? We don't go where the other can't follow. We don't hide where the other can't find. That's the story."

Lips pressed tight, Trueblood shook his head. "I didn't know about this one."

"Pé, don't you…"

The old question bubbled up like foam in Fen's throat. Twenty years he'd been swallowing it down, but now it tumbled out, spitting and snarling. "Don't you love me anymore?"

"Fen, I'm sorry."

Fen shook him harder and the mariner allowed it.

"I'm sorry," he said, over and over as he rattled in Fen's desperate grip. "I'm sorry" while stumbling back as Fen pummeled him. "I'm sorry" when they were crushed up against the wall of Nydirsil's trunk and Fen crumpled, cursing through tears in Trueblood's arms.

"I love you," Trueblood said into Fen's hair. "You're the love of my life and you're the only one who can survive what—"

"Stop *saying* that. My heart can't take this shit anymore."

"I have a godsdamned *star* in my heart, Fen. It's going back where it belongs, whether you're willing or not."

"So everything that happened with us means nothing?"

"Don't say that. You're the best thing that ever happened to me."

"Then how can you—"

"Because it's *written*."

They stared at each other, breathing hard through clenched teeth, fingers white-knuckled in each other's clothes and hair.

No, Fen thought. *Not again. Not one more time. I cannot.*

"I have to do this," Trueblood said in a voice thinner than air. "And the only way I can is if you're watching the whole time. I need you to be with me until the end. Your job isn't to just kneel there and *take* it. Your job is to watch and remember and then *give* it to the rest of the world. You're the rakcntistos, Fen. You have to survive so people will know."

Fen thought he would die. He knew Trueblood was right and it hurt. Breathing hurt. Living hurt. Even loving Pé hurt. But denying him anything hurt even more. "Gods fucking dammit," he whispered.

"I can get up that tree," Trueblood said. "But you're the only one who can get me down. I'm going up a man and coming down a story. You have to tell the story and not let it be forgotten. Fen, please…"

"Pé," Raj called. "It's time."

The two lovers pulled one another to their feet.

"Here," Trueblood said, sliding the ringos off his finger.

"No, keep it."

"Put it on. And don't let anyone take it from you again. When you get back to Nyland and get your moonstone back, I want you to *swallow* it. Nobody is ever going to own you, in any way, shape or form. Ever again. Do you understand? Answer your commander."

"Aye, Kep." Fen put the ringos on and wished he were dead.

"I need you to promise me something else."

"Héjo, you're not in the position to be making demands right now," Fen said, thinking maybe he could joke this whole fucking thing away.

"Shut up and listen to me. If the tree starts making spice again? I mean like it starts falling down right away from the branches? You bring some back to Belmiro. I don't care if it's one grain or ten, you catch it, keep it and give it to him."

"I will."

"You tell him more is coming and he's free now."

"All right."

"Come here."

They held each other as if trying to become the same person. Fen whispered, "I can't do this again."

"Do it for me. You survive for me. I want you to live. I want you to sire an heir and show him what it means to be a good father. Whenever you think you can't do something, you do it for me."

"Gods, I hate your guts." Packing sarcasm around his broken heart was the only way Fen could maintain any sense of dignity. If he spoke the true words, he would start screaming and not stop.

"I hate you too," Trueblood said. "I hate you so fucking much, Fen il-Kheir."

"Say my name. Go on, let me hear you slaughter it one more time."

"*Tehvani…*"

The syllables rolled forward like he was born for no other purpose than to speak them. The near-perfection hurt Fen's ears so bad, he ended it by kissing Trueblood hard. He pushed the mariner up against the tree, slid his tongue in Trueblood's mouth, swallowed his soul name and shut the beautiful bastard up good.

"I'm going to kill you," he whispered. "I love you so much, I'm going to *kill* you."

The son of a bitch whipped around and Fen's back slammed against Nydirsil. "Shut up and kiss me."

Fen's arms locked around the giantsblood's neck, pulling him in. His mouth opened and the frantic, furious heat in his body pawed the ground like an enraged bull. The nerve of this gods-damned wharf rat, thinking he could order Fen il-Kheir around. This idiotic sailor had some set of balls, making the heir to the kheiron herd show his best side, making him actually want to survive this horseshit.

"Pé," Raj called.

"I'm in the middle of something," Trueblood mumbled.

Fen stepped away, digging his ringed fingers in his hair. He drew in a powerful breath and let it go, abruptly changing his attitude and deciding none of this was happening.

"All right," he said. "It's time. You go. And we're going to talk about this later."

"Be with me until the end." Trueblood was still trying to hold him. "And I'll be with you forever."

Fen was having none of it. "No, don't go being cute. We're going to have a really long, really unpleasant conversation later. You are in a world of deep shit."

Trueblood touched his face. "You made me a better man."

"Yeah, we're going to talk about that, too."

"Fen."

"Go on. Do your thing. It'll be a lot more fun than the chat we're having later." Boldly, Fen took Trueblood's face and kissed him with open eyes. "Go on now."

As Trueblood turned, Fen backhanded his ass. "You're getting more of *that* later, too."

Trueblood looked around. "I'll see you in a little while."

"Oh believe me, you will. What you got for leaving the nyellem door open is going tickle in comparison."

"I love you," Trueblood said. "Don't you fucking leave me until it's done."

"You wish," Fen said. "You're stuck with me until the end."

THE GREATEST LOVE STORY

TODAY, LEGANTOS, WE call Trueblood's sacrifice *The Naŭtag-giad*. The Epic of the Nine Days.

Some call it the greatest love story ever told.

Others have no name for it.

You decide.

Listen to learn, learn to tell, tell to teach.

And then call it whatever you want.

THE WRONG MAN
FOR THE JOB

PELIPPÉ TRUEBLOOD WASN'T afraid during the ascent of the tree, when the ground disappeared beneath him like last night's dream. He wasn't afraid when Raj and Lejo placed the crossbeam and tied him to it, their hands sea-strong and ship-sure as they secured him around the chest, wrists, elbows and shoulders.

He only feared for Fen.

The kheiron wound a rope of his own around the tree, flying in slow spirals. Accompanying the climb, as was his job. There in case of panic or a fall on the mast. He was excellent at it. All that long afternoon, from zenith to twilight, he glided and hovered around Nydirsil, not resting once.

His excellence made Trueblood afraid. None of this could start until Fen went to the ground.

The sun was an orange disc in a sky streaked pink and amethyst when the flight of pegasos came. The herd mentality declared it was time for Fen to come down. Darea, the beautiful copper mare, flew in closer and said, "It won't begin until you begin. And you must begin as Khe did."

"Go on down now," Trueblood said to Fen. He almost said *you're tired,* but he knew Fen was a proud creature. And Trueblood had promised to be careful with all the things he knew about Fen.

"I can't do this without you," he said. "But I need to start now. Go down with Darea and help me start."

Fen was tired. His face pale as ash, wincing with every rise and fall of his wings. His lips trembled against Trueblood's one more time.

"Right now," he said. "This."

"Right now." Trueblood filled his lungs with Fen's scent. "Only this."

Pulling back, Fen's feathers drooped and he plummeted a sharp foot before regaining himself. Darea was at his side at once.

"Tehvan, will you honor me by riding?"

"The honor is mine," Fen whispered. His wings retracted as he mounted her back and slid his shaking hands into her dark mane.

So the kheiron went down to begin as Khe did, as a man bound to earth.

Trueblood was alone now. The twins had climbed out of sight and the ground was farther away than yesterday. The sun charged down the bowl of the sky, burning behind the lowest branch on Nydirsil's western side. If the tree were a kheiron's hands, the sun would set on the fourhand's last finger. The one that bore ringosol, the ring of Solos.

His fingers were tingling. He pushed down on his feet, taking some of the tension off his shoulders.

This is going to get a whole lot harder before it gets easier, he thought.

A lick of anxiety in the back of his throat as he thought about nine long days ahead.

I want to do a good job. I may have to settle for good enough.

The sun was nearly down. The apex of the sky had darkened to indigo and the first stars were shimmering through when, in a flash of copper and gold, Darea flew toward the tree like an arrow.

Nydirsil trembled against Trueblood's back. A beat of pure silence, then the pegaso flew due west with Lejo mounted between her wings. Sparkles in their wake flooded across Trueblood's eyes, blinding him with clarity. He knew the last finger on Fen's four-hand was empty now. His ringosol would be used to anchor one of the stars inside Lejo's heart to that lowest, westernmost branch.

But why Lejo? he thought. *That makes no sense. Lejo isn't the sun.*

It should be Raj in the west. Raj and his sunny handsome-ness, his laugh that could light up a room. His aura that glinted at the edge of Trueblood's vision. Bold, fearless Raj who, if he didn't know the answer, didn't hesitate to make something up. His solid, dependable nature that never wavered. Raj was con-sistent as sunrise and sunset. He was the very definition of sun.

Why was Lejo anchoring the branch of Solos?

The sun slipped out of sight and Nydirsil shuddered against his shoulders. Then the entire sky rumbled, pierced by the force of pinning the branch like a brooch to her cloak.

Once, Kepten Trueblood thought, *long ago, the first time Nydirsil was anchored, Nyos accidentally made a hole in the sky, and the winged horses came through it. Their hooves tore a second hole open, and the birds came through.*

Once, not quite that long ago, the minoro Trueblood sat at old Rafil's feet, reluctant to take stories at face value. "What was on the other side of the hole?" he asked. The sitting room hissed with shushing noises but little Pelippé was unwavering in his curiosity. "Where were the winged horses and birds before?"

Far away on the western horizon, a tiny hole opened in the sky. Through it, Trueblood saw a golden temple, its central dome sur-rounded by minarets. Gorgeous indolent lions lazed on the wide steps, tamed by the massive field of red poppies planted around the edifice. He saw an altar of topaz and tiger's eyes and rubies, heaped high with sunflowers, marigolds, dandelions, goldenrod and heliotrope. The potent perfume of the poppies caressed his eyelids and nose, along with the scent of burning cassia and sandalwood.

Oh, he thought. As he thought on another long-ago day when Lejo's body slid against his and the universe whispered secrets into his ear.

Oh. I see. It's Lejo because he made *me see.*

"Exactly," Solos the sun god said from everywhere. "Now go to sleep, lad. You have a lot of work ahead."

Trueblood's eyes closed as the new star burst into life at the tip of the lowest, most western branch.

BY NOON ON the second day, he was certain they'd picked the wrong man for the job.

The only thing taking his mind off the growling knot of hunger in his stomach was the salty thirst swelling his tongue within his mouth. The only thing taking his mind off the thirst was the pain in his arms, which was diminished by the cramping in his legs, which was overshadowed by the war in his head.

All of which paled in comparison to the agony of loneliness.

Nothing in the history of his life, anywhere, ever, had prepared him for doing this alone. He'd been raised within a crew mentality. To work together at difficult tasks and stay together in dangerous places.

I can't do this alone, he thought desperately.

He knew Fen would have to kneel heartbroken at the roots, but he assumed the twins would be right next to him for the ordeal. Starsilver and giantsblood. Instead, in a cruel betrayal, the twins climbed far above him, as if they'd received outside instructions he wasn't privy to.

"You said you'd be with me until the end." Within their bonds, his hands went to fists, wanting to punch and throw things. An apple sailed through his starving memory, hitting a marble column with a dull thud. Followed by a sensory rush that was almost erotic and he *wanted* that apple.

His teeth wailed for a bite. A luxurious, crunching chomp and the skin would wrinkle under his lip while a slice of flesh would glide across his palate and drop onto his tongue. Dry then juicy. Tart then sweet. Crisp in his mouth giving way to soft in his throat. He'd eat it the way Fen ate a grasshopper once—stem, seeds, core, calyx. Not a scrap left. Then he'd spend an hour going after the bits left between his teeth.

He'd worship that fruit. He'd build a religion around it.

He swore he'd never complain about a bruised apple again.

Then he cried, because he'd never have to.

He cried a lot that first day. It was all right. Nobody could see. After weeping, he dozed off. Or maybe the cramping ache in his limbs made him pass out. He woke and was positive he was never going to do this. They had the wrong giantsblood. Surely someone in charge would be climbing up any minute, shaking their heads in regret. "Sorry, lad, afraid you're not the one we want. Good try, though."

It was all a mistake. Any minute they'd be here.

The walls of his mind folded down. He went away, but came back when feathers brushed his cheek.

Fen.

His eyes popped open. It was over. Thank Gods. Fen was here to take him down.

A two-tone whistle corrected him.

It was the lark.

"You came," he said.

She swooped left and right, then settled on a small twig by his hip.

"I'm so glad to see you."

A long trill like an explanation.

"It's all right. I'm just glad you got here."

She flew up and perched on his outstretched arm. Hopped shoulder to wrist, examining the ties that bound him.

"I'm really up the mast, aren't I?" he said. "Don't ask me how I got into this mess. Between I and you, I wish I was out of it. This ship is too big. I'm not ready. I'm not the one."

She flew across his chest and examined his other arm.

"Did you see Fen? Is he all right?"

As if she understood, she looked down and whistled.

"I don't think he can hear you. But maybe you can… Héjo, come here. Come close to me. Please."

She hopped back to the cap of his shoulder and nestled by the cheek he leaned toward her.

"Tell Fen I want him so bad," he said. "Tell him I could do this better if he were near me. Maybe Raj is the compass and Lejo is the conscience, but Fen is the courage. The valentos. He's the bravest person I know. Tell him I'm scared out of my mind and I want him. Please. Can you do that?"

She rubbed her head against him, then canted off his outstretched arm and flew down.

Trueblood exhaled, then noticed the sun was lower in the west. Company made the time go by. Anything could be endured if you had someone to talk to.

Gods, he was so thirsty.

He dozed.

When he woke, the sky was lavender and the full moon was rising in the east. Lunos faced him dead on, peeking through the lowest branch on that side of Nydirsil. A kheiron's fivehand pinky finger with a ringolun, the ring of the moon.

A wind blew his plaits around and a pegaso scorched the sky like a reversed lightning bolt, flashing creamy white from ground to branches, then out to the east with Raj on his back.

Through the tiny rift in the stars, Trueblood beheld the realm of the moon goddess. Her temple built of overlapping circles of light at the center of a perfectly round lake. Swans glided along its surface, barely making a ripple. The altar within the luminescent spheres was heaped high with round objects. Trueblood crammed his eyes with creamy white eggs, silver apples, globes and orbs and...

He squinted. *And compasses?*

"Of course," Lunos said. "A circular journey is a noble thing. Always start as you mean to end, Pelippé Trueblood."

She rose higher on her course and the second star dazzled to life at the tips of the easternmost branch.

The lark flew back to Trueblood and nestled in the curve of his neck and shoulder, fluffed up round and warm. As she slept, she made a funny thrum. A tiny whistle in her slumber that sounded exactly like Fen's breathing when he slept in Trueblood's arms.

Trueblood drank that little sound all night.

The Rakontistos

THE THIRD DAY it rained.

The ground beneath Fen's knees turned to mud. He pinched off bits and whispered his khenom into the wet earth, then rolled it into small balls that he pressed into Nydirsil's bark.

He remembered climbing the Kaleuche's main mast and the kepten's counsel to give the spine of the ship a hug. It spent so much time being hated, it liked to be appreciated every now and then.

Fen stretched his arms wide against the massive bole of the world's mast. "You were taken away from your home and everything you loved. You did nothing wrong. Things were done to you. You had no choice and you gave no consent. All these years you've been lost, waiting for someone to find you. I know what that's like. If you think no one understands, please know I do. We're here now, valentos. You're home."

His fingers pressed into mud and bark. He spoke his name again and again, begging Nydirsil to draw it up like sap and deliver it to Trueblood.

I miss you so much, Pé. I love you and my heart is breaking.

The rain came down harder. Darea stepped behind him and curved her wings around, making a little shelter. All this time, she'd been by his side. She kept a respectful, emotional distance from his vigil, but she didn't stop guarding him a minute.

The world will have to go through her before it can get to me. She's the witness to all of this. The rakontistos. She'll remember everything in perfect detail and help me tell the tale.

"Thank you for staying," he said into the circle of her damp feathers.

"It's an honor," she said. "The most important thing I'll ever do."

Fen sank his knees deeper into the earth. He spread his hands wide on the trunk of Nydirsil and let go of both the past and the future. He stayed in place and stayed in the present, knowing it was the most important thing he ever did.

ARGUING WITH A GOD

TRUEBLOOD DRANK IN the rain. Gulp after delicious gulp along his tongue and throat, the cells of his body perking up with joy before slumping back into exhausted pain. When he sensed the storm was letting up, he let the water collect in his mouth, the same way Fen had pooled up his spit while being marched across the desert.

Grumpy and bedraggled, the lark preened her feathers while balanced on her twig. Except it wasn't a twig anymore—with each passing day, it had grown longer and was now a proper branch. A nice place for visitors to sit.

Wrevos came on that third day. The god of wisdom was gray as the clouds blanketing the sky. An owl perched on one shoulder, a crow on the other. His opal eyes were somber but kind as he told Trueblood more stories in an afternoon than the lad had heard in his whole life. He had so many questions, but the water he was carefully hoarding in his mouth kept him silent.

"All a story needs is a listener," Wrevos said. "An aŭskultantos. The kheiron trusted you with his terrible tales. Quietly listening and promising to be careful with them was best thing and the only thing you needed to do, my one."

Trueblood nodded, missing Fen desperately. The day was sliding into evening, but the clouds kept the stars hidden. He felt the wind of the third pegaso flying up into the branches, but didn't see it, nor the new star, nor what lay on the other side of the hole in the sky.

Ele-Kheir said not everything was for the waking world, he thought as he fell asleep. The owl and the crow each left him a feather, which the lark tucked in between his plaits.

VELOS VISITED HIM on the fourth day. She smelled of fertile earth, corn and grains. New flowers and dried leaves tumbled from her hair, for it was she who plowed the earth at springtime and reaped it in fall. Her realm on the other side of the sky was pink with new beginnings and brown with endings. Cows heavy with milk and possibility walked among the busy squirrels and beavers who loaded the holds of the earth's ship.

"Balance," she said. "It's all about the correct distribution of weight, Pelippé. Knowing what the right amount of ballast is and when to let it go."

"And knowing that outside dimensions don't always match the inside."

The goddess nodded. "Secrets take up a lot of room. It's why Fen looked thinner when he came back from Altynai."

"It's why a hiding serves some purpose—it makes your skin sting as much as your conscience, and then you feel balanced again."

She laughed a cornucopia, which he nibbled on as the sun went down. Lejo had now anchored two branches in the west, while Raj had fastened just one in the east. Nydirsil listed on her roots. Trueblood's eastern peripheral lit up hot and glaring with the pilot's effort to equalize Nydirsil's scales. He could feel

Lejo, whose soul went down fifteen flights of stairs into a warren of secret rooms and passageways, frantically re-organizing the world's cargo into a counterweight.

Isn't that what love is though, Trueblood thought. *Helping the one you love stay balanced on the journey?*

THE FIFTH DAY was terrible. Meros, the war god, filled Trueblood's dry mouth with the taste of metal, flooding his eyes and nose with the smoke of burning pine and cypress.

"You've learned how men make love with each other," Meros said. "But how they make war on each other is as important a lesson. From the horrors of battle, we learn the value of gelang."

"I don't like gelang that comes at a price."

"Everything has a price, Trueblood. Something as priceless as love is worth fighting for."

Through the choking haze, Trueblood glimpsed an ironbound land criss-crossed with veins of bloodstone and sardius. The air rang with the clashing of swords and the whistling of arrows. Warriors screamed on the offense, bellowed in retreat, cried out on the giving and receiving ends of death blows. Chains rattled in the blood-soaked earth, dragging enslavement and rape behind, tearing open wounds that could never heal.

The furious day went on and on until it killed itself. When Meros's star burst into being, it shone angry red all night long.

The sixth day it rained again. Trueblood filled his mouth but his jaw trembled and the water leaked out his teeth and ran down his chin. His feet and hands had long disappeared. The pain in his body so profound, he couldn't remember a time it wasn't there. He welcomed the end of it all.

Sweet Nyos came to him in a dress of green velvet, embroidered all over with red and gold leaves. She gathered up his plaits, kissed their ends and murmured, "You are an especial monster, Pé."

Mami, he cried in his head. *Mami, Mami…*

The goddess of love wrapped him in beaded, emerald softness. In especial beautiful penmanship, she described a temple of diamond and carnelian, its domes topped with copper. She wrote of butterflies, hummingbirds and dragonflies that followed Minos around the verdant fields of wildflowers. He wore a ridiculous crown of daisies around his horns and his muzzle was forever sticky and slick with honey. Every night Nyos shot him dead and every morning he forgave her.

Trueblood was a slave to the thought of death now. He hurt all over and between the razor-sharp spasms, he recalled Fen's description of the fadara addicts in Arcodolori, their veins howling in withdrawal, begging their captors for mercy.

This is what it's like for Belmiro, he thought. *All day long, every day, nothing but pain.*

He begged Nyos for compassion. He cried for his mother, saying he was done, he was tired, he wanted to go to bed, he wanted a story, he wanted her lap, he wanted to be picked up and taken away and godsdammit, wasn't that Noë's job?

Please, Mami, don't you love me anymore?

Up from the ground flew a pegaso, then out to the east with Raj. The goddess drew her mighty bow, its arrow fletched with peacock feathers. The eyes of the stars were in her aim. She never missed. It was her triumph when she brought down Khe, and her undoing when she slew the thing she loved most.

Please, Mami.

The string dropped with a twang. Nydirsil shook as she was pierced in both branch and trunk.

Trueblood opened his eyes. He leaned his head against the shaft of the arrow embedded a hairsbreadth away. Exactly where Nyos aimed it.

"I guess you do love me," he whispered.

SO GREAT WAS Nyos's love, it allowed him to go away and stay away until twilight of the seventh day. He opened his eyes. The sky reeled with seagulls and a new visitor sat on the branch. His back to the trunk, long legs stretched out, clad in white breeches and black boots. His braids moved in a gentle breeze.

Trueblood pried his mouth open and croaked, "Da?"

The black face turned to him. Gold eyes twinkled above a giant grin. "What's troubling my Trueblood?"

"Da, I can't finish this job."

"Oh, horseshit you can't." The black man tossed his head, clattering the little shells tied at the end of each plait. He crossed his triple-spear over his lap and extended his arms, beckoning two of the gulls. Golden scales circled his wrists.

"Oh, it's you," Trueblood said unhappily.

"At your service," Truvos said, posing with a bird in each hand.

"Hold still while I get my oil paints."

"I detect some sass here, Pelippé Trueblood."

"This is all your fault."

The sea god's mouth fell open, the portrait of indignation. Then he sighed and looked away. "I'm afraid it is, my one."

"I hope it was worth it." Trueblood never imagined he'd be arguing with a god, but his abject misery gave him both courage and audacity. "You fucking ruined everything. Cracked the world open, took the Nye away, unleashed war and killed my mother. Opened the sea floor and let Murder take my father. Was it some kind of joke to let Misery almost kill me? That was fun. I bet you had a great time watching me suffer through the worst moments of my life. Did you watch I and Fen make love and laugh your ass off, knowing what was coming?"

"Of course not."

"Why me?" Trueblood cried. "Why am I the one cleaning up the mess you made? Why am I bringing back what you stole? You're a god. I'm just a sailor. You could've fixed this ages ago. Instead you chiseled some bad poetry into a rock, then sailed off and fucking sulked for millennia. When you were done moping, you couldn't man up to put the stars back where they belonged so you fobbed them off on ele-Kheir. What the fuck was up with that? No, don't answer. I don't want to know. I just hope you're happy with how it all turned out. I hope you're at least fucking grateful."

"Thank you," Truvos said.

"Kiss my ass," Trueblood yelled, spooking the gulls into a cloud of shrieking, flapping chaos.

The sea god blinked at him, a portrait of confusion. Then he smiled like one who'd discovered the meaning of life.

"I see," he said. "You're trying to get me to kill you."

"You couldn't kill me if you tried."

"Oh, my one, I assure you—"

"Go on," Trueblood said, straining against his bonds with the last bit of muscular strength he could find. "Kill me, you son of a bitch. I dare you."

"Let's not bring my mother into this." Truvos slid off the branch and walked across the air to stand in front of Trueblood. He put a knee down on nothing, then the other.

"I'm sorry," he said. "If it's any consolation, Pelippé, I love nothing and no one the way I love you."

"Shut up," the mariner cried through his teeth. "Only my father tells me that. You're not allowed to say those words."

"It's you because it could be no one else," the sea god said. "It's you because you were born for this job. It's you because you strive for excellence at a task which everyone else would settle for being mediocre. It's you because of all the people who had the privilege to come along on your voyage. It's you because no one else can tell this story."

He touched the tips of Trueblood's boots. "It's you because I love you."

"I hate you," the mariner whispered.

"I know. And that's the beauty within the tragedy, Pé. You'll go on being excellent at this job even though you hate it. Because you know no other way."

The sea god glanced to the west. His braids lifted off his shoulders in the gusts made from pegaso wings. His hand shot out and the triple-spear flew into it. His elbow bent and aimed three golden, deadly points at Trueblood's heart.

Thank you, the mariner thought, slumping against the tree. *I did my best.*

Truvos fired. The tree shuddered. The gulls scattered. The seventh star appeared.

Trueblood leaned his head against the pillow made by the embedded trident and slept.

HE OPENED HIS eyes on the eighth day to find himself awash in feathers. Brown and red and yellow. Larks and finches clung to every inch of his body.

"They don't quite know if you're to be born or if you're to die," said Helos. The goddess of birth and death lay on her side along the branch, elbow bent and head propped on her hand.

"Please let me die," Trueblood said.

"Soon," she said, sitting up. "It's almost over. You're doing beautifully. But then again, we knew you would."

"You did?"

"Oh yes, but you gave us quite a scare, though. We thought for sure we lost you that one time."

"When? After my father died?"

She shook her head. "Ele-Kheir had that under control."

"When Misery got me?"

"Goodness, no. Fen would never let you die. We barely worried."

Trueblood was barely human now. All physical aspects of himself had fallen or floated away. Hunger, thirst and pain no longer had description. Trying to remember the close calls of his life was like trying to piece together someone else's dream. His exhausted mind squeezed like a fist, wringing out his encounters with death.

"Was it when the minotaurs killed my mother?"

"No, you idiot. It was when you jumped off the Cay's main mast when you were six. Holy horseshit, I still get nauseous when I think about it."

"But I was fine."

"Fine?" she cried, sending birds flying in every direction. "Have you ever seen eight gods have a simultaneous heart attack? Truvos nearly impaled himself on his trident when you jumped. What were you thinking?"

She paced back and forth in the air, waving her arms. "Do you know what kind of bargain we had to strike with Os to stop time long enough for me to get to you? You would've broken your neck if I hadn't backhanded you into that pratfall, and then we would've been *fucked*."

"Oh," Trueblood said, too tired for anything else.

"If you ever wondered why your father's disappointed expression made you feel like shit that day, it was because eight gods were looking through his eyes, wanting to take turns spanking you."

"I'm sorry."

"Don't do it again."

"I won't," he said. "I learned not to grow careless once the end was in sight."

Her stern expression softened. "And you never make the same mistake twice." She took his face in her cool hands and kissed his brow. "You have no idea how proud you've made us."

"I'm so tired," he said.

"I know, my one."

"It hurts."

"It's almost over. Raj is giving up his last star." She kissed each of his eyelids. "Soon, Pelippé. The end is in sight. You don't have to be perfect. You don't have to be brave. You only have to be careful and finish the job."

"Then die?"

"Then die. I promise."

Trueblood sighed under her kisses. "Thank you."

That night, the lark slept on one of his shoulders and a gold-finch on the other. A redfinch pulled a few of Trueblood's plaits into a nest and slept on the crown of his head, filling his dreams with Fen.

ESTELOS

ALL THE PEGASOS were gone, except for Zoria.

Fen's hands were empty, except for the thumb on his five-hand. Tonight at sunset, he'd give it up forever.

I'm still keeping my promise to Pé, he thought. *If I wear no rings, no one can take them from me.*

No one can take what I freely give away.

I fly no more. I begin and end as a man bound to earth.

I do this willingly.

I do this because I love you.

He had only one regret: that he hadn't the time or the means to engrave the mariner's name on the inside of his ringos. He and Pé, together, could hold the last branch to the sky and be as one within Estelos, the star of Os, who was One.

He whispered his khenom through the ring's circle, then whispered, "And Pelippé Easy Trueblood Cay."

Take us into your merciful heart.

Zoria carefully took the bit of silver in her mouth. Through her transparent shadow, Fen could see it sitting between her teeth. Her head passed through Fen's body and her love soothed him an all-too-short moment.

Then she spread her wings and flew up the tree.

ONE OF MY ONE

THE MORNING OF the ninth day, a bud swelled on the branch next to Trueblood. At the sun's zenith, the pale green calyx split, revealing white petals within. One by one they unfolded as the sun dropped and the sky softened to periwinkle at the western horizon. A black stigma extended from the flower's center, surrounded by eight slender filaments, each topped with powdery gold.

"Good job," Trueblood said to Nydirsil.

They were his last words.

Zoria hovered before him, the breeze from her wings soft on Trueblood's fevered skin. Her head bowed a moment, then she gently set Fen's ringos in the little hollow at Trueblood's throat.

One of my one, I honor thee.

The mariner glowed bright. A lamp in the branches. Light both glaring and sparkling poured from his heart, through the silver circlet and into Zoria, giving her form, turning her transparency opaque. Alive and magnificent from hooves to feather tips, she ascended to the end of the central branch and anchored it.

The ends of the divine loop touched as Zoria became the new pegaso living atop the Tree of Life. Bird and horse, the two faces of Os, who was One.

The circle closed as Pelippé Trueblood died.

ONE OF MY OWN

When the Ĝemelos came down from Nydirsil, both were thin and pale, but Raj looked rattled at a cellular level. The eighth day had shaken him badly—the day when Lejo was finished with his stars but Raj still had one to go.

"It was hard," he said. Even his voice trembled. "Having to carry it alone. Not being able to feel Lé anywhere. It…" His eyes welled up and he couldn't go on. Lejo put arms around him from behind, his sweet, tired smile framed by dimples.

"See, everyone thinks I'm the more sensitive twin," he said. "Raj is really the sap in the family."

"Fuck off," Raj said softly, holding tight to his brother's wrists. "I always told you of the two of us, you're the better man."

"Stop crying and let Fen in."

Six arms wove together and three heads pressed into a triangle. That the twins wouldn't survive the ordeal had never entered Fen's mind. His thoughts had been with Trueblood alone. Now, held up tight by the Ĝemelos, he fought through a retroactive anxiety, intensely grateful they were alive, wondering what he'd do without them right now. They clung and clutched. Two took turns consoling the third, until they were cried out and wrung dry.

"Gods, I need a drink," Raj said hoarsely.

"I feel so old," Lejo murmured.

"Telling you," Fen said. "I don't think anything will upset me or surprise me for the rest of my life."

His heart lurched in his chest when the twins put his rings back in his hands.

"I take it back," he said. "What the fuck?"

"Exactly what I said," Lejo said. "I anchored the first branch, thinking I'd be using your ringosol as a nail."

"It was more like a hammer," Raj said.

"And a spoon. First I used the ring to scoop the star out of me."

"Right, right," Raj said. "Then put it into this little hole in the sky. Gods, Fen, the things on the other side?"

"Beautiful things," Lejo said, his eyes dreamy.

"The star fit right in," Raj said. "A key in a lock."

"Then your ring fit on top and pressed it into place."

"Everything perfectly made for the job."

"And once it was done, the ring came away. Its job was done."

Raj pulled at his thick, dun hair. "Who saw that coming?"

As Fen breathed over the little pile of silver, he couldn't help a stab of insult, as if the rings hadn't been good enough. Then his delayed rationale caught up and he quickly shoved the bands onto their proper fingers.

"I'm going to get him," he said, and unfurled his wings without taking his shirt off. The split garment floated to the ground as he flew up the trunk.

The lark was hopping along one of Trueblood's arms, pecking at the ropes around his wrist and elbow. She was crying. No sound in the world was more terrible than a bird crying. Fen's heart broke as he closed a hand around the trembling feathers and held her to his cheek.

"Shh," he said. "It's over. It's all right now. I'll get him down and we'll go home."

The rope had swelled with the days of rain and then tightened as it dried in the sun. Fen had no knife and he didn't want to leave Trueblood for a single second to fetch one from the longboat. If Trueblood hung here nine days with nothing, Fen would get him down with nothing.

The lark tried to help. Still, Fen's fingertips were rubbed raw as he loosened the knots. Coordinating the freeing of limbs and the management of deadweight was anxious work. He'd kill himself if he let Trueblood fall.

"You told me once that in the whole history of the world, anywhere, ever, no one ever fell off the mast of a giantship. I'm not changing history today."

Fen brought his commander safely to earth. He knelt heartbroken in the roots of Nydirsil, not looking up at his love in the branches but down in the circle of his arms. He didn't cry. It wasn't the time. Later was for weeping. Now was for holding still, cradling Trueblood close. Smoothing his brow, letting his plaits trail through Fen's hands and nursing the tiniest flame of hope he'd wake up. As silver rings peeked through the long black braids, the hope kindled higher.

I got these back, he thought. *Maybe it means I'll get him back.*

"Fen, your father's here," Lejo said softly.

Fen looked up and the flame snuffed out. Il-Kheir spiraled in the sky above the inlet, here to collect Trueblood's soul. An honor bestowed on only the most righteous of men.

As the Horselord touched down, hair and coat wet with salt spray, Fen felt his eyes widen.

Holy Helos, he got old.

Silver hooves sank into the damp earth where Fen kneeled. Blue eyes ringed with shadows gazed down from a gaunt, lined face. The stare didn't pierce, nor did it comfort.

"It's time, Fen," he said.

"Can you take me with him?" Fen asked.

A single drop of water fell from the moonstone around the Horselord's neck. His expression softened the tiniest bit and he said, "I can't." A beat and then, as if pulling his teeth or breaking his heart apart to say the words, he added, "I'm sorry."

The tone was gentle but non-negotiable. Il-Kheir took a step forward but Lejo put a hand on his arm. "When Fen's ready, mysire," he said.

"And not a moment before," Raj said.

We all have jobs to do, Fen thought. *Finish this one the way Trueblood would. You said you'd be there until the end and you were.*

Fen kissed the mariner's head and held it to his heart for one last breath.

Now be excellent at letting him go.

"You can take him now."

The Horselord held out his hands. Up from Trueblood's scarred heart rose an orb of light, swirling in black and white and blue and gold.

"Be careful with him," Fen said.

Sevri nodded. "As if he were one of my own."

The words were glass in Fen's throat but he pushed them out. "Thank you."

The Horselord stumbled backward as if spooked. He shifted into equos and reared a little, giving a pained neigh.

"Father?" Fen said.

Sevri came back to kheiros, shaking his head hard. "It's time," he mumbled. "By gods, it's time to end this once and for all."

His wings unfurled and he flew away with Trueblood's soul, leaving Fen and the twins staring helplessly after.

"Come on," Raj finally said. "Let's take him back to the ship where he belongs."

"Héjo," Lejo cried, pointing up. "Look."

Down from the tree drifted a single flower, tilting this way and that on the breeze and settling on Trueblood's motionless chest.

Its nine white petals fell away, leaving a pale brown pod dusted with yellow-gold powder.

"Godsdamn," Raj said slowly. "We're the first to see one of those in a long time, lads."

Fen held the Nye pod to his nose and inhaled the familiar fragrance before putting it in his pocket. He'd put it in the nyellem when they got onboard. He could see it already, resting neatly on the bed's pillow. A promise kept safe for the voyage home.

Because it's both my reward and Belmiro's cure.

TEHVAN'S PRICE

IL-KHEIR'S JOURNEY TO the moon with Pelippé Trueblood's soul isn't a tale that will ever be told aloud or read in books. But, my legantos, it's a truth you must know even if no one else does.

For the second time in his life, Sevri il-Kheir came to make a bargain for his son. This time, he had a partner in trade. Ele-Kheir came with him and she offered the moon Sevri's soul in exchange for Trueblood's.

Where did you get that? The moon's voice was everywhere and nowhere. Soundless yet filled with all the sound of the universe.

"He sold it to me," ele-Kheir said. "Which makes it mine to do with as I please."

I see. This for that.

"As is the way of the world," the Horsedam said.

In the mere presence of his soul, the Horselord was sucked back into his full experience, remembering everything he'd done for Fen. And everything he did to him. A father's love buckled his legs and flayed his chest open. The immense weight of everything Fen suffered stabbed him like a hundred arrows, each tipped with the poison made by twenty years of apathy, abuse and neglect.

"Give Trueblood back his life," he said. "Take mine instead."

Your life is already mine to take, the moon said. *I don't negotiate for what belongs to me.*

"It's a fair trade," ele-Kheir said. "A soul for a soul."

A long silvery silence.

I have my reputation to think of, children of Khe. I don't make bargains or barter. Tehvan must pay a price as well.

Il-Kheir stomped a silver hoof on the cold dead surface. It rattled his bones but made no sound. "It's time to end this," he cried.

The moon was cool and unfazed. *It's time when I say it is and not a moment before.*

Trueblood's soul rose from Sevri's hand into the immobile air, defying the laws of gravity and nature as it turned in a slow dervish of gold, white, blue and black. A voice within the spirals spoke a khenom, so perfectly that both the Horselord and Horsedam gasped.

"Please," the kepten's soul said. "Take us into your merciful heart."

The feathers of both kheirons ruffled, as if the celestial body beneath them were sighing.

Pelippé Trueblood, you are indeed an especial monster.

"Isn't he, though?" ele-Kheir murmured.

Very well, Sevri il-Kheir. This for that. Fly home. Take True-blood's soul and bind it to Tehvan's ringos. Pass your reign to your son and return to me.

"Bind the mariner's soul to my son's ringos?"

Trueblood must wear it always to live. It will be Tehvan's price to pay.

"My soul plus Tehvan's wings for Trueblood's life," the Horselord said slowly.

This for that.

"It's fair, little brother," ele-Kheir said. Always so poised and confident, her hooves shuffled backward in the dust, eager to go.

The Horselord stood his ground. "Is it? After what Fen's suf-fered?"

"Loving Trueblood the way he does, I don't think he'll view being grounded as a sacrifice. Take the bargain while she's still in a good mood."

The Horselord closed his eyes and raised his voice. "What if I give Fen my ringos to wear?"

The ensuing silence was confused.

"Does the power transfer?" il-Kheir asked. "Or is it like a khenom? It can only fit its owner's finger?"

More silence, and when the moon spoke, the tiniest grudge was in her voice. *It might work.*

"It might?"

It's never been done.

"It's never wanted to be done," ele-Kheir said thoughtfully.

"Which isn't to say it can't be done."

The sighing wind made feathers ripple and ele-Kheir's hair blow back.

No one truly knows the magnitude of power within starsilver rings, said the moon. *Or within khenoms. Tehvan spit his into the dirt of Arcodolori to no avail. He left you a trail of his name you never heard. What if he spit yours instead? Could you have heard him then?*

Sevri il-Kheir's lips moved. Only a thread of sound reached his ancestral aunt's ears and it sounded like "Gods, my foalboy."

Tell me, children of Khe. Is anything greater than the power of a name?

"Forgiveness," ele-Kheir said.

Indeed. But as we know, Tehvan has little love for his sire. Which makes the premise even more intriguing. What magical, soul-saving power exchange would come to pass if Tehvan were to call his enemy by name?

"Call me by name," the Horselord said.

It might be asking too much of him.

The moon's tone jeered now and the Horselord's hooves pawed at the ground again.

"My son is capable of more than you could possibly imagine," he said. "You'd have to take the world apart to find a braver, more resilient soul than Tehvan il-Kheir."

His body shuddered, shrinking in on itself, as if it broke his heart to say it. Or he *had* to break his heart apart to say it.

CONSOLATION PRIZE

THE KALEUCHE SAILED back to Nyland, Trueblood's body on a bier. In between their mourning, the crew raised telescopes to look back at Nydirsil.

"Do you see any flowers?"

"No."

"None, lad?"

"Not yet."

"Will there be?" Melki asked. "Will Nye grow again?"

"Give it time, lad," Abrakam said. His voice was reassuring but his body was tighter than a bowstring.

"She needs to trust that she's safe," Lejo said, with a little more confidence.

"How long will that take?" Melki said.

"It takes as long as it takes," Raj said.

Abrakam sighed. "Could be years before she begins to drop seeds."

"When she's ready and not a second before, Abe."

Numb with grief, Fen wandered the ship. Hiding and waiting for Trueblood to find him. He went into the nyellem, rubbed his hands against the walls and held them to his face. Yelled at an imaginary Trueblood, giving him a piece of his mind before throwing him down on the narrow bed and taking a piece of his ass.

He didn't dare sleep in their bed in the kepten's room. He wasn't that strong. He either slept on deck next to the bier, or in his old cabin. Waiting for Trueblood to find him.

"Fen, come sleep with us," Raj finally said.

"Please," Lejo added.

So Fen did, and found the space between the twins a restful, blameless place where he did not dream.

Raj and Lejo ran the ship. They were subdued, with their moments of intense grief, but stalwart. In truth, Fen had expected the twins' loss to be more debilitating. Their hearts were empty of stars. The space between them a vacuum. Without their ringos, they ought to have been severed, separate entities, wandering around lost.

"We're all right, Fen," Raj said. He was sober, but as steady and dependable as before.

Lejo smiled his agreement. He didn't talk much, but he remained accessible and kind. All the crew treated each other gently, helping one another through.

Abrakam was Fen's rock on the hard days. Fen spent long stretches of time sitting on the afterdeck, leaning on the centaur's broad flank. The lark came to perch on his shoulder and nestled her soft head against Fen's jaw. He covered her with a palm.

"Nothing in this story makes sense," he said.

"Because it's still being told," the centaur said.

"I don't like my part in it."

"Neither do I, lad."

Fen chewed on that, wondering if Abrakam meant he didn't like his own part or didn't like Fen's.

IN A DELAYED epiphany, he had to process all over again that Raj and Lejo were kheirons. Naturally he had three thousand questions but the twins could answer few. Some of their revelations were as recent as his, namely that their rings and moonstones were used to hold the stars in their hearts. They'd been sacrificing all their lives, living as men bound to earth.

"But it's not like we knew any other way," Lejo said.

"I just wonder who our father was," Raj said, tapping the side of his big nose with a finger.

"So do I," Lejo said. "But I'm not instigating that conversation with ele-Kheir."

"Good point. Sometimes it's better not to know the truth."

"Well, on a less sensitive topic," Fen said, "why do you each have six fingers?"

Raj shrugged. "Consolation prize?"

"Makes sex interesting," Lejo said.

Fen closed his eyes. "You know, you two…"

As the words faded out, he realized the Gêmelos were the closest thing to brothers he'd known in his life. His throat was tight with emotion as he told them so.

Lejo laughed. "Fen, if it feels like we're brothers, it's because we're first cousins."

"A thousand times removed," Raj said.

"Well hold my holy horses," Fen said.

The twins laughed, slung arms around his shoulders and pulled him into the safe place between them.

"You're one of us," Raj said. "Cousin and crew. If you want, the Kaleuche can always be your home."

"If you stay, it would be like having Trueblood here," Lejo said.

Fen gave a pained glance to the ship's wheel. "Who's going to be the next kepten?"

Raj pulled at his hair and Lejo rubbed at his jaw. "I don't know," they said together.

"Does another member of House Tru have to take over? Did Trueblood have uncles or cousins?"

The same unison answer, "I don't know," made the miniscule flame of hope kindle in Fen's heart again. He paced the ship that night, his ringed fingers trailing over walls and railings and masts. Touching all those godsdamned little holes the lark pecked, driving Trueblood crazy.

He stared a long time at the ship's wheel. Imagining Trueblood's tall form before it, his touch light on the spokes but his strength and control absolute.

His imagination morphed the mariner into a young boy.

Trueblood has no son, he thought.

Is this the end of House Tru?

How could it be?

He cupped furtive hands around the fire in his heart, both to conceal and shelter it.

Maybe he's not really dead.

How can he be dead? It would be the end of the ships.

It can't be the end.

It just can't be.

HIS FINGERS STARTED to inexplicably itch. The skin beneath his rings was cold, then it was hot. It pulsed. It throbbed. Sometimes water ran down his palms and it tasted salty, like the ocean. Or tears.

One night, his fivehand thumb started to bleed beneath the ringos. No matter how he pulled, the silver band was stuck tight and wouldn't come off.

What, he thought, staring at the blood. *Are you looking for me? Are you trying to tell me something? I'm here, Pé. Talk to me. I'm right here. Tell me. Where are you?*

Come back to me.

Rather than coming to grips with Trueblood's death and finding peace, he grew increasingly desperate.

"Pé, come find me," he said in the dark of his cabin.

Don't you love me anymore?

"Gods, I miss him so bad," he said in the light of day.

"I know, lad," Abrakam said. "He misses you too."

"Does he?"

"He loved you. Why else would you have shown your best self the first time you saw him?"

"And then I shit on his feet," Fen said through his tears.

"Well, you do like to do things the hard way, Feños." The centaur opened his arms and gathered the kheiron close.

"Give him back to me," Fen cried.

"I would," Abrakam whispered in his hair. "Gods know I would do anything, my one."

Fen was crazed with grief. Bones and cells split apart in mourning. Anger and despair and abandonment and betrayal foaming in his stomach, slashing like knives through his throat and bubbling over the centaur's shoulder. Silent screaming that tore Fen's ears apart, echoing in his skull and blinding him.

"Give him back to me," he said. "Give him back…"

He woke from a smoldering dream with a ragged shout of ecstasy. Trueblood had been taking him, giving him, loving and fucking him in a vivid rush of skin and mouths and fingers and sex. The cry turned agonized as Fen's eyes opened and Trueblood slipped from his arms.

It was over.

He hadn't been found, it wasn't later, they didn't get to have that conversation, no giant was at the helm and this was the last voyage of Trueblood Cay.

Fen pulled himself from bed and went above. It was a little past dawn and the world was quiet as prayer.

"You said you'd be with me to the end," he said to Trueblood's body. "Why are you hiding where I can't find you?"

With a yell of rage, he whirled around and smashed a fist against the railing, startling the lark from her perch. He went on kicking the ship, right near the place where Misery had breached. The planks, already loosened off their nails, rattled in protest, followed by a delicate spray across the deck. Like a handful of beads flung.

Fen kicked the wall of the hull again and again, each blow of his boot causing another scattering of tiny sounds.

Breathing hard, Fen looked at the deck. Then he stooped and looked closer.

"My Gods," he whispered. He pressed a fingertip to the ship's floor and raised it to his eyes.

"No..."

He scrabbled on his knees and pulled a plank free. Turned it so the side pecked with holes was facing down, and tapped it carefully on the deck.

"Holy horsesh—... *Abrakam*!"

He started pulling more boards down. Yelling his head off for the centaur, he turned them over and tapped them out onto the deck. The lark swooped in and puffed herself up, her expression smug.

"You newborn-soul-bringing little bitch," he said.

Abrakam was coming out of the aftercastle. "What is it?" he called. "Feños, what's wrong?"

"Seeds," Fen cried, one arm wide, the other indicating the little pile starting to grow by his knees. "Every godsdamned board on this ship is full of Nye seeds."

THE MOST GIANT
OF GIANT WORDS

GREAT WAS THE day when the Kaleuche sailed into Valtourel. The waterfront was lined with good citizens with
beautiful, broken hearts. Bands of black silk wrapped each arm.
Ebony bunting festooned storefronts. Handkerchiefs pressed to
eyes and noses.

Naria Nyland waited at the end of the pier, enormously preg-
nant. The hopeful fire in Fen's chest extinguished and he knew
it was over.

He does have a son after all, he thought.

*And if it's a daughter, she'll be the first keptenne of a giant-
ship in the history of the world, anywhere, ever.*

His heart broke, even as it dedicated itself to this unborn child.

You haven't even begun yet, but I'll be with you until the end.

The Kaleuche would be dismantled carefully, board by board.
Every plank loaded onto wagons and carted out to where land
was being cleared. They'd be laid in the earth, seeds, wood and all.

No one person knew to do this. Nyland had a herd mentality
of its own and every soul knew it was what had to be done. The
same way everyone knew another ship would come soon. The
Kaleuche came back for the Cay. No doubt, now that Nydirsil

was anchored to the sky, the Khollima was on her way back to replace her sister.

And she would endure.

A NINE-DAY VIGIL was held for Pelippé Trueblood Cay in the mariners' crypt. Crew members took turns keeping watch from sunrise to sunset. They came and went like the tide. The Ĝemelos. Merevhal, Dhar and their baby boy, Ikharus. Calvo and Beniv. The Sisters. All came to pay tribute.

Fen wasn't present for the daylight shifts. Much as he had on his flights across the desert, he slept when the sun was out and kept watch from twilight to dawn. Darea often came to stand with him in the wee hours, and as he leaned his head on her smooth coat, a bit of his future tapped his shoulder. He turned to face it, at last recognizing who Darea was. Not the great love of his life, the way Zoria was for Sevri. But a noble, courageous and compassionate pegaso who might give him an heir someday.

"If you're willing," he said.

"Only when you're ready." Her velvety muzzle caressed his head. "And not a moment before."

NARIA SAT WITH Fen on the seventh night. He lay his head and hands against her round belly and listened to the sounds of truest blood.

"This will be your child as much as mine," the queen said, stroking Fen's head. "I promise. We'll be a family. I and you, this baby. Raj and Lejo. We'll raise a new kepten together. We'll build new ships. We won't be complacent and just wait around for spice to grow. We'll keep being the goodness in the world. We can do it. We can do anything, Fen. And we will."

"Thank you," Fen whispered, and could say no more.

ON THE EIGHTH night, Belmiro came. He lit his candle and kneeled beside Fen.

"I'm so sorry, *Tehvani…*"

The flawed soul name rose above the pews, making the candle flames flicker.

"Thank you for coming," Fen said.

"I had to," Belmiro said, his voice tight. "Gods, he was something."

"He was everything." Fen reached in his pocket for the spice pod and held it out to his old lover. "Here."

Belmiro stared. "Is that…?"

"It's Nye. And it's from Trueblood. He told me to give it to you and tell you more is coming. As much as you need to stay clean."

"Khe l'khe."

"You're free now, Bel."

Belmiro put his head in his hands and cried. Fen gathered him close, rested a cheek on the kheiron's nape, and let himself feel everything.

"I'm sorry, Bel," he said. "I'm so sorry about everything."

"I never got to explain," Bel said. "Why I waited so long to tell your father I'd seen you that day. I don't even know why. I was…"

"Young," Fen said, rocking him. "We were both young and it's nobody's fault why young creatures in love do foolish things."

"I'm so sorry."

"It wasn't your fault. All you did was ask me to wait. I chose to follow you. I'm the one to ask forgiveness."

"It's yours," Bel said. "It's forgiven. I'm so tired of unfinished business. I hate that Trueblood left Valtourel when he was pissed off at me. My heart hurts so bad about it. And if I can…" He glanced at the pod in his palm. "If I can turn things around, I'm not saying I and you can be best friends again, but I'm so sick of the estrangement."

"Then let's end it. I and you. It stops now. We forgive, we go from here and we see what happens."

The two kheirons kneeled quietly together and kept watch. At the end of an hour, Belmiro picked up Fen's fourhand and held it to his mouth a moment. "Thank you."

"You get clean and you stay that way," Fen said. "You don't have a price anymore. You're no longer for sale. You understand?"

Answer your commander, he thought as Belmiro nodded and got shakily to his feet.

"Promise me, Bel."

"I promise. It'll be a new life."

"All right then."

Belmiro hesitated in the aisle. "Maybe I'll see you later?"

Fen smiled. "I'd like that."

Sunset on the ninth day. Fen felt no shame in not being able to shift into equos for the last watch of the vigil. He knew humos was the most noble form he could take.

He knew so many things now.

The hours passed. Fen dozed on his knees, then shivered awake. The crypt was dim and cold and behind him came the distinctive sound of four hooves on stone.

He thought it was Abrakam, and said, "When you carried us to the ship, the day we left? That was his idea, wasn't it?"

No answer.

Fen's arms crossed, hugging the chill in his bones. "I believed he was still alive, because he had no son. But when we came into port and Naria waited on the pier for us...I knew then. That's when it became real. He's gone and he isn't coming back. We don't get a later."

A hand touched his shoulder. Fen leaned into its warm strength.

"I'm going back to the herd," he said. "Darea's chosen me and I like her. I never gave much thought to my own children but maybe... If one were friends with Pé's child, then—"

"Give me your ringos, Fen."

Fen looked over his shoulder and reared back a little.

His father stood in the aisle, the swirling cloud of a soul in his cupped palm.

"Hold out your ringos to me," he said. "Do it now."

His tone was so dire, Fen pulled the winged band from his thumb and held it up.

"Stay still." The orb of light in the Horselord's palm began to turn. Round and round. Faster. Brighter. Drawing out long and threading the loop of the ringos. The eyes in the horse head flashed. The wings fluttered. The metal surged hot in Fen's fingers and he nearly dropped it. Then it cooled and went quiet. Fen let it roll into his palm.

"What just happened?" he said.

"The starsilver will sustain him," il-Kheir said. "But his heart won't beat without it. He has to wear it always. Which means you cannot fly."

"Sustain him?"

"Keep him alive."

Fen's heart lurched in his chest. "You mean...?"

"I brought you later."

"But..." Stunned to incoherence, Fen looked back toward the bier, then down to the ring in his palm. "I don't understand."

His father's fingertip touched the feathered edge of the silver band. "Given my way, I wouldn't make you choose," he said.

"I'd give you back everything. It's no less than you deserve." A trembling shook him. "This was the best I could do."

Fen closed the ringos up in his hand. It was everything he wanted, but he'd been here too many times before. Suckered by the hidden prices of things. Tempted by candy filled with poison. Lured by a demon turtle disguised as a beautiful island. Lulled by a swirl in the water with the potential to suck him down to a watery grave.

Is this real? Can this be mine?

"Did you hear me when I said his heart won't beat without your starsilver?" the Horselord said.

"I heard."

"A love like that? You only read it in stories."

"No, not only." Fen looked at him. "I was born from a love like that."

The Horselord shivered. "You were."

"Mami is so beautiful. And the way she said my name was—"

"Please," Sevri whispered, his face twitching in pain. "You don't need to tell me what's in my eyes and ears every single day. What I miss every minute of my life."

"I know, Father. I know now how it feels."

"Put it on him then. Gods know I would, if it were me."

Fen glanced backward at his shoulders, assessing wings he'd never see again. Then he sunk his teeth into life's sweetness and put the ringos on Trueblood's finger.

"It will take time for his heart to wake up," il-Kheir said. "Don't be afraid. He'll come back." He cleared his throat. "You have no reason to take my word but I give it. He'll come back to you."

Fen had been kneeling a long time. He leaned a hand on the edge of the bier to get up, putting weight on one stiff leg, then the other. He turned to face his father, who now held something between his thumb and forefinger. Milky-white with veins of opalescence.

"Yours," he said. "No conditions. No choices to make."

Fen took his moonstone and held it in his fist for one inhale and exhale, then put it in his pocket. "Thank you."

"And this." Sevri slid his ringos from his thumb and held it out to Fen.

A long staring moment.

"Take it," Sevri said.

"Why?"

"Because I…" The Horselord's mouth worked several times around the words before answering, "Because I want to see you wear it?"

I must be dreaming. Dazed, Fen slid his father's ringos onto the empty thumb of his fivehand. *Gods, if I'm dreaming, don't let me wake up.*

It's a good dream.

Il-Kheir had been watching intently, the lids blinking over his pale blue gaze.

"What's wrong?" Fen said.

"I thought it…" Sevri shook his head. "Nothing. Never mind."

"Well." Fen forced a little laugh. "We both know the day isn't complete until I've disappointed you."

Such a look of consternation came over Sevri's face, Fen was filled with a bewildered shame.

Khe, he's gotten so old.

"I'm sorry," he said. "That was uncalled for."

The Horselord's head moved slowly side to side. "You were only a foalboy."

Fen felt a loosening in his heart. Some old, tight grudge moving over a hair.

Abrakam said Father lost his mind when Mami died. Then lost it again when I was taken.

He went mad.

He went literally and excusably crazy.

I know how it feels. I've barely started to mourn my gelangos. He's been enduring it thirty-five years.

The bitterness in his heart moved over some more, making room for Sevri's mad cruelty. Not quite forgiving it, but creating a place where it could live.

It belongs in my nyellem, along with Arcodolori. And Trueblood stands at the door, guarding it.

This is a better way. If I'm willing.

Fen extended his hand. Elbow to the ground, thumb to the sky, offering gelango.

His father reached. Palm clasped palm. Then forearms. A single, shared inhale and exhale. Their free hands came to rest on each other's shoulders. Then their brows pressed.

"I haven't felt your head on mine in a long time," Fen whispered.

"*Tehvani...*" His father spoke his khenom. The syllables light and beautiful. Slightly wrong.

Fen dug deep in the hold of his memory. He had to push aside boxes of anger, barrels of resentment and crates of vindictive hate before he found it.

"*Sevri...*" The sounds were more than just slightly wrong. He butchered it badly and embarrassment burned the back of his neck. "Like I said, a long time."

"Try again."

Fen did. Better this time. Not perfect, but no one could say it perfectly but Sevri himself.

The gust of his father's sigh blew gentle on his face. "Gods, what enemies I made of us."

Fen closed his eyes. This was a new piece of cargo for his ship and he didn't know where to put it.

"I tried, Fen."

"You did everything you could."

"I wanted to do more."

"It's enough," Fen said. "Da, it's en—"

The chamber lit up as if by lightning. A stabbing, soundless flash. Blinding, deafening. A jolt and a crackle through hands to skin into bone and soul and a waft of burning flesh.

When the light fell away, Fen stood on four hooves and Sevri il-Kheir stood naked on two swaying, buckling legs. Where once his moonstone hung was a broken cord of dark purple horsehair. Where once were tiers of alabaster feathers was a charred skeleton frame with a few smoking tufts.

"Da?"

The Horselord stumbled back against the pillars of the nave and the protruding bones crackled, disintegrating into clouds of ash.

Fen lunged to catch the frail old man. Frantically he beat out the last smoldering embers around one pathetic shard of cartilage protruding from his father's back.

Diminished, burned and broken, Il-Kheir slid to the stones at Fen's hooves. With a grunt, the last shard of his wingspan trembled, folded, and slipped beneath the skin of his shoulder blades. A hiss of finality. A last curl of smoke. Then they were gone.

No silver etchings marked their place.

Fen's wings exploded. Again the crypt was filled with light as he morphed from humos to equos to kheiros and back again. Over and over from best to worst, from strength to vulnerability, hidden to exposed. A blur of limbs and mane and hair and tail and wings and skin and feathers. Until finally he stood, breathing hard, half-man, half-horse, his wings shivering. He stared at his nine ringed fingers, then reached up to touch his brow and feel the stone embedded there. Not dangling from a hoop but inexplicably and miraculously fused within his skin.

"Well," il-Kheir said in an old man's rasp. "I didn't think that would work."

The smoky air of the crypt was bitter in Fen's open mouth. "Think *what* would work?"

"I wasn't sure you'd say it."

"Say what, what are you talking about? What the fuck is happening?"

The Horselord rocked to his knees. Slowly his head turned to look at his son's magnificence. "Help an old man up?"

Speechless and bewildered, Fen reached down to take his father's shaking hands. Once on his feet, Sevri brushed off each ashy arm, then turned and made his slow way down the length of the crypt. Wrinkled and twisted and naked, but dignity in his slow, shuffling steps.

"Da," Fen called, following him. "Da, wait…"

The Horselord stopped, a hand on one of the pew backs. Tears dripped clean tracks down his dusty face as Fen's hooves rang on the stones, coming to a slow stop.

"You see, Fen," the old man said. "Names have tremendous power. But Da is the most giant of giantwords."

Words of all sizes swirled through Fen's astonished mind, gradually becoming realization.

The Altyn witch said no word exists in the world for how much my father loves me.

But it does exist. A word both name and noun. Father and the courage to be a father.

Fen bent his forelegs, then his rear ones, sinking to his father's level.

"Da, will you honor me by riding?"

The old kheiron reached a shaking hand to pat his son's cheek. "The honor is mine."

Fen helped his father onto his back. He folded his wings tight around the Horselord and started walking toward the pavilion.

"Go slow," Sevri said. "I have so many things to tell you."

Fen walked with deliberate precision, each hoof placed and lifted on the road. "All right, Da?" he asked over and over.

"All right," his father answered, sounding more and more sleepy each time. "So many things, Fen."

"Almost there."

Sevri's arms tightened around Fen's waist. "Take your time. I'm enjoying this."

Fen put his hands over his father's. "Me too."

"I'm so sorry, my one."

"I'm here," Fen said, holding on tight as the roles reversed. "I'm taking you home, valentos."

"I'm sorry. I love you, *Tehvani*..." His voice was a thread as he spoke his son's soul name perfectly.

Fen was crying too hard to answer.

Kheirons and attendants gathered at the pavilion gate, open-mouthed and pale with shock.

"Please help my father down," Fen said. "Carry him inside. He needs to rest."

He unfolded his wings as the kheirons approached. At the collective gasp, he looked over his shoulder.

His back was empty.

All heads rose as a charm of goldfinches took to the sky.

HOME

ELIPPÉ TRUEBLOOD WALKED on shaky legs out of the mariners' crypt, turning his palm over and back, looking at the ring on his finger. He gazed up at the brilliant sky, squinting under his hand at the newborn day. Then he looked blinking around the portico.

And smiled.

"There you are," he said.

Fen il-Kheir stood on four magnificent legs. The sun shone on his mercury-gray flanks and caught the silver in his hooves, one of which was poised on the edge of its coronet.

"We need to talk," he said.

Knees wobbling, Trueblood put a shoulder against a column. "This is going to be really unpleasant, isn't it?"

Fen crossed his arms, head nodding slightly. The sun glinted off the moonstone in his brow.

"You look different," Trueblood said.

"I made another side quest."

"I can't turn my back on you a minute."

"I'm never letting you out of my sight again."

Trueblood smiled. "Promise?"

Fen nodded, lips pressed tight.

"I love you," Trueblood said.

"I know. And you're still in a world of deep shit."

"Come here, you moron."

They were in each other's arms, wrapping and weaving, trying to find a better fit, a tighter grip, one trying to disappear in the other. Fen's wings burst free and closed around them, sunlight leaking through every feather.

"I missed you," Trueblood said into Fen's neck.

"Never again. You hear me?"

"Never."

Fen drew his wings back. "I'm going to kill you." He put his hand on Trueblood's face and pressed their brows together. "I love you so much, I'm going to kill you."

The apple of Trueblood's smile filled Fen's palm. "Gods, I'm so fucking tired."

Fen kissed him. Took him by the shoulders and shook him, then kissed him again.

"Climb on my back, gelangos," he said. "We're going home."

EPILOGUE

*The Most Private Journal of Noelippé Cay-Nyland.
An especial accounting of her
voyages on the Khollima.
As written in the ninth year of her life,
and her first year as a minoro.*

These are the people I love.

*My father. His name is Pelippé Trueblood Cay and he is
the kepten of the Khollima. He is the only mariner in the
history of the world, anywhere, ever, to sail on all three
of the giantships built by Truvos.*

*My mother. Her name is Naria and she is Queen of
Nyland. And my brother, Rafil, who is my twin. He is
home with Mami while I'm at sea with Da.*

*I'm not going to say more about Mami and Rafil right
now because this is the first time we've ever been separated and writing about it hurts my heart. Da understands
because his Mami (who I was named for) died when he
was very young and it hurt him so bad, he couldn't speak
and he almost forgot her. He doesn't want this to happen
to me but it won't. I think about Mami all the time. I'm
not going to say anymore. I will when it's time and not
a second before.*

I love my uncles, Raj and Lejo Ĝemelos (they are not really my blood uncles, but they were raised by my grandfather and grew up with Da as if they were brothers). Raj is the pilot of the Khollima and Lejo is the boatswain. They are twins, which means they understand best how much I miss Rafil and they give me really good words to describe how it hurts to be away from him. Well, at least Lejo does. Raj teaches me words I'm really not supposed to say. (He's wonderful.)

Hadevri il-Kheir is a minoro like me. He is a kheiron, meaning he can change from human to horse, or be half of each, like a centaur. Except he can fly, which centaurs can't. Hadevri is beautiful. His coat is dark blue, almost black. He has gorgeous red hair and deep purple eyes. He's a year younger than me, quiet and shy, but I must be honest and say I'm a little afraid of him. Sometimes when I come near him, he looks at me funny and quickly changes into a horse. Da says he does this because he likes me. Which makes no sense. Hadevri likes lots of people but he only turns into a horse around me. It makes my chest feel strange.

And I love Fen il-Kheir, who is Hadevri's father. Fen is the Horselord, meaning he rules all the Horsefolk. He lives at the pavilion in Valtourel and he's kept very busy being king, but he often flies out to meet the ship and sail with us a few days. He also takes me flying, which I love a tiny bit less than sailing.

Fen and Da are gelang. That means they are together and love each other and when Fen is onboard the Khollima, they sleep in the same cabin.

APPENDICES

Character Pronunciation Guide

Ikharus-Lippé (ICK-are-us LEE-pay)
Pelippé (pel-ee-PAY)
Raj (RAHJ)
Lejo (LAY-ho)
Osla (OH-sla)
Sayenne (sigh-ENN)
Rona (ROE-nah)
Dhar (dar)
Beniv (ben-EEV)
Merevhal (mere-ay-VAL)
Calvo (CAL-voh)
Rafil (rah-FEEL)
Melki (MEL-kee)
Naria (NAR-ee-ah)
Noë (NO-ee)
Sevri il-Kheir (SEV-ree ill-KEER)
Tehvan il-Kheir (tay-VON ill-KEER)
Zoria (ZOR-ee-ah)
Belmiro (bel-MEER-oh)
Noelippé (no-LEE-pay)
Hadevri (ha-DEV-ree)

GLOSSARY

Agnom (AG-nahm): Kheiron name used by outsiders, usually the first few syllables of their khenom

Algolerta (al-go-LEHR-ta): A lubricant made from seaweed oil.

Alon (AL-on): Giantword meaning "lark."

Alondra (al-LONE-dra): Former capital city of Nyland, destroyed by Minotaurs during the reign of Queen Nysiemi.

Amatos (ah-MAH-tohs): "Until the morning."

Arcodolori (ar-co-do-LORH-ee): Northeast region of Minosaros noted for its red rock formations. Legendary place where Minos the bull was slain by Nyos, hence its name, "Arrow of Sadness."

Aspida (ah-SPEE-dah): giant turtle released from the sea floor when Nydirsil pulled off her roots. Disguised himself as an island and lured sailors to their doom

Aŭskultantos (AUJH-kool-tahn-tos): Giantword meaning "beloved listener." One who heeds an oral storyteller (see Rakontisto), as opposed to legantos—those who read a printed story.

Aybar (AYE-bar): City in the Arcodolori region of Minosaros.

Altynai (al-tyn-EYE): Land west and north of the Altyn Range, including the Old Forest.

Caracaros (cara-CAH-ros): Falcons of Altynai who nest exclusively in Nye trees. Used as messenger birds.

Cay (KAY): Giantship built by Pel. Named Khe in antiquity, spelling later became Cay.

Centaur: A horsefolk race. Half-man, half-horse.

Da (dah): Giantword meaning both "father" and the steel-hearted courage to be a father.

Danysh (dah-NESH): Region in Arcodolori irrigated by the Bull River and noted for its fadara plantations and slave labor system.

Ele-Kheir (el-KEER): The Horsedam. Immortal queen of the Horsefolk. Daughter of Khe and a pegaso, and twin sister of il-Kheir.

Equos (eh-KWOSS): A kheiron's state of being in pure horse form.

Fadara (fah-DAH-rah): A highly-addictive narcotic made from poppies.

Fen: Giantword meaning "finch." Also the agnom taken by Tehvan il-Kheir following his escape from captivity in Minosaros.

Fivehand: A kheiron's five-fingered hand.

Foalboy: A male kheiron. Typically used from infancy to adolescence, but also as an endearment into adulthood.

Fourhand: A kheiron's four-fingered hand.

Gelang (gell-ANG): Giantword meaning "at hand" or "together with." Used to describe great romances or great friendships.

Gelango (gell-ANG-oh): A ritual handshake where first palms are clasped, then forearms. Opposite hands touch shoulders and brows are pressed together.

Gelangos: Endearment from gelang, meaning "my one at hand" or "the one I belong to."

Ĝemelos (jah-MAY-lohs): Giantword meaning "twins." Surname taken by Raj and Lejo, the foster sons of Kepten Ikharus-Lippé True.

Héjo (HEY-oh): Casual greeting, "hi" or "hello." Also an exclamation for attention, "hey."

Helos (HEY-lohs): Goddess of birth and death.

Hokosia (ho-KOH-see-ah): Continental empire to the west of Nyland, ruled by the emperor Xuan-Gavriel. Capital city is Lak Thennes.

Horsedam: Alternate title for ele-Kheir.

Horsefolk: Collective noun for kheirons, centaurs and pegasos.

Horselord: Alternate title for il-Kheir.

Humos (HUE-mos): A kheiron's state of being in pure human form.

Il-Kheir (ill-KEER): The first male kheiron, son of Khe and a pegaso, and twin sister of ele-Kheir. Also the title given to the reigning Horselord, and the surname used by him and his heir.

Kaleuche (kah-LOOSH): Giantship built by Raj and Lejo (not to be confused with Raj and Lejo Ĝemelos, the fosters sons of Ikharus-Lippé True, who were born millennia later). Disappeared with all on board. Sightings remained undocumented and legendary until she appeared during the marinership of Kepten Ikharus-Lippé True. True's son, Pelippé Trueblood, took command after his father's death.

Kepten (KEP-ten): The commander of any ship, but as a proper noun, specifies a giantship mariner.

Kharbidis (car-BEE-dis): Sea monster released from the ocean floor when Nydirsil pulled off her roots. Her mouth formed a whirlpool that sucked any ships nearby beneath the ocean.

Khe (kay): The first kheiron. Born human, he became the lover of Truvos, the sea god, who gave him the power to shift between man and horse, and to fly. Slain by Nyos during the Nyvosok. Her arrow impaled Khe to Nydirsil's trunk, where he hung for nine days before his body was taken away by Truvos.

Khe l'khe (kay-leh-KAY): An expression meaning both "what's up?" or "what the hell?"

Kheiron (KEER-on): A horsefolk race with the ability to shift between man and horse, and to fly at will by means of wings that can retract beneath the skin.

Kheiros (KEER-ohs): A kheiron's state of being in half-man, half-horse.

Khenom (KAY-nahm): A kheiron's soul name. Unpronounceable to anyone but himself. Shortened to an agnom which is used by outsiders.

Khollima (ko-LEE-mah): The first giantship, built by Truvos. Towed away Nydirsil following the Nyvosok.

Kvartermastisto (kvar-tar-mahs-TEE-stoh): Quartermaster of a giantship, in charge of cargo.

Kyrrh (cure): Rare, healing resin made from the sap of stave trees, an evergreen cultivar that grows only in Altynai.

Legantos (lay-GAHN-tohs): Giantword meaning "beloved reader."

Loĝigos (loh-JHEE-gohs): Lodges and hostels built and maintained by the giants in various cities.

Lunos (LOO-nohs): The moon goddess.

Majoro (may-JOR-oh): A giantship crew member between the ages of sixteen and twenty-one.

Maristo (mah-REE-stoh): "Mariner." A giantship crew member over the age of twenty-one.

Meros (MERE-ohs): The god of war.

Minoro (meen-OR-oh): A giantship crew member under the age of sixteen.

Minos (ME-nohs): Legendary bull companion of Nyos, who accidentally slew him during the Nyvosok. A bastardization of his myth led to the radical Cult of the Bull in Minosaros, who view him as a martyr.

Minosaros (me-no-SAHR-ohs): Lands east and south of the Altyn Range, including the red rock region of Arcodolori. Its southern region, Sanpago, was annexed to Nyland after Tehvan's War.

Minotaur (MIN-oh-tor): Half-man, half-bull race of Minosaros. Unlike horsefolk, their heads are beast and their bodies human.

Moonstone: A kheiron's magic stone that allows shifting between equos, humos and kheiros. If lost, stolen, or given away, the kheiron rests permanently to humos.

Murder and Misery: Twin kraken released from the ocean floor when Nydirsil pulled off her roots. Murder's venom causes instantaneous death. Misery's causes slow, excruciating death during which the victim relives his or her worst moments.

Mydam (MY-dam)/Mysire (MY-seer): Honorifics for female and male horsefolk, respectively.

Naŭtaggiad (nowj-TAH-gyadd): The nine-day hanging predicted in the *Truviad*.

Nydirsil (ny-DUR-sill): The Tree of Life. Tended by Nyos, her roots are deep in the ocean bed and her nine branches anchored to the sky with stars. Love is drawn up through her trunk and her flowers produce Nye spice. Only Nydirsil drops seeds to create new trees, which are sterile.

Nychet (NYE-shay): linen or muslin bag used to make Nye tea.

Nye (NIGH): Spice contained in the flowers of Nye trees. The spice of life, the source of love and the birthplace of happiness.

Nyellem (nye-ELL-em): Hold in a giantship used exclusively to store and transport Nye.

Nyland (NYE-land): Empire consisting of a mainland continent divided into three regions: Nordater, Arbaro and Sudenlo; Pellandro, the eastern portion of the Hokosian continent; and Sanpago, the southernmost region of Minosaros.

Nyos (NYE-ohs): Goddess of love and tender of Nydirsil. Slain by her brother Truvos during the Nyvosok.

Nyvosok (NYE-voh-sock): The feud between Nyos and her brother Truvos. Started when Truvos stole the nine stars of Nydirsil and gave them to his lover, Khe. After he refused to restore the stars, Nyos shot Khe. Truvos then slew his sister and towed Nydirsil away on his ship, the Khollima.

Os (ohs): God of gods, who is One.

Pegaso (peh-GAH-soh): Horsefolk race. Winged horse. Plural pegasos.

Rakontistos (rah-kahn-TEE-stohs): Giantword meaning "story-teller."

Ringos (RIN-gohs): Ring worn on the thumb of a kheiron's fivehand. Carved as two wings that wrap around the finger with a horse head between. Has no distinctive power, but holds great emotional weight. Symbolizes Os, who is One, and often engraved within with a name or credo or sentiment.

Ripozo (rih-POH-zoh): Afternoon rest hour.

Salutos (sal-LOO-tohs): A formal greeting meaning "hello."

Salu (sal-LOO): A more casual form of Salutos. "Hello" or "hey" or "hi."

Ŝnuromastistos (schnur-oh-mahs-TEE-stohs): Sailor in charge of rope rigging on a giantship.

Solos (SOH-lohs): The sun god.

Sorĉi (SOR-zhay): Giantword meaning "witch." Proper name given to the female shaman of Altyn tribes.

Ŝuo (Shoo-oh): "Shoo" or "go away."

Tehvan's War: Conflict following the abduction of Sevri il-Kheir's heir, Tehvan. The kheirons joined forces with Nyland under Queen Nysiema to invade Minosaros.

The Teeth: Treacherous channel between Altynai and the north coast of Hokosia.

The Truviad (TRUE-vee-add): Epic poem about the life of Truvos, the sea god. Depicts his building of the great ships, his love affair with Khe, the theft of the nine stars from Nydirsil and the ensuing Nyvosok. Carved into three monoliths, of which the third was lost, along with Truvos' prophetic conditions for the return of the stars. Printed copies of the *Truviad* had their last page torn in half to symbolize the lost portion. The third monolith was eventually discovered in the hold of the giantship Kaleuche.

Truvos (TRUE-vohs): The sea god. Creator of the giants and twin sister of Nyos. Built the giantships Khollima, Kaleuche and Khe. The last named after his lover, Khe, the first kheiron. Truvos disappeared after the Nyvosok, last seen sailing away on the Khollima with Khe's slain body and towing Nydirsil behind.

Ukhor (EWE-core): Blue minerals found at the roots of Nydirsil. Used for dye until the Nyvosok, after which the stones and the dye were extinct.

Valentos (vah-LEN-tohs): Giantword meaning "My brave one."

Valtourel (val-tour-EL): Capital city of Nyland after the sack of Alondra. Originally the shipyards of the giants, and the burial place for the kheirons.

Velos (VELL-ohs): The goddess of fertility and harvest.

Vicreĝo (vik-REJH-oh): Elected regent.

Wrevos (RAY-vohs): The god of wisdom.

Xeromo (zher-RO-moh): Literally "slave of a slave."

Zeuxis (zoo-SHEES): Capital of Sanpago.

AUTHOR NOTES

OFF THE COAST of Jamaica is a tiny island called Trueblood Cay. Its good citizens have beautiful hearts.

That's actually a lie. Trueblood Cay is a bump of coral reef you couldn't pitch a tent on. This was told to me by Philip "Flip" Trueblood, a musician I met in the summer of 2001. I hesitate to say it was love at first sight, but one glimpse of his face and my weird mind started throwing things down. *His face could launch ships. His face could sail ships. The Adventures of Trueblood Cay.*

No, wait.

The Voyages of Trueblood Cay.

All this before I even got a glimpse of his beautiful heart.

I started writing the story. I wrote it all summer long while Flip and I became friends-and-a-bit. Then on September 11, he boarded United Flight 93 and the rest was history. A venomous, multi-tentacled kraken named Murder attacked the country and cut short the jobs of thousands of good citizens with beautiful hearts.

I'd heard everything happens for a reason. I didn't like this reason. After Flip died, I put *The Voyages of Trueblood Cay* away in a drawer and didn't touch it for seven years. During which time many things happened that allowed me to love again, write again and dig an old story out of a drawer and finish it.

You hold in your hands both the story I promised Flip, and a love letter to my life. All the people and things that touched me, shaped me, hired me, abused me, valued me, found me and loved me are in its pages. This is the first book I wrote while I was in love, the first I wrote as an openly bisexual man and the first I wrote when I wasn't for sale. All of which makes *Trueblood* priceless to me.

Most of the giantwords in *Trueblood* come from the Esperanto language, created by L.L. Zamenhof with the hope it would serve as a universal language to foster peace and understanding. The word Esperanto translates to "one who hopes." It sounded good to my ears and many of its words end in O or OS, which suited my needs perfectly.

I drew on numerous sources of mythology, with a heavy emphasis on Greek and Norse legends. Nydirsil is a nod to Yggdrasil, the Tree of Life that bridges nine different worlds. Odin hung in its branches nine days to learn the secrets of the runes.

Winged horses are prevalent in the international folk narrative and I worked as many as I could into Trueblood's world. Anything with a C or K sound was a sure thing. For example, Chollima is a flying horse in East Asian myths, which I changed to Khollima. The winged steed al-Buraq comes from the Islamic tradition and I adjusted the prefix for my kheirons, il-Kheir and ele-Kheir. Kheiron is a variant of Chiron, whom the Greeks held up as the superlative centaur. I simply added feathers and held him up higher.

The Caleuche is a mythical ghost ship and one of the most important myths in Chilean culture. I'd say I discovered it by accident, but my friend Alex would say it was no wonder it found me.

I thank everyone who trusted me to weave bits of their life stories into the canon of *Trueblood Cay*. I thank my nephew, Ari, who took the map I scribbled on the back of a dry cleaning receipt and made it into Trueblood's world. I thank my agent, Lorraine for being so kind to the emotional importance of this project, and my editor Mike, who was so gentle with the first draft, I thought he had a fever. I thank my weird head for being a pipeline to the Thing on the other side that comes up with all this stuff.

Most of all, I thank my husband. Tehvan is the Estonian version of Steven, which in Germanic languages is Steffen, which ends in Fen, which is the giantword for Finch, who delivered this gods-damned soul and is everything, everything, everything to me.

—Javier Landes (Gil Rafael)
Chelsea, New York City
September 2011

About the Author

GIL RAFAEL IS the pen name of Javier Landes. His short story collection, *Client Privilege,* includes "Bald," which was shortlisted for an O. Henry Award and made into the 2004 movie of the same title. His bestselling works include *Gloria in the Highest, The Trade,* and a collection of Latin American folk tales, *The Chocolate Hour.* He has written articles for *The New Yorker, GQ* and *Esquire* magazines and appeared on NPR's *Moments in Time.*

When not writing, Landes is a founding member of Reveno, a shelter and community outreach program for Latino LGBTQ youth in the Bronx. He's also editor-in-chief for Reveno's newsletter, *Unavoz/Onevoice,* and co-producer of the *Unavoz* podcast with NPR's Camberley Jones.

A native of Queens, Landes lives in Chelsea with his husband Stef, who makes him a better man.

Visit him on Instagram or Twitter, @javierlandes

ABOUT THE OTHER AUTHOR

Javier Landes, aka Gil Rafael, is the creation of author Suanne Laqueur.

A former professional dancer and teacher, Suanne Laqueur went from choreographing music to choreographing words, writing stories that appeal to the passions of all readers, crossing gender, age and genre. As a devoted mental health advocate, her novels focus on both romantic and familial relationships, as well as psychology, PTSD and generational trauma.

Laqueur's novel *An Exaltation of Larks* was the grand prize winner in the 2017 Writer's Digest Book Awards and took first place in the 2019 North Street Book Prize. Her debut novel *The Man I Love* won a gold medal in the 2015 Readers' Favorite Book Awards and was named Best Debut in the Feathered Quill Book Awards. Her follow-up novel, *Give Me Your Answer True,* was also a gold medal winner at the 2016 RFBA.

Laqueur graduated from Alfred University with a double major in dance and theater. She taught at the Carol Bierman School of Ballet Arts in Croton-on-Hudson for ten years. An avid reader, cook and gardener, she started her blog EatsReadsThinks in 2010.

Suanne lives in Westchester County, New York with her husband and two children.

THE LAST WORD

I WAS GOING TO stay out of it and let Jav have the limelight. I'll keep it brief.

Do the scary things. Like writing a fantasy novel when you have *no* idea what you're doing and you're sure it's the dumbest thing in the whole history of the world, anywhere, ever. Write it anyway.

Be sure to read a lot of outstanding fantasy books while you're writing your idiotic one. Load up on Leigh Bardugo, V.E. Schwab, Phillip Pullman, Neil Gaiman and Catherynne Valente. Read all their magnificent works, just to stay aware of how you are *way* out of your wheelhouse. Cry a lot. Keep writing.

If you're lucky enough to have a terrible friend who recommends Laini Taylor's *Strange the Dreamer* to you, be sure to jump on it immediately. And then have a breakdown because honestly, after that masterpiece, what's the point of trying to write anything? She took all the good words.

I had that breakdown because I have that terrible friend. Her name is Camille and after she ruined my life, she told me what to do with *Trueblood Cay:* "Just write it from the heart."

Be a valentos. Do the dumb, scary things. Do them from the heart. Dumb and done is better than perfect.

This isn't the most perfect book I ever wrote, but I done it.

—Suanne Laqueur
Somers, New York
December 10, 2018

THANK YOU

IF YOU ENJOYED *The Voyages of Trueblood Cay*, I'd love to hear about it. Please consider leaving a short review on the platform of your choice. Honest reviews are the tip jar of independent authors and each and every one is treasured.

If you're a Facebooker, join others who enjoyed my books in the Read & Nap Lounge:

LQRWRITES.COM/LOUNGE

Stop by my website

SUANNELAQUEURWRITES.COM

or look for me on Instagram at

@SWAINBLQR

Wherever you find me, all feels are welcome. And I always have coffee.

ALSO BY
SUANNE LAQUEUR

A Small Hotel

THE FISH TALES
The Man I Love
Give Me Your Answer True
Here to Stay
The Ones That Got Away
Daisy, Daisy

VENERY
An Exaltation of Larks
A Charm of Finches
A Scarcity of Condors
The Voyages of Trueblood Cay
Tales from Cushman Row
A Plump of Woodcocks

SHORTS
Love & Bravery: Sixteen Stories
An Evening at the Hotel

ANTHOLOGIES
Flesh Fiction